MISCREANT

THE DARKOV SERIES

KYNSIE COLE

Cover by Lindsey Sorensen
Map by Shepengul

ISBN 979-8-9925818-0-5
ISBN 979-8-9925818-5-0 (ebook)

For my brother, Cody

Our scars are the stories of our lives
Oh, the stories you have

Hiayda Mansion

Darkov Mansion

the Spire

Bloodthorne Mansion

CHANDRIA

ISLE OF NADIR

Spora Forest

Falls Forest

Garden Of
Remembrance

Ridge

ONE

The wail of a siren pierced the forest air, rising and lowering to a prolonged moan. Nova gritted her teeth, longing to dampen the noise with her abilities. But that skill required a focus she couldn't spare while fleeing. Her black hair whipped wild as she ran behind Denali, branches snapping under her feet.

She risked a glance behind and caught sight of armored figures closing in. "Catch the vagrant!"

How had they discovered her secret? The truth she and Denali had buried so deep, had bled to protect, had woven lies upon lies to shield. The question festered beneath her panic, but there was no time to dwell on it now.

Denali had prepared her for this scenario—they'd rehearsed it countless times—but the reality of their escape plan unfolding was far more terrifying than any practice run. "Keep going!" he said.

"I—I can't." Nova's legs were on the brink of collapse. Her brother's footsteps matched hers stride for stride.

"We'll lose them, Nova. Don't stop!"

Every bone in her body screamed to give up. To surrender. If she gave up now, perhaps they would be more lenient.

Maybe they would let her have a longer goodbye with Denali.

He sped up, pulling her harder behind him. As the distance

between them and their pursuers widened, the forest seemed to conspire against her, branches lashing out, thorns seeking flesh.

"Here!" Denali said.

They ducked into a rocky crevice. Nova pressed her back against the rough surface, her lungs burning with the effort to stay silent as she willed herself to blend into the shadows. She looked up at the slice of sky overhead where dark clouds loomed, promising a heavy rainfall. The stampede of footsteps grew louder as the approaching figures scanned the area with an eerie precision, eyes cutting through the darkness like predators seeking their prey.

"Check the glades," one of them ordered. "I'll go to Nadir myself before I let a miscreant best us."

The siren's wail intensified. Nova clamped her hands over her ears, but the sound seeped through her fingers, stabbing into her skull. She dug her heels into the dirt, fighting the impulse to scream. Now wasn't the time for a breakdown. As the world began to spin, Denali's warm fingers cupped over her hands.

"Breathe," he mouthed.

Denali pulled her beside him, enveloping her in a warm embrace. She drew in unsteady breaths, her body shuddering against his. Gradually, her racing heart began to slow.

Calm down, Nova.

She began to focus inward, aiming to avert a full-blown panic attack. In her mind, she visualized dials and carefully turned down each channel of noise. The siren's wail dampened to a distant, muted hum. Her fingers, still trembling, gently withdrew from her ears as the soundscape became bearable, thanks to her hard-won control over her senses.

Nova's rigid posture began to soften. She exhaled shakily and her shoulders dropped from their hunched position.

The figures drew closer and Nova squeezed Denali's hand. Every muscle tensed for flight as she heard their muffled shouting. She buried her face into her knees, shutting out the world as the fear overwhelmed her. She waited a few moments before peeking up at Denali. As he scanned the area, his grip on her hand eased. His eyes met hers and they exchanged a look which showed they both

2

appreciated the magnitude of what they had narrowly escaped. He mouthed, "I won't let them take you."

Tears blurred Nova's vision, spilling over as her body quaked.

This wasn't real. It couldn't be real.

Denali's bloodless face confirmed that it *was* real. Nova dreaded the final step of his plan, which involved running to the beach where a boat waited. It would take them far away from here . . . if they survived. The current was strong, and Nova had heard of people who had drowned—

Stop, she reminded herself. *We are going to make it out.*

Nova had no clue where the boat would take them, she only knew the plan for getting out of Ghandria. Denali had made the plans and she followed. The burden of decision-making often triggered her anxiety and following his lead kept her calmer. He'd made her rehearse his plan nearly every week since she was twelve, so she had played through this exact scenario for years. She'd *memorized* it, but she never thought it would be needed. They had both been so careful.

Her thoughts were overtaken when she noticed streaks of thick liquid running down Denali's arm.

Blood.

She scooted toward him and carefully lifted her fingers to tap his fresh wound. It was a deep gash on his upper arm, probably snagged by a branch. Denali offered her a faint smile, though the lines of strain around his eyes betrayed his effort. "Just a scrape."

Nova stiffened, her gaze lingering on the wound he was trying to hide.

"Later," he said.

"Please."

He sighed and rested his arm on his knee. As he closed his eyes, his brows drew together in concentration. Nova studied his face, watching a single strand of dark brown hair fall softly against his forehead. Her gaze trailed down his arm where the torn skin began to pull inwards, stitching itself back together. Taking deep breaths, Denali drew strength from the air itself, steadying his focus. In seconds, the wound closed, leaving behind a thin pink line. His arm was still smeared with fresh blood, but the injury had vanished.

He had become a prodigy in their land. He'd achieved the highest degree of honor in his classes and excelled at nearly all of his skills, though healing was certainly his best. He lived up to their family name. He was someone to be looked up to . . . a true Darkov.

Yet, here he was, risking all of that to help her.

Nova's face fell. She hated herself for it.

Denali used his shirt to wipe up the blood, then pushed himself up and held out his hand.

Nova eyed the direction of the ocean. It would take eight minutes to run there. She took Denali's hand. The forest's embrace loosened as they cautiously emerged from the hollow rock. Denali gestured for Nova to follow and they navigated through the underbrush. Once they were sure no guards were near, they picked up their pace and hurtled through the trees toward the ocean. As they neared the shore, the ground beneath their feet became increasingly rocky and uneven.

Nova's heart pounded within her ribcage. This was their world, their sanctuary, and yet every step drew them closer to a confrontation they couldn't avoid. Finally, they reached the edge of the forest where the trees gave way to a small, craggy cliff overlooking the bay. A thick blanket of fog hung low over the ocean, rolling against the shore.

Before them stretched the vast expanse of sea, its surface broken by a line of massive, jagged rocks jutting from the water. Though the water near the shore was relatively calm, farther out Nova could see larger waves crashing against the stacks, sending sprays of foam high into the air. At the center of one rock formation, a whirlpool churned, its dark vortex powerful enough to pull entire waves into its spinning maw.

They carefully made their way down the rocky incline. At the bottom, where the cliff met the shore, Denali crept along the black sand until he reached a dense patch of underbrush nestled against the rock face. He glanced back once more before pushing aside the foliage, revealing a small, sleek vessel about ten feet long.

The *Marmoris*.

Its hull, crafted from the silvery-blue wood of the celtian tree, shimmered and shifted, reflecting its surroundings. In water, it would be nearly invisible. The sharply pointed bow was designed to cut through the roughest seas. Last year, Denali had leveraged Father's status to borrow it from Ghandria's small flotilla. Once it was hidden, he'd swum back to the guard tower and reported it lost. It was the first and only thing he'd ever stolen.

Nova had expected search parties to comb the waters for months. Instead, their father had simply commissioned another vessel without so much as a whisper about the missing one.

Denali grasped the boat's edge. Nova joined him and together they began to drag it through the sand. Inside the vessel, a pair of oars lay ready, their handles wrapped in soft leather. Nestled between the oars was Denali's waterproof bag, bulging with supplies for their journey.

They pulled the boat in until the water reached their knees. Nova looked out at the expanse of ocean. This part of the plan would prove to be the most dangerous, but with the Marmoris, they stood a chance. She shuddered, remembering the tales of miscreants who had tried to cross without it. The waters were a death trap of whirlpools, and their violent currents turned normal boats to splinters. The remains that sometimes washed ashore were a grim testimony that none could survive the journey without the Marmoris.

The first drops of rain began to fall. Denali turned back, extending his hand to help her into the boat. She glanced at the ocean again, its surface now choppy with growing waves, the rain creating a tapestry of ripples across the water.

Were they going to survive this?

Denali placed his hand on her shoulder, then slid it to grip the nape of her neck. His eyes met hers with an intensity. He gave her a firm nod.

Nova straightened, willing her quivering muscles to show more courage than she felt.

Denali released his grip to steady the boat against the waves. Nova was about to climb in when he tensed beside her. His sudden alertness made her whirl around just in time to see a group of seven guards charging down the beach, their boots kicking up sand as they raced toward them.

Denali's mouth moved as he yelled, but she couldn't make out his words with her hearing diminished. He grabbed her arm, trying to haul her into the boat.

Nova's vision tunneled, the edges darkening as panic set in. She scrambled to obey Denali, but the shifting sand beneath her feet gave way. The splash of the approaching guards grew louder. Denali pushed the boat deeper into the waves. Nova's hand shook violently as she grasped the edge of the boat. The world around her seemed to spin, nausea rising in her throat.

A hand clamped down on her waist. A strangled cry escaped her lips as she was yanked backwards. Her fingers scrambled for purchase on the boat's edge.

Two guards seized Denali while the others dragged Nova through the shallows back to the beach. Her chest heaved with rapid breaths, each one feeling insufficient.

When they reached the beach, her legs gave out. A guard roughly hauled her up. She could see Denali being manhandled nearby, but her vision kept swimming in and out of focus. She lost control of her senses and the sound of the siren returned in full force. She winced at the pounding in her skull and tried to lift her hands to shield her ears, but they were trapped in the man's grasp.

Through her haze of horror, she became aware of a figure approaching. It was Merek, their father's head guard. His white-blonde hair was slicked back meticulously. He drew himself to his full height as he inspected Nova from head to toe. His nose crinkled in disgust.

"Miscreant," he hissed. Then, he spat at her. Nova flinched as the secretion hit her cheek and slowly dribbled down her jawline.

Denali stepped forward and several guards intervened, reaching for their dualfates at their backs. The twin daggers, balanced on their length of wrapped center grip, glinted menacingly as they leveled one blade at his pulse. Nova could see the battle in her brother's eyes as he fought the instinct to retaliate. The veins in his neck were like twisted vines, bulging under his strain.

"Don't touch her," he growled.

Merek's attention snapped to Denali. "Your title . . . your *existence* can be revoked. The world will see what becomes of those who stand with miscreants."

Denali ground his teeth. "She's not a miscreant."

Merek considered him for a moment. "We shall see." He gave a nod to his underlings and they lowered their dualfates. "Return the Marmoris to its place."

They moved toward the boat. At a gesture from Merek, another guard advanced, rope in hand. Everything slowed to a treacle, trapping Nova in place. She counted heartbeats as he bound her hands.

"Move," Merek said.

Her limbs refused to obey. He shoved her to get her moving forward. With every tug pulling her from their escape route, her breath grew more frantic.

Nothing would ever be the same again. Somehow, her secret had been revealed. If only her body would crumble to dust right here, right now, so she wouldn't have to face what came next.

TWO

Nova itched to wipe off the sweat of her clammy hands, but a guard was already retying them in front of her. She winced when he pulled the cord taut. Behind Nova, her maid finished lacing up the back of her gown. The dress, a vision of tyrian purple, was her most expensive. It was made of the finest silk, the bodice cinching tightly around her small waist before flowing gracefully to the floor.

It was suffocating.

Nova tried to draw in a proper breath, but the fabric that constrained her ribcage wouldn't allow such freedom. The urge to tear at the fabric, to rip it away and free her lungs was overwhelming. But everyone was expected to wear their best in the presence of the syphon. A quick shiver jolted through her as she thought of the syphon exposing her for who she really was.

A fake.

Two guards flanked Nova, forcing her into her chair. Anxiety crept along her spine, so she focused on the faint background music in her room—a melody mimicking a flowing waterfall. Nova let the sounds wash over her. Her trembling hands betrayed her as she willed them to still. Behind her, her maid's fingers worked through her hair, weaving small braids that cascaded down to her hips. Her raven black locks, now adorned in tiny crystals, served as a symbol of her status. Only those of highborn families were allowed the privilege of embellishing their hair with braids and crystals. The jewels laughed at her, mocking her for being what she was.

A blemish on the Darkov name.

She peeked her head around the mirror to the hallway. Another guard stood blocking her escape route. She looked around her chambers. Her bed was a sprawling expanse of deep mahogany. To anybody else, it was a lavish masterpiece. To her, it served as a reminder that sleep was a treasure she could never truly obtain. Ever since she was a child, she'd lain there unable to quiet her mind. Back then, Denali came in every night to tell her stories while she lay restless.

Towering windows stretched up to her high ceiling, their velvet drapes drawn tightly to block out all light. Her chambers were lit only by the gentle glow of a fireplace. It was the perfect amount of lighting for her to see without triggering a blinding headache. Years ago, when he started noticing her sensitivity, Denali removed all the bulbs from her room.

Nova eyed the guards again, then her windows. Maybe she could run to them, but what then? Even if she could pry them open in time, the drop from three stories was far too daunting to consider as an escape route.

Or perhaps being paralyzed and comatose was a better fate than the syphon revealing her.

Her father's voice in the hallway made her blood turn cold. "She is my blood! My hair! My eyes!" A loud crash on the other side of the wall made her jump. "Fix this or I'll banish you myself!" His screams rattled the walls of her room.

Nova tensed and felt the maid behind her flinch in response. Slowly, the door creaked open. Nova braced for the worst. When Denali's face appeared in the doorway, terror released its claws. With a subtle nod, he dismissed the maid, who slipped out without a word.

"I thought you were Father," Nova whispered.

Denali shook his head slightly as he approached. "He's gone to the syphon."

Nova sunk her head into his chest. Her shaking escalated to full-body tremors. Denali circled his arms around her.

"How did they find out?" Nova asked.

"I'm not sure," he said. "I think someone may have been in the cavern while we were practicing."

Nova pulled back and searched his face. "Last night? But we made sure everyone was gone before we went in."

So someone had followed them, or had been hiding inside . . . But if someone had seen her, why had they waited until today to reveal her?

Nova's bottom lip quivered. "I'm sorry."

Denali knelt down and grabbed her shoulders so she looked at him squarely. "This is *not* your fault. Do you understand? I'm going to get you out of this."

A tear slipped down her cheek. "How?"

Denali ignored her question and grabbed an amethyst jewel from her vanity. "Wow," he said, lifting it in front of his left eye. "Wowwww."

Nova sniffled and gave a soft laugh. *Not this again.*

"I've never seen such a beautiful jewel," he paused. "You know my favorite thing about jewels?"

"What?"

He tucked the crystal into one of her braids. "They sparkle brighter when they are placed on a bigger jewel."

Nova wiped at her nose. "You made that up."

Denali traced an imaginary X over his heart. "Honest, I swear." He turned her chair so she was facing the mirror again. "See, it just got a little brighter."

She offered a faint smile. He had been doing this ever since she was a child. "I'm seventeen, Denali, and you're still doing that?"

"You'll always be my kid sister." He winked.

Despite his teasing demeanor, there was a rawness in his eyes. The fragile stillness fractured when Merek loomed in the doorframe. "Time's up."

Nova shook her head, lips parting, but the words "I can't do this" died before they could escape.

Merek's firm grip clamped around her arm.

"Hey!" Denali said. "Be careful with her."

Merek scoffed. "We don't show regard for *miscreants*."

"She's not been labeled a miscreant."

"*Yet.*" Merek escorted her down the marble staircase of their mansion, past walls where ivory crept between dark stone, and outside to the iron-gated entrance. The sudden onslaught of light triggered an instant throbbing in Nova's head. She raised her bound hands to shield the sun that peeked through a hole in the clouds.

She replayed Merek's words in her mind as he led her closer and closer to her undoing. They descended into town, and Nova glanced backwards to ensure Denali stayed close behind, past the half-timbered houses with their steep terracotta roofs and dark wooden beams that lined the cobblestone street. The contrast never failed to strike her—how the grandeur of her family's estate gave way to the medieval charm of Ghandria proper, where citizens lived much as they had for centuries.

A cascade of chills rippled across her pale skin. The secret she and Denali had hidden their entire lives hadn't been revealed yet, not fully at least.

Not yet.

After this, all three highborn lines would know of her indiscretion. *Perhaps my title will pardon me,* she thought.

Deep down, she knew it would only bring more disgust, more consequences, more *disgrace*. She passed houses where faces quickly withdrew from the windows, wooden shutters snapping closed as the path gradually inclined, leading her toward a low, forested hill.

As her traitorous feet approached, a natural stairway of stone emerged, winding its way up the hillside. Each step took her a little higher until she found herself staring at the heart of their world—the cavern protecting their most sacred possession. She halted at the wide entrance. The walls of solid rock towered above her, engulfing her entire being and casting shadows that reached out and lured her in.

Nova's every instinct urged her to turn back. The ropes binding her hands seemed to tighten with each breath, feeding the knot of fear in her stomach.

Escape, her mind screamed. *Escape now.*

She swiveled on her heels, but then Denali lowered beside her. "Not now," he said so only she could hear.

Did he have a new plan?

A force from behind shoved her forward, causing her to stumble almost to the ground.

"Move," Merek said.

Nova steadied her feet beneath her. She extended her shaky leg into the mouth of the cave. Merek mumbled something as he moved ahead of her, his torch casting a feeble light on the jagged walls that surrounded them. The air inside was thick and musty, carrying a hint of dampness that clung to her skin. They ventured deeper, and the cave swallowed the glow of the torch. As it darkened, the throbbing in Nova's head gradually subsided.

The sound of dripping water echoed through the chamber, each droplet splashing into a shallow pool at the cave's base. The pools of water glistened like black-glass mirrors. The reflections of fractured light in the water rippled and distorted, creating an illusion of movement. The walls of the cave were a tapestry of textures, rough and uneven. An eerie sensation crawled over her skin as they continued to go deeper, as though the cave already recognized her as an intruder. The weight of her unworthiness was about to be exposed to the highborns of Ghandria. She lifted her bound hands to do a final check on her hair, brushing through the ends. Then, she turned a final corner and her eyes were lured straight to the syphon.

The black mass hovered in the center of the cavern, a sphere that pulsed with dark mists. Its obsidian swirls resembled inky veins. Its mass was nearly the same as hers now. She remembered a time when she could have fit it in her palm.

She stood watchful, observing as the three highborns occupied their imposing thrones of solid rock. Though she couldn't bear to make eye contact with him, her father's presence was the most daunting. His throne seemed to cast a longer, darker shadow. His silver-peppered hair and clean-cut scruff framed a strong jaw set in grim determination. Beside him sat Morianna and Archaelus. It was rare for all three of them to be there. The ritual required only one highborn to be present, and usually it was her father, Cronian.

From her position, Nova could see the highborns in their seats watching a man kneeling before the syphon. The man knelt with his back partially to her, his hands outstretched toward the syphon, palms upturned as he prepared to make his offering to the sacred entity. His body tensed and the cave responded, growing darker and casting a dark aura around him.

Nova began to sense the whispers of his memory echoing through the cavern. Initially, the voices blended into an unclear jumble of sound, but with time they solidified, unveiling a painful memory. A glowing transparent picture materialized in front of the man's forehead. The highborns leaned forward and Nova did the same, compelled to witness the profound act.

A man's voice escaped his memory: "If you walk out that door . . . you can't undo this. Is that what you want?"

A woman's voice came next: "I haven't decided anything, Roric. I just need more time."

It was a breakup. This was a familiar occurrence, one that hardly caught Nova by surprise. Most people used the syphon to erase memories like that—breakups, family deaths, and other traumatic experiences. She even heard someone had used it to obliterate their memory of a bad test score which, to her, seemed excessive. But in a world where you can forget all of the pain, where you can simply erase all the heartbreaks, sadness, and disappointment . . . why would you not?

Nova's gaze locked on a pair of dark blue eyes in front of her. *Father.*

Even in the dimly lit chamber, the clench of his jaw was unmistakable. His penetrating stare bore into her soul, causing her to break the connection and lower her head. His cutting words repeated in her mind. *You are a disgrace.*

He was right. And she was about to prove it. In front of the highborns. And then, in front of *everyone.*

Her legs shook relentlessly as she listened to the man's memory repeat.

"If you walk out that door . . . you can't undo this. Is that what you want?"

"I haven't decided anything, Roric. I just need more time."

The projection lingered in front of the man's face like a wisp of cold mist. Nova nervously fidgeted with the fabric of her dress as the words repeated a third time.

". . . I just need more time."

His floating memory descended to the syphon. When it was just inches from the black mass, the syphon reached its tendrils forward and absorbed the memory into itself. Faint whispers of the memory replayed in the syphon one last time until fading out to silence.

I just need more time.

The aura around him began to dissipate, and he lowered his arms. Nova quietly moved from her position, edging closer to get a better view. She circled cautiously, careful not to disturb the solemn moment, until she could see the man's profile. His eyelids dragged open, revealing irises glazed over in white. Nova watched, transfixed, as he blinked several times, the natural color gradually seeping back into his eyes.

The highborns nodded their heads to the man and her father spoke, "The syphon has accepted your offering. May the burden of this memory be lifted from your soul."

The man bowed before the syphon, then strolled away, rubbing his temples as he walked.

And just like that, it was done. He would eventually be reminded of his breakup, but the pain associated with it had vanished. The emotional weight attached to that memory was gone. Forever.

This was the gift of syphoning, the cornerstone of their society's emotional wellbeing. No longer did their people have to suffer through sleepless nights reliving painful memories or struggle with debilitating anxiety about past mistakes. The syphon offered a chance at true emotional freedom. Trauma, grief from loss, the sting of rejection, the paralyzing fear of failure—all could be erased at will.

Nova burned with jealousy.

The highborns shifted their focus to her. Morianna's and Cronian's gazes were heavy with judgment, while Archaelus kept jerking his head up every few seconds as he fought to stay awake.

Morianna cleared her throat, pulling Nova from her thoughts. "Give praise, youngborn."

Nova turned toward the entrance of the cavern, hoping to see Denali there.

But he wasn't.

They hadn't permitted him to enter. It was law that only highborn blood was allowed to witness syphonings. Since Nova and Denali were Darkovs, they were sometimes permitted to observe. But not today.

Morianna gestured for Nova to approach.

Move, she told herself. Still, she remained motionless, gripped by an icy paralysis that left her knees trembling. Merek untied the ropes around her wrists and, at the highborns' signal, left the cave. Nova slowly stretched out her hands, flexing her fingers to restore circulation. As she edged toward the syphon, reality warped into her worst fear.

Just last night, she stood in this very spot with Denali, practicing in secret before the syphon.

Just last night, she had been a respected Darkov, above any suspicion.

Only yesterday, nobody had known what she was.

If only she had known someone else was in the cavern. If only she had been more careful.

The syphon swirled like a cloud of black mist and pulsed with ghostly whispers. She felt her father's cold gaze on her and she shifted on her feet, adjusting her stance. She used one hand to hold the fingertips of the other in an attempt to calm them.

Breathe, Nova.

She drew a shallow, hesitant breath. Then she lowered to her knees and turned her palms upwards. The shadowy substance of the syphon danced in front of her, waiting to welcome another memory. Nova closed her eyes and offered the recited words of praise.

"In release, we find freedom," she said. "In forgetting, we find peace. Praise the syphon. For through it, we are healed."

As the last words left her lips, Nova opened her eyes and looked to the highborns, waiting. Morianna's face was impassive, but after a moment, she gave a slight nod. It was the signal that granted Nova permission to proceed.

The silence in the cave helped her remain focused. The setting around her faded away as she concentrated solely on one memory. It was the memory that haunted her each night when she lay awake for hours. She stilled her thoughts, and her mind was transported back to her home.

Nova found herself looking down on the scene. She saw her young self lying on the floor. Wood crackled in the fireplace. A younger version of Denali knelt beside her, sobbing. Nova watched as her younger self's eyes fluttered, struggling to open fully. Towering above them both stood Cronian, holding his whip decorated with hundreds of tiny crystal shards.

Nova brought herself back to the cave and peeked through a crack of her eyelid to see the projection floating steadily between her and the syphon. *So far, so good.* As the memory solidified, the syphon stirred. Phantom tendrils crept from its form, reaching toward her memory.

The fireplace came into focus, its flames licking at the edges of the projection. Young Denali's tear-stained face materialized, his mouth moving in silent sobs. As Nova strained to hear his words, to push the memory further, something changed.

The projection began to flicker. The edges of the memory blurred, and Denali's face became hazy.

Sweat beaded on Nova's forehead as she pushed harder, willing the memory to stabilize. But the more she pushed, the more unstable the projection became. Portions of the image disappeared, leaving gaping holes in the memory, only to reappear moments later in a different part of the projection. The flickering intensified and then the image dissipated into the air. Nova still felt the buzz from the syphon's tendrils centimeters from her fingertips.

Then, it happened.

Images, sensations, and emotions that weren't her own flooded her mind in a dizzying rush. In one heartbeat, she was on her knees, cradling a cold, still body. A wail tore from her throat, but the voice wasn't hers.

It was a man's.

The world collapsed into this single moment—these masculine hands clutching a body gone cold. The loss consumed everything—past, future, reason—until there was nothing but this moment, this agony, this *shattering*.

The world shifted.

Nova blinked, and she was sitting in a classroom. Her hands were smaller now, and they stung from a sharp smack. A professor's shadow stretched across her desk like a dark tide. The room contracted, twenty pairs of eyes witnessing her shame as each word the professor spat carved shame deeper under her skin, marking her as different, wrong, *broken*.

The classroom blurred and dissolved.

Heat exploded around her. Fire erupted from nowhere, everywhere, consuming her whole. Each breath sucked in flames that scorched her from inside out. She thrashed against the ground, her screams stretching past human sound. Her flesh bubbled and blackened—she could smell it, taste it, *feel* it peeling away.

The inferno snuffed out. Now, darkness pressed against her aged skin as she gripped a book, her arthritic fingers finding strength in rage. Years of sacrifice, of devotion, reduced to lies printed on paper. She shredded every false promise, every hollow word, until her lap was filled with the confetti of a wasted life.

The scene twisted again, and suddenly she was drowning in eyes the color of autumn leaves. It was the woman from the syphoning earlier. She was looking straight into Nova's eyes.

"I haven't decided anything, Roric," she said. "I just need more time."

Each word was a blade sliding between Nova's ribs. Time. Such a gentle word for abandonment. Such a soft way to say *I don't love you enough to stay.*

A shrill screech shattered the image, thrusting Nova back into reality. The cavern ground began to shake beneath her feet. Pain shot through her head. She covered her ears and gaped at the syphon. It pulled in all directions, like a tempestuous whirlwind. The sound swelled, mingled with remnants of memories—hundreds of different voices merging together. Pressure built up in her brain. Nova felt like it might burst. The cave quaked harder, and Nova's palms fell to the cold, damp ground. The syphon lowered until it was in front of her face again. Nova's eyes widened.

"Get her out!" Cronian yelled.

The syphon's hiss sent a shudder down her body.

A hand ripped her arm, yanking her to the exit. Her father had grabbed her. She tried to stand, but he was dragging her with such force that she continued to stumble. Once outside the cave, the terrible sound faded and the earth began to still. A string of people from town were running in their direction. Denali raced toward Nova, reaching his arms out to tend to her.

Their father scowled at him. "Make your next moves carefully, boy."

"Cronian, what's going on?" someone in the gathering yelled.

"Is the syphon okay?"

Murmurs of concern rippled through the crowd. "The syphon—check on the syphon."

Cronian clenched his jaw and tightened his grip around Nova's forearm. She let out a quiet squeal.

He turned to Merek. "Take her to the spire, *now.*"

✦

As Nova approached, the spire loomed before her—a dark stone tower piercing the blanket of swirling storm clouds brewing above.

Upon entering, worn steps spiraled along the interior wall, leading to rows of tiered seating that surrounded a central platform.

Guards flanked Nova as she was led across the chamber floor to the pedestal. She felt the weight of countless eyes upon her from the seats above. Finally, her captors secured her wrists with chains anchored to the floor.

The highborns sat on their thrones, looking down on her. Now that they were out of the cave, Nova could study Morianna's appearance, which always demanded attention. Though she shared years with Father, time had touched her with remarkable grace. Her gown of shimmering gold pooled around her like molten metal, contrasting strikingly with her rich, black skin. Her hair, styled into an extravagant display of braids, was piled high upon her head.

Nova's braids had been taken down at Cronian's insistence—a highborn facing trial was too big a spectacle, he'd said—and she felt vulnerable with her hair hanging free in front of everyone. The loose strands fell around her face, occasionally obscuring her vision and reminding her of how she'd been stripped of even this small aspect of her identity. Her hands tingled unpleasantly, the circulation partially cut off by the tight metal cuffs.

Archaelus, the eldest of the three highborns, sat on Morianna's left. He wore a dark green robe. The sharp contour of his cheeks gave him a stern, almost skeletal appearance. He stared forward lifelessly. He could fall over dead any moment and nobody in the building would be surprised. Somehow his heart kept beating. It was probably because he had no living offspring to inherit his title.

On the other side of Morianna sat Cronian. His black suit fit his broad form with precision, as did the crisp black shirt underneath. He reached down and tugged at the ends of his sleeves, straightening the cuffs.

Each of the highborn's bloodlines discovered one of the three abilities. Morianna's grandfather learned how to train the mind to enhance sight and hearing, by taking from one sense and giving to another. Archaelus's great-great-grandfather discovered healing. It was Nova's own grandfather, Lucien Darkov, who had introduced syphoning, the newest and most sacred ability, allowing one to discard whichever memories they did not want to keep. He became a sovereign for his offering to Ghandria and the Darkov line earned its place as highborns. But now, Nova wasn't so sure that title would hold true. If there was one thing which drew more attention than a highborn, it was a miscreant.

Two women in the stands were eyeing her, and Nova could feel their judgmental gaze hanging over her as they leaned close, trading secrets behind cupped hands. Nova focused on her senses. She extended her hearing past hundreds of voices until it found them. Their faces were now mere blurs, unrecognizable in the periphery of her diminished vision. Enhancing one sense always came at the cost of another. Stretching her hearing meant sacrificing her sight.

"Surely they'll exile her," one of them said.

The other woman spoke, "That's two transgressors in these past five weeks."

"Who else?"

"That Taos lad, do you recall? The boy who lost his parents."

"Shhh. You could get us both in trouble, throwing his name around like some fumbling fool. You know we mustn't utter the name of a miscreant after exile."

"It was such a shame. Then again, his parents were the worst kind of people. Good riddance, I always say."

"Surely. But what is to become of this one? You know . . . I heard she's of distant relation to the *Darkov line.*" The woman spoke the last words in a quiet hush, as if saying it aloud was unholy.

"Surely not."

"Look at the child, midnight hair, fair skin, the Darkov eyes."

Nova's eyes were mirror copies of her father's and grandfather's —a bright blue that easily identified her as their offspring. Denali's eyes were the same rich hue as his hair, a deep chestnut brown that Nova had always envied, mostly because those were their mother's eyes.

The two women inspected her a few moments longer.

"How absolutely terrifying."

"My word," one of them said, watching the entrance. "Here comes Vivian, if you can believe it."

"Carrying *another* newborn," spat the other with a disdainful click of her tongue. "It's unheard of. Does she aim to populate the entire land single-handedly?"

They watched as Vivian navigated the mass of people, holding an infant in her hands.

"Three children," the other woman sneered. "It's disgusting."

More vicious gossip slithered into Nova's ears—speculations about her indiscretion and potential banishment. The walls seemed to bend inward, thousands of eyes pressing down until Nova's bones felt brittle beneath their judgment. Each breath turned to broken glass in her lungs.

Desperate to shield herself from their words, Nova tried to raise her hands to cover her ears. The heavy shackles bit into her wrists as she strained against them, barely managing to lift her hands to shoulder level before the chains pulled taut. She was a sparrow thrashing against iron bars, each heartbeat a frantic wing beat against her cage. Her inner turmoil swelled, like a mental scream only she could hear. Her rising anxiety threatened to consume her until a familiar voice called out to her.

"Breathe, Nova," Denali said. "Just breathe."

She opened her eyes and found him in the first row. "I'm getting you out of this," he said.

His words rang hollow. She didn't care if anyone was listening in. She was defeated. "They know, Denali."

He frowned. "We'll figure something out, Nova."

She froze at the mention of her name. After today, he wouldn't ever be able to say it again. She would be erased from existence. She felt like a fool for ever believing it could be any different. The stiffness of her cold blood turned to a flash of hot anger. She shook her head. "It's over, Denali."

A flicker of pain crossed his features. "Don't say that."

"Stop trying to fix this. I don't belong here, Denali. I never will."

Denali held her gaze in silence. Would he finally admit defeat?

After years of shielding her, of hiding their secret, would he finally accept what she was? A *miscreant*? She waited for him to speak. When he did, his words were steady. "There's never been a moment you didn't belong here. Not one."

Nova released a hot breath and dropped her head. Staying calm was nearly impossible with such a huge group of people surrounding her. Her anxiety always heightened around crowds. Denali was the only person she could talk to without having the feeling that her brain was screaming in her skull.

Morianna rose from her seat and the room instantly fell silent. Everyone shifted to direct their attention.

"Esteemed citizens of our beloved Ghandria," Morianna began, "we gather here today to perform a most crucial duty—the identification and removal of those who hinder our society's inexorable march toward perfection."

She paused, allowing her words to sink in before continuing.

"For generations, we have ascended beyond the limitations of our base ancestors, honing our senses, sharpening our minds, perfecting our very essence. Yet among us lurk those who would drag us back into the mire of mediocrity—the miscreants."

Morianna's lip curled in disgust as she uttered the last word.

"These flawed creatures are not merely useless to our society— they are a pestilence. Their inability to evolve alongside us is a genetic aberration that threatens the very fabric of our evolution. To allow them to remain, to breed, to infect our pristine bloodlines with their impotent genes, would be to invite our own devolution. We view this process as a purification and we excise these malignant growths from our society, ensuring the continued ascension of our species. Our society, our very future, depends on our unwavering commitment to this principle."

She gave a wicked grin. "The weak are pruned so the strong may thrive."

The chamber burst into thunderous applause and cheers. Morianna's grin grew wider the longer the cheers went on. When it didn't die down, she lifted her palm and the building fell silent. "And now, to the matter at hand."

Nova braced herself for what would come next, the three questions she had dreaded her entire life.

"Our dear, young Nova," Morianna called out, "do you possess the ability to heal?"

Nova's body stiffened. Morianna had purposefully neglected to say her full name. Cronian would do everything in his power to keep his people from knowing Nova was his daughter. She would bring disgrace to their name. Nova took in the crowd of unfamiliar faces, strangers to her after a lifetime spent within the walls of her mansion. She caught Denali's eyes again and he nodded at her. The simple gesture steadied her, but she couldn't entirely quell the tremor in her voice as she forced out the words, "I do."

True. Thanks to her father, she was rather good at it. His lashes had given her and Denali plenty of practice healing wounds. She wasn't nearly as skilled at it as Denali, but no one had more practice than him.

"Do you possess the ability to enhance your senses?"

Simultaneously, the onlookers leaned forward, waiting.

"I do."

Gasps and stunned voices filled the room. People began to shift and look at each other. Yes, she'd had tutors and extra lessons from Denali, and she had learned how to take from one sense and give to another. Nova held her breath, waiting for the final question.

"Do you possess the ability to syphon?"

Nova's entire frame shook and it took everything in her to stay upright. The question lingered in the air, holding the entire room captive. They were waiting—waiting for her to reveal the secret that had plagued her her whole life.

The secret that would strip her of her title.

The secret that would remove her from existence.

And separate her from Denali forever.

Morianna repeated her question, firmly. "Do you possess the ability to syphon?"

This was it, this was the end. Every effort she and Denali had expended, all of their training, all of the *hiding* had led them to this point. It was all for nothing. She was foolish to believe she could ever escape her fate. She looked up at Denali. His expression carried the same determination she had seen countless times before. They had done all they could. If there was a way out, they would have found it by now. With the only ounce of courage Nova could muster, she whispered her answer—

"No."

The chamber erupted with cries of horror. They jumped out of their seats. Someone in the front row shrieked. Others became rageful, yelling at each other and directing protests at the highborns.

"That's not possible," someone yelled. "Nobody has ever failed to syphon!"

"How can this be?" another person asked.

Pressure built in Nova's head like a drumbeat. Her fingers dug into the fabric of the dress, threatening to tear the fine silk.

A booming yell came from Cronian, "Silence!"

Archaelus startled awake, clutching at his heart with bony fingers.

The room fell silent, all eyes on Archaelus. He sagged back in his throne, already drifting off again.

Morianna looked directly at Nova. Her gaze was dark and cold like Cronian's.

"Nova, you have proven incapable of mastering one of the three abilities. Your failure to evolve alongside us marks you as inferior to our kind. You are hereby declared . . ." She paused before uttering, "a miscreant."

The crowd broke into anxious conversation and Morianna raised her hand to silence them. She waited until they returned to their seats.

"Nova, I hereby condemn you to exile on the Isle of Nadir, effective at dawn's first light."

Nova's knees gave out beneath her. As she fell, the metal links of her chains scraped against the floor. Panting heavily, she struggled to orient herself. One hand covered her thudding heart while she fought for air. The floor was like a magnetic field, pulling her weight down . . . down . . . down.

Being sentenced to Nadir was a banishment, a life sentence.

Nobody had ever returned. She wasn't sure why she had ever thought it might be different for her. All miscreants were sent there. And Nova wasn't any ordinary miscreant. She had been rejected by the syphon, the most sacred ability in their land. Other miscreants lacked the abilities to heal or to enhance their senses, but nobody else had ever failed to erase their memories. Nova had just become the first miscreant charged with the indiscretion of syphoning.

✦

From his seat in the front row, Denali had a clear view of Nova on the platform below. The low partition wall separating the audience from the central stage was barely waist-high to him. Nova seemed both impossibly close and frustratingly out of reach. Denali stared forward numbly. He couldn't shake himself from the reality of what had just been declared.

Nova . . . you are hereby declared a miscreant.

Murmurs and protests from those around him blurred together as he tried to regain control of his spinning head. He had dreaded this possibility, and had never come to terms with it. Now that it was here, he was not going to accept it.

He stood from his seat.

No weakness. Show only confidence, he told himself. Though that was hard with so much on the line.

Denali lunged over the low partition wall and onto the platform where Nova sat shrunken and helpless.

"People of Ghandria"—he lifted his head to address the spectators—"I am the son of Cronian Darkov, grandson of Lucien Darkov."

Ghandrians stared back. He didn't need to remind them of his title, but he needed their attention for what he was about to do. He brought his gaze to the highborns, specifically to Morianna Bloodthorne, the woman who finalized all banishments.

"As a member of the Darkov line, I lift an appeal for Nova's indiscretion."

The assembly broke into stunned muttering. Denali felt his father's dark stare. He met it, challenging him.

"You surprise me, Darkov." Morianna spoke casually. "You are aware of the consequences for interrupting a trial, are you not?"

He gave her a cutting smile. "I am quite aware."

"And you are aware that no one has ever succeeded in altering the course of a banishment?"

"I am," Denali said. He began to move, his steps calculated as he circled the platform where Nova was chained.

As he paced, his voice carried to every corner of the chamber. "It's true, only a handful of people have ever had the courage to challenge a banishment." He completed half a circuit around Nova.

"It has only ever been family members or lovers, desperate to save their beloved from exile." His path brought him directly between Nova and the highborns. He paused there, facing the tribunal. "However, it has always ended in a lifetime in the dungeons for speaking against the highborns, and the banishments took place nonetheless." Denali's voice grew harder. "Over time, our people have learned to stay quiet."

A smirk played across his lips. "But not today."

He resumed his orbit, completing his circle around Nova and addressing the people now. "I am sure the people will agree that this is no ordinary trial."

"Oh?" Morianna perked up. "And why is that?" She was egging him on, daring him to betray his father. She loved a good scandal. And he was about to give it to her. Ghandrians sat on the edge of their seats, waiting. Denali's fingers twitched when he met his father's cold glare, a look that warned of the consequences of what he was about to share.

Denali rested his eyes on his little sister. She slowly shook her head. She had no idea he had planned this. He hated to catch her off guard, but this was Plan B. It was his *only* Plan B. She would never have agreed to it because it meant bringing shame on their family. But Denali was no stranger to shame.

"Because, dear Ghandrians . . ." He practically spat the words. Below him, Nova shook her head desperately.

"Denali, no," she pleaded.

He flashed her a wink and continued, "What the highborns have neglected to tell you is Nova's full name . . ."

Cronian rose from his seat. "Boy!"

"Ladies and gentleman, may I introduce . . ." He took Nova's hand and lifted her up so she stood. "My dearest kid sister, Bellanova Darkov."

The audience recoiled as one. Their shock quickly turned to outrage.

"Did he say Darkov?"

"Bella Darkov?"

". . . the daughter he keeps hidden."

"It can't be true!" someone yelled.

The Darkov name rolled through the stands like thunder.

"Silence!" Cronian's voice boomed.

The cacophony ceased and a sea of faces turned in Cronian's direction. His gaze grew darker and Denali shuddered, fully aware of the punishments that would follow. Right now, all that mattered was Nova. Her hand was stiff in his.

"Foolish boy!" Cronian yelled. "No miscreant is a daughter of mine."

Denali watched Nova's head drop low. He couldn't imagine the hurt she was feeling. All she had ever wanted was to make their father proud. Denali learned a long time ago that it was a lost cause.

He squeezed her hand and then continued, "Ghandrians, if the progeny of Lucien Darkov, the creator of the syphon, has not been accepted by the syphon, then what is to become of the rest of us?"

Morianna raised her head.

Denali's hand slipped from Nova's and he took two steps toward the highborns. He didn't want to get too close while Cronian had that look on his face.

"The syphon would not reject that which created it. So instead of blaming Nova for the failure, consider—does this not mean that the syphon has become unstable?"

Archaelus stood, wobbling as he yelled, "You dare question the syphon?"

A guard reached out to return him to his seat.

"Choose your next words carefully, boy," Cronian growled.

"My loyalty has always been to the syphon," Denali said. "I am simply raising the point that if the syphon rejects the blood of its own creator, then people may begin to question it."

Cronian gritted his teeth together. He knew Denali was right. This would spark rumors throughout Ghandria. Protecting the syphon was Cronian's most sacred duty. It was Denali's only loophole.

"And if the people begin to question what the highborns have created, what stops them from beginning to question the highborns themselves?" Denali said.

Uneasy glances shifted through the crowd. Cronian glared down at him.

Yes, he would surely get his lashes for this.

"What is it you are suggesting, youngborn?" Morianna asked.

Denali hated it when the highborns called him that. He was nearly nineteen. In a week, he would be allowed to officially sit as a witness of the syphon rituals. After that, Morianna had no right to refer to him as a youngborn.

"My suggestion is to give Bellanova more time. She can still learn to syphon." Even as he said the words aloud, he had to try to convince himself it was possible. Thirteen was the age at which girls were supposed to prove their abilities to evolve. Nova was four years past that. Luckily, being a youngborn granted certain privileges. Exemption from testing was one of them. It's how Nova was able to hide her indiscretion for so long.

"When she does," Denali continued, "everything will go back to normal. The highborns' rule will be absolute and the syphon will never again be questioned."

The collective gaze shifted back to the highborns. Whispers

fluttered through the crowd as they cast uneasy glances toward them.

Perfect. That was exactly what Denali needed in order for this to work. If there was one thing his father hated, it was being challenged.

Cronian clenched his jaw. Beside him, Morianna contemplated for a long moment. She parted her lips to speak, "Very well, Darkov."

Denali's heart pounded.

"Seeing as you are so sure, Nova will be given extra time to prove she can syphon."

Relief flooded through him.

It had worked. His plan had actually worked.

She looked at Nova. "Sixty days, youngborn. That is what you get."

Nova turned to Denali, her face a mask of disbelief. Denali straightened his posture. He could work with that. Morianna's sixty-day reprieve would give him and Nova another chance to *escape*. It would be plenty of time for him to come up with a new plan to get them both out.

Denali shrugged. "Well, everything is in order then." He reached a hand out to the guards signaling for the keys to Nova's chains. "I'll just release her and we'll be on our way—"

"Not so fast, youngborn," Morianna said.

Denali's head snapped up at her smug grin.

"I never said the girl would be staying here."

His heart dropped. *Surely she can't mean . . .*

"Bellanova Darkov, you are hereby sentenced to the Isle of Nadir."

No.

"You will have time there to learn to syphon. If you have done so within your timeframe, you will return to Ghandria by way of the boatman and your miscreant title shall be revoked. If you fail to do so, you will remain in Nadir." She glanced at Denali with a smirk for her last word— "Forever."

Denali's fingers quivered at those ominous words. This wasn't right. This wasn't the plan. Legends of Nadir whispered of the miscreants within, being devoid of mercy, steeped in cruelty and malice. Nova wouldn't survive there. Denali knew that. He also knew Morianna knew that.

"My dear child," she said with a feigned look of sorrow, "you didn't think we would allow her to stay here with *you*? Surely not after your scheme in the forest today."

The weight of Morianna's words hung heavy in the air, suffocating Denali's hopes. His mind raced, searching for a loophole, a way to defy Morianna's decree. But the realization slowly settled in—he was powerless against the highborns' authority, especially when they were determined to make an example of Nova.

He turned his head and his gaze flickered to his sister, whose eyes brimmed with unshed tears. There had to be something else he could do, some other loophole he could find. Time was slipping through his fingers like grains of sand, and the trial was drawing to its inescapable conclusion.

A heavy silence settled in the building, broken only by the soft sound of Nova's ragged breaths. Denali's thoughts splintered while he searched for a solution. Morianna's smirk widened as she reveled in her triumph over his failed rebellion. She relished the opportunity to assert her dominance, to remind him of his place in the hierarchy of Ghandria.

Denali's hands curled into tight fists. He refused to accept defeat. It was his job to stop this. Nova was led away, her steps faltering beneath the weight of her fate. He snapped out of his trance and bolted toward the band of guards holding her, but before he could reach her, strong hands closed around his arms, pulling him back with a force that made him lose his footing. Two guards restrained him and he struggled against their grip. His roar of defiance bellowed through the building.

One of the guards bent down, grasping a large metal ring set into the floor near the platform's edge. With a grunt, he heaved upward, revealing a dark opening beneath the metal slat. Another guard unlocked Nova's chains from the floor.

Something broke inside Denali as he watched them lower her into the opening, her raw eyes meeting his one last time before she sank into the darkness.

THREE

Nova huddled in her cell beneath the spire. Cold stone leeched warmth from her skin as she leaned against the wall. A single narrow beam of moonlight filtered through the high barred window, inching away from her as the night deepened. She counted her breaths until the numbers blurred together, trying to prove she was still solid, still here. But she was fading at the edges, like ink bleeding into water. Soon there would be nothing left of Nova Darkov at all.

And what about Denali?

Surely, he was receiving his punishments as she sat there.

Why did he act so recklessly?

He had just poisoned the Darkov name. And it was all her fault. She wrapped her arms around herself, trying to hold together what Nadir would tear apart. Denali's voice came to her mind. *Don't think the worst.*

At least here, she was alone.

At least now, it was dark.

At least tonight, it was silent.

A knock sounded on the wall, but Nova ignored it. Her gaze was fixed on a crumb beside her on the cold floor. Tales of Nadir haunted her—creatures feeding on fear, feral miscreants, poisonous soil. Nova's skin prickled.

A tiny bug scurried over to the crumb. It grabbed it, pushing with no luck. Nova absently nudged a smaller crumb closer. The bug claimed it, inched toward a crack in the wall, and vanished. Nova's finger traced circles around what remained.

The tapping came again, louder this time. Nova stretched her hearing.

"If you can hear me," Denali's voice drifted from outside the spire, "there's something I need to talk to you about."

His words cracked something inside her. She closed her eyes, gathering each syllable close before they could slip away. Soon enough, she'd forget the sound of his voice entirely.

"Do you remember our nights stargazing?" she asked.

It was their most exciting pastime. With their sights stretched into the sky, they witnessed wonders. Shooting stars blazed across the darkness, trailing stardust that felt as though they could reach out and touch it.

"All the stories you told me when I was a kid . . . Tell me my favorite one again. The one about the star girl."

It was silent for a few moments. Then, Denali began to rehearse the story he'd told her so many times growing up. "In the vast sky, filled with sparkling stars, there was one star named Astraea who was different from the others. While most stars shone in the usual golden light, Astraea radiated an azure hue that was unlike anything the others had ever seen."

As Denali continued, Nova imagined the stars above.

"But being unique sometimes made her stand out in a way that made the other stars uncomfortable. They didn't understand her light and it made them worried. One night, the other stars decided to take Astraea's light from her. They surrounded her, covering her glow with their golden radiance. They blocked her light until she became dimmer and dimmer, fading and fading in the dark sky. Astraea was on the verge of disappearing when the mother star, Cassiopeia, reached out to her.

Cassiopeia was the eldest star in the sky and had the most brilliant light in the entire galaxy. She embraced Astraea with her warm radiance and, in a selfless act of love, Cassiopeia began to give Astraea her own light. As Cassiopeia's glow dimmed, Astraea's light intensified, casting a blue brilliance that outshone all the other stars. Cassiopeia smiled at her daughter as her light continued to dwindle. Before she disappeared completely, she said to Astraea, 'Lu mea evoradara.' That is to say—"

"I will always give you my light," Nova whispered, finishing his story. "Denali?"

"Yeah?"

"Why would Cassiopeia sacrifice all of her light?"

It was silent for a moment before he answered. "Because, Nova. Some stars are meant to be bright. And some are meant to keep the light alive in others."

Nova tilted her head back, resting it against the wall.

"Promise me, Nova," Denali said. "Promise you won't give up. You have to keep going without me. I'll find a way to bring you back."

It used to be common for a miscreant's family to rebel. Some had tried to steal the Marmoris and failed. Others had braved the ocean without it and were swallowed by the currents and whirlpools. Once, a parent had purposely lost her vision to get banished and be reunited with her loved ones. It was all in vain, though. The highborns couldn't allow them to outsmart the system.

Instead, they offered them the choice to erase their most painful memories of the exiled, and, over time, people became more and more reliant on the syphon. They became more supportive of the banishments, too. Now, people turned on family or friends when they were suspected to be a miscreant.

But not Denali.

He knew what she was and had spent years helping her hide it. Keeping her safe. But how long could he last without erasing their memories together?

A tear slipped down her cheek.

"Tell me the star story again."

The guards came to take Nova at the break of sunrise. Hands bound, she was led through a line of people—more than had ever before shown up for an exile. That was to be expected—she was a descendant of the Darkov line. The spire cast a long shadow across the gathering. Sunlight bore through Nova's brain. She had lowered her auditory level before leaving her cell, so she could only detect faint muffles coming from the gathered mass. Even though she couldn't hear their words, she could feel their feral hatred crawling on her skin. Faces twisted into masks of revulsion as she walked the gauntlet. An elderly man's spittle caught the light as his mouth worked furiously. Nova struggled to remain calm. One crack in her composure would unleash the full force of their voices—and with this many people surrounding her, panic would devour her.

The onlookers continued to jeer and sneer as Nova walked toward the ocean's edge, less than a mile away from the beach where she and Denali had tried to escape the day before. A thick blanket of fog hung low over the water. Some in the throng dared to reach out and lay hands on her. Fingers clawed at the delicate fabric of her dress. Someone tore at the shoulder of her gown. Another aggressive yank ripped the seam at her waist, and the mob's hysteria escalated. Hastening her steps, Nova clung to the last vestiges of her attire.

Amid the chaos of grasping and shoving, a hand slipped something into her palm. She darted a searching glance, but the throng of unfamiliar faces blurred together, and the mysterious giver was lost in the churning of the mob. The clamor of their yelling and the tearing at her attire intensified. The pressure in her head built until the crowd peeled away like vultures from poisoned meat. Nova was left in the tattered rags of her once extravagant dress. Her hair was now a tangled, disheveled mess.

Cronian and Morianna stood on the shoreline. Nova, unwilling to meet her father's gaze, kept her eyes fixed on the black sand beneath her feet. She could sense the seething rage radiating from him. Meeting his eyes would etch the haunting image of his wrath into her memory forever. Denali was wedged between two guards. One gripped his arm in warning. Surely their father had ordered them to contain him lest he do anything reckless. Though Nova knew that wouldn't stop him from trying.

At the exact moment Nova was passing, Denali threw his elbow into his captor's face and leaped out toward her. Before they could reunite, another guard's grip seized Denali. He threw his head back, striking the guard squarely on the nose. As soon as that grip loosened, three more were on him. Denali struggled to break free, but they had pinned his arms behind him.

A chill came over Nova as she realized this might be the last time she would see her brother's face. She broke, losing control of her hearing, but it no longer mattered. Tears streamed down her cheeks as she watched Denali wrestle against his restraints.

"Nova!" he yelled. "Don't let them know who you are!"

The guards dragged him away from her. Nova started to run forward when a guard's grip closed around her waist, keeping her rooted in place.

"No!" She sobbed. Her arms reached out for her brother, but they continued to be pried apart.

Nova was hauled to the dock. Waves crashed against massive, jagged rocks jutting out of the water, sending sprays of foam high into the air. The Marmoris sat waiting in the churning water. The boatman, a grim and haggard figure, stood at the bow of the boat, waiting with a black hood pulled low over his eyes so that no part of his face showed.

A forceful shove from behind propelled Nova onto the boat, sending her sprawling onto her hands and knees. As she hit the wood planks, the tiny piece of paper slipped from her fingers. The world tilted and spun. She clung to the edge of the boat, her knuckles white with the strain.

Someone tossed a bag beside her and the boat lurched forward. The sound of Denali's yells rang in her ears. Tingling numbness spread from her fingertips up her arms. She forced her head up, straining for one final glimpse of her brother. He was running to the dock, his figure already shrinking across the waters.

The numbness continued to creep up her limbs. She tried to draw in a breath, but as her chest heaved, no air entered. Tears streamed down her face as she gulped frantically for oxygen. Her throat felt impossibly tight, as if her father's hands were squeezing it shut. Her eyes widened.

"I can't breathe," she gasped. "I can't breathe!"

She dug her fingernails into the skin of her collarbone. Her muscles tensed as the tingling sensation spread up her neck to her face.

The Marmoris continued its journey, carrying her farther and farther from land. The colossal rocks began to obstruct her view of the shore, their dark shapes cutting off her last sight of Denali.

Nova's entire body was heaving now, begging for air. Her eyes darted around wildly, looking for anyone to help, but the boatman's focus stayed on the horizon.

And Denali was gone.

Nova lowered her tense body to the floor of the boat. She tried to imagine him sitting beside her, holding her hand.

Breathe with me, he would say. *Just breathe.*

Denali stood motionless on the dock as he watched Nova grow smaller and smaller against the mist-shrouded horizon. Even as her face disappeared into the fog, the image of her expression, etched with fear, seared itself into his mind like a brand.

A desperate longing to erase this moment into the syphon invaded his thoughts. It was a tempting escape from this weight. He clenched his eyes shut, resisting the impulse.

No.

He vowed a long time ago to never offer any memories of Nova to the syphon. His mind raced with a million thoughts and regrets, each one cutting into his soul, reminding him of all the things left unsaid and undone.

A knot of onlookers huddled together behind him. "The poor thing," they murmured. "What a shame it is, having to bear this burden of his sister's sins."

The sound of their pity dragged against his skin. His fists tightened at his sides as he forced himself to maintain his composure.

"Come, boy," Cronian said.

Denali's nostrils flared with barely suppressed anger at the ease with which his father accepted Nova's banishment. He kept his gaze on the shoreline where his sister had disappeared. With grinding teeth, he managed to mutter, "Leave me." The air crackled with tension as he dared his father to defy him, to issue another command and provoke him.

Come on, you heartless wretch, he thought. *Give me another reason to despise you.*

But the only response was the heavy silence that hung between them, suffocating in its weight. Then came the creak of footsteps retreating across the wooden dock. Time blurred as Denali stood there, staring at the empty expanse of the sea. A nagging guilt gnawed at his conscience. He had failed Nova. He should have done more to keep her safe. Now, with miles of ocean between them, there was nothing he could do to protect her.

FOUR

The Marmoris cut through the waves, rising and falling with each swell. All that echoed in the quietude was the deep, sucking rush of the whirlpools, punctuated by gurgling eddies. Nova was slumped against the side of the boat. Her limbs felt heavy, but at least now she could feel them. Her face sagged in exhaustion the way it always did after her anxiety attacks. The world slowly came back into focus, leaving her with a dull achiness. The swaying of the boat had long since ceased to bother her. The boatman remained fixed at the bow of the vessel. In his grip was the strange tool of his trade, a dual-ended blade. On one side, it appeared to be a solid, silver paddle, which he dipped into the water to navigate the boat. On the opposite end, a crooked hook like a farmer's sickle jutted out, gleaming ominously in the pale, foggy light.

She half wondered what the purpose of the weapon was, but her mind was too tired to come up with any scenarios. A drop of water on the boat's rim caught her eye, standing strangely upright against the edge. She pulled her eyes from it and stared forward blankly, numb of any emotion.

Thoughts of Denali began to surface. She saw his face in her mind's eye. He was her protector, her constant. He always knew what to do and remained unwaveringly strong.

How was she supposed to do the same?

Promise me, he had said the night before. *Promise me you won't give up. You have to keep going without me. I'll find a way to bring you back.*

A tear slid down her cheek. Denali had never asked anything of her before, so she wanted to do this for him. She owed him that much. Whatever awaited her on the other side of these waters, whatever dangers lurked in the land of the exiled, she would have to endure them.

"I promise," she whispered.

Sixty days surviving in a world that represented her deepest fears—this was the promise she had made, and she would see it through.

The distant sound of howling broke through Nova's senses. She pushed herself upright and stared out.

The thick fog made it impossible to tell what time of day it was. The boatman stayed in the same spot, his back to her as he navigated with his oar. Nova noticed a flicker of movement beneath her. A small piece of paper, disturbed by the rocking of the boat, slid across the planks near her feet. She plucked it from the weathered wood. Curiously, she unfolded it, revealing a single word written in black pen: *Berkshire.*

Nova looked down to the bag that had been tossed in with her. She opened it, and her fingers closed around a small dagger at the bottom.

Another strange sound pulled her attention, but this time it was more of a shriek. Nova shifted herself to the side of the boat and peered through the swirling fog, though her vision proved frustratingly inadequate.

Nova closed her eyes and inhaled a measured breath. She began to retract her hearing and the howling wind faded to a hum.

With her auditory senses tuned down, her eyelids fluttered open, and she harnessed her seer ability. She stretched her vision, delving deep into the misty veil until she reached a horizon, where an island gradually came into view. It was covered in a bizarre landscape of gigantic flora. Enormous mushrooms stood on the shoreline, their caps glowing with an inner luminescence that ranged from deep amber to pale gold, though the fog obscured everything beyond the first few rows. The stems were sturdy and tall, supporting caps that spread wide like umbrellas. A short sandy beach encircled the island's perimeter. It was here that a chilling sight caused Nova's heart to momentarily stutter.

A hundred figures lined the beach, their elongated bodies pressed together, shifting and twisting in a chaotic mass. Skeletal frames contorted at odd angles, skin stretched taut over protruding bones. Their clothing, if it could be called that, hung in tatters—grimy rags that clung to their forms like a second skin. Some of their faces bore twisted grins, their yellowed teeth bared in savage snarls. Others twitched and jerked. Nova's gaze swept over their gaunt faces, taking in the dried blood caked on cheeks, the deep scars etched into skin, and the layers of grime that obscured their features.

At the front of the crowd, two figures stood out. Their milky sightless eyes stared blankly ahead, yet their necks were craned at an unnatural angle, as if straining to hear the slightest sound.

Miscreants.

They were every bit as horrifying as the stories made them sound. They shoved and clawed at each other, their bony elbows and sharp nails leaving fresh scratches on already marred skin. One man near the front convulsed violently, foam bubbling from his pale lips and spilling down his chin.

Nova's vision rushed back to her. Her breathing intensified.

"Boatman," she said, "they are waiting—"

He shot up a hand to silence her. Immediately, screams cut through the fog. Nova's stomach dropped. She must have signaled their arrival. The boatman brought them close enough to see the blackness of figures barreling into the waters. Nova's hands flew to her mouth. A small whirlpool formed in front of the boat, trapping two of the creatures in its spiral. Other figures were making it close to Nova.

Too close.

The boatman jerked his hooded head at Nova and pointed to the waters with the hooked edge of his oar.

He wanted her to get out? Here?

Suddenly, the boat rocked and Nova fell forward, her palms slapping against the deck. Sinister hands thrust from the murky depths, latching onto the vessel's side. A horrifying figure emerged, pulling itself up and causing the Marmoris to teeter perilously on its side. Nova frantically looked to the boatman, who was retracting his hook. He spun and brandished his weapon, unleashing a deadly arc toward Nova.

She ducked, and the blade cleaved through the air, striking the ghastly figure, sending it plummeting back into the abyss with a splash. Nova's flood of relief was halted when three more sets of hands clamped onto the boat's edge.

Nova squeezed her eyes shut and covered her ears to block out the screeches, wails, and splashing. When she finally mustered the courage to peer again, she recoiled at the sight of more figures dragging themselves aboard.

The boatman fought to expel the intruders one by one, but the tide of miscreants surged faster than he could repel them. Among the swarm, a particularly menacing figure climbed up, his face marred by a wicked scar. He was a blind man, his pupils clouded like frosted glass. Nova shrieked as he reached out, sinking his clawlike nails into her shoulder. Her desperate response was swift, plunging her dagger into his arm. He released her with a guttural howl of pain, only to be replaced by another pair of clammy hands that seized her from behind, yanking her over the boat's edge and plunging her into the dark waters.

FIVE

The waters engulfed Nova, their icy grip sending shockwaves through her senses as she was mercilessly dragged beneath the surface. Her lungs burned with a fierce craving for air, and desperation coursed through her as she fought to claw her way back to the surface. The clutches of the creature behind her were unrelenting, pulling her deeper into the watery abyss. Her movements grew wild, frenzied, each thrash weaker than the last.

A sudden surge of the ocean's current propelled Nova forward. She used it to break free from her captor's grasp and surfaced, gasping. She found herself distanced from the chaos on the Marmoris, where the boatman's struggle against the miscreants continued. Her bag bobbed beside her. She grabbed it and began swimming toward the shore, veering around small whirlpools, pushing through waters that teemed with miscreants rushing to the boat. Each stroke brought her closer to solid ground. When the water grew shallower, she could feel silt stirring beneath her kicks. Finally, she crawled onto the sand.

She coughed out water and flinched as more figures streaked past her into the ocean. She glanced back. The Marmoris was engulfed by a swarm of miscreants, their figures shrouding the boatman from her view. The blood drained from her face as comprehension crashed over her. They were trying to get back to

Ghandria, and the boatman was their only passage. A leaden weight settled in her gut as she witnessed the boatman's blade dancing through the air, each arc leaving a trail of crimson in its wake. As she shielded her eyes from the gruesome sight, Nova noticed a lone miscreant standing on the shoreline, frozen in time amidst the mass. It tilted its head at her.

"Darkov," it rasped in an otherworldly whisper.

The bustling crowd of figures came to a standstill. The splashing in the water ceased, and they all turned to Nova. In that dreadful moment, she understood the gravity of her situation—why Denali had warned her not to reveal her identity. These miscreants were all exiles, like her, condemned to never return home or see their loved ones again. Erased from existence, all because of the highborns. In Ghandria, being a Darkov brought honor . . .

Not here.

The miscreants crept toward her. Nova sat rigid on the sand, muscles coiled like a spring. A blood-curdling screech emanated from the boat, and they all turned as one to look as the boatman dispatched his final victim, sending a headless body tumbling back into the water. Then, the boat began to move, pulling away from the shore. A wave of wails rose from the miscreants on the shoreline, and Nova seized the opportunity to escape.

She jumped up and charged into the forest of towering mushrooms, her feet sinking slightly into the pitch-black soil. As she brushed past the massive stems, a distant sound filtered through her mind—a baby's gentle laugh and a woman's soft humming.

People.

Nova changed direction, following the sounds. Maybe they could help. The laughter grew clearer with each step.

After a few minutes, she rounded a massive stem, certain she'd find the source, but found only more mushrooms standing in the fog. The sounds shifted, coming from a different direction now. She spun in place until she realized with growing dread that no one was there at all. Then she heard it distinctly and her eyes were lured to the source. One particular mushroom beside her was throbbing with light, brightening with each echo of laughter, dimming with each pause between sounds. Nova drew closer, mesmerized by the strange synchronization.

Keening split the air and broke her trance. She glanced over her shoulder and saw a horde of miscreants charging after her, their figures barely visible through the fog.

Then, a blur of black fur launched at Nova from behind a mushroom—a feline creature twice the size of a normal cat. The force of the impact knocked Nova off her feet, sending her sprawling onto her back with a painful whoosh as her lungs emptied.

The cat, now entangled in the tattered purple silk, thrashed wildly, ripping the dress clean off Nova with its teeth, leaving her in only her thin black underdress.

As the sound of the approaching miscreants grew louder, the cat bolted and Nova's shredded dress trailed behind it like a banner. Nova rolled to the side, concealing herself behind the base of the glowing mushroom. She held her breath as the miscreants burst into view and rushed past, stampeding after the dress.

As their silhouettes faded, Nova's adrenaline began to ebb. She reached out and grasped the base of the mushroom to pull herself up.

The forest began to fade away as a vivid mental image overtook her mind with surprising force. The eerie mushroom forest and the waning sounds of the miscreants' pursuit vanished, replaced by an altogether different setting.

Nova spun around and found herself inside a room bathed in soft yellow light. The image was still forming, as if her consciousness was painting a detailed scene before her eyes. Her gaze drifted from one emerging detail to another, drinking in the fantastical sight with growing awe.

Healthy green vines adorned the stone walls, twisting and winding their way through intricate patterns like an enchanting tapestry. Thick wooden beams supported the ceiling, while glass windows reflected the light from a fireplace. A baby's wail tugged at her heartstrings. Her gaze lowered to discover an infant nestled in a crib.

Nova leaned over the crib, a soft melody humming from her lips. Without her consent, her fingers reached down to stroke the infant's rosy cheeks, brushing them like petals against silk. Her fingertips traced the tiny nose and the child stopped crying, crossing his eyes to see her finger. Nova felt her frame shake with laughter. Then, the baby began to giggle, reaching his tiny hand up and wrapping his fingers around hers.

Nova shook herself from the picture and stumbled backwards. She was back in the forest now. *What just happened?*

Panicked, she backed away and began scanning the surrounding forest for an escape. As she turned to flee, she noticed a peculiar formation: two enormous mushrooms had grown so close together that their stems had fused, creating a conjoined pair. Nova pried her eyes from the sight and steered in a different direction than the miscreants had gone, marveling at the fungi as she moved.

Now and then, a single mushroom glowed amid the others. Her footsteps disturbed the low-lying mist, leaving ghostly ripples in her wake. As Nova ventured deeper, she saw another cat sitting at the base of a mushroom and one perched atop its stumpy cap. Her body tensed instinctively and she braced herself, ready to dodge or run at the slightest sign of aggression.

To her surprise, the cats barely acknowledged her presence. They licked their fur, and their eyes slid past her as if she were invisible.

Strange.

She continued her journey, staying alert to the felines as she passed. The sun descended as Nova put more distance between herself and the ocean behind her. The mushrooms themselves were a diverse tapestry of shapes and sizes. Some resembled towering trees with sprawling canopies of bioluminescent foliage, while others took the form of colossal umbrellas, their caps casting a soft, dappled light below.

Nova's senses were awakened by a tantalizing aroma that made her stomach rumble. As she ventured onward, strains of music began to weave through the air, drawing her forward despite her exhaustion. Each step felt heavier than the last, her feet dragging across the damp, spongy ground as she moved. Gradually, the mushrooms surrounding her began to thin out.

Nova pushed through the last curtain of fungi and found herself at the edge of the forest and at the top of a small rise. Before her stretched an expanse of open land, dotted with plots of cultivated earth—a patchwork of farms and a cotton field surrounding a village. In the near distance, perhaps a few hundred yards away, she saw the silhouettes of brick cottages, smoke rising from a few chimneys. The town was substantial, with several hundred structures spread across a few square miles. Beyond the village and its farmlands, a line of dense forest extended across the other end of the island. Unlike the flat fungal forest behind her, the forest on the eastern side of the island rose into craggy highlands, where traditional trees clung to rocky slopes. She could make out the silver threads of waterfalls tumbling down the rocky face.

Nova took a moment to stretch her sight into the village in the center of the island and saw an entire town of people. To her surprise, they appeared . . . normal. They were moving about the streets, exchanging food and other goods. She brought her sight back and tugged down the long sleeves of her underdress to hide her scars, but as her hand brushed her shoulder, she froze. The fabric was torn open, and a sharp sting drew her attention to blood trickling from the wound on her exposed shoulder.

She grimaced, focusing her mind to close the wound enough for the bleeding to slow. She could finish healing later, when she was far away from this miscreant-infested forest. Once satisfied, she made her way to the center of the town. Now that there were no more giant fungi to hide behind, she ducked behind cottages as she went. The sun was setting, casting a light that was soft enough to not overwhelm her with a throbbing headache.

Once she was in the heart of the village, Nova ducked behind a barrel. She studied the townspeople, noting their clothing was much different from home. Tunics and trousers were the norm, made from coarse fabric. The colors were muted, blending seamlessly with the town's earthy palette. Even their shoes looked humble—they were sandals held together by strings or ropes. A small group of people used their hands to communicate with each other. There were stands selling fruit and bread, and others with flowers. At one, a man held out dualfates.

"Hot off the forge!" he hollered.

A small group of kids rushed toward a gathered crowd and pushed through to the front. There were "oohs" and "ahs." It piqued Nova's interest enough to draw her in. She stayed at the back where she could go unnoticed.

In the center, two boys around her age stood poised in fighting stances. One had almond-shaped eyes with straight black hair styled in a short, spiky cut. He gripped his dualfate in his right hand. Nova quirked her head to the side when she noticed he wasn't wearing any shoes.

The other boy had tousled golden brown hair. He was wearing a loose white top with the first few buttons undone. The sleeves of his top were rolled to his elbows, revealing forearms tensed for battle. He wore a sash around his hips that was meant for a sword—an antiquated choice. Most had abandoned traditional blades when dualfates were created.

"Your footwork is getting sloppy, friend." The one with golden hair smirked.

The dark-haired one shrugged. "Surely, you know, I'm only halfway sober."

The clash of their weapons echoed on the cobblestone. The audience watched in awe as the duel unfolded.

"Go, Xander!" some of the children yelled.

"Go, Taos!" others cheered.

The latter name rang in Nova's ears. She remembered it from her trial—the orphan boy the women had spoken of, the one that had been exiled just before her. As the duel reached its climax, it became clear that the golden-haired boy was the superior fighter. He executed a series of flawless moves and, with a swivel of his sword, he disarmed his opponent.

The crowd broke into wild cheers for their victor. "Taos, Taos!"

Nova's eyebrows arched, her mouth slightly agape. She was astounded that a *miscreant* could hone such skills. He looked so different from everything she'd heard about miscreants. Everyone in the village did.

Taos threw his arm around Xander and ruffled his hair.

"Ninny want one more fight," a young girl pleaded, tugging on the bottom of Taos's blouse. "Please, Taos!"

Xander freed himself from Taos's hold and knelt beside them. "Come now, children, you wouldn't want your beloved commander to challenge me again and get injured now, would you?"

Commander?

"*Him* get injured?" the young girl said, followed by a ripple of laughter from the young children.

"Another time." Taos smiled. "Berkshire is expecting me"

Berkshire. Hearing the name from her note made Nova's heart skip.

The kids mumbled their goodbyes and the gathering dispersed. Nova tracked Taos as he made his way around a corner. She fell into step behind him. When she rounded the corner, she ducked behind another barrel and watched Taos disappear around a cottage.

She half ran, leaping in giant strides toward him, when a man shoved a basket at her. "Bread it is you want, miss."

Nova shook her head. "No, thanks."

"Jimmy give you deal, he will."

Nova's eyebrows knitted together at his broken grammar, then she shook her head again, rushing to the next corner. When she reached it, there was nobody there. She turned in circles, trying to make out where he could have gone. Suddenly, a figure whipped her around and pressed her against the side of a cottage wall. Her frame hit it with a thud and she winced. Taos was holding his elbow against her, pressing into her shoulder.

"Not very subtle, are you?" he said.

Nova kept her face carefully blank. Inwardly, she willed him not to see through her facade. She steadied her breath, attempting to conceal any sign of discomfort.

"I don't know what you mean," she lied.

He squinted at her, probing for any sign of deception.

Nova fought the urge to break their eye contact. She felt the inside of her cheek caught between her teeth. Forcing her jaw to relax, she pondered her next move.

Could she tell him she was looking for Berkshire?

Surely he would want to know why. What then?

His brown eyes, flecked with gold, narrowed. Strands of his tousled curls fell beside them. He kept his forearm pressed against her, maintaining an intense presence.

"Who are you?"

Nova parted her lips to speak, but she hadn't come up with a lie yet.

He raised an eyebrow. "Most people know this one."

The feeling of her heart pounding was all Nova could focus on.

A name, a name . . . Come on, think of a name! Any stupid name!

A screech tore through the marketplace, followed by a chorus of screams. Nova shielded her ears.

"Krall!" a voice yelled from a distance. People began to run past them, doors slammed shut. In the spaces between the cottages, Nova saw some of the grotesque figures rush past. None of them had seen her yet, and she needed to keep it that way. She needed to get inside.

An entire market stand selling pottery was flung over the cottage and crashed beside Nova and Taos, dishes shattering and littering the ground.

Taos let her go and turned, reaching for his blade. Nova grabbed his forearm.

"Wait, please," she said. "I need to find Berkshire."

He looked back, studying her.

The door behind them swung open. An elderly man with deep brown skin stood in the frame. His expression was solemn as he observed Nova, his form blocking the doorway. The sounds of destruction from the marketplace drew nearer.

She looked up at the man and begged, "Please."

The old man stepped to the side, clearing the entrance. Nova rushed through the door. As Taos secured the latch behind them, she crumpled to the concrete floor. In her panicked haze, the interior of the cottage slowly came into focus.

Through an archway in the wall, she glimpsed packed dirt and grass, with straw targets standing at attention in what appeared to be a practice yard. The cottage was built in a perfect square, with narrow hallways forming a continuous loop around the central courtyard. Multiple archways lined the courtyard's perimeter, suggesting that every part of the home had direct access to the hidden training ground.

"This doesn't make sense." Taos peeked through a crack in the splintered door then turned to the man. "We need to get out there now."

The man stroked his beard as he inspected Nova. His intense gaze on her added to her anxiety. His eyes were set deep beneath a curtain of wrinkles at their corners. Furrows etched deep lines around his nose and mouth. A short, silver beard framed his face.

He placed a hand on Taos's shoulder and bobbed his head toward Nova. "Aid kit, boy."

Nova covered her bare wound, which she had yet to finish healing.

Taos nodded and turned, taking a few steps toward an archway immediately to their left. Through the opening, Nova could see a small kitchen tucked into the corner of the home. Rustic cabinets lined the walls, with a small window perched above a worn sink. A modest table with two chairs squeezed into the limited space.

The older man used his foot to push a chair closer to Nova. She looked at the seat, but shook her head. She was too dizzy to pull herself up. In the room beside them, drawers slid open and shut as Taos rummaged through them.

"I need Berkshire."

The man gave her a flat look. Taos walked back in, holding a rag and a bottle of liquid. The man turned and retreated from the front hallway, failing to acknowledge her demand.

She started to stand, reaching out her hand. "Wait—"

Her knees buckled and she stumbled, but instead of falling to the floor, she was caught by strong arms.

"Whoa, there." Taos lifted her to the chair.

He kneeled down on one knee in front of her and poured the

liquid on the cloth, then dabbed it to her shoulder. Nova squirmed at the stinging sensation.

"Now, how about that name?"

Nova gave no answer.

"I could play at this all day."

She shook her head. "It's not important."

"Which means it's *very* important." A smile curved his lips, revealing a single dimple on one side of his mouth. He added more liquid to the cloth in his hand, and dabbed it onto the wound again. Nova bit down on her tongue to keep from crying out.

"I need to know where Berkshire is."

With one hand on her chair, Taos tipped her forward. She caught herself against his frame, palms pressed to his chest as their faces hovered inches apart. His smile quirked to reveal that dimple again. "Fair trade—I'll answer your question when you answer mine."

He waited. Nova's mind was reeling, preparing a lie. She could pretend she was one of Denali's old friends. She tried to recall their names, but they kept slipping away. She could give him her partial name. There was a slim chance he knew that. She opened her mouth to speak, "It's No—" She bit her cheek. What if he *did* recognize her partial name?

Taos looked amused. "No?"

"Berkshire!" someone yelled from outside the door. Nova stilled. *Berkshire?* The elderly man that had let her in came back into the front hallway. Nova gawked up at him. He opened the door halfway, shielding them from the visitor's sight.

Berkshire nodded. "Quentin. Has anyone been hurt?"

"No. The Krall are on their way out now. But we may not be so lucky next time. They think—" He lowered his voice. "They think a youngborn is here in the village."

Taos eyed Nova suspiciously and tilted his head. Nova's frame tensed. Taos parted his lips to say something, but Nova jumped forward, grabbed his shirtfront and pressed her other palm firmly over his lips, silencing him. His expression turned to a scowl.

"And, what do you think?" Berkshire asked.

"Bollox, no. Cronian is a monster, but he's not low enough to banish his own daughter."

Taos's frame stiffened beneath Nova's touch and she cautiously loosened her grip.

"Sending a Darkov here would be a death sentence. There's not a soul that would hesitate to take their revenge."

Another crashing noise came from outside.

"Tell us if you see anything!" Quentin yelled.

Berkshire shut the door, then turned to Taos, who was backing away from Nova.

"She's a Darkov," Taos muttered.

When he said nothing, Taos raised his voice. "Berkshire!"

Berkshire spoke calmly. "I know."

Taos snapped his head up, and now the contempt was aimed at the man.

"You *knew?* You knew and *helped* her?" He spat the last words out like daggers. Berkshire only stared back. Nova looked back and forth between them.

"You let her come in here knowing what they did to us? What they did to *you?*" Taos shook his head and grabbed a coat that was hanging on the wall. "I'm giving her away."

Nova jumped from her chair to block his exit. "Wait, please!"

"You are in dangerous waters, Darkov," Taos growled. "Step back."

Nova blinked up at him and then at Berkshire.

"I suggest you listen," Berkshire said.

Nova tentatively retreated. "Please, give me a moment."

Taos stepped around her, ignoring her comment and reaching for the door.

Nova's heart raced. She hadn't even gotten to speak to Berkshire. She didn't know what she needed from him yet.

Berkshire rested one hand on Taos's shoulder and grabbed onto the back of Taos's neck with the other. He lowered so they were parallel. Then he spoke with a steady tone. "Not today."

Taos held his gaze for a few seconds, like they were having a silent conversation. Finally, Taos turned from him and hung his sword sash beside the front door. He stopped there, facing the wall. His hands balled into fists again. Without a word or glance in Nova's direction, he strode through the archway into the central courtyard. He disappeared through another archway on the far side and the sound of a door shutting resounded across the open space.

Nova looked up at Berkshire. His attention lingered on the archway where Taos had vanished. Nova opened her mouth to thank him, but something told her she should stay quiet. Berkshire crossed to a bin in the corner by the front door, opened it, and lifted a blanket from it. Dropping it on the floor beside the wall, Berkshire then crossed the hallway. He paused briefly at an archway, his hand resting on the weathered brick. With one last glance toward where Taos disappeared, he entered his own room, positioned in the right corner of the house.

The door closed with a soft thud and the cottage fell into complete silence.

Nova looked at the blanket he'd left for her on the cold concrete floor. She stared at it for a long moment, then sighed and spread the blanket out. Sitting down on top of it, she wrapped it around herself. The ache in her heart deepened as she thought of Denali and the life that she may have lost. The day had been so rushed she hadn't had time to really let the truth of her situation sink in.

She missed home.

She missed *Denali*.

She lay down and curled into herself, knees drawn tight against her body. The thin blanket did little to cushion the floor. In the distance, Krall cries shattered any illusion of lasting safety in Berkshire's cottage.

✦˙

Denali's fists clenched and unclenched as he tried to ignore the searing pain that radiated from his raw, burning arms. His flesh was torn in all directions. His father spoke with a chilling detachment as he pulled the strings of the whip through a cloth, clearing off the blood.

"Don't think about healing this time," Cronian said. "Not after what you've done."

Denali bit down hard in an attempt to manage the agony coursing through his body. If he didn't tend to the wounds right away, they would scar, joining the collection of slashes and cuts that already marred his arms.

I asked for this, he reminded himself.

"Morianna requests your presence in the morning," Cronian grunted. "It will not bode well for you if you try something. I won't have you tarnishing my name further."

Fingers trembling slightly, Denali picked up a roll of unraveled cloth bandages and began to wrap them tightly around his injuries. Each wrap elicited heavy, controlled breaths.

"I never meant for this to happen," Denali muttered, his voice strained.

"And yet . . ."

"There's still time. She's stronger than you think."

Cronian slammed his fists onto the table in a fit of rage, causing the walls to shudder. He pointed an accusatory finger at Denali, his voice thundering.

"You will learn your place, boy! My Darkov name is linked with a miscreant." He was screaming now, his face grew red and spittle flew from his lips. "She is my blood!"

Anger stabbed at Denali's core.

"Now I will have to find a way to rid us of this embarrassment."

"Don't talk about her that way," Denali growled.

A sting of pain shot through him as Cronian's backhand connected with his face. "Mind your tone!" Cronian yelled. "I am being merciful today in light of what you have done."

Denali scoffed. How typical of Father to give him twelve lashes and call it mercy.

"Consider yourself lucky, *boy*. Your punishments would be far more severe were it not for you being the sole heir to the Darkov line." He clicked the whip back into its holding place on the wall. "I need you in one piece for next week."

Denali glared at his father and spat hot blood onto the floor. The red liquid splattered across the polished marble.

"Be sure not a spot of that filth is visible when I return," Cronian said. "I won't have you spoiling my decor." He strode out of the room.

Denali relaxed his fists and noticed the nail marks dug into his palms. One week remained until he would claim his highborn birthright. If only he could have kept Nova safe until after his nineteenth birthday—maybe then his word could have carried more sway. Thoughts of her made his heart drop.

Had she made it to the Nadir safely? Would her identity remain a secret? What if someone recognized her? What if . . .

No.

He stopped his wandering thoughts. It wouldn't do any good to think the worst. Nova had to be alive. She had to survive this. Otherwise, Denali wouldn't be able to live with himself. He was her older brother. He was meant to protect her. Instead, he was to blame for—

Stop, he told himself. *Stop thinking the worst.*

✦

The next morning, Morianna's guard led Denali toward her estate where a grand limestone manor commanded a hillside. A sweeping staircase descended from ornate double doors to the geometric splendor of her private grounds—trees and shrubs forced into unnatural shapes, sculpted hedges forming a green maze. A marble statue stood watch: Morianna's grandfather, Magnus—the man who first discovered the ability to adjust one's senses. As they neared, the air thickened with the scent of damp earth. Dew clung to every surface.

Morianna's golden blazer caught Denali's eye as she glided

through her grounds, surveying her creations. Her hair, like her garden, was its own work of art. The top of her head featured a series of braids, dotted with golden cuffs, that formed an elaborate, crown-like structure, with more braids gathered and twisted into a bun at the nape of her neck.

Without turning to face him, Morianna's voice broke the stillness. "Ah, young Darkov," she purred. "Come."

She continued to glide past, hands interlaced in front of her, and Denali followed. The foliage parted, revealing a clearing. There, standing in majestic solitude, was a tree of breathtaking proportions.

Its impressive trunk twisted skyward in a mesmerizing spiral, each curve and contour speaking of centuries of growth. The bark was smooth and unblemished. From its powerful base, branches extended outward in a perfectly symmetrical array, forming a vast canopy.

Every leaf, every twig was meticulously groomed. The foliage was a stunning tapestry of emerald and gold. Clusters of plump, violet plums hung like jewels. The fruit was uniform in size and placement.

"This tree, magnificent as she is, is both an anchor of our past and the beacon of our destiny."

Denali felt a twinge of unease at the reverence in her voice. Something about this felt . . . off.

"Her roots run deep, her trunk strong." She traced the backside of her long, polished nails along the bark's contours. "Each branch, each leaf, each budding plum blossom precisely where it should be."

Her fingers moved to circle a plum fruit, blooming from a branch. She plucked it off, rotating it delicately in her grasp. "Is this not the very embodiment of divine order?"

Denali stared dully at the tree.

"Look at it," she ordered.

Reluctantly, Denali's gaze dropped to the fruit in her hand. The plum was a perfect sphere, its deep purple skin unmarred by even the slightest blemish. No bruises marked its surface, not even a single indentation from an insect's tentative nibble.

"Flawless. As all things should be," she said. "But such beauty . . . such *order* . . . does not come without sacrifice."

She strolled around to the back of the tree and Denali forced himself to follow. There, on the backside of the tree, a small twig branched off. It was rougher than the other branches and a small rotten fruit bud hung from its tip.

"For in every tree, there are branches that grow wild, that drain her strength without bearing fruit."

She reached for a pair of golden shears in her blazer pocket.

"And so, we prune." With a swift, practiced motion, she sliced off the wayward branch. Denali winced at the impact. The wild shoot fell onto the ground beside their feet.

"Tell me, youngborn, what effect does this have?"

Denali didn't answer. He wasn't sure he would be able to control himself if he opened his mouth to speak.

"You fear speaking, child, but you mustn't. It is not the sign of a confident ruler. Surely not one who is ready to take his place."

Denali's jaw tightened, his teeth grinding silently as he fought to hold back a scathing retort.

Morianna clicked her tongue. "We direct the tree's energy to where it's most needed, to the branches that can truly contribute to the tree's growth. Some may think it cruel, but true mercy lies in maintaining the health of the whole. Herein lies the secret to our prosperity, our advancement."

Suddenly, a cry rang through the courtyard. A guard escorted a woman toward them.

"Caught this one trying to sneak into the cavern," the guard said.

The woman collapsed onto the floor in front of Morianna, on hands and knees. Denali could barely make out her words through her sobs.

"My husband . . ." Her voice broke. "He's g-gone."

Morianna stared down at her.

"I c-can't . . ." Her fingers pressed against her sternum, shaking. "I can't bear this. I n-need the s-syphon."

Denali's gaze softened, the harsh lines around his mouth easing as he listened to her plea. Meeting with the syphon was only possible with an appointment and most were filled at least a week in advance. Of course, it was up to the highborns whether they would make an exception.

"Please," the woman begged. Snot began to pour from her nose. "I can't g-go on. It h-hurts."

Denali pitied the woman. This kind of hurt looked torturous. Syphoning had become sacred to their people because it allowed them to live without ever knowing grief or pain. Growing up, he had tried to imagine what the world was like before Lucien introduced the ability. How did people survive? How did they move about their day-to-day tasks with such sorrow?

Of course, Nova had been enduring sorrow her whole life. Denali had wished so many times he could help her erase all the bad.

Guilt settled like lead in his stomach.

Because Nova couldn't syphon, he felt that he shouldn't either. Her inability was responsible for Denali's decision to cap his syphoning sessions to once a year. Even then, the memories would never include Nova.

Below him, the woman continued her sobs.

Morianna bent down and lifted the woman's hands into hers. "My dear, this feeling of pain is one that mustn't ever be felt here." She stood and motioned to the guards. "Alert Cronian at once to halt the syphonings until hers is complete. This poor soul needs refuge."

The woman dissolved into tears of relief. "Th-thank you. Thank you." She reached out to embrace Morianna, but Morianna declined, waving her off.

"P-praise the syphon."

Morianna gave a toothy smile. "Praise the syphon, indeed."

The guards carried the woman away, and Morianna pulled a golden cloth from the pockets of her blazer to wipe her hands clean. As she did, she turned to face Denali. "It is my deepest hope that as you take your place, you will understand what it means to display the kind of mercy I have spoken of."

Denali studied the tree. Its flawless appearance was undeniable. But he had long learned that when something looked perfect on the outside, it rarely was within.

"Are we done then?" he asked.

Morianna's eyes darkened. "You may mock me, youngborn, but you do not comprehend the lengths it takes to keep a society evolving," she spat. "The miscreants will continue to be exiled and we are better off for it."

Denali's nostrils flared with each sharp intake of air. A vein pulsed at his temple.

"Oh, my." Morianna feigned sympathy. "How cruel of me to bring up such a sensitive subject. It must be perplexing, carrying around the weight of a sister who does not wield such a monumental ability. What would it be like, I wonder, to be her. To have to feel so deeply all the time? To have no escape from one's emotions? To have *no* syphon."

"Do not speak of her."

Morianna bent down and picked up the discarded twig from underneath the tree. "I wonder, will she survive? With her anxiety I hear she can barely function on her own. She is a weak little thing, is she not?"

Something snapped inside Denali. He stepped forward, but a guard restrained him. He held Morianna's gaze, unflinching. "She's stronger than you think."

Morianna's lips curled into a predatory smile. "We shall see."

She gently took his hand, placing something in his open palm before closing his fingers around it.

"Do not turn your back on the secret to our prosperity, youngborn." Her eyes blazed as she delivered her final pronouncement. "The weak are pruned so the strong may thrive."

After she glided off, Denali grunted and tugged a shoulder forward so the guard released his hold. He opened his fist. The severed, lifeless twig lay in his palm.

SIX

Nova pretended to be asleep when Berkshire and Taos awoke. They didn't speak to one another, but she could hear their footsteps moving around the cottage. After about an hour, new sounds began to filter through the quiet morning air: the creak of a door opening and closing, followed by a sudden burst of chatter and laughter. Young voices filled the space.

Taos's voice rose above the others, giving instructions that were met with a chorus of "Yes, commander!"

The patter of multiple feet echoed about. Then came a series of dull clacks and thuds. Curiosity finally overcame her, and Nova's eyes cracked open. As she shifted to sit up, soreness bloomed in her joints, her muscles protesting after a night on the hard floor. With a grimace, she pushed herself upright, only to shriek at the sight of a tiny mouse gnawing at her underdress. The creature scurried away.

She craned her neck and peeked through the archway into the courtyard, wincing at the open sky above. In the middle of the space, Taos commanded the attention of a group of young students. Their wooden practice blades moved smoothly through the soft morning air. The students, ranging in age from around six to thirteen, moved with excitement.

Nova watched as Taos guided them through the art of combat.

The clacking and thudding of wood striking wood filled the air. Taos's voice rang out with instructions, guiding and shaping the skills of his eager students.

"Remember, Enzo, keep your stance lower. You'll have more balance and control that way."

The little boy nodded up at him, then bent his knees and held out his blade again.

"Better," Taos said, then crossed his arms as he walked through the group of students, surveying them as they took the proper steps and blocked their attackers.

It was captivating that a miscreant had such a role. Nobody ever took miscreants seriously. They condemned anything that came out of a miscreant's mouth, and they certainly never took *lessons* from them. Nova's heart skipped a beat as someone cleared his throat behind her. She whirled around and found Berkshire standing there.

Without a word, he shoved a bundle of fabrics into her arms. "Change," he said.

Startled by his manner, Nova unfurled the fabric and lifted the first cloth. It was a long piece of beige linen.

When he exited the room, Nova called after him, "Wait! I need to talk to you."

Berkshire ignored her, shutting the door to give her privacy.

Nova sighed and stared at the cloth. Hesitantly, she attempted to put it on, first trying to wrap it around herself like a towel, but the excess fabric left her feeling clumsy and restricted. She then tried to pull it over her head like a tunic, only to find herself tangled in the voluminous cloth. As she struggled, a thin rope bundled with the fabric fell to the floor. She picked it up, pausing to consider its purpose.

She peeked out at the students again and found a young girl wearing the same rope tied around her waist. Ducking back out of view from the archway, Nova removed her underdress, and copied the girl. She draped the fabric over her left shoulder, leaving the other bare that she had healed last night when she couldn't sleep. At her waist, she cinched the cloth with the leather cord. Beneath the draped cloth, she slipped on brown, form-fitting leggings.

Nova glanced down at herself, feeling like a stranger in her own skin. She drew in a quick breath when she noticed that her lower arms were bare, leaving her scars completely vulnerable. She tore a long strip from the edge of fabric on her top and wound it around her forearms. The rough fabric chafed slightly, but it was a small price to pay for concealment.

The door to Berkshire's room opened. Nova watched as he walked past her, a pair of leather boots in his hand. He moved through the hallway into the adjacent kitchen, where he took a seat and dropped the boots on the floor for her. Turning back to Nova, he motioned toward the chair that had been left in the hallway the day before. "Sit."

Nova dragged the chair into the kitchen and sat down across from him. "Um," she said. "Thank you for the clothes."

She waited for him to speak, but he remained silent, his expression unreadable. She tapped her fingers on her knee and looked around the room to avoid eye contact. He folded his arms and sat back in his chair. Clearly, he wasn't going to break the silence. Nova finally looked at him and spoke again.

"I need your help. I have to get back to Ghandria."

"That isn't done."

"My father will allow it if I correct my indiscretion," she said. "He's given me sixty days. I think you can help me."

He gave no response.

"Someone gave me a note with your name on it. I assume it's because you can teach me," she said.

His eyes clouded for a moment. Nova watched as he stared at the far wall. Then his demeanor shifted again, and his expression closed off entirely.

"You're mistaken." He rose from his chair and began to walk out of the kitchen.

It was as though an extra twenty pounds had been draped over her. "You're my only hope of seeing my brother again," she whispered. "Please."

Berkshire halted under the archway, his back to her for a few moments. "Show me the note."

"What?"

He strode down the narrow hallway leading to the back of the cottage, leaving Nova alone with one major problem—she didn't *have* the note.

Why did he need to see it? Did he think she was lying?

Her mind reeled, retracing her steps from the previous day. She must have put it back in her bag. But where had she put the bag? Even if she could find it, the note would be soaked and likely ruined.

She backtracked through her memories until realizing where she must have left it—in the forest, at the base of the glowing mushroom. Her spirits plummeted. She had no idea how to find that one mushroom in a forest full of them. And even if she did find it, the place was teeming with Krall on the prowl. It was a death trap. She would have to find another way to convince Berkshire to help her.

She stood and started to follow after him. Right as she turned the corner, Taos came striding through the archway from the courtyard, nearly colliding with her. He was focused on the blade in his hand, a whetstone in the other.

"Watch it," he muttered, barely glancing up as he brushed past her and into the kitchen.

She bit her lip, hesitating to speak. "Do you know where—"

"He left." Taos continued to sheath his blade.

"Where?"

"Not your concern."

"It's important."

"Surely."

"Do you know when he'll be back?"

He lifted his sword to inspect his work, not looking up at her when he replied, "Yep."

Nova chewed on her bottom lip and decided to change tactics. "I, uh, I never thanked you for not giving me away yesterday."

Taos's eyes flashed at her. He set his stone on the table and started walking toward her, forcing Nova to take a few steps back.

"Listen, Darkov. The only reason I haven't is because, for some reason, Berkshire wants you here. Don't think for a second that I won't turn you in if the Krall hurt anyone in their search for you."

Nova swallowed hard, knowing his threat was not to be taken lightly. She found herself trapped against the wall. "What are the Krall?" she asked. "Why do they look so different from you all?"

Taos's expression darkened. "They all started off the same as us. They were exiled here, banished from their homes and families. Everyone fights to get back at first . . . You learn to give up over time. Accept your fate and try to make a life for yourself here. But some of us . . ." His voice trailed off.

Nova had seen them on the shoreline. They were so strange, so *inhuman*. "They never gave up," she said. "But they were so different?"

"Stop talking about things you don't understand. Berkshire asked me to tell you to stay out of the spora forest. The spores release toxins some nights that can be detrimental to . . ." He paused. "On second thought, feel free to go whenever you'd like."

"Toxins?" Nova asked. "Is that what made them monsters?"

Taos's eyes whipped back up at her. "Don't call them that. They've spent years, some of them their entire lives, in that forest, fighting to get back to their families. Fighting to get back to a place where they no longer exist."

"Surely they understand they can't go back."

"Do *you*?" he challenged.

Nova was taken aback by his comment. She had hope of getting back, yes. In her case, she *did* have a chance.

"It's different," she said.

"Different, how? Because you're a youngborn? Because you're *better* than them?"

His voice dripped with bitterness. "Let me clue you in, Darkov. Those *monsters* were people taken from their families and erased from the only life they ever knew. They became that way because of *you*."

"But . . . I've done nothing to them?"

"Oh? Has your father not been training you and your brother to take his place? Has he not been bringing you with him to witness the syphonings?"

Nova flinched as Taos took another step closer and slid his sword into his sash. "To me and everyone else here, you are the reason we live this way. Think about that before you call *them* the monsters."

His words hit Nova like a physical blow. Her cheeks burned with shame and the effort to hold back tears.

How could she be the reason for their suffering when she had suffered too?

She looked down at the floor as she struggled to process his accusation. In Ghandria, she'd been singled out as different, a *freak*. Now, here she was among people who had endured the same rejection and fear she had, yet she was still somehow separate from them.

Still the one who didn't belong.

Taos's face was mere inches from hers, and she could see the years of pain etched in his features.

"Taos!" a child yelled from the courtyard. "Enzo need help!"

His voice dropped lower. "If Berkshire hasn't handed you in by the end of the day, I'll do it myself."

With a huff, he retreated, leaving Nova against the wall, heat rising to her face. She clenched her fists, her nails digging into her palms as she struggled to regain control of her thoughts.

How dare he accuse her of being responsible. She had done nothing wrong. She was just a pawn in her father's game. She brushed the thoughts aside, unwilling to entertain them further.

Nova pushed herself away from the wall and turned on her heel, striding back through the kitchen and grabbing her new boots on the way out. She would prove Taos wrong. She would show him that she was not the weak, privileged girl he believed her to be. If he wouldn't tell her where Berkshire was, she would find him herself. He couldn't have gone far. She swung the front door open and light flooded into the room. Nova flinched as searing pain shot through her head. She quickly shut the door. Once the pressure in her head subsided, she grabbed her blanket off the floor and wrapped it around her like a shawl, pulling a hood over her eyes for shade. She opened the door again and took her first steps outside.

As her vision adjusted, she noticed something peculiar. Outside nearly every door along the street, small piles of food were neatly arranged. Some houses had baskets filled with fresh produce, while others had wrapped parcels. A creaking sound drew her attention to a bald man pushing a wheelbarrow down the street. He stopped at each doorstep, collecting the food offerings and placing them in his barrow. With a last glance at the scene, Nova turned and hurried to the market square. As she rounded the corner of a cottage, her hand flew to her mouth, stifling a gasp.

The market was in ruins. Stands were knocked over and shards of glass littered the cobblestone floor, reflecting sunlight. Nova used her hand to shield her eyes. Her head started to pulse. She had to make this fast. She turned in a circle. There were three directions Berkshire could have gone. In one area, a man was sweeping debris. Nova approached him.

"Excuse me, sir."

The man didn't acknowledge her in the least.

"Him no hear you."

Nova whipped around to see a petite old woman facing her, holding a broom in one hand and a clay pot in the other. Her hair was a thick mane of white and her face was marked by deep-set wrinkles and skin that softly sagged, framing her old age. Nova looked back at the man, who was still sweeping, completely oblivious to their conversation.

"Lost him hearing long time ago."

The woman didn't recognize her, which meant Nova was safe to speak with her. "Do you know Berkshire?"

She grinned from ear to ear. "Well, 'course Lottie know Berkshire. Him Lottie's friend. Said hi just now."

Nova smiled with relief. "Lottie, where did he go?"

"Him did not say. Him go that way." She pointed beyond Nova, deeper into the village.

Nova began to jog that way, yelling a thank you as she fled. She ran past cottage after cottage, ducking her head around each of them. She shouldn't be out here, but she didn't have any time to waste . . . not with so much on the line. Nova was in the middle of another marketplace now. She turned in circles, realizing that she was lost. Every building was identical.

The structures started to blur together, closing in around her. Her heart was picking up speed. *Not again, not now.* She pleaded with her body to stay calm, but panic hummed beneath her skin. A tap on her back sent terror shooting through her veins.

She spun around to find a woman studying her with a faint smile. Small, delicate lines framed her eyes and mouth. Sandy blonde hair, mixed with strands of brown, fell loose. Nova flinched when the stranger lifted her hand, holding out a small bunch of flowers, fresh-picked from their stems. Nova looked down at the vibrant array and noticed the woman's hand was discolored and shiny with scars which webbed over her skin as if from a serious burn. Nova reached forward uneasily and took the flowers.

"Tulips are a child's window to the soul," she said in a hushed whisper. "See the stars, yes, a lovely time to garden."

Stars? It was the middle of the day. Nova glanced up at the bright sky and was awarded with a keener throbbing in her skull.

The woman began to hum as she recited a phrase: "Tulips and lilies for they, and Astraea, her brightness, she'll display."

A flicker of emotion softened Nova's expression at the mention of her favorite childhood story. It was the story she'd made Denali tell her over and over again growing up. Two nights ago, he'd told it to her outside her cell, perhaps for the last time.

The woman began to waltz away. "Such a lovely time to garden," she sang. Then, she stopped in her tracks and turned back toward Nova, inspecting her closely. Nova pulled her hood low over her eyes. Another woman, short and plump, approached from the back. "There you is, Clara." She wrapped a blanket around the woman. "Time come home now."

Clara paid her no heed and continued to study Nova. "Those eyes," she said. "I know those eyes."

Nova's bones stiffened. The plump woman looked back and

68

forth between Clara and Nova. "Sorry, miss," she said. "Clara been sick lately, she has."

Nova forced a shaky smile. "It's uhhh . . . It's all right."

The woman struggled to turn Clara away because her gaze remained locked on Nova, as if in some kind of trance. She finally got Clara to move and they disappeared behind a cottage.

Nova focused on the delicate flowers in her hand. The story of Astraea played out in her mind, like Denali was telling it to her again. She ached to hear his voice again. The longing carved into her.

She wasn't supposed to be here. She was meant to be home, in Ghandria with Denali. Instead, she was here, surrounded by people who resented them both. The irony of the situation struck her suddenly. She, a Darkov, was now among those her family had exiled.

She didn't want to live like this, not for any longer than the sixty days she was forced to. Her gaze traveled to the spora forest in the distance. She had made Denali a promise. If retrieving that note from her bag was the fastest way to get Berkshire to help her, then she had to try.

She could go to the edge and stretch her vision to find it and make sure no Krall were close by. Then, she would run in, grab it, and run out. It would be quick and easy. Perfect. Now she just had to move.

The sun pelted down on her as she headed to the edge of the forest. Her head was throbbing, but she kept her hood low and pressed on.

Once Nova made it to the edge, she hid between two mushroom caps. She minimized her hearing until she could hardly hear anything around her. Then, she opened her eyes and stretched her vision, cautious not to stretch it too far lest her hearing would dip too low and be gone forever, giving her another indiscretion. Her vision shot through the forest, whizzing past mushrooms and a sleeping cat. She continued for several minutes, shifting the angle of her sight, pulling it in and pushing it out, seeing more of the same as she aimed it in different directions. At last, it zeroed in on the figure of a Krall dragging one foot on the forest floor. In its hand, it was clutching a piece of tyrian purple fabric.

Her dress.

Nova shivered. Then something else caught her eye. Beyond the Krall, she recognized the distinctive shape of the conjoined sporas she had seen earlier. At the base of the mushroom beside it lay her black bag.

Nova tapped her finger against her knee, waiting for the Krall to get far enough away from the bag for her to safely retrieve it. She'd underestimated how long it would take. The Krall moved at such a slow pace when they weren't chasing her. It had been nearly an hour and she still felt it was too close, worried its hearing might still reach her.

After another twenty minutes, Nova got to her feet. She moved with a purposeful swiftness across the spongy ground between the towering mushroom stalks. Bioluminescent spores drifted through the air like lazy fireflies, casting shifting shadows across the pale caps high above. She flinched at every movement, every whisper of the spores. Pieces of her ripped dress were scattered on the ground. Then, she spotted her bag. It lay undisturbed, just as she had left it the day before. She returned her vision and hearing back to their normal states. With a few more strides, Nova closed the distance, her fingers wrapping around the strap of her bag. She crouched down and sifted through it.

Please let it be in here.

She pulled out her dagger and looked into the bottom of the pouch. The tiny, damp note was still there, impossibly intact.

She went to push herself up, but hesitated at the sight of the mushroom. Its veins pulsed with an ethereal light, casting an intoxicating glow. Faint whispers reached her ears—a baby's distant laugh. A woman's voice. Nova leaned closer and the sounds grew clearer: *"I won't hide from what I believe . . ."* The mushroom's veins throbbed brighter with each sound, drawing her in. Slowly, she reached her fingertips toward the mushroom's base and touched the roots. Immediately, the forest blurred around her, fading away . . .

Nova was back in the vine-covered house. She dropped to the dark wood flooring and her legs folded beneath her into a criss-cross posture. She wasn't in control of her body. Well, it wasn't her body at all. It was a peculiar sensation—being a passenger within someone else's form, moving with their motions.

Before her, a baby crawled with determination. Nova's hands were stretched out, beckoning the child to come into them. It was the same child she had glimpsed a day before, only now a little older. Bright blonde curls bounced on the baby's head as he crawled closer.

Nova's frame shook as a feminine laugh echoed in the room. She extended her arms farther, scooping up the giggling child and cradling him tenderly. She traced her fingers gently along the baby's soft, button nose. His tiny hand wrapped around her finger and his joyful wail filled the air. The moment was interrupted by a voice behind her, revealing that she wasn't alone in the house.

"You have to be more careful," the deep voice cautioned.

Nova turned to see a man with a trimmed dark brown beard framing his jawline. He approached and spoke solemnly, his eyes holding a hint of concern.

"The syphon is sacred to these people."

Nova continued to cradle the baby, her resolve unwavering. Her mouth began to move. "I won't hide what I believe."

"It's too dangerous. You don't know the lengths they would go to protect it."

"They don't know the lengths I would go to protect my baby. To protect us. I've spoken with the others and they agree. The syphon must be destroyed."

"It's my job to protect this family," he said.

"By hiding behind Cronian's laws?"

"If that's what it takes to keep us safe."

Nova tenderly placed her free hand on his cheek. "My darling, how do you expect anything to change if you aren't willing to do something?"

A screech split Nova's ears and made the walls fade from her vision. Her hands dropped from the mushroom and clutched onto her bag. Her mind was reeling.

If the syphon was in danger, she had to warn her father.

What would happen to her people if it was destroyed?

Images flashed through Nova's mind: Ghandrians overwhelmed by painful memories they could no longer erase, chaos erupting in the streets as citizens grappled with emotions they'd never learned to handle. The syphon wasn't just a tool. It was the foundation of their entire way of life. It was their *savior*.

Without it, Ghandria would crumble. If she could get back and warn the highborns, maybe they would allow her to stay. She imagined bursting into her father's chambers to tell him what she had seen. For once, she wouldn't be the daughter who disappointed him. She would be the one who *saved* the syphon, who protected their way of life. Maybe then she'd see that look in his eyes—the one she'd spent her childhood chasing, the one that said, "I'm proud." Then, she could finally come *home*.

Nova swirled around at the creak of wheels behind her. It was the bald man, pushing his wheelbarrow, only it was empty now. The food that he had collected was gone and he was headed back in the direction of town. Nova squinted, wondering why he was bringing it out to the forest.

When he saw Nova, he halted mid-stride. A spark of recognition flicked in Nova's mind. She knew this man. Years ago, he had been a servant in her home. He used to deliver Cronian's meals, always with his head bowed, always with trembling hands that made the silverware rattle against the plates.

He gaped at her, blinking rapidly. As his initial shock wore off, the man's demeanor darkened. Nova tugged her hood forward, attempting to hide her identity, but it was too late.

He pounced, abandoning his wheelbarrow and nailing her back against a mushroom trunk. Her bag fell from her hands and she grasped onto his bulky forearms. The man lifted his hands to her neck, tightening his grip until black spots danced in her vision.

"Please," Nova wheezed.

Her limbs began to tingle with the onset of numbness. The

edges of her vision darkened, but then a screech sliced through the tension, compelling him to release her. Sucking in air, Nova clutched her throat. Beside her, the man stood petrified, riveted on something beyond her. Nova followed his line of sight. A single Krall dragged its feet toward them, hunched forward and twisted. One arm was raised as if suspended by unseen strings, while the other dangled at its side, gripping a fragment of purple cloth.

SEVEN

The Krall's gaze pierced straight through Nova, but it saw nothing. Blindness had claimed its eyes, yet the way its head pivoted, listening, betrayed a dreadful compensation. The air around Nova thickened. A blind Krall meant its hearing was incredibly sharp, every whisper a thunderclap, every breath a roar. So Nova held it, as did the man, until their lips turned blue. The standoff stretched on, seconds feeling like minutes as her lungs begged for air. Her dagger lay tantalizingly close, but reaching for it would have been suicide. In the heightened hearing of the Krall, any sudden movement would give her away. The creature emitted a harrowing cry—a sound so raw it seemed to shake the ground. It masked the sharp intake of breath Nova couldn't suppress any longer.

The man beside her, though, waited too long. His lungs betrayed him only after the savage sound had faded. In that moment of vulnerability, the Krall pounced on him. Its nails sank into the man's shoulder, piercing through fabric and flesh with ease. A gut-wrenching scream tore from his lips before his body went limp in the creature's grip. Nova clamped her hand over her mouth, crushing her own cry into silence. The man's head lolled to the side as consciousness left him, his face slack, but his chest still rising and falling. The Krall began to drag him away.

Nova shrank to the ground, her hands now shielding her eyes from the scene, but she couldn't block out the sound of flesh dragging across the earth. She wanted to flee, but her body was locked in a state of paralyzing fear. She was trapped within herself, screaming for action, but her limbs were unresponsive. The violence had triggered something inside her.

Denali was usually there to pull her out of her episodes, but now, she would have to wait it out.

✦

Whispers spread through the class and Denali tried his best to ignore them.

"Some say it's contagious," a classmate behind him said. "That means he might be one too."

Denali's hands tightened into fists and he shot a glare at his friend Blythe, who mouthed, "Stay calm." Denali forced his fisted hand off the table, letting it rest on his lap. He attempted to focus on the demonstration at the front of the class.

His professor, who stood with another student, was wearing her signature lavender blazer and matching pencil skirt. Silver accents embellished her outfit, complementing the silvery highlights in her pale brown hair tied neatly into a bun. Professor Pippington was certainly the kind of person to adorn her hair with braids, were it allowed. However, that was a privilege for only highborn blood. Pippington held a small blade and used it to make a slit in the palm of Denali's classmate for healing practice.

"Professor?" Blythe called out, interrupting the demonstration.

Their professor raised an eyebrow. "Ahem?"

Blythe rolled her eyes and corrected herself. "Professor Pippington?"

Unsatisfied, Pippington crossed her arms, tapping her foot with impatience.

"Professor *Lavender* Pippington?"

Pippington held her head high. "Yes, my pupil?"

Blythe shot Denali an annoyed look. She tucked her vivid blue, shoulder-length hair behind her ear, revealing the collection of silver studs climbing from lobe to helix. "Isn't learning more effective if we actually *do* something? Sitting here watching one person at a time is such a waste of—"

Denali strained to concentrate on the lesson, but the voices behind him persisted.

"I knew there was a reason she never left their home. How embarrassing for Cronian to be associated with such a lowlife."

Unable to contain it any longer, Denali slammed his fists on the table and stood. He aimed his finger at the boy with platinum blonde hair and cold gray eyes. Slater's pale, freckled face twisted into a sneer, revealing a prominent gap between his front teeth.

"Slater," Denali warned, "If you don't shut up about Nova—"

The class gasped, and Blythe facepalmed. "Dude."

Professor Pippington calmly strode over. "Ah tut-tut, Mr. Darkov. You may be top of this class, but that does not exempt you from the rules." Her voice laced through the air like silk, and her hands did the same as she talked. "The utterance of a miscreant's name post-trial is strictly forbidden." She bowed her head. "It would be a pity for your father to hear of this."

Denali bit his tongue, his jaw hardened in frustration. He knew the rules. After miscreants were sent to Nadir, they were removed from all records. They were never to be seen or heard of again. But this was different. Nova's case was different.

"She's coming back," he said.

Pippington placed her hand on his table and leaned toward him, using her other finger to stroke a piece of loose hair on his forehead. "Return from the Isle of Nadir is not possible, my dear pupil. I fear not even a Darkov can breach its bounds." She flounced to the front of the classroom, placing her hand on the back of his classmate who stood before them. There was still a cut on her palm, and blood was spilling onto the drip tray beneath her.

"My dearest apologies for the interruption, Miss Gullinsby. You may now proceed."

Denali observed as his classmate closed her eyes, immersing herself in the task at hand. The room fell into a hushed anticipation, the only sound being the steady, focused breathing of the healer. Denali watched, transfixed by the intensity of her concentration. He remembered his early lessons, how he'd been taught to heal while seated, eyes closed, visualizing the process. Standing while healing led to his advancement to Professor Pippington's class at the age of eleven, making him the youngest student in history to earn a place in the group.

As time stretched on, the edges of the girl's cut began to move. After ten minutes, Denali could see a noticeable change. The tips of the gash were coming together. A sheen of sweat had formed on the girl's forehead, the beads tracing paths down her cheeks.

Another fifteen agonizing minutes crawled by, each one longer than the last. The cut finally sealed, leaving behind no trace of its existence except the drying tracks of blood. The moment the wound closed, it was as if a spell had been lifted from the room, a collective exhale filling the space.

The girl's eyes dragged open and she reached up, wiping away the sweat now dripping from her chin with a tired but satisfied smile.

"Average time, Miss Gullinsby," Pippington said, then added, "Next time, shall we aim to beat the average? As a society, we don't progress anywhere by keeping with the status quo. We must mature past our boundaries." She gracefully waved her left hand in the air. "Or, shall we say, become more improved versions of ourselves."

"Yeah, so we never have to worry about becoming *miscreants*," Slater mocked. "Praise the syphon for that."

Denali gritted his teeth together.

"Mr. Darkov, might I request your participation for the next demonstration?" Professor Pippington's voice cut through the tension.

Denali stood and walked to the front of the classroom, doing his best to compose himself. Everyone leaned forward in their seats, like they always did when it was his turn. He could barely feel a sting when Pippington made a cut in his palm. Then, she grabbed his other hand and did the same. Two cuts.

"Show my pupils what we've been practicing," she said. Her words danced with a light giggle.

Denali took a moment to center himself. He turned his attention inward, focusing on the lingering pain in his hands. Within the quietude of his state, Denali visualized the damage, the open wounds as clear in his mind's eye as they were in physical form.

Beneath the surface, his body was already at work. Blood vessels constricted at the edges of the wounds, slowing the bleeding while his cells swarmed the injury. He could feel them—platelets rushing to form a protective seal. The real work, however, was just beginning.

Denali willed his cells to move faster, to weave the tissue back together, filling the gaps. The sensation was subtle but present—a tingling warmth, the hum of restoration.

Despite the complexity of managing two healing processes simultaneously, Denali's concentration was unwavering.

The process unfolded in less than a minute. Upon opening his eyes, Denali immediately looked at his hands, now seamlessly healed. He flexed his hands, the blood streaks still wet and sticky, marveling at the swift absence of pain. The thrill of using his ability never waned. Each time felt as exhilarating as the first.

He turned his hands, examining them under the light, looking for any sign of imperfection, any hint that what he had accomplished was less than flawless. But there was nothing—no scar, no discoloration, just unblemished skin, as pristine as if the injuries had never existed.

His classmates stared after him with gaping mouths, except for Slater. He was reclined in his chair, arms folded casually as he blew a bubble with his gum. Pippington clapped her hands together with delight, her excitement bubbling over as she did a small, jubilant hop. "The most extraordinary display of healing power I've seen. Truly a testament to my teaching, of course," she beamed, her eyes sparkling with pride. "You are to show your father the heights you've reached under my guidance."

"Healing *ability*," Blythe corrected her. "Calling it a power implies it was a birthright or given to us. But it's a skill that can be learned and honed, not innate supernatural talents."

Pippington narrowed her eyes on Blythe. "All pupils are to raise their hands before speaking. And when doing so, you are to address me by my proper title, Miss Pierce."

Blythe huffed.

"Very well, then," Pippington said as she pulled out a silver star sticker. "Let's congratulate my star pupil."

Denali cast his eyes to the floor as his classmates applauded. His mastery over healing far surpassed anyone else's, but the credit didn't belong to Pippington's teachings. It stemmed from a source far more personal and profound. Fortunately, nobody had ever asked why he was such a skilled healer. Not even Blythe. The true foundation of his talent was a secret closely held between him and Nova.

Once he got home, Denali headed straight for the library. The massive double doors swung open silently, revealing the grand space. Polished marble floors stretched out before him. Their intricate patterns gleamed under the warm light of ornate chandeliers. Towering bookshelves of rich mahogany lined the walls, reaching up to the tall ceilings.

Denali's footsteps echoed in the room as he began his search for books that might explain the syphon's bizarre behavior. If he could find record of it ever happening before, he could use it to save Nova. He could prove that the syphon was to blame. If he could find some glitch, he could show others that it was unsteady. At the trial, he had already cast suspicion on the syphon. Now, he needed to press further.

He scoured one corner of their library, methodically examining the shelves and piling all the books he could find that mentioned the syphon. Though, he doubted he would find anything meaningful in these. If there were even a sliver of knowledge, a mere hint capable of undermining the syphon, it surely wouldn't be somewhere so accessible. His gaze wandered to the glass windows of his father's library—his *forbidden* library.

That's where any valuable information would be. He moved closer.

Cold prickled his skin.

He shuddered and backed away. He couldn't go back in . . . not after what happened when he foolishly broke in as a child. He would have to find another way.

His hand hovered over the selection of books sprawled across the table. He opened and scanned through each to get a feel for what they contained. Then he selected one with an aged spine. As he opened the book, the scent of old parchment and ink unfurled, and a whisper of dust rose into the air, its particles dancing in the slanting light. The pages were delicate under his fingers, filled with elegant script that told of the Great Choice. In that distant time, humanity had stood divided between two paths: the advancement of machines and weaponry, or the mastery of mind and spirit. Their ancestors had chosen the latter, turning away from the allure of technology to explore the depths of human potential. Denali flipped through the thin sheets, skipping over the next chapters containing photos of the original highborns. He stopped on a page titled "The Four Abilities of Ghandria."

Four?

The chapter detailed their abilities of healing, sense enhancement, syphoning, and, to Denali's surprise, levitation. Denali leaned in, studying the section. According to the text, these four abilities were once considered the cornerstones of their civilization—each held equal esteem. Denali flipped to the section on levitation. It was described as a tangible manifestation of harmony between the wielder and the world's essence. Practitioners of levitation were said to achieve a state of grace, floating through the air with ease of thought. The ability was revered, symbolizing a profound connection to one's consciousness.

Denali closed the book and inspected its binding again. There was a small inscription near the spine, faded but still legible. The publication date made him pause. This book was forty-nine years old.

If the levitation ability was revered, then lost, the highborns would surely have ordered all records of it purged. This book had somehow escaped notice. He set it in his backpack, making a mental note to dig into it later. For now, he needed to study the syphon.

He sighed as he poured water into the small pot of soil where he'd planted the twig he had brought home from Morianna's grounds. The plant was long past saving, but discarding it felt wrong.

His gaze rested on the pile of thirteen books left to study. It was going to be a long night.

EIGHT

Tick-tick-tick.

The sound reached Nova's ears like a metronome, pulling her back to awareness.

A whisper floated through the darkness—

"It didn't have to be this way."

The air was frigid and fog began to settle into the forest after the sun had set. Light rain misted down. Sensation crept back to Nova —first the throbbing in her temples, then the rhythm of her breathing.

Lifting herself off the ground, she started making her way back to the cottages. *Run*, she urged herself, but her body refused. Pushed to the edge of total exhaustion, she mustered what strength she could, though her efforts yielded little more than a sluggish pace, insufficient to escape a Krall should one approach. She was exposed, vulnerable.

The fog obscured her path, but she knew the direction from which she'd come, so she trudged forward, using bits of precious energy to stretch her sight for a moment now and then to ensure she was on the right path. The cottage town below lay in the cloak of night. The distant, shrill cry of a Krall from behind triggered an adrenaline rush, propelling her into action. She forced herself into a jog before finding the strength to run. She didn't dare look back—

getting to Berkshire's was all that mattered now. The miscreants in the village were all inside their cottages and the warm light spilling from their windows illuminated Nova's path.

She burst through the door of Berkshire's home, stumbling into the front hallway. Taos and Berkshire sat at the table, their conversation halting upon her sudden entrance.

"Wonderful," Taos said. "She returns."

Nova pressed both hands on her forehead as she paced from the hallway to the kitchen. "There was a man in the forest. A Krall . . . it attacked him. I don't know where it took him. It might have killed him."

Berkshire stood. "Who?"

Nova continued to pace, words tumbling out, "He was a servant in my home. I don't remember his name."

Taos shook his head. "That doesn't make sense. Krall don't attack our people."

"They don't raid our village either," Berkshire said.

Taos bit down. "If the Krall are turning on us now, it's because of *her* arrival here."

Berkshire placed a restraining hand on Taos's shoulder. Taos huffed but fell silent. Berkshire motioned for Nova to take a seat in his chair. "Describe him."

Nova sat. "Uh . . ." She swallowed. "He was bald. He was pushing a wheelbarrow."

"Taos, alert the others. One of our collectors has been taken."

Taos rushed out, the front door slamming behind him.

Silence fell over the cottage. Berkshire moved to the stove, where a pot sat.

"Why are you feeding them?" Nova asked. "The Krall?"

He kept his back to her as he grabbed the ladle in the pot. "I am Krall," he said, his voice low. He turned and set a bowl on the table in front of her. "*You* are Krall."

Nova recoiled slightly. "I don't understand."

"Eat."

Nova peered into the bowl. Chunks of root vegetables and green leaves swirled in an orangish broth. Her stomach growled. She picked up the spoon, looking up at him again.

"They had never raided the village until I came?"

Berkshire pulled out the chair opposite her and sat down. "They never had a reason to. Our people donate a portion of food to them each day. It's collected and taken to the forest every morning."

Nova frowned, her spoon hovering over the soup. If she really was putting everyone in danger, why was Berkshire letting her stay? She revealed the note in her hand and placed it in front of him.

Berkshire took it, his fingers barely touching the paper as he stared at it.

"So . . ." Nova said, "will you teach me?"

Berkshire shoved the note into his pocket.

"Eat," he said.

Nova complied, spooning the soup into her mouth. As she ate, Berkshire sat back in his chair, arms crossed, his gaze fixed on a point beyond the kitchen walls.

Time stretched in the tense silence. Nova's spoon scraped the bottom of the bowl, gathering the last bits of broth. The front door burst open with a bang that made her jump.

Taos strode in. "The collectors will organize a search."

Berkshire nodded, pushing his chair back with a scrape. He turned, moving toward the hallway that led to his room.

Nova set down her spoon with a clatter. "Wait," she called out. "There's something else."

Berkshire stopped but didn't turn to face her.

Nova braced herself. "I think someone's trying to destroy the syphon."

Taos scoffed. "And you know this how?"

She kept her eyes on Berkshire. "I've been seeing things. Visions, maybe?"

Taos leaned toward Berkshire, his whisper carrying to Nova's ears. "She's insane."

"I'm not insane," she defended. "I don't know exactly what it was, but I know what I saw. We have to warn them."

Taos's eyebrows shot up. "You want us to help the people who banished us?"

After a long pause, Berkshire turned to study her. "What was your indiscretion?"

"What?" Nova said.

"Your indiscretion?" he repeated.

She glanced at Taos and then back at Berkshire. "I, uh—I don't see why that matters."

"It matters if you want help."

Nova stared at her feet. She *did* need his help. Desperately. She closed her eyes and cringed as she whispered, "Syphoning."

"Not possible." Taos huffed. "Nobody is rejected by the syphon. Certainly not a Darkov."

Nova's blood boiled. She didn't need one more person reminding her how much of a disappointment she was. "You think I don't know that?"

"I wouldn't put it past a *miscreant*."

She grimaced. "Is that supposed to be an insult? Aren't you a miscreant too?"

Taos opened his mouth, but then his gaze shifted to Berkshire, who wore a smug smirk. He waited for Taos to speak, but instead, Taos closed his mouth and backed down.

Berkshire redirected his attention to Nova. "You've never syphoned?"

Nova's shoulders slumped, her eyes downcast. "No."

After a beat of silence, Berkshire looked at Taos.

"You can't be serious," Taos said. "She can't be trusted, and she can't help you."

Nova lifted her gaze to Berkshire, her curiosity piqued.

Taos folded his arms. "No."

Berkshire turned to Nova. "Leave us."

Nova glanced back and forth between the two, then backed out of the archway, but she could still hear them.

"*Cronian's* daughter, Berkshire."

"Quiet, son. Heaven forbid anyone close by hears you." Nova shuddered at the thought of a Krall overhearing.

Berkshire sighed. "She *is* his daughter, which is why she might be our only chance."

Nova walked into the courtyard until their voices were too distant to make out. She began to kick at some scattered pebbles as she waited. Taos came out of the kitchen and paused by the front door. He cast a glance in Nova's direction. His eyes met hers for a brief moment before he turned to Berkshire. "I hope you know what you're doing."

Once Taos was gone, Berkshire passed through the yard. "Come."

Nova trailed behind him. They passed the weapon racks, heading toward the far corner of the open space. As they neared the opposite end, Berkshire ducked through an archway, leading into a narrow hallway she hadn't explored yet. They reached a door tucked away in the back corner of the house.

As they entered, Nova was enveloped in an unexpected sanctuary. Upon her first step inside, she was greeted by the gentle creak of polished wood beneath her feet, contrasting the concrete that dominated the rest of the house.

The room's beige brick walls exuded a welcoming warmth. In the corners, plants thrived in large terracotta pots—varieties that flourished in low light. Candles of varying heights and widths were arranged throughout the room, standing directly on the wood floor. Some of the tallest candles reached as high as the plants, their flames flickering softly and creating dancing shadows on the walls.

High up on one wall was a window whose closed shutters blocked out the outside world, preserving the room's atmosphere. Beneath it, a hefty chest rested on the floor. Its dark polish resembled the flooring. In front of it, a simple, charcoal-colored mat lay perfectly positioned in the center of the room.

Berkshire motioned for her to sit.

"There is a particular subject we will study, but which has fallen out of the current curriculum of Ghandria. Do you know the history of levitation?"

Nova shook her head.

Berkshire bobbed his head and began, his voice deep and

measured. "Levitation used to be one of the four abilities in Ghandria. Decades ago, beginning about the time syphoning was discovered, there was a sudden dearth of the levitation ability among Ghandrians, and hundreds of miscreants were exiled. Over time, the highborns decided to remove that ability requirement altogether."

Nova's body stilled as she absorbed his words. How long had he been here?

Berkshire knelt beside the chest and lifted its lid. He rummaged briefly before pulling something out, his broad frame blocking Nova's view. She craned her neck in curiosity, but couldn't see what he had taken. He reached for her hand, and she offered it.

Berkshire revealed a small blade and drew it briefly across her palm, leaving a precise cut no longer than half an inch. "Ow!" she yelped, pulling her hand back. Berkshire gave a silent nod toward her hand, urging her to look. As she did, she cupped her other hand beneath it to catch the trickle of blood before it could stain the floor.

Berkshire waited, watching. Ah, so he needed her to prove that she could heal, that it really was syphoning that was her indiscretion. With a deep inhale, she shut her eyes. As she concentrated, she sensed a subtle shift beneath her skin, a magnetic pull as the edges of the wound began to draw together. She held onto this sensation, encouraging the natural healing process with the power of her mind, feeling the skin tentatively knitting itself together, stitch by invisible stitch. When she finally opened her eyes, two ends of the cut had come noticeably closer together, making the gash a little smaller. She wasn't nearly as skilled at this as Denali was. He'd had much more practice.

Without comment, Berkshire handed her a bandage. Nova wrapped it around her palm while he pulled out two items: a brass-cased device with its paired gauge faces, and a small glass vial filled with clear preservative fluid. Inside the vial, white nerve fibers floated like delicate strands. Using forceps, Berkshire carefully extracted the first fiber from the solution, letting excess fluid drip off before attaching it to one of the brass fittings beside its corresponding gauge. He repeated the process with the second nerve, each preserved fiber hanging like a wet thread from the device. It was an old model of the neurotuner used to track their hearing and visual senses. Fine cracks spiderwebbed across both gauge faces, where the needles rested at their center marks of one hundred percent. The brass was dulled with age, but as long as the needles still moved smoothly across their arcs—from zero percent on the left to two hundred percent on the right—it didn't matter.

Nova tilted her head back slightly and led the nerve fiber through her nasal cavity. There was a strange pressure as it wound upward, finding the natural channel where her optic nerve ran. The tissue made its connection deep behind her eye, joining with her retina. The sensation always made her eyes water.

She guided the second one into her ear canal and it sought its path to her eardrum. The real discomfort came as it found a way past the delicate membrane to connect with her ear's inner nerve network. Feeling another person's nervous system joining with her own always made her queasy—it wasn't painful, but impossible to get used to.

Keeping her encumbered eye closed, Nova focused on the first gauge. As she diminished her hearing, the needle swept counterclockwise. She stopped when she went below forty percent, not daring to venture too close to zero and risk permanent deafness. Thirty-nine would do. She shifted her attention from her eardrums to her vision.

With her one open eye, Nova cast her gaze at a crack in the brick wall across from her. She peered through it, allowing her pupils to contract and her vision to extend into the dark, sleeping town. Through a narrow gap in another cottage's wall, she could make out every detail of the room within—the wood grain of ceiling beams, the individual threads of a tapestry, even the tiny footprints a mouse had left in the settled dust. A spider's web held a struggling moth, its wings leaving powder traces with each desperate flutter.

"One-sixty-one." With her diminished hearing, Berkshire's voice was muffled, but Nova was grateful for the information. Enhancing her vision to one hundred and sixty-one percent was more than enough to prove her ability.

With a swift reversal, her vision retraced its path, back through the cottage and into the meditation room. Then she relaxed her grip on her hearing, watching the gauge's needle move back to its center mark. She turned to Berkshire, her one open eye meeting him.

"The other," he instructed.

Nova focused on her eyesight. The world blurred as she watched the second needle sweep left from center, and her vision dimmed like a dying light. Nova honed her hearing, capturing the sound of rainfall in the courtyard. Among the steady patter, a different rhythm caught her attention—a single droplet hitting the dirt. *Drip. Drip. Drip.* The sound had to be coming from the showerhead hidden in the corner of the courtyard. She stretched her hearing farther, past the walls of Berkshire's cottage. Boots were scuffing against cobblestone in the street. Taos's muttering drifted to her ears: " . . . a damned youngborn . . ."

"Enough," Berkshire said.

Nova complied, letting her hearing return to its normal state, and then bringing her vision back. She had proven that she could wield two of their abilities, which only left syphoning. She extracted the nerve fibers, suppressing a shudder as they disconnected from her ear and eye, and held the device out to Berkshire. He ignored her offering and stroked his beard.

"Fascinating."

Weird, she hadn't ever heard of anyone referring to an indiscretion that way. Horrifying? Disgusting? Disgraceful? Yes. Never *fascinating*. She set the device on the floor.

"When you tried to syphon . . . ?"

Nova pressed her lips together. "I saw other people's memories they had erased. It was like . . . like I was living their experience in their own bodies and feeling everything they felt." She wrapped her arms around herself. "What's wrong with me?"

"Your question is misdirected."

She raised her head. "I don't understand."

"You will."

Nova looked up at him with eyes full of hope. "Does that mean . . ."

"We start tomorrow."

✦

Nova sat on the mat, eager to start her training. High on the wall, the worn shutters remained closed. Thin slivers of morning light streamed through the cracks. She had already lost two valuable days, but she had gotten Berkshire to agree to train her, which was a major victory. In fifty-eight days, she would be home with Denali, with the ability to forget all of the horrific events that had plagued them growing up. She could erase all the times their father had punished them—her arms burned just thinking about it. She could erase the trial. She could forget her time here in Nadir—it would be like it had never happened. She could make her father proud. Her heart thumped with anticipation.

Berkshire strolled into the room and Nova straightened her posture. She was ready to soak in his wisdom, desperate for her ticket home. He approached the chest and lifted its brass latch. Reaching inside, he pulled out a wooden box and set it on the floor in front of her. Nova's heart quickened as she lifted the lid, hungry for her first chance to become normal, to leave behind the painful memories of her past. When she saw what was inside, she paused and then leaned in closer.

The box was divided in half by a slat rising from its base. On one side, it was filled with rice—thousands upon thousands of grains, an endless sea of them. The other side was empty. She reached a hand into the full side and scooped a handful into the air, letting them cascade through her fingers and back into the pile.

She scrunched her face. "What is this?"

"Your first lesson."

"What do I do?"

"Count it."

Nova scoffed, half-expecting him to reveal that he was joking.

But his face remained sincere, leaving no room for doubt. She looked back into the box, her heart sinking.

"Berkshire, I'm already on borrowed time. I need to learn how to syphon—"

"Restart at any error. No grouping or pile-making," he instructed. "Notify me upon completion." With that, he left the room, and his footsteps faded down the hall.

Nova was left staring at the box of rice. She had expected to learn deep breathing techniques or perhaps some advanced combat skills. Counting rice grains seemed mundane and utterly pointless. Frustration gnawed at her skin as she considered the enormity of the task before her. No way was she doing this. This wasn't going to cure whatever was wrong with her.

Yet, in the quiet, her promise to Denali floated through her thoughts.

She took a moment, reconsidering her situation. Berkshire was her only lead, her only hope to *fix her* so she could get back to Denali and take her place in Ghandria.

Nova picked up a single, tiny grain, brought it close to her nose, and went cross-eyed to inspect it. Then, she let it fall into the empty side of the box.

"One."

NINE

"Nine hundred and fifty-two, nine hundred fifty-three, nine hundred fifty-four . . ." Nova focused intently as she counted, she had already restarted five times. The faster she could get this done, the faster she could get on to a *real* lesson. She groaned. It had been over an hour and the pile of rice looked exactly the same, despite nine hundred and sixty of them being removed.

Or . . . was it nine hundred and sixty-one?

Nine hundred and sixty-two?

With a frustrated sigh, she poured the rice she'd separated back into the collective mound. Another hour slipped by and three more attempts collapsed under the weight of distraction. Each time she approached fifteen hundred, her mind wandered to Cronian's proclamation during her trial.

A miscreant is no daughter of mine. His statement tore through her like a fresh wound.

She fought the sting in her eyes and started again. This time, more voices infiltrated her mind.

You know . . . I heard she's of distant relation to the Darkov line, the women from her trial mocked.

How absolutely terrifying.

Surely they'll exile her.

Nova gasped from the pain these words had caused her. She grabbed at her heart and took in measured breaths.

Why did she have to be such a failure? Why couldn't she syphon like everyone else? Why did she have to be the *only* person who couldn't?

Tears traced paths down her cheeks, the saltiness tingling on her tongue as they brushed her lips. She had lost her count again so she started from one. Upon reaching fifteen hundred, the whispers grew in volume and intensity.

I heard the brother was concealing her existence. Another voice from the crowd rang in her mind.

The poor boy, he must have been so embarrassed.

Taos's voice came next. *Nobody is rejected by the syphon. Certainly not a Darkov.*

Nova pushed the voices aside and focused on the sequence of numbers. Pressure started to build in her head, like the voices were demanding to be heard. Nova winced as she exerted every ounce of her will to silence them.

"One thousand four hundred and seven, one thousand four hundred and eight . . ."

The pressure in her brain continued to build as the minutes passed, but she didn't stop.

"One thousand six hundred and thirty, one thousand six hundred and thirty-one . . ."

An onslaught of voices clamored for dominance. Her mind felt dangerously close to shattering under the strain. Finally, she stopped counting and the voices immediately subsided. The pressure in her head began to calm, and she took a few moments to recover. She massaged a tender area on her tailbone and shifted her position, lying down on her stomach to resume her task. "One thousand six hundred and thirty-two, one thousand six hundred and thirty-three . . ."

A chomping sound made Nova jerk upwards. She groaned and peeled her flyaway hairs from the crusted drool that had collected during her slumber. A couple of grains of rice that had been stuck to her cheek fell to the floor.

Taos stood across the room leaning against the wall of the archway, arms folded across his chest while holding an apple in front of his mouth. Nova looked down at the pile of rice that was scattered across the floor and groaned again.

Glancing behind him into the courtyard, she caught sight of the sun beginning its descent in the western sky.

She rubbed her eyes. "Where's Berkshire?"

"Out," he said. "Get up. It's time to train."

Train? With him?

"I—" She hesitated. "I can't. I have to finish this."

"Yes, you've been making great progress." He pointed to his cheek, close to his dimple. "You've got another piece of rice, just there."

Nova's glare was icy as she plucked away the stray grain, letting it fall into the pile. He took another bite of the apple and tilted his chin toward the courtyard, signaling for her to follow. Hauling herself up, Nova followed after him. Luckily, the high walls shaded the entire courtyard at this time of day, but it was still bright enough to make her head pound. Taos snatched a blade from the rack.

"Grab a weapon," he ordered. Nova took in her options, which were limited to only swords and dualfates. She chose the latter. She wrapped her fingers tightly around the hilt in the middle of the daggers.

"Today, we practice footwork," Taos said. "Focus on maintaining your stance and anticipating your opponent's next move."

"I've had training in footwork before," Nova said. "Can we start further along?"

Taos's response was a single raised eyebrow. Then, in an instant, he was on her. Nova barely had time to raise her weapon in defense before his blow crashed against her guard, driving her backwards. She stumbled and Taos dropped down and swept his foot, kicking Nova's out from under her. She landed hard on her butt.

Taos started rolling his sleeves to his elbows. "Like I said, we start on footwork."

"You didn't give me a warning," Nova said as she rubbed her sore hip.

"Real fights don't come with warnings," he said. "Get up."

Drawing in a deep, steady breath, Nova pushed herself to her feet. She assumed her stance once more.

"Lower."

She did as he said. As Taos advanced, he launched a series of swings toward her. Nova responded with swift blocks—first to the left, then to the right, and finally one down low. A triumphant smile flickered across her face, a silent boast of her skills, hoping it was enough to prove that beginners' lessons were beneath her.

"Too slow," he said.

Nova's scowl deepened. She returned to her stance, this time focusing harder. She deflected a flurry of blows, barely keeping up with his movements. The training stretched on, each minute blending into the next until an hour had passed. Nova's legs burned from her efforts to maintain a low stance. Whenever she dared to straighten to relieve them, Taos would knock her feet from under her.

"Real fights don't give breaks," he reminded her each time.

Taos's strikes were a blend of agility and skill so refined that Nova found herself struggling to anticipate his moves, which surprised her. In the span of a single lesson, he had displayed a level of expertise that surpassed any of her previous tutors. It was most impressive considering his miscreant status. At this moment, however, it was infuriating. No matter how effectively she blocked or maneuvered her feet, Taos was three steps ahead of her. A rash decision to go on the offensive left her disarmed and, once again, on the ground.

"Not this lesson," he said, his attention shifting to the courtyard entrance where three figures walked in—two young men and a tall, slender girl with her blonde hair pulled back into a tight bun. They all looked to be around Denali's age. Nova recognized Xander, the barefoot friend Taos was dueling on her first day here.

Taos slid his blade into its sheath, turning to face the group. "I said no training today."

The three of them eyed Nova as she got back on her feet. Xander responded with a casual shrug. "You know how I like to follow orders, *Commander*."

The girl crossed her arms. "Since when do you cancel training, anyway?"

Xander's grin grew smug. "Since he's got a girl, apparently."

"Enough," Taos said. "Leave."

"Gus want practice," the final boy said. He was shorter and plumper than the other two, and had curly red hair. *What's with his grammar?*

"We can't let Gus Gus here down." Xander turned to Nova. "Besides, your girl won't mind, will you, lovey?"

Being referred to as "Taos's girl" made Nova want to scrub the words from the air.

Taos's expression darkened. "How many times do I need to tell you to leave?"

Xander spun around, ignoring Taos's commands. "Kiera, I do believe I could best you in a duel."

"Be my guest, Xander. You saw how that went last round," she said, her tone laced with amusement.

"Eh. I was taking it easy."

"Gus do think Kiera to win."

"Ha," she said. "Gus Gus only ever speaks the truth. Now, are you going to introduce us or not?"

Nova's heartbeat spiked. *Please don't tell them.*

"Not," Taos said.

Nova's gaze sharpened on him, surprised that he hadn't given her name away.

Gus, meanwhile, seemed charmed by her. He smiled and a noticeable blush tinted his cheeks as he sheepishly approached. He took her hand in his and bowed his head, planting a respectful kiss on her hand. "A beauty, her is."

Nova withdrew her hand and blushed.

"Like Kiera said, Gus only speaks truth," Xander said, his grin wide as he looked her over.

"She wouldn't know truth if it hit her between the eyes," Taos mumbled under his breath.

Nova's cheeks flushed darker at his dismissal.

"Ah, but the lengths I would go to stare at those eyes," Xander said with a distant look. "An exquisite blue, indeed."

"Shut it," Taos snapped.

"Gorgeous," Xander cooed as he began to swing his dualfate at an invisible opponent. "Will you be joining us for duels?"

Nova shifted uncomfortably on her heels. If dueling with them was anything like dueling with Taos, she was done for.

"She will not be." Taos turned to Nova. "Our lesson is finished."

Nova held her tongue. She wanted to demand her participation out of sheer defiance. But as much as she cared to hold onto her pride, she wanted to get away from him more. And now that he was giving her the opportunity, she was going to take it.

"What's got you in a knot?" Kiera asked.

Nova chimed in, not wanting to give him any more chances to spill her secret. "It's all right, actually. I have another lesson to get to."

"Gus Gus go easy."

Nova offered him a smile. "I wish I could, Gus. Maybe another time."

"I'll be waiting till then," Xander said with a wink.

"Quit it," Taos warned. "I won't tell you again."

With Xander's hands raised in a gesture of surrender, Nova took it as her cue to exit. As she headed for the meditation room, the murmur of their continuing conversation trailed after her and she enhanced her hearing to listen in.

"Well?" Taos asked.

She heard Kiera's voice next. "Dead ends everywhere. I'm beginning to think there's really no way out of here."

"There has to be a way out," Taos said.

"Maybe. But the Krall have been territorial these past couple days. I don't know if they'll let us scope out the forest without bothering us."

"Something's up with them," Xander said.

"Gus think they look for something."

"Or *someone*," Taos muttered.

Nova bit down on her teeth and sat on the mat. She reached into the rice heap and pulled out a handful of grains. The sooner she could get this over with, the sooner she could get away from Taos for good.

TEN

"Today's challenge, my dearest pupils," Professor Pippington began, "will test not only your healing abilities, but also your mental acuity and focus." Her hands moved in fluid motions, emphasizing her words with elegant gestures. "You will each heal a minor injury and my first pupil to do so shall be bestowed with a special reward."

The entire class exchanged knowing glances. One girl groaned. "But, Professor, Denali wins every time."

"Hush, child," she said. "I have made a few alterations to today's challenge."

Denali struggled to keep his eyes open, the exhaustion from last night's fruitless search for information on the syphon weighing heavily on his mind. He had spent hours pouring over the ancient texts, hoping to find some clue that would help him discredit the syphon. Despite his efforts, he had come up empty-handed. The lack of sleep was taking its toll, and he hardly cared that today was his nineteenth birthday. Right now, all that mattered was getting the information he needed. Last night's search had proved that it wouldn't be in the public library—it would be in the forbidden one. But he couldn't go in. He wouldn't.

Not again.

Professor Pippington smiled, her eyes twinkling with

amusement. "Yes, my dear pupils, today's challenge will require both skill and concentration." She picked up a small box from behind her desk, brought it to Denali's desk, and tipped it over. Hundreds of tiny pieces of cardboard spilled out.

"Spread out on the table before each of you will be your very own puzzle." She clasped her hands together as she let out a bubbly giggle. "My first pupil to successfully mend their wound while simultaneously completing the puzzle wins today's challenge."

Denali picked up a piece, his fingers tracing the edges as he studied its shape. Then he eyed the whole pile. There must have been five hundred pieces.

Pippington clapped her hands together twice. "Come now, my pupils. Your puzzles await."

The class formed a line. Denali drummed his fingers on his desk while he waited. He had never tried to multitask while healing before, but he couldn't imagine it would be much more difficult.

How much of a difference could it make?

Once everyone's puzzles were poured out in front of them, Professor Pippington situated herself on top of her desk, one leg crossed over the other.

"Now," she said, "you may proceed."

Denali reached for the blade tucked under his desk. The rest of the class did the same. He watched as Blythe made a cut in her palm.

Here goes.

Denali made a single slice in his left palm. He immediately placed his hand on the sterile gauze pad that lay on his desk. The cut remained visible, facing upward for Pippington to observe, while the pad caught any blood that might drip down. Then, he began to manipulate the puzzle pieces with his good hand. The healing energy that flowed through him wavered and flickered, threatening to dissipate altogether as his focus split between his injury and the puzzle. Sweat gathered on his brow as he fought to maintain his concentration, the demands of both tasks pulling him in opposite directions.

Without being purposeful, his brain switched to focusing single-mindedly on his wound, willing it to mend and knit together in a split second. He lifted it from the pad and inspected it.

"Ah tut-tut, Mr. Darkov," his professor said. "My instructions were to complete the puzzle's assembly whilst in tandem nurturing your healing. You are to start anew."

Denali gnawed on the inside of his cheek as he made another cut in the same place.

Slow down the healing?

Going fast was the only thing he'd ever learned to do. It's what he was good at.

He studied the others. Their fingers fumbled over the puzzle pieces. Some let out frustrated sighs, their wounds stubbornly refusing to close as they divided their attention. Blythe grunted as she tried to balance both tasks. Her hand shook slightly as she attempted to force a piece into place, only to have it slip from her grasp again.

Denali closed his eyes and forced himself to maintain a heightened awareness of the injury in his palm. He concentrated on the sensation of the wound, visualizing the flow of healing energy as it coursed through his body. With each breath, he willed the energy to temper its pace, to linger in the damaged tissues just a fraction longer before moving on to the next. He peeked one eye open and focused on the puzzle with one part of his mind, while the other remained ever vigilant, monitoring the progress of his healing efforts. His thoughts threatened to wander and he had to physically shake his head to keep it focused.

He moved slowly, matching a handful of puzzle pieces together one by one until he had formed a fragment of the picture. He looked at the cut in his hand. When he did, his mind wavered slightly and that fleeting moment of distraction caused his healing energy to surge forward. The wound in his palm sealed. The sensation was overwhelming, a rush of warmth and tingling as his body responded to the sudden influx of energy. Alarm shot through him when he realized what had happened.

"Swiftness, though a commendable trait, is not the only measure of success, Mr. Darkov," Pippington said. "Indeed, true mastery requires a harmonious blend of discipline, patience, and the ability to maintain control over one's powers."

"Not a power," Blythe mumbled.

With a frustrated growl, Denali grabbed his blade again. Forty minutes passed and nobody in the class had completed the challenge. Their professor clapped her hands together twice.

"My cherished pupils, it pains the very fibers of my being to utter such words, yet I fear I have no star pupil today. We shall weave the threads of our learning tomorrow. Please dazzle me upon our next meeting." She rested her hands gracefully in her lap. "Particularly you, Mr. Darkov."

✦

"Mr. Darkov, my star pupil, my shining, *sparkling* pupil," Blythe mimicked their professor after they left the class. "Honestly, D, you ever get tired of being the class pet?"

Blythe, a good foot shorter than Denali, had to crane her neck slightly to meet his gaze. She was a bite-sized spitfire, as Denali had learned a long time ago.

A mischievous smile played at the corners of his mouth. "No, but clearly you do."

"Yeah, well, it's just 'cause you're a dude. Everyone knows Pippington favors the guys—"

"Ahem," Denali interrupted. "I think you mean Professor *Lavender* Pippington. Do remember to address her by her full name next time, please."

Blythe rolled her eyes. "The chick's exhausting. How does one person have so much . . ." She creased her forehead as she tried to come up with the right word. "Exuberance?"

Denali raised an eyebrow, amused. "Exuberance?"

Blythe shoved him. "Shut up."

He placed a hand over his heart and did his best to look

offended. "Now, how would the professor feel if she knew you had just insulted her star pupil?"

"I'll knock those perfect teeth right out of your mouth."

Denali chuckled. "Oh, I don't doubt it."

"Good. Don't mock me."

Denali lifted his hands in a gesture of peace.

"Darkov, I need your help." The quiet voice came from behind them. Denali turned to find Finnian, a former classmate, shifting his weight from foot to foot. Dark circles shadowed his eyes, and his usually neat uniform was wrinkled, as if he'd been sleeping in it.

"Uh, yeah," Denali said. "What's up?"

"I need a session with the . . . you know."

Denali pressed his lips together. It wasn't uncommon for people to ask this favor. It certainly wasn't Finnian's first time trying to see the syphon without an appointment.

"I tried setting up a session, but the soonest one is weeks out."

"I can ask," Denali said, "but my father doesn't usually make exceptions. You know that."

Finnian scratched behind his ear. "Can you tell him it's important?"

"Sure, man."

A heavy shoulder slammed into Finnian, sending him stumbling to the side. Slater stepped into Denali's path, his gap-toothed smirk spreading across his face as Finnian scurried away without a backwards glance. Slater folded his arms. "Well if it isn't the nasty's big brother."

Denali tried to step around him, but Slater was quick to cut him off. Denali's jaw tightened, muscles working beneath his skin.

"Tell me, why didn't we ever see your lil' sis in the first place? Why were you and your dad hiding her? Did you know what she was?"

Tension rippled through Denali's body. His hands curled into fists, knuckles blanching with the force of his restraint. The urge to plant them on Slater's jaw became almost irresistible. Instead, he grabbed Blythe's hand and turned around. "Let's go."

"One more question," Slater called out. "What's it like being the grandson of Lucien Darkov and the brother of a filthy *miscreant*?"

Blythe swung her head around as they walked. "What's it like sporting twiddles the size of a grape?"

Around them, students in the hallway paused mid stride. Hushed laughter fluttered through the corridor. Meanwhile, Slater's face flushed a deep shade of red.

"Come on," Denali said. He pulled her away and they wove through the hall until they passed through the archway leading outside. A courtyard spread before them, its stone benches dusted with fallen golden leaves. "You're riling him up."

"I could take him, you know. The secret is to go straight for the eye sockets." She lifted her thumbs and dug them into the air as a demonstration.

Denali chuckled. "I'll remember that."

She inhaled deeply as she straightened her worn jean jacket. She insisted on wearing it rather than abide by the school's fine cotton blouses and tailored uniforms because, as she put it, "conformity is the death of the soul, Denali."

"You in for the hang tonight?" she asked.

Denali rubbed the back of his head. She invited him every week, as if she didn't already know his answer. "I'm not ready for that, Blythe."

"D, rejecting an invite?" She threw her hands up and said in a sarcastic tone, "How could anyone have guessed?"

A decade of guilt pressed against Denali's sternum. After classes, he devoted all of his time to Nova. It had to be that way. He turned down his friends until they finally understood he wouldn't be spending time with them anymore—not when Nova needed him. It hurt to shut them out, but it was a sacrifice he would make again and again for her.

"Things are . . . serious right now."

"You need to help your sis, yeah, yeah. Before she was exiled it was always 'I have to stay home with Bellanova tonight,' or 'Bellanova needs my help.'"

A couple crossing the courtyard gasped. The girl covered her mouth in shock.

Noticing their reactions, Blythe flashed a cheeky grin. "Your ears didn't deceive you. Yes, I said the name that *shan't* be said. Shall we wait for the sky to fall together?"

The boy's mouth opened slightly, as if to protest or perhaps call for others, but no words came out. Instead, he took his girlfriend's hand and they hurried away.

Blythe turned back to Denali. "Look, losing someone is rough, D. Seriously sucks. I've been there. You can't let it freeze you out from, you know, actually living."

A pang of sympathy hit Denali. Blythe's uncle, who had basically been her father, was exiled. Her parents were always so focused on experimenting and trying to discover the next evolutionary ability that they'd alienated their only child. Luckily, her uncle took her in, until a couple years ago when he lost his ability to stretch his hearing. She was devastated at first. It took Denali months to get her to leave her house.

"It is your birthday, after all," Blythe said. "You're officially no longer a youngborn."

Denali pursed his lips together. "Oh, that. Right."

It was supposed to be the most important day of his life, but celebrating was the last thing he had time for right now. He had hours of research waiting for him at home. Suddenly, a thought struck him, and his face lit up with a mischievous grin.

"B," he said, "how would you feel about helping a friend?"

She scowled at him. "I know that look, man. You're about to try something stupid."

Denali shrugged, pleading innocence. "I don't know what you mean. I just need help with some light research."

She ticked a finger at him. "Don't even try to make it sound innocent, D. You're up to something. I can see it brewing on your angel-faced mug."

Denali wrapped an arm around her, though he had to lean down to reach. "Come on, B. Would you really leave a friend hanging in his time of need?"

"So, let's get this straight. You're rejecting my invitation to come to the party tonight *and* you're asking *me* to ditch and come 'research' instead?"

"Yep." Denali flashed a wink. "It is my birthday after all."

She sighed. "Lead the way."

✦

Blythe coughed as a cloud of dust swallowed her. She waved away the particles and set the book aside. "So, what are we looking for?"

Denali plopped three more books on the marble floor in front of her. "Something we aren't supposed to find."

"Helpful, thanks."

He took a seat beside her. "We need to find any information on the syphon's creation."

"Okay," Blythe said. "Why?"

"It's . . . complicated. I can't go into detail right now. Just trust me—it's important."

She leaned back on her hands. "You're being really vague, man. If you want my help, you gotta give me more."

"I need to understand how it works and why it's acting so weird."

"Hmm," Blythe said. "If you can prove there's something wrong with it then you have a chance of bringing Nova back. Okay, I'm on it." She grabbed the first book off the stack and started reading.

Hours passed. Blythe was laying on her back now, flipping pages of a book as she held it over her head. Denali's back ached from hunching over for so long. He found another section on the syphon, but all it mentioned of its creation was that it was "an entity created by Lucien Darkov." Denali slammed the book shut and threw it at the wall.

Blythe peeked an eye over her book. "Calm down, D. What did you find?"

"Nothing. That's the problem. We're not going to find anything in these." He looked into his father's library.

Blythe followed his gaze. "You think we'll find something in there?"

Denali paused, his eyes trailing to the lock on the heavy, wooden door.

Blythe stood. "So, do we waste time hunting for this key, or opt for a good old-fashioned break-in?"

Denali's breath hitched. He knew exactly where the key was hidden. He crossed the room to a potted plant beside the door. He bent down and sifted through the soil until his fingers brushed against the cold metal.

Blythe moved closer. "A potted plant. How innovative. Truly groundbreaking security."

Denali's fingers curled around the key, his grip so tight that his knuckles turned white. He traced the ornate "D" on the front and his mind flooded with memories of the last time he held this key.

His tongue felt heavy and numb, and a tingling sensation spread from his throat to his lips, leaving them rubbery.

Blythe stepped forward and placed a gentle hand over his, covering the key and pulling Denali from his trance. Sensation slowly returned to his lips as he struggled to find his voice. Color seeped back into his face. Blythe's steady walnut eyes bore into his, unraveling his carefully constructed walls, as if she could see past the scars that had shaped him.

Denali tried to withdraw his hand, but she tightened her grip. Then, she pried the key from his grasp. She smiled softly and knelt beside the pot. Denali watched as she nestled the key back into the soil. She smoothed the dirt over the metal and patted it down.

Blythe rose to her feet and dusted the dirt from her hands. "That's enough for one day. Get some rest, D. We'll get back at it tomorrow."

Denali swallowed hard, unable to pull his eyes from the soil where the key had been buried. "I start witnessing the syphonings tomorrow."

"Already? I thought you weren't supposed to start until a few weeks after your coming of age?"

Denali turned his head toward her voice, though his gaze lingered on the soil for a moment longer before finally meeting hers. "The town is still shaken up over what happened when Nova tried to syphon. My father thinks it will help to get another Darkov in there."

"You really think it'll help?" she asked. "No offense, but the Darkov name has all the charm of a dead fish at the moment."

"It's what my father wants."

"And what about you? Are you ready to keep those secrets? If you speak of anything you see there, you could end up . . ."

Denali nodded. He was aware of the consequences of repeating anything he witnessed during a syphoning. Erased memories were never to be spoken of again. It was one of their highest laws. Whatever happened in the cavern was meant to stay between the offerer, the syphon, and the highborn families.

After walking Blythe out, Denali closed the door and let out a deep sigh. It was time for dinner, which meant facing Father. They usually ate at separate times, but his coming of age meant a shared meal. He braced himself for the uncomfortable silence that would inevitably fill the room. He put on an impassive face and strode toward the dining area.

✦

I heard she's of distant relation to the Darkov line
How absolutely terrifying.
Surely they'll exile her.

Nova shook her head, trying to chase away the distraction, but she had already lost her number. She poured the rice back into the pile and began again, facing more and more of the conversations that haunted her. She started to see the faces of the people mocking her and she strained to push them out.

After an hour, the faint silvery glow of the moon seeped through the window shutter's cracks. Nova had successfully made it past seven thousand, but it was at the cost of a major migraine. Voices were screaming at her. Her brain was throbbing. One pebble of rice looked like it was moving. Nova drew closer and swore she could see the tiniest face on it. It looked at another rice grain beside it and spoke. "The syphon doesn't reject anyone. Certainly not a Darkov." The words, whether real or a product of her fraying sanity, cut deep.

She slapped her face in an attempt to dispel the illusions and continued, "Seven thousand, three hundred and twelve. Seven thousand, three hundred—"

The creak of the front door swinging open halted her counting. *Berkshire must be home.*

She jumped up and rushed across the courtyard to see him. He was talking to Taos when she came through the archway.

Berkshire was shaking his head. A heavy sigh escaped Taos. He turned to go out, brushing past Nova as he muttered something under his breath. She couldn't help but wonder why there was so much animosity between them. Nova watched as he shut the door to his room, leaving her and Berkshire in an awkward silence. She opened her mouth to ask a question, but before she could utter a word, Berkshire cut her off.

"Have you finished counting?"

"Not yet, but I—"

"Then no." He backed into his room and shut the door in her face once more.

The next few days blurred in repeats of the same events. Each morning, Berkshire left while Taos taught the students, then trained Nova, and Nova continued to count in the meditation room. As the days stretched to weeks, Nova's frustration with the task grew. It didn't help that the voices in her head were pushing her to the brink of insanity. It had been three weeks since she arrived, and her determination was waning as the grains stared up at her. She was definitely closer. She'd made it all the way to fifty thousand and didn't need to start over nearly as many times as she had at the beginning. When she did start over, it meant hours of counting to make it back to the same number and hours of fighting the voices. Nova stretched out her arms and massaged the knots in her back. It wasn't just her back that was sore, though. Weeks of training sessions with Taos had left colorful marks on her. Her arms throbbed with the strain of countless sword blocks. Even in a seated position, her legs felt numb. She scooped up another grain and began to count.

Before she made it far, she heard the front door open and close. She stood up and walked out of the room, pausing at the archway. Across the courtyard, Berkshire was hanging a coat on the wall. He was home early today. Taos, Xander, Kiera, and Gus were practicing with their blades in the courtyard. Berkshire made his way to Taos.

"I'll start again tomorrow, kid." He rolled his shoulders, grimacing at the tension in his muscles.

Nova couldn't help but wonder what Berkshire was looking for each day.

Taos waved it off. "Tomorrow, then." He turned to see Nova watching and his eyes darkened. He veered back to his friends.

What was that about?

Xander broke away from the group and crossed the courtyard to Nova, that familiar smirk playing on his lips. "Gorgeous, will you be joining us today?"

Taos stabbed his sword into a training dummy. "No."

Nova stiffened when Xander grabbed her hand and pulled her forward. She stumbled into the center of the courtyard. "I'm making an executive decision for yes," he said.

Taos turned on Xander and grabbed his shirtfront in his fists. "I said no."

Nova's fingers pressed to her lips in shock.

Xander only smirked. "Gus, what think ye?"

"Gus say yes!"

"Kiera?" Xander asked.

"Hey, I wouldn't mind having another girl around. Sorry, Taos."

Xander inched his head closer to Taos's. "Ha."

"Fine," Taos conceded. "She starts in the pit."

The three others all winced simultaneously. Kiera mouthed, "Sorry."

Unease prickled at the back of Nova's neck. Xander, still holding her hand, led her behind the training dummies. Her eyes fell on a hollow in the ground, only a couple feet below ground level. With a sinking feeling in her stomach, Nova stepped into the pit. Xander, Taos, Kiera, and Gus circled her, holding their blades in hand. Nova gulped. "What is this?"

"The purpose of this exercise," Taos instructed, "is to anticipate your opponent's movements." He tossed a dualfate at her.

Nova flinched but managed to catch it. She blinked rapidly, processing the ratio of four to one. "All of yours?"

"We strike one at a time. Your goal is to block," he said.

Nova stared back. Surely, they wouldn't actually strike her. *Right?* Taos nodded at Kiera, who immediately jabbed out her dualfate. Nova barely dodged it. Before she had a second to recover, Gus's blade flew in her direction. Nova managed to block a couple of blows. Luckily, they weren't coming in very fast.

"Stop taking it easy," Taos barked at them. He returned his attention to Nova. "What are you forgetting?"

Lower your stance, she reminded herself and did just that.

A blade grazed her arm, leaving a shallow cut that stung. Nova released a pained grunt.

"Sorry, rookie." Xander shrugged. "You gotta be quick."

Nova looked at Taos, who was unbothered. "You can heal, can't you? Get back down."

She ground her teeth and got back into her stance. Yes, she could heal, but that cut would take nearly a half hour of concentration to close up. The walls of the pit seemed to stretch higher. Taos's blade whistled past her ear, slicing a small gash. She stumbled backwards. Gus's strike came next—too close, too fast. The circle was tightening. Four figures boxing her in, weapons raised, looking down on her—

Nova's lungs couldn't get enough air. Each breath came shorter than the last.

Another blade grazed her arm and hot blood trickled down her skin. The metallic scent filled her nose. Her heart slammed against her ribs.

The dualfate grew heavier in her trembling hands, slick with sweat.

Her vision tunneled. The faces above swam in and out of focus. Metal clanged against metal, each strike jolting through her bones.

The walls were definitely closer now. The pit was shrinking, closing in—

Taos held up a hand and the blows halted.

Nova's chest heaved as she fought for air, her pulse thundering in her ears. A flash of concern shone in Taos's eyes, but Nova convinced herself she had imagined it.

"Now," he said, "you have met the pit."

Xander reached down and pulled her out. Nova winced as the movement tugged at her torn flesh.

"Not bad for a rookie," he said. "Can't wait for next time."

Nova shuddered. *Next time?*

She hugged herself and turned toward the meditation room, wanting more than anything to get back to counting her rice grains.

"Nova," Taos called out.

She stopped, but didn't turn around to face him.

"When you start to hear the voices, don't push them away," he said. "Listen to them. Accept them. Don't try to silence the past. That's what he's trying to teach you."

Nova hugged herself tighter.

"Dude," Xander said. "What are you talking about?"

Nova wondered if this was another jest aimed at her vulnerability. Even so, it was worth a try. She'd been working on this lesson for weeks with no luck. She navigated her way to the outdoor shower, hidden partially by a small divider wall behind the pit. It offered a semblance of privacy. As she cleansed herself, pink water trickled off her and stained the floor. She drowned out the sound of clinking blades on the other side of the wall as she focused on healing her wounds. After an hour, she had pulled her torn skin back together. Pink, raw skin still remained, but the pain was much more bearable now.

Nova rinsed one final time, dressed herself, and made her way to the mat. She took a few minutes to calm her senses. Then, she lifted the lid from the box.

After five hours of counting, the voices began their relentless assault on her consciousness.

A miscreant is no daughter of mine.

Nobody is rejected by the syphon. Certainly not a Darkov.

Each word felt like salt being ground into her barely-healed cuts. Her instinct screamed at her to push the mocking away, to shield herself from the torment they inflicted. But in that pivotal moment, she remembered Taos's words.

Accept them.

Nova hesitated, her hands trembling slightly as she held a grain of rice between her fingertips. Then, she let the voices in, unfiltered.

You know . . . I heard she's of distant relation to the Darkov line.

It is a shame for Cronian to be associated with such disgrace.

"Twenty-four thousand, one hundred and thirty-two," she counted through heavy breathing.

The poor son, having to deal with that embarrassment of a sister.

Nova's skin became hot. It felt like the words were being hammered into her. Each repetition was another blow. These were her biggest insecurities. The idea of accepting them was unfathomable. She couldn't do it. Her hands turned to fists. Their words weren't true. She wouldn't let them be true. And yet, here she was, exiled to Nadir, spurned and bearing the weight of her last name.

Anger swelled within her and she punched the pile of rice. Being accepted by her father was always far out of reach. If she could be different, if she could be *normal*, everything would be perfect. She would lose her miscreant title, forget everything about Nadir, and live up to the Darkov name. She would make Cronian and Denali proud. She would banish her memories of these insignificant specks of rice. She looked down at the pile, glaring at each miniscule piece. She swore that, once she made it back home, she'd never eat rice again.

She picked up a grain from her pile. "Twenty-four thousand, one hundred and . . ." *Oh no. What was I on again?* She cursed and pelted it back into the pile. She would have to start again and it had taken her over five hours to make it this far.

She lifted her hands in defeat. "Nope, I'm done." With that, she hoisted herself to her feet and made her way toward Berkshire's room. She had a bone to pick with him. When she walked into the courtyard, though, she found the front door wide open.

With her curiosity piqued, she approached the doorway on her tiptoes. It creaked on its hinges as it swayed back and forth with the wind. Through the opening, she could see the sky ablaze with the colors of sunset. Oranges and pinks painted the horizon. Nova reached out to close the door. Before she could, a bag was thrown over her head and strong arms encircled her, pinning her arms to her sides.

Panic ripped through Nova as she struggled against her assailant, trying to scream. The bag muffled her voice, though, and, despite her efforts to break free, her abductor's grip was unyielding. Her movements grew weaker with each passing moment. Nova felt another pair of hands grab her. The first shifted to one side and the second assisted in dragging her out of the house.

A heavy blow struck the back of her head. A burst of white-hot pain shot through her skull, and her vision blurred. Nova's world spiraled into darkness as her body went limp, and she collapsed into the arms of her captors.

ELEVEN

"Fool! How could you crash here again?" A man's voice echoed through the cave.

Denali inspected the memory that floated in front of the syphon. He had witnessed plenty of syphonings before, but today was different. Today was the first time he sat as a highborn. He occupied the throne usually reserved for Archaelus, who never came anymore. These days, Archaelus rarely did anything besides snore in his chair.

Denali focused on the man syphoning. It was Hubert Tumbleton, a waste collector. In their land, Hubert was one of eight people licensed to operate Ghandria's muck carts—massive wooden contraptions that rattled through the streets. Why they kept renewing his license was anyone's guess, given how often he crashed the carts.

"This pothole here's the reason!" Hubert's projected voice declared. "Came outta fishin' nowhere!"

Cronian kept records of every person's syphonings. They were stored away in his library. Each person was given a limit on how many times they could syphon annually. Hubert was the first to reach his limit every year. He came in for the tiniest of inconveniences. The man couldn't deal with the smallest form of embarrassment. Today, Hubert was erasing his memory of crashing a muck cart into his neighbor's house.

At the beginning of the ritual, Cronian had reminded Hubert that he only had two sessions left. He would have to reserve his last appointments for more important things than this.

The reason for the syphon's imposed limit remained a mystery to Denali. He had asked Cronian once, and his curiosity had earned him a lash.

Denali's gaze drifted to Morianna's empty seat beside Cronian. Her son would typically take her place in her absence, had he not been sent away on "Bloodthorne family business."

Denali imagined a world where Nova took the empty seat beside him. His heart dropped at the thought of her.

Where was she now?

Was she learning to syphon?

Had she succeeded in concealing her identity, or had the miscreants recognized her?

The last question made his limbs go numb.

What if she had been hurt? Or worse . . .

It would be entirely his fault. He was meant to be her protector. And yet he was the cause of her downfall.

He woke from his trance when he heard Cronian clear his throat. Hubert had his head bowed before Denali.

Denali straightened his back. "The syphon has accepted your offering. May the burden of this memory be lifted from your soul."

The man walked out and the guards left to bring in the next Ghandrian.

"If you cannot focus . . ." Cronian said, "then perhaps you are not prepared to take your place."

Denali gritted his teeth. "It won't happen again, *sir*."

"See that it doesn't," he snarled.

Denali clenched his jaw. The last time he had called Cronian "Father," it had earned him a backhand to the face. Over time, Denali had learned which titles were safe to use.

When the next person walked in, Denali submitted his full attention.

A middle-aged woman approached the syphon and knelt before it. She raised her palms upwards and offered words of praise. After she finished, Denali nodded, and she began to project her memory.

It was a picture of a young face—a girl in her teens. Tears streamed down her face. She choked on her words. "Mother, please. Please don't do this."

The offerer's voice came next. "You have left me no choice."

"I can still learn." The girl's voice shook.

"You are of age, child. If you could heal, you would have learned by now."

Heart-wrenching sobs escaped the girl. "You can't send me there. I'll never see you again. Please, Mother. If you love me, you won't tell."

A heavy silence lingered. Then, her mother's words poisoned the quiet. "How could anyone love a miscreant?"

The words struck Denali deeply, but he forced himself to remain focused.

The cruelty intensified as the girl was dragged toward a mansion Denali recognized as his own. The girl's sobbing persisted. "Please, Mother. Please don't do this."

Upon reaching the door, the mother let her drop, and the girl crumpled to the ground like a discarded doll. She pleaded at her mother's feet while her mother, unmoved, knocked on the door.

"Silence, child. You are only embarrassing yourself further."

The door swung open, revealing Cronian.

"She's one of *them*," the mother declared.

Guards moved to restrain the girl, binding her wrists together.

"Don't do this!" she sobbed. "Mother, don't do this to me!"

The girl's screaming faded until it was nothing more than a whistle in the cold air. Denali inspected the mother as the syphon reached outward with its ink-like tendrils and swallowed the memory into itself. The woman blinked until the color returned to her irises. She regained her composure then turned toward them and bowed her head.

Had she even felt regret or grief after turning over her child?

He'd seen plenty of people turn in their loved ones, but they usually showed some kind of sorrow. This woman showed none. It didn't look like she was fazed for a moment. But then again, the memory must have been bothering her for her to bring it to the syphon.

"The syphon has accepted your offering," Denali said. "May the burden of this memory be lifted from your soul."

He watched the woman turn and leave. He could purge himself of his guilt, too, if he lost Nova. If she didn't come back . . . he wouldn't be able to live with himself. Erasing the memory of her exile would make things so much easier.

No. He reminded himself of his vow. He would never bring his memories of Nova to the syphon.

✦˙

Nova stirred at the sound of distant yelling. Her vision was blurry, but she could tell that it was her home.

Dim firelight filled the room. Nova was lying on the marble floor, attached to something. Her wrists were strapped to a chair. Blood pooled around her, staining the dark floor crimson. Denali unbuckled her hands and pulled her tiny body into his arms. He looked to be about six years old.

This is a memory.

Denali's voice was trembling as he cried. "Hold on, Nova," he said, cupping her face in his hands.

She heard another voice yelling at her. "Wake up!"

A sharp, stinging sensation cut through the fog as a hand made contact with her cheek. The impact jolted Nova awake, her eyes snapping open. She tried to move, but her limbs felt heavy and unresponsive. Panic surged through her once more as she realized she was tied to a chair. Ropes bound her wrists behind her.

Groggily, she attempted to speak, but the gag in her mouth silenced her. She could taste the bitterness of the cloth against her tongue. She squinted against an oil lamp that hung above her, its flame magnified by a metal reflector that directed the light straight into her eyes and intensified her headache. As her eyes adjusted, she found herself in a cramped, single-room dwelling. The red brick walls were stained with patches of water damage. A small window to her left was caked with grime, its murky pane allowing only a faint sliver of moonlight to filter through. To her right, a hearth overflowed with half-burnt logs and forgotten plates with moldy remnants of meals scattered around it. Dirty dishes and empty bottles littered every surface, some teetering in precarious stacks. The air hung heavy with the stench of rotting food and unwashed clothes.

A pudgy man stood and stared at her. Seated, she was roughly the same height as him. His bristly burnt-red hair and beard had been left to grow unchecked, giving him an unkempt, wild appearance. His imposing, bulbous nose dominated his features and his nostrils, wide and flared, twitched as he inspected her. A tall, skinny man stood beside him. He had a thin, angular face with high cheekbones and a pointed chin. His most striking feature was his thick, jet-black hair.

The skinny man studied her, tilting his head to look at her. "You were right, Hognose."

"Hognose told you she'd be there, he did," the squat man said.

Nova scrunched her face. *Hognose?* She'd never met someone with quite as fitting a name. His mother must have picked it out when she took her first glance at him.

He leaned in, his hot breath on her skin. "What you up to, huh?"

Nova bit down hard on the gag. She didn't have the time or energy for this after weeks of monotonous counting and the bone-deep weariness from enduring the pit.

Hognose grabbed a large stick from a table beside her and waved it in front of her. Then, he jabbed the rough tip into her ribcage, forcing the breath from her lungs.

"Want talk to Hognose now, sunny?"

He jammed it into her side again, eliciting a pained groan from Nova. She hunched forward. As she did so, she became aware of a slight give in the ropes binding her hands. Careful not to draw attention, she began working to loosen them further.

"Tell Hognose what you up to."

"Perhaps, if we want her to speak, Hognose—" The skinny man said, "we should first remove her gag."

Hognose looked up at him, then at the gag in Nova's mouth, and his face relaxed as realization dawned on him. He plucked the cloth from her mouth.

Nova stretched her jaw once it was free.

"Start talkin'," he said.

Nova's lips curved into a smirk and she let out a soft laugh.

Hognose recoiled, taken aback by her response.

"A *stick?*" Nova said, slipping the last coil of rope from her hands.

The only thing they had in here that could hurt enough to the point of torture was their reflector lamp. If they'd shone two or three more of those on her, she would have lost her mind.

Hognose let out a frustrated huff. Then, with an exaggerated lunge, he brandished the stick again, holding it menacingly before her nose.

In one motion, Nova grabbed the stick and yanked it from his grasp. He shrieked as she stood from the chair, the ropes sliding to the floor with a thud.

"Listen closely," she said, taking one step forward, while he retreated a step backwards, visibly flinching at her approach. "I am a Darkov that can't syphon. I've been humiliated, rejected, exiled by my own father." She raised her hand and tugged her wrist covering up, revealing her marred arm. "*Tortured,*" she spat. "I am the biggest disappointment in Ghandria and the most hated person in Nadir."

Hognose was against the wall now. Nova closed the remaining distance and pressed her elbow to his neck.

"If I am to break one day, it's not going to be because of a puny, *dull* stick."

She eyed it again and scoffed. It was an insult to the punishments she and Denali had endured growing up. All the rejection and hate was something she was learning to live with. Being threatened with a stick was mockery. Hognose shut his eyes tightly. "Oscar!" he shrieked. "Grab her!"

Oscar pounced and Nova whipped the stick up to his neck with her other hand, stopping him cold. The three of them exchanged glances, unsure of what to do next. Suddenly, the front door swung open and Taos bounded through. He stopped abruptly, taking a moment to inspect the scene.

"Oscar," he said, nodding at the tall man. Then, he turned to Hognose, who Nova still had pinned against the wall. "Horace, always a pleasure."

He surveyed the scene more and then relaxed, giving an amused smile. Nova released the pressure on Hognose and he gasped for air, grabbing onto his neck and falling to the floor.

"Hognose been attacked!" Hognose wheezed.

Oscar ignored his friend and looked at Taos. "Everyone knows she's here now."

"I'm aware," Taos replied.

"Attacked!" Hognose yelled again.

Oscar raised his chin. "Those who stand with highborns stand against miscreants."

Taos reached for the door, gesturing for Nova to follow. She promptly obeyed.

"Trust me," Taos said, "I don't stand with her."

He shut the door behind them. There was a long silence before Taos looked at her. "A stick?" he asked flatly.

"He used it first," Nova said. After a moment of hesitation, she added, "Why do so many of them talk like that anyways? Hognose, Gus, and the others?"

Taos remained silent as they walked toward Berkshire's. Nova thought he would ignore her question entirely.

"The spora release toxins," he said finally. "They affect brain development in children."

Nova eyed him, waiting for an explanation, but Taos offered nothing more. "Just children? Not adults, too?" she asked.

Taos exhaled sharply, clearly annoyed at having to elaborate. "I'm not here to give you a biology lesson. I'm not your teacher."

Nova crossed her arms. "Why are you here, then?"

Taos stopped, turning to face her. "Berkshire sent me." He squinted at her. "Is a stick really the best you could do?"

Nova groaned, suddenly feeling like she was back in one of his training lectures. "It's not like I had a choice, okay? He was the one using it."

"Right," Taos said, "because there was absolutely nothing else in that hoard house you could have used as a weapon."

"That's not fair," Nova snapped, feeling her frustration rise. "You weren't there. You don't know what happened."

"Just try not to embarrass us if we ever get into a real fight," he said. "You're still holding it, by the way."

Nova looked down and saw her hand clutching the stick. She dropped it like it was poisonous and wiped her palm on her shirt. Suddenly, Taos's expression shifted, his gaze fixed on her arm. Noticing the scars on her bare arm were visible, she quickly pulled her covering back down to hide them. His eyes trailed up to meet hers, piercing in their intensity.

She looked away, unable to bear the weight of his silent questioning. "Just take me back to the rice." She side-stepped him.

Taos remained silent, though she could feel him watching her as she moved ahead.

"Nova," he said. "Not that way."

She slowed her pace but didn't turn around. "Isn't Berkshire's right over—"

She rounded the corner and froze. A sprawling crowd had gathered outside Berkshire's cottage. They were shoving into each other and yelling.

"Show yourself, Berkshire!"

"Hand over the girl!"

TWELVE

Taos grabbed Nova's arm and yanked her behind a small cottage.

"They found Wendell."

"Who?"

"The collector. And he's brought some friends over to visit."

"He's alive?" she asked, relieved that she hadn't inadvertently caused a man's death. "How did they find out I was at Berkshire's?"

"The kids have seen you there. My friends too," he said. "Doesn't take a genius to put it together."

She pressed her lips together as she contemplated. "What do we do now?"

Taos's hand clamped around hers. "Follow me," he said.

Pulling her behind him, Taos weaved through the shadowed spaces between cottages until they reached a small, overgrown yard a few doors down.

"Where are we going?"

"Quiet." Taos's attention was fixed on something on the ground near the corner of a cottage. He led Nova to a spot between some unkempt bushes and knelt down. Brushing away dry leaves and debris, he uncovered a trapdoor. He grasped the edges and swung it open. A bottomless pit gaped before them and Taos motioned toward it.

Nova grimaced. "I'm not getting in there. For all I know, you'll close it and leave me there."

Taos rolled his eyes. "It's a tunnel, Darkov. It leads to the courtyard."

Nova's suspicion didn't wane. She studied him as she weighed her limited options.

"Would you just get in?" he said.

"Why do I have to go first?"

"You're impossible," Taos said. "Because I'm going to confront the angry mob."

Nova bit her lip as she hesitated, conjuring visions of dropping twenty feet and breaking her legs.

What if she became paralyzed?

Or worse, what if there was no end?

What if she fell and fell forever?

Her face drained of color as she stared into the darkness. She gulped audibly.

"It's six feet deep, Darkov."

Nova crossed her arms. "So you *say.*"

The creak of a door opening nearby shattered their discussion and pulled Taos's attention away. Then came the sound of footsteps descending wooden porch stairs, each step groaning under the weight. In a split-second decision, Nova pushed Taos, ramming her shoulder into his midsection.

Caught off guard, Taos stumbled backwards toward the opening. His arms wrapped around Nova as he lost his balance, pulling her with him as they tumbled into the dark hole.

They landed in a jumbled heap, the impact knocking the wind out of both of them. Above, the trapdoor slammed shut, sealing them in complete darkness. Nova attempted to disentangle herself from the awkward knot of limbs she and Taos had become.

"Ouch, watch it," Taos muttered as Nova's elbow found an unfortunate landing spot on his arm. She shifted again, trying to stand, but his movements under her made her slip.

"Ouch!" he yelped again as another elbow jabbed into his rib.

Nova twisted her weight. "Just—let me try to—"

Her words were cut off by a sharp groan from Taos as she accidentally kneed him in a particularly sensitive area. The impact was immediate, and Taos let out a series of heavy, pained breaths. Nova finally managed to shimmy off him. She was standing hunched over, hands on her knees.

Between strained breaths, Taos mumbled, "Serves me right for helping a Darkov."

Nova ignored his comment, feeling around in the blackness for a way out of the pit. "Ready?"

He huffed. "Just keep your elbows and knees to yourself."

The sound of him searching the ground echoed in the cramped space. "I know it's in here somewhere," he said. After a few seconds of fidgeting, a flint sparked, and a torch flickered to life.

Taos squatted down next to a tiny tunnel entrance near their feet. He squeezed through it feet first, momentarily disappearing from Nova's view.

"You next," he said, poking his head back through the opening.

She followed his example and descended into the main tunnel. It was narrow and the ceiling sloped so low that it forced them to crawl single file. Nova trailed close behind Taos, his torch light bobbing and swooping with each stride forward. As Nova brushed against the damp walls, she noticed Taos's labored breathing rasping through the confined space.

She tried to make conversation. "So if this leads to the courtyard, did Berkshire build it?"

"Yep," he replied, his voice tight. He came to a stop in front of her, and Nova nearly bumped into him. He muttered, "Damn Berkshire and his rabbit holes."

Nova bit back a smile, realizing the usually stoic Taos might be struggling with the enclosed space. "By himself? How long ago?" she pressed, hoping to keep him talking.

"I don't know, Darkov," he huffed. "He said something about his family being tunnel diggers for the highborns. What's with all the questions today?"

Nova absorbed the new information. She had heard rumors of

secret passages that the highborns used, but she had never pressed it. Father wasn't one to entertain questions.

Taos gave a grunt and started moving again, his pace noticeably quicker. As they finally reached the end of the tunnel, they found a ladder leading up to a trapdoor. The glow of the moon filtered through its edges.

"Up you go," Taos said.

Nova climbed up, pushing the door open with a quiet creak. The cool night air hit her face as she rose into the courtyard. A noise sounded behind her. Before she could turn, arms wrapped around her from behind. Someone kicked the back of her leg and she fell to her knees. The impact sent shockwaves through her.

Taos emerged a second later, torch still in hand. His white shirt was covered with streaks of dirt and grime. He went still, taking in the scene before him.

Three men stood in the courtyard.

"So it's true, then," one man announced, coming forward. "You are protecting the Darkov spawn."

The man holding Nova pulled her arms behind her back. Her muscles locked, her body turning to stone in his grip.

"What are your intentions, Quentin?" Taos asked.

Quentin ignored him as he circled Nova like a vulture, looking her up and down. Nova's skin crawled under his scrutiny.

"Using her as leverage won't work," Taos said. "Cronian won't change his mind."

"I don't want leverage." Quentin gave a big, toothy grin. "I want revenge."

He looked at the men holding her. "Take her to the Krall."

A cold dread seeped into Nova's veins. With a violent shake of her head, she pleaded, "No."

Taos positioned himself in front of their exit. "It won't change anything."

"Taos Bladen." Quentin advanced on him and put a hand on his shoulder. "Of all the miscreants here, I'd have never expected *you* to be the one to protect the blood of a highborn. Not after what they did to your parents."

Taos's head snapped up, his eyes locking onto Quentin's.

"They fed us lies about the sickness that took your parents," Quentin said. "You and I? We know better."

He paused, then gently pressed a finger under Taos's chin, guiding his gaze toward Nova. "She has his *eyes*. Can you honestly look at her without seeing *him*?"

Nova studied Taos, noticing his tightly set jaw. Quentin's words had struck a nerve.

"I won't tell you again," Taos warned. "Let her go."

Quentin released his hold on him and withdrew. "Your loyalties surprise me, Mr. Bladen."

"My loyalty is to Berkshire."

Quentin sighed. "Very well." He gestured the two burly men forward. They let Nova go.

The first assailant hurtled toward Taos, but Taos sidestepped and swung the torch hard into the man's ribs. The torch splintered from impact, its flame snuffing out. Taos tossed the broken handle aside as the other attacker stepped in with a dagger. He delivered a series of jabs, but Taos blocked each of them.

Nova's eyes darted around the courtyard, landing on the rack of wooden training weapons Taos used with the children. She dove for the nearest one.

Taos caught his assailant's arms mid swing, redirecting the momentum to unbalance his opponent before delivering a sharp elbow to the man's face. The first assailant was back on his feet. He reached for him, attempting to encircle Taos from behind in a chokehold. Taos ducked and pivoted, but the attacker caught onto his shirt, yanking him forward and delivering a blow to his abdomen.

Nova gripped the prop sword with both hands and swung it at Quentin, but he stopped it midair and ripped it from her grasp. He tossed the weapon aside and seized Nova's wrists.

"Enough games," he growled, twisting her arms behind her back.

Nova struggled against his grip, but Quentin was too strong. He forced her through the front hallway. He yanked the door open and a wave of startled whispers rippled through the gathered miscreants outside. Quentin shoved her off the front steps to the ground in front of them. They backed away, forming a conspicuous space around her.

"That's her." The words had come from the bald man—Wendell —pushing his way to the front. Bandages wound their way up his arms and circled his neck.

The spectators gaped at Nova. A woman pulled her daughter behind her for protection. Kiera, Xander, and Gus pushed their way to the front of the half-circle.

Taos burst through the door and halted at the sight.

Nova's cheeks burned with humiliation as she shrank into herself. Her fingers and toes curled inward, stiffening beyond her control.

The moon's harsh beam cut through the night, spotlighting her on the ground.

The crowd loomed over her like a collapsing tunnel, stealing what little air remained.

Their whispering swelled into a roar, each word battering against her skull.

"Her is Taos friend," Gus said.

"Yeah, well, now we know why he's been hiding her," Kiera mumbled.

Nova grabbed her head with both hands and squeezed. Through squinted eyes, she caught Taos's gaze. His brow furrowed as he took in her state.

Two more figures pushed their way through to the front. It was Hognose and Oscar. Hognose raised an accusatory finger at Nova.

"Her!" He stretched his finger out farther. "Her attacked Hognose!"

"What do you want from us!" someone yelled.

"Who cares?" one woman said. "We can use her as leverage."

"Give her to the Krall!"

The air around Nova thickened and she started to suck in sharp gasps.

"You don't want to do that." One familiar voice towered above the rest, causing everyone to fall silent.

Nova's hands fell away from her head as she searched for the source of the voice. There, parting the crowd, stood Berkshire.

Quentin spread his arms wide, encompassing all of the assembled miscreants. "The people demand answers, Berkshire." As he spoke, he descended the front door steps.

Berkshire said nothing.

"He hid her here," Quentin called out as he walked in a circle around Nova. "He *protected* her. He let her around your *children*."

The town erupted in outraged cries. They held up fists, and Nova flinched.

Breathe, Nova. She repeated Denali's words to her growing up. *Just breathe.*

Berkshire raised his hand, and a hush fell over the gathering. He ascended the three steps leading to his door and came to a stop next to Taos. Berkshire's gaze roamed over the gathered miscreants, waiting until every eye was fixed upon him.

"The girl can help us," he said.

Nova's mind stumbled over the words as the people shared concerned glances.

"With the proper guidance, I believe she can master the art of levitation."

Nova's jaw dropped. Berkshire had told her that ability had been lost long ago.

Quentin scoffed. "Not this again." He addressed the miscreants. "Do not be fooled. Levitation is a lost art."

"Or perhaps the introduction of syphoning is the very reason we are no longer capable of it," Berkshire offered.

"A tenuous theory at best," Quentin said. "How can you prove this?"

Taos descended the steps and stood beside Nova, offering his hand. "By teaching someone who has never syphoned, and who has been invited back to Ghandria."

Laughter skittered through the crowd.

"Do enlighten us, then," Quentin said. "Where will you find a miscreant who has been invited back?"

Nova let Taos help her to her feet, her legs stiff beneath her.

Quentin threw his head back and laughed out loud. "You expect us to believe that a *Darkov* has never syphoned?"

Berkshire met Quentin's eyes with a steady look.

"It can't be true," a woman said.

"It is," Taos said, one arm anchoring Nova upright. "The highborns have given her another chance to prove she can syphon. If she shows them she can levitate instead, then we can prove Berkshire's theory . . . that syphoning is corrupt. It could give us a chance to go home."

"Corrupt?" Quentin sneered. "Syphoning keeps us sane. It *protects* us."

"What if it doesn't?" Taos said. "It's portrayed as our savior, but what if that's false? The loss of levitation happened right after the creation of syphoning. Think about it."

Everyone looked to Berkshire, waiting for a response.

"It would be wise to consider the possibility," he added.

Some faces soured, others inspected Nova, as if they were trying to decide if she was capable of doing it. Some, though, looked hopeful.

Nova mulled over the information in her head. Berkshire thought there was a chance for them all to return—but miscreants couldn't get back into Ghandria. Her case was the only exception. Still, she wondered why the miscreants cared so much for the syphon when they didn't have access to it. Why did they care so much when it was an ability they couldn't even use? Even if they succeeded in showing that the downfall of levitation was a direct result of the uprising of syphoning, Cronian wouldn't allow exiles to return. Doing so would be admitting that he had made a mistake —and Father wouldn't be proved wrong.

"The highborns took our lives from us," Taos said. "We've all been rejected. We've all lost someone because of it."

The crowd murmured and spat at the mention of the highborns.

Quentin approached Nova, edging closer to her, but Taos cut him off.

"You have a nephew there, right?" Taos said. "She might be your only chance to get back to him."

Quentin's expression faltered. The fire in his eyes dimmed and for a few seconds, he went still, lost in thought.

"If we do nothing," Taos said, "the banishments will never stop."

Nova noticed one elderly woman grab onto her necklace, rocking back and forth with words too quiet to hear. The miscreants all stirred for a few minutes.

"You better be right about this." Quentin's eyes flickered to Nova. "For her sake." Then, he pointed at Berkshire. "Keep her away from the children."

"The kid won't go near the children," Berkshire said, "so long as she poses a threat."

"You best hope she doesn't betray you, Berkshire. Heaven knows you should never trust a Darkov."

"You don't have to trust her," Taos said. The words felt like a jab at Nova. She frowned. "You have to trust Berkshire," he added.

Nova felt the glares from more than one person, but, surprisingly, they began to disperse. A few people lingered there. Wendell was one of them. He stood still, nostrils flaring. Taos pulled Nova inside, locking the door behind them.

Nova winced, her head throbbing, as she turned to confront Berkshire. "Levitating, Berkshire? You can't be serious."

He continued toward his room.

"Are you ever going to answer me?"

"Finish your lesson."

Nova couldn't contain her anger any longer. She let out an exasperated groan and tugged at her hair in frustration. Her cheeks flushed with irritation as she paced back and forth.

"Hey," Taos said. "What happened out there?"

Nova tensed and a knot formed in her stomach. The memory of her public vulnerability flashed through her mind—her hands shielding her face as she curled into a tight ball. Taos had seen it. She avoided looking at him. "Nothing. It was hot, that's all."

"You're gonna pretend that was nothing?"

Her pacing slowed, and she stopped altogether, turning to face him with steady eyes. "Please stop pretending to care."

Taos leaned forward, his voice low. "I was defending you out there."

"If by *defending* me you mean nearly killing me in the pit earlier today, then telling the whole village not to trust me, *and* keeping this levitation business a secret from me, then, yeah, thanks for all of it."

Taos scoffed. "Fine, that's the last time I try to rescue you."

"Rescue *me?*" She laughed. "I was handling Hognose just fine on my own."

"Yes, you and your stick were making terrific strides."

Nova dug her fingers into her palms and stormed past him, making her way to the meditation room. She plopped down onto the mat and opened the rice box. Each grain she counted was a declaration of her impatience, a mini-rebellion against the endless task of tallying rice.

Hours passed and the voices began their assault on her consciousness.

No miscreant is a daughter of mine.

Nova tried to focus, but her anger made it impossible. Heat rushed to her face.

Why did Berkshire hide his plan from her?

She paused her counting. She wouldn't get anywhere with this on her mind. Instead, she focused on memories of Denali.

Stay positive, he would say. *Don't think the worst.*

She drew in a measured breath. Once her anger cooled, Nova lifted a single grain of rice. She hesitated, her hands trembling slightly as she held it between her fingertips. Then, she surrendered. She allowed the voices to flood in, unfiltered, overwhelming her thoughts as she continued to count.

I heard she's of distant relation to the Darkov line.

Nobody is rejected by the syphon.

"Sixteen thousand, five hundred and—" She choked on the numbers, swallowing hard before pushing out the word, "—forty." The room was still dark, the soft glow of candles her only companion. Berkshire and Taos had gone to bed several hours ago. Nova's bones ached with exhaustion, her muscles spasming in protest. Morning light began to seep through the shutters.

She was at fifty-thousand now and had made it through half the pile. The voices persisted, but gradually lost their control over her. Nova began to realize that everything they had said about her was true.

I heard she's of distant relation to the Darkov line.

True, Nova thought, though only "distant" because they were in Ghandria and she was here.

Nobody is rejected by the syphon.

Also true, she told herself. *Nobody but me.*

The sounds of children practicing in the courtyard came and went and Nova counted on.

"Seventy-thousand, thirty-two."

As the judgments sank in, Nova felt oddly calm. She *was* the first youngborn to be exiled. She was also the first miscreant with the indiscretion of syphoning. Her chest felt a little bit lighter. It was the first time she hadn't denied being a miscreant. The voices seeped into her consciousness, fading into mere echoes.

As the day wore on, the room gradually darkened. Nova's voice, cracked and dry, continued its steady rhythm. Hours slipped by unnoticed as she worked under the soft glow of the candlelight. Through the cracks of the wooden shutters, the deep blue of night gradually gave way to a warmer, golden hue and Nova found herself holding the last grain of rice. She stared at it intently, feeling its weight in her hand, as if it bore the collective burden of all the judgment she had endured.

"It's over," she whispered as she dropped the last grain into the awaiting pile.

THIRTEEN

"Ninety eight thousand, five hundred and six." Nova plopped the box down onto the kitchen table where Berkshire sat. It had taken thirty-two hours.

He eyed his bowl of food and looked up at her like she was interrupting his breakfast.

"You promised answers," she demanded, taking the seat next to him. "Do you really think you can teach me to levitate?"

Berkshire brought his spoon to his mouth, but Nova continued.

"I don't understand how syphoning and levitation are connected?"

Berkshire sighed and plopped his spoon back into his bowl. He leaned forward in his chair until they were parallel. "When you syphon, what do you lose?"

Nova thought about it for a moment. "Humiliation, embarrassment." She paused, then added, "Pain."

"More than that?"

Nova wrinkled her forehead. "What's more than pain?"

Taos walked in and made his way to the cabinets. Nova did her best to ignore him.

"Our experiences," Berkshire said. "We feel anguish due to transgressions inflicted upon us or those we have perpetrated ourselves. The discomfort serves as a catalyst, prompting us to reflect and transform. It is an evolutionary journey in which we emerge as new beings."

Nova gave a blank stare.

"Pain forces us to think and change," Taos chimed in as he rummaged through drawers.

"So . . ." Nova said. "You think when people erase their pain, they become . . . dumb?"

Berkshire scowled. "No."

"Then, what?"

"They're hindering their own growth. Erasing a memory is a grave injustice to themselves, effectively erasing a fragment of their own identity. Consequently, they lose sight of their true selves and struggle to manage their emotions. They become consumed by anger. That's why they don't hesitate to isolate their friends. It's why they will even go as far as to cast out their own family."

Nova looked down. Her father had exiled her without a second glance. Deep down, she knew he would. The syphon came before everything else. It was their most sacred possession. Was it really *corrupting* her people? Ghandrians had been syphoning her entire life, so if it made them act a certain way, she would have no way of knowing the difference.

"How does this affect levitation?" she asked.

"Levitation manifests through profound meditation. *Meditation* is a journey of self-discovery. That becomes impossible when one is erasing crucial parts of their identity." He lowered his head to catch Nova's gaze. "The syphon opposes levitation. If someone syphons, even just once, they altogether lose their ability to levitate."

"But, everyone in Ghandria has syphoned."

"Everyone . . . except you," Taos said, now leaning back against the counter.

Nova glanced from him to Berkshire.

"You think I'm the only one who can . . ." her voice trailed off as the implication of his words finally dawned on her. "You've been teaching me to meditate this whole time?"

She stood up and waved her arms in the air. "You mean to tell me I spent three weeks counting rice grains so I could *meditate*?

Berkshire, I have to learn to syphon so I can get back home, so I can see my brother again. This isn't a time to test a theory!"

She waited for an answer, but he stayed silent.

"What about the miscreants who grew up here?" she asked. "They haven't syphoned. Why can't they do it?"

Taos raised an eyebrow at her, giving her a look as if she were dumb.

Nova crossed her arms. "Stop looking at me like that, *miscreant*."

"Nice insult, coming from the miscreant of all miscreants."

Nova pressed her lips in a thin line and drew a deep breath through her nose.

"Quiet," Berkshire demanded. "Sit down."

Nova sat, but kept a harsh glare on Taos.

"I never lied to you," Berkshire said calmly.

Nova brought her attention back to him.

"I am helping your mind heal and I am teaching you to master it. Once you have, the choice to syphon or levitate is entirely yours."

Nova frowned. *Heal from what, exactly?* And why would she choose to levitate when nobody else could? She didn't need one more reason to be a freak. She wanted to get home . . . to be normal.

To belong.

"In return for teaching you," Berkshire said, "I ask that you show Cronian and the others what you achieved here—that you can levitate."

"*If* I can levitate," she corrected him.

Berkshire gave a single nod.

Nova eyed him suspiciously. "So if this works. . . I can syphon?"

"You'll be able to erase any memory you wish to, although I hope you consider the consequences before taking such dire action."

"Yeah, yeah." Nova waved her fingers through the air. "I'll lose my identity."

"And the ability to levitate."

Nova mulled over the information. She didn't care to levitate, not when it was a lost ability. Learning to syphon would be her savior. That's what would bring her home. That's what would remove her miscreant title. She held her head high. "When's the next lesson?"

Berkshire sat back. "Eat."

Nova's stomach growled. She hadn't stopped to eat during her rice counting. Taos lowered a bowl onto the table for her. She grabbed the spoon to start dishing, then scowled at what was inside.

Taos smirked. "It's all we have at the moment."

"I'm not so hungry anymore," she said, pushing the bowl of rice away.

Taos crossed the room and opened a cupboard. "Aw, don't be such a buzzkill." He tossed an apple at her and she caught it in front of her face.

"I'm ready for the next lesson," she said.

"No," Berkshire said.

Nova jerked her head back. "What do you mean, no?"

He pushed himself up from his seat. "Rest."

Nova paused, staring at the half-ripe apple in her hand. Physically, every fiber of her being cried out for rest. Her muscles were knotted with tension and her bones were weary from the relentless events of the past two days. Still, the idea of rest seemed indulgent, wasteful, given the ticking clock that governed her time here.

"I don't have time to sit around, Berkshire. The trial is a few weeks away. I need to start the next lesson."

"Rest is not idleness," he said. "Often, the art of stillness teaches us more than constant motion can."

Another one of his mystifying lectures.

He glanced at Taos. "Take her to town tomorrow."

Taos let out a sigh. "Really? She can't just stay here and rest on her own?"

Nova crossed her arms defensively. "Yeah, I'd much rather stay here and rest—*alone*," she added pointedly.

Berkshire turned to leave, but threw his words over his shoulder. "Take her."

137

"So much for my rest," Taos mumbled.

✦

"Get up." Taos's gruff voice cut through Nova's sleep. She struggled upright from her makeshift bed on the concrete floor, her body fighting every inch of movement. The blanket slid off her. Her eyelids felt weighted, resisting each blink as her body sank under its own heaviness.

Taos's silhouette filled the open archway. The pre-dawn sky was visible in the courtyard behind him. She'd slept for nearly a full day, and sleep still pulled at her with greedy hands.

"I'm leaving in five minutes. With or without you."

Nova rubbed her left eye with the heel of her palm. "I'm up," she muttered, already reaching for her boots.

Minutes later, she followed Taos into town. His hand gripped the strap of a bag—something like a duffle bag, but worn and scuffed.

As they walked, a door creaked open and a sleepy-eyed resident emerged, carefully placing a small basket of food on her doorstep for the collector. Farther down the road, vendors were busy setting up their stands, unfolding tables and arranging their wares. Nova did her best to ignore the stares of those who recognized her. The air was filled with sounds of crates being opened, awnings being unfurled, and sleepy greetings exchanged between neighbors.

Some merchants were arranging fresh produce, while others hung handcrafted goods from makeshift displays, all working under the light of the lowering moon.

Eventually, Nova and Taos arrived at a house on the outskirts, away from the market. Nova's steps faltered as she took in the sight. The door hung off its hinges, and one window's shutters had been torn away. A sense of unease crept over her.

"What happened here?" she asked.

Taos led the way inside, with Nova trailing closely behind. More chaos greeted them as they entered. Furniture was overturned, belongings scattered and broken. The knot in Nova's stomach tightened.

"Taos," she said. "What happened?"

"There was a Krall raid last night, while we were asleep." He set the bag down and unzipped it, revealing supplies and tools.

Nova's heart sank. The Krall were searching for *her*, which meant that this destruction was because of her. Her expression dropped. "Was anyone hurt?"

Taos paused in his work, a piece of broken shutter in his hands as he turned to face her. "No, nobody was hurt," he reassured her. "There was another home raided last night, though. Xander and the others are helping take care of it."

He turned his attention to the shutter as he attempted to secure it to its hinges. Nova took in the disarray that surrounded them. She entered the main room, scanning the mess for a place to start. She bent down, grabbing the edge of an overturned chair, and set it upright. Moving from one piece of furniture to the next, Nova felt like her efforts did little to make up for the damage that had been caused. Her eyes caught on the deep claw marks gouged into the couch. She shivered, a chill running down her spine as she imagined the terror those marks must have caused.

What was stopping the Krall from raiding more houses tonight? What if they started killing? How long would it take for someone to give her away?

Sunlight now streamed through the windows, illuminating motes of dust stirred up by their cleaning efforts. As Nova worked alongside Taos, she was drawn to a line of clay pots on a shelf that had miraculously remained intact. She approached the collection. Each pot was uniquely shaped, and engraved with surprisingly detailed faces. Some were smiling while others showed much different emotions.

"What's with the faces?" Nova asked.

Taos glanced over, following her gaze to the shelf. His expression softened. "Lottie, uh—" he began. "It's her way of keeping her family around."

Nova spent a few minutes looking over the faces on each pot, then she backed away to focus on the larger task at hand.

As the hours passed, the house began to resemble a home once more, though the claw marks remained. Nova and Taos surveyed their work when footsteps creaked on the porch. Nova watched a short, petite elderly woman step through the door. She gripped the door frame for support. Nova recognized her, remembering their encounter on her second day here. Lottie shuffled around the room, taking in the familiar landscape of her home.

She clasped her hands together. "Lottie is so thankful. Yes, very thankful. Brave and kind, you is."

With a tender reverence, Lottie approached the shelf where her collection of pots resided. Standing on her tiptoes, she reached high to grab one and then brought it close to her lips.

"Maggie," she breathed. "Look who's come to help us." Her fingers grazed the rim of the pot. "Lottie is just so grateful you is okay." With a gentle smile, she leaned in closer, her ear almost touching the pot's mouth as if expecting to catch whispers from within the clay.

The room was quiet, the only sounds coming from the creaking of the house settling. Nova turned to Taos and searched his face for any sign of confusion that mirrored her own. Taos, however, remained unfazed by Lottie's interaction with her inanimate friends.

After a few seconds of silent communication, Lottie straightened, a look of resolve crossing her features. "Right you is, Maggie," she said. "Lottie should get them something."

Taos shook his head and flung his bag over his shoulder. "No need, Lottie."

She waved off his refusal. "Follow Lottie."

With a warm smile, she led them into the marketplace. The air was alive with scents of herbs, freshly baked bread, and the tangy sweetness of fruit. Voices clamored in a symphony of haggling and laughter as the inhabitants of Nadir engaged in their daily trade and barter.

Nova observed a woman trading a basket of ripe tomatoes for a hand-knitted shawl. She noted a young man offering a few hours of work in exchange for a pair of sturdy boots.

As they walked, Nova shifted her path to stay within the shadows cast by the market's tents and awnings. The afternoon sun was beating down on her, and her head was hammering.

Approaching a vendor, Lottie pulled a pot out of her bag and presented it with pride, placing it on the makeshift table for inspection. It was a beautiful handmade piece, its surface decorated with floral patterns. The vendor examined the work, turning the pot over in his hands. After a moment of consideration, an agreement was reached with a nod, and Lottie was handed two loaves of bread and a wedge of nut cheese. Her face lit up with a smile as she presented the food to Taos and Nova. "Friends help Lottie, Lottie help friends."

Nova and Taos reached for the food, but Lottie quickly pulled the cheese back. "Lottie keep cheese, though."

Taos chuckled and grabbed the bread. "Thank you, Lottie."

As they continued to navigate the tent lanes of the marketplace, they passed a tent shop adorned with fabrics of neutral hues. The woman working it picked up a dress and held it against Nova's frame. "This would be lovely on you, dear."

Her skin was a black so deep, it was radiant under the canopy's shadow. Her hair was gathered up into a turban, with a few braids escaping, each embellished with brown and orange beads. Nova found herself momentarily taken aback by the woman's audacity to wear braids. That was a privilege reserved only for highborn blood. It was a rule so ingrained in Nova's social order that the sight of this woman, proudly wearing her hair this way, challenged everything she had been taught.

"Name's Rita Weaver, dear. I've clothed half of Nadir with these two hands." She pulled the dress back and gave it a shake.

Nova's gaze shifted to the dress. Its fabric was a dull brown tone that absorbed rather than reflected light, giving it a rough appearance. She reached out, her fingers grazing the surface. The fabric felt coarse under her fingers, much different from the silks she was accustomed to in Ghandria.

Taos, picking up on Nova's evident distaste, chimed in with a cautious nudge. "You need more than one outfit."

Nova glanced down at her attire. The fraying leather cord around her waist barely managed to cinch the fabric in place. Despite her efforts to keep it clean, washing it alongside herself during each shower, the cloth had begun to show signs of wear.

"Rita?" Nova asked. "Do you have anything black?"

Rita tapped her chin thoughtfully. "Black, you say? That's a rare color around these parts, dear. Costs the most, too." She paused, considering. "Wait here."

She disappeared into the depths of her stall, rummaging through her inventory. Seconds later, she returned, holding out a set of garments that consisted of black cloth, similar in style to Nova's current beige one, accompanied by a thin black cord and a pair of form-fitting black leggings.

A smile tugged at the corners of Nova's lips, delight flickering across her face at the sight. She allowed herself to imagine wearing something that felt more like her again. But reality quickly set in, and her smile faded.

"I . . . I don't have anything to trade."

Rita let out a soft sigh.

"You know," Taos said, "you might have more to trade than you think."

Nova looked at him, puzzled. "What do you mean?"

He shot a knowing glance at Rita before returning his focus to Nova. "Knowledge can be just as valuable as goods or services here."

With a coy smile, Taos turned back to Rita. "Rita, what is the name of your mother back in Ghandria?"

The question sparked an immediate reaction from Rita, her eyes lighting up with recognition. "Jamila Weaver."

Taos's hopeful look toward Nova was met with disappointment as Nova shook her head, unable to connect with the name. "I'm sorry. I don't know her."

"More names, Rita?" Taos said.

"Mateo Crouch, Ticus Wassim, Posey Hayes . . ."

Nova felt a growing unease, biting her lip in frustration as none of the names resonated with her. Taos, his amazement poorly masked, whispered to Nova so only she could hear. "I thought you were a youngborn. Aren't you supposed to know your own people?"

Nova fidgeted uncomfortably with her hands. Her isolated upbringing, filled with private tutors and confined mostly to her mansion, had prevented her from meeting many people.

Rita kept spilling names . . . "Vivian Earl, Bryson Miles—"

"Wait!" Nova said. "Vivian," she repeated—a name that had surfaced in a snippet of conversation overheard at her trial. The memory came flooding back to Nova in vivid detail, including the significant news about Vivian that might just be of value.

"I do know something!" Nova announced.

Rita perked up. "Well, dear?"

"Would it be enough for the dress?"

Rita studied Nova for a moment, considering the offer. "That depends on the news, dear."

"She just had a child. Her third, I believe."

Rita put a steadying hand over her heart. "Goodness me, three of them?" She laughed out loud. "I suppose she always said she wanted a big family. Is she well? Do you know the child's name? How far apart are the ages? What about her father—"

Taos chuckled. "Easy now, Rita."

"I'm sorry," Nova said. "That's all I know."

It didn't take long for a nearby vendor to overhear the exchange. He peeped his head in. "What about the Elsons? Are they well?"

One by one, people began to drift closer, drawn by the prospect of news from home. As the gathering around Nova grew, people reached out, some holding goods in their outstretched hands, hoping to trade for a piece of information from Ghandria.

Among the voices, one man's demand cut sharply through the rest, his approach more forceful than the others. "Blythe Pierce."

That name rang familiar in Nova's ears. She was one of Denali's friends.

"I—"

Another man reached forward and cut Nova off, tugging on her dress. "Geraldine Hunter! She's an architect—"

"Asher Stokes—"

Nova's body tensed. Hands reached for her from every direction, blocking any path to escape. Her head swirled as she tried to navigate the sea of desperate faces. The goods held out to her—loaves of bread, a scarf, a dagger, a handful of berries—blurred together. Each new voice, each grasping hand, pushed her further into the chaos until the world seemed to shrink around her.

Taos stepped in, trying to create a buffer between Nova and the more insistent demands, but the intensity of their need was unrelenting. Nova grabbed her head. "I . . . I'm sorry," she managed to stammer out. "I don't know. I can't . . ."

Taos leaned in and whispered something to Rita, who nodded. She placed a hand on Nova's lower back and guided her deeper into the tent, motioning for her to take a seat.

Taos kept the crowd at bay while Nova struggled to catch her breath.

"Geraldine Hunter," Taos said, "the architect someone asked about. Last I saw her she was—"

Nova's fingers gripped the edge of her seat.

"Look around you, dear, and choose something steady," Rita suggested, pulling Nova's attention away from the scene. "Focus on it. Let it be your anchor."

Nova's gaze settled on a potted plant whose leaves stirred in the wind.

"Focus on your breathing. In four counts, hold four counts, out four counts."

Nova followed her instructions, and her racing pulse began to slow, the tension in her muscles easing with each exhale.

"Just breathe, dear," Rita instructed softly, sitting beside her.

After a few minutes, Nova steadied herself. Rita remained beside her, offering silent support until Nova felt ready to speak. "Thank you," Nova managed softly.

"The world can wait," Rita said, "even if just for a few breaths."

Nova kept her gaze on the plant. She gave a slight tilt of her head when she noticed the carvings of a face sculpted on its pot.

With a solemn smile, Rita explained, "A gift from our beloved Spottie Lottie. The poor dear has been through it."

Someone in the front of the tent shouted out a name. Rita and Nova both looked up at Taos, who was addressing the few remaining onlookers. He took goods from their hands one by one as he answered each question.

"They're not usually so forceful," Rita said. "Helga announced a curfew today, what with the recent Krall raids. It's got everyone worked up."

"Helga?"

Rita nodded. "Our leader, dear."

"I didn't know you guys had a leader."

"Well, now you do." Rita waved her hand dismissively. "Enough about that. Let's get you changed into your new outfit." She grabbed a piece of fabric hanging nearby and draped it over a rack in the corner of the tent to create a makeshift changing area.

"There you go, dear."

As Rita turned away, Nova stood and began to change. She draped the black cloth over her left shoulder, leaving the right bare. She wrapped the fabric around her body and fastened the thin cord around her waist. After pulling up the leggings and slipping her feet back into her boots, she stepped out from behind the sheet.

Rita turned back. A broad smile spread across her face as she took Nova's hands in hers. "Black suits you, dear." Her smile faltered slightly as her gaze fell to Nova's forearms, still wrapped in beige cloth. "Oh, this won't do. It clashes terribly."

Nova started to protest, but Rita's nimble fingers were already unwrapping the fabric. As she pulled it off, Rita's hands stilled. Nova tensed, and Rita's face softened. She reached for a pair of scissors and a folded length of black cloth, cutting off two wide strips. She then discarded the scissors and began to rewrap Nova's forearms.

"Scars are the stories of our lives, my dear—stories of what we've endured written on our skin." Rita's eyes crinkled with warmth as she looked up at Nova. "What lovely stories you must have."

After securing the wrap, she gave Nova's hands a gentle squeeze.

Taos ducked into the tent, market goods piled high in his arms. The stack teetered and Nova quickly reached out to stabilize it. As she stepped closer to him, his gaze finally swept her over. For a split second, his eyes widened and a faint flush crept up to color his cheeks. He quickly looked away.

"We should go," he said. "Before more people show up."

Rita lifted a pile of neatly folded fabrics from her table. "Do come back if you remember more . . . about Vivian."

Nova smiled at her new friend. "Of course."

"Come on," Taos said. "We have one last stop."

Nova followed him out of the marketplace. They wound their way through the cobblestone streets and the noise of the market faded behind them. As they walked, the closely packed cottages gradually gave way to open fields.

At the edge of the settlement, Taos led her to a secluded area. A low, intricately woven fence of living vines and flowers marked the boundaries of what appeared to be a sacred space. Beyond the barrier, a garden was divided into small, irregular sections, each separated by meandering paths of smooth river stones. Plants with vibrant blooms filled every corner. In one section, a group of people knelt on the ground, holding polished stones to their hearts. Soft whimpers and quiet cries occasionally broke the garden's reverent silence. Some of their faces were streaked with tears.

Nova's gaze drifted across the garden to a corner where the plants grew more dense. There, she spotted what looked like a freshly covered burial mound. A short, plump middle-aged woman stood in front of it. Her burnt orange dress fluttered slightly in the light breeze, and her red hair was adorned with a crown of yellow blooms.

As Nova watched, the kneeling people began to rise one by one. They formed a procession, slowly making their way to the burial mound. A young boy at the front of the line approached the grave first. He murmured words into the stone he held, then placed it atop the mound of dirt.

Nova noticed the grave wasn't alone. Surrounding it were other mounds, each covered with a collection of stones. Some were entirely blanketed by the river rocks. The ritual continued as each person in turn laid their stone, adding to the growing pile.

"What is this?" Nova asked.

"The Garden of Remembrance."

"Remembrance for who?"

"The Krall that died."

Nova eyed the mounds. "What happened?"

Taos bent down and picked up a rock. "They tried to get on the boat."

"You mean the ones that tried to get on when I arrived?" Nova said. "That was almost four weeks ago."

He nodded, brushing dirt off the rock. "They were buried as soon as their bodies were found. The Garden is always open."

Nova's throat tightened, her mind reeling back to the chaos of her arrival. The boatman had slaughtered so many of them. A chill ran down her spine as she thought about the bodies that had gotten sucked into the whirlpools or swept away by the current.

She watched as a woman stopped in front of the pile, kissed a stone, and gently laid it on the dirt.

"So this is a way to honor them?" Nova asked. "I don't understand. The Krall just raided this village. Why do you praise them like this?"

"We aren't praising them, Darkov," he said. "We are giving them the one thing they wanted . . . to be remembered."

Nova fell silent, pondering his words. After a moment of thought, she bent down and picked up a small rock. Her eyes met his. "Can you show me how?"

The questions seemed to catch Taos off guard, his usual composure slipping for a moment. He glanced around at the other mourners before his eyes found Nova's again. She held her breath, suddenly aware of how exposed she felt under his stare. She willed him to see her genuine desire to participate, to understand.

147

Finally, his posture eased, and he gave a small, almost imperceptible nod.

"Follow me," he said quietly.

He turned and walked through the opening in the barrier to the burial mounds. Nova hesitated for a split second before falling into step behind him. They stopped at the edge of the gathering, partially hidden behind the last row of mourners.

Taos turned his stone over in his hands. He closed his eyes and held it close to his chest, over his heart.

"We think about the lives lost," he explained softly, barely loud enough for Nova to hear, "about the families they may have left behind. We acknowledge their dedication to making it back home."

He paused. "In some ways," he said, "they are stronger than the rest of us, because they never gave up."

As his words sank in, Nova's brow furrowed in painful understanding. She looked back at the burial mound. How many of them had children who would never see their faces again? How many had siblings hoping that somehow they would make it back home?

Her lower lip trembled as she remembered Denali running to the dock the day of her exile. She struggled to maintain her composure, but the quivering of her chin betrayed her.

Taos moved forward through the crowd, approaching the mound. As he did, a little girl near the back of the gathering turned around. When she saw Nova, she tugged on her mother's shirt, pointing.

Her mother waved her off, but a couple more heads began to turn. Curious and suspicious glances swept over Nova. She shifted uncomfortably and tugged the fabric of her top away from her neck, suddenly feeling constricted. The sacred garden now felt suffocating. The sun's rays were piercing right through her skull and she squinted against the harsh light.

Taos deposited his stone and made his way back. He passed the onlookers and grabbed her hand. "Time to go."

When they turned to leave, Nova's gaze locked briefly with that of the flowered woman in the orange dress. The woman studied her with quiet intensity. Taos tugged her hand, breaking the moment. His fingers slipped away as they walked briskly, leaving the space behind before the whispers could grow into anything more.

Minutes later, as they approached their cottage, Nova spotted Berkshire standing out front with a woman she didn't recognize. Her hands were clasped tightly in front of her.

Taos froze mid-step at the sight of the woman. He swallowed hard, his voice tense. "Wait here."

He strode up to them. Nova fought the urge to extend her hearing. The woman wavered forward, her eyes fixed on Taos's face. When he stopped in front of her, she reached out an unsteady hand, almost but not quite touching his face, as if afraid he might disappear.

Taos stood stock-still, his back to Nova. She could see the tension in his shoulders. The woman's expression shifted. She shook her head slowly, tears welling up.

Berkshire frowned. The woman offered an apology before walking off, wiping the tears from her cheeks as she did.

Nova edged toward Taos. She wanted to ask if everything was okay, but the words got trapped somewhere in the bottom of her throat. He kept his gaze on the ground, his jaw locked. Without a word or glance in her direction, he turned and brushed past her. He opened the front door and disappeared into the cottage.

Nova turned to Berkshire, questions forming on her lips, but he cut her off.

"Get inside. The next lesson starts tomorrow."

FOURTEEN

The following morning, Berkshire led Taos and Nova east through the steadily falling rain. Unlike the fungal forest that dominated the west side of the island, here ancient trees ruled, their shadows falling over a carpet of ferns. As their path climbed higher, the sound of rushing water began to fill the air. The atmosphere grew cooler and more humid, carrying the fresh scent of water and damp earth.

The vegetation changed subtly as they continued upward. The trees became taller, their trunks slick with moisture. Vines and epiphytes clung to the bark. Ahead, a waterfall came into view, cascading from the towering cliffs above. Its waters plunged into a pool below, which fed into a stream that wound its way down the slope. Berkshire halted at the water's edge, where Nova could feel the gentle mist of the falls against her skin. There was a large flat rock in the shallow pool of water, with enough area for a few people to sit.

He gestured for her to take a seat on the rock. Nova climbed onto it.

"Sit," Berkshire said. "Cross your legs. Palms up."

Nova awkwardly folded her legs into a cross-legged position.

He scowled. "Sit up straight."

Nova obeyed. Berkshire stroked his beard and addressed Taos. "Tell me when she's ready."

He walked away and disappeared into the trees. Taos positioned himself before the rock. "Inhale for ten seconds, hold for ten, exhale for ten, and hold for ten."

Nova closed her eyes. She took a deep breath, following his instructions. She inhaled quickly, puffing out her chest.

"Stop," Taos snapped. "Breathe from your diaphragm, not your shoulders."

Nova paused. "I don't know what that means."

"Put your hand on your stomach," he said. "When you breathe in, it should expand. Inhale through your nose, not your mouth."

She placed her hand on her abdomen. This time, she focused on making her hand rise as she inhaled.

"Better," Taos said. "Now, do it for ten seconds. Count in your head."

Nova tried again, but only made it to six seconds before her lungs filled.

"I said ten seconds. Start over."

She made it to eight.

"You're not focusing. Block everything else out."

This time, she managed a full ten-second inhale and hold.

"Good," Taos said. "Go again."

As Nova repeated the cycle, she found her rhythm improving, though Taos's sharp corrections continued. After several more attempts, she finally performed the sequence to his satisfaction.

He lifted his fingers to his mouth and made a loud whistle. Nova flinched and covered her ears, the sound drilling into her skull. That whistle promised a headache for the rest of the night.

Footsteps drew closer and Berkshire appeared in front of them.

"What's next?" Nova asked.

"Breathwork," he replied.

"But," Nova said, "that's what we just did."

Berkshire gestured toward a massive rock emerging from the pool, standing its ground against the downpour of the water. "There," he clarified.

Nova's gaze sharpened. "Under that?"

Berkshire ignored her, turning his attention to Taos. "Take her."

Taos bowed his head and descended into the water, making his way to the rock. Nova turned to Berkshire with pleading eyes.

"Go," was all he said.

Reluctantly, Nova followed after Taos.

Behind her, Berkshire ordered, "Don't drown."

Nova approached the rock. Taos pulled himself up first and extended his hand. As she gripped it and climbed up, the water slammed into her with astonishing force, blinding her. Water filled her mouth as she tried to draw breath. She slipped from Taos's grasp and the current swept her off the rock.

The force of the water pinned Nova to the riverbed. She thrashed against the current, desperate to break free, but her struggles grew weaker as the roar of the waterfall faded, and everything went black.

✦

Nova's eyes fluttered open to a soft patter of rain against her skin. The rocky shore was rough against her back. Her body convulsed and she retched up water. Through blurred vision, she made out Taos kneeling above her, water dripping off the tips of his curls.

Berkshire was scowling. "I said not to drown."

Nova tried to sit up but her arms gave way. She rolled to her side, her body still purging water. She had just *drowned*.

"Again," Berkshire said.

She stared up at him, his words not registering at first. Her voice rasped, "How many times am I supposed to do this?"

"Until you cannot feel the weight," Berkshire replied, his gaze steady.

Nova's head dropped before she forced it back up. "Berkshire, it feels like eighty pounds coming down on my head."

Taos stood beside her, waiting for her trembling to subside

before helping her up. Her legs wobbled as she followed him back into the water, doubting her teacher's sanity.

Would he let her die? What if this was all an elaborate revenge against Father? Nova's face paled as the dark thought took root. First, the rice-counting madness, and now this torture.

Nova shot a suspicious glance between Berkshire and Taos. They were probably conspiring together.

Her confidence wavered with each step toward the rock. Taos climbed up first, extending his hand. Once on the rock, her fingers scrabbled for purchase, but the moss-slicked surface betrayed her grip. The water hammered down, and she slipped. The current drove her to the bottom. She planted her feet against the riverbed and pushed, launching herself sideways out of the crushing cascade. She burst through the surface and sucked in air.

Nova turned to Berkshire, who nodded with approval. Turning back, she found Taos already in the water beside her. She swam to him.

"Find a pocket of air," Taos yelled over the crashing water.

He scaled the rock first, then pulled Nova up as she wedged her feet into the crevices. Beneath the waterfall's overhang, they settled cross-legged on the slick ledge. Nova's fingers dug into the stone as she searched for air, turning her head from side to side to avoid the rushing water.

When panic threatened to overtake her, she found it—a tiny pocket of air, barely wider than a straw, but accessible through one nostril. It was enough. Gradually, her racing pulse steadied.

Once settled, she shifted her senses—dimming her hearing until the waterfall's roar faded to a whisper and her heartbeat became clear. She focused inward, trying to draw air through the tiny space. Her lungs screamed for more, every instinct demanding she pull away.

The water's weight pressed harder and her grip failed. She slid, and darkness claimed her again.

Nova woke on the shore, sputtering water from her mouth. Taos sat beside her, wiping his mouth off.

Wait.

Nova's fingers touched her lips. "Did you just—?"

"Rather I let you drown?" he asked. "Fall again, and I might."

Nova's head was still spinning as she looked to Berkshire, waiting for him to reprimand Taos.

Berkshire merely stared at the waterfall, unfazed by the entire exchange. "Take five minutes," he said.

Nova collapsed back against the rocky shore. Her stomach heaved and she rolled to her side, expelling water. Taos backed away to give her space. Another wave of nausea hit and she pulled her knees under her, pushing up onto her hands and knees while the dizziness subsided. Her ribs throbbed and she winced at the tender spots where Taos's hands had compressed them.

They gave her an extra ten minutes, a mercy that Nova couldn't deny.

"Ready?" Taos finally asked.

She wasn't, but she nodded anyway.

Every muscle screamed as she pushed herself up. Though the ground still swayed beneath her, she forced herself forward, back into the water. She used Taos's shoulder as a footstep this time. As she pushed off, her foot slipped, accidentally bumping his face.

"Watch it," he grunted.

Back on the rock, Nova found her air pocket and focused on the pattern Taos had taught her. Her bruised ribs protested with each deep breath. Time stretched as she fought to maintain her position. She couldn't fall again. Taos had made that clear.

Gradually, her body surrendered to the water's pressure and her panic ebbed. She followed the count—in for ten, hold, out for ten, hold. She risked a glance at Taos, seeing him mirror her movements, but the slight shift cost her balance. Her hand shot out instinctively, catching his. His fingers tightened around hers. The gesture surprised her, but she welcomed the anchor.

With each exhale, the weight against Nova's back softened. The water's touch transformed, its assault mellowing into something almost . . . bearable. Nova's grip loosened. She started to slide. Taos yanked her hand, but the motion pulled him off balance. They slipped and the waterfall claimed them both. Nova fought the current, and with a forceful push from Taos, she broke free. They surfaced together, water streaming down their faces. For a minute, they simply floated there in silence.

Nova smiled triumphantly in Berkshire's direction. "What's next?" she asked.

"Again."

✦

Denali massaged his temple with his free hand as he struggled to concentrate in Pippington's classroom. Over half of his puzzle lay completed before him, revealing Professor Pippington in her signature lavender attire, seated regally on a throne. In her arms was a white cat, though its details remained elusive. This attempt marked Denali's furthest progress in the past seven classes. He peeked at the wound in his left palm. The cut was noticeably smaller. He reminded his body to slow the healing energy. Beside him, Blythe shifted with a huff of frustration. He cast a brief look at her puzzle. Unlike his methodical edge-first approach, Blythe had opted for a chaotic start-from-the-middle strategy.

Who starts a puzzle from the inside? The thought caused a flicker of amusement to dance in his eyes.

Her puzzle was slowly taking shape, showing parts of a red cat. However, many pieces were missing, leaving large empty spaces yet to be filled. He glanced at another classmate, who had managed to assemble a few sections of her puzzle, showcasing a different red cat nestled in their professor's lap. The feline wore a black bowtie. Denali returned his attention to his desk. He reined in his urge to pour energy into the wound, keeping it a careful trickle as he worked. Each puzzle piece he placed was accompanied by the subtle sensation of skin mending.

Around him, occasional groans and the sharp sound of desks being kicked in frustration punctuated the air, but Denali's world had shrunk to the immediate task, his concentration unbreakable.

Finally, with a soft click, the last piece fell into place, revealing a golden jeweled crown atop the fluffy white cat's head. Denali lifted his hand as the final stitch of his torn skin knit back into place. Professor Pippington leapt from her desk and approached with a brisk stride.

"Ah, Mr. Darkov!" she exclaimed, beaming with pride. "My star pupil. You have dazzled me today, just as you have always done!" Reaching into her blazer pocket, she retrieved a silver star sticker and affixed it to his forehead. The class erupted into a low murmur. Blythe rolled her eyes at the display. Denali shot her a cheeky grin.

Pippington lifted her hand over her mouth in awe as she stared at the completed picture. "Oh, and how fitting for you to get my favorite feline . . . my dearest King Kitty!"

Blythe groaned. "Are we finished, then?"

Pippington placed her hands on her hips as she narrowed her eyes on Blythe. "Ah, Miss Pierce. I see your efforts continue to fall dismally short of expectations." She looked down at the jumbled mess of puzzle pieces. "What a shame the rest of my pupils won't get the chance to see Sir Whiskerbottom in all his glory. And to think, it is predicaments such as these that affirm my preference for only nurturing *male* felines."

Denali bit his cheek to stifle a laugh. Blythe's face flushed with embarrassment, and Denali could sense she was considering making good on her earlier threat to knock his teeth out.

✦

After class, Denali and Blythe headed straight to his library. As they worked, Blythe reached down into her bag and pulled out a large bag of chips. She tore it open with a loud crinkle. Denali glanced up.

She popped a chip into her mouth with an obnoxious crunch. "I can't focus on an empty stomach," she said, her words muffled by the food.

As they continued to read, Blythe kept snacking on her chips, the crunching and rustling of the bag punctuating the silence. Denali tried to ignore the noise and focus on the pages in front of him. However, as he glanced down, he couldn't help but notice the small pile of crumbs that had accumulated on the rich, dark marble around Blythe's feet. He bit into his cheek. His father's no eating rule was in the forefront of his mind. He opened his mouth to speak, but Blythe beat him to it. "D, look at this."

She pushed a book across the floor to him, her finger pointing to a passage on the page. Denali leaned in to scan the words.

"Lucien's creation of the syphon was a complex process, involving the extraction of . . ."

Denali's fingers traced the edge of the smeared ink, where legible text gave way to an indecipherable blur. "It's been redacted," he said.

"Must've been some real spicy info here for someone to throw a hissy fit with an ink pen."

Denali shook his head, finally realizing that the reason they weren't finding any useful information was because they weren't *allowed* to. In two days, Nova would reach her halfway point on the isle, and Denali still had nothing to show for it. His gaze fell back to the door separating them from the forbidden library.

"Don't you have access now?" Blythe asked. "With your coming of age?"

Denali scoffed. "Cronian would never allow it."

"Hey," Blythe said. "I saw a book I wanted to read over on shelf G12. It's high up so I couldn't reach it. Could you grab it for me? I think it might have something useful."

Denali nodded and headed over that way, already knowing that it would be a lost cause. Cronian had covered his tracks too well. When he found shelf G12, he hollered back to her, "What's the title?"

No answer.

"The title, Blythe."

Still, she gave no response. He turned around. The spot where she'd been sitting was empty, marked only by a trail of chip crumbs on the floor. The wooden door to Cronian's library was wide open, and a flash of blue hair disappeared into the room.

Denali's world narrowed to a pinpoint. He sprang forward, rushing to the door. He skidded to a halt at the entrance.

Blythe was already scanning shelves, her fingers tracing over the spines of several books as she went.

Touching them.

Denali's stomach churned. He began to pace the length of the doorway.

What if Father notices her fingerprints?

What if she knocks over a book, leaving a dent in the flooring?

He paced faster, hands running through his hair.

What if she sneezes, and the force of her breath disturbs the delicate placement of the dust on the shelves?

What if a strand of her hair dislodges from her scalp and falls to the floor?

Blythe opened a book and Denali's lungs seized. He stopped and gripped the doorframe.

What if the oils from her fingertips seep into the paper, leaving behind an indelible mark on its pages?

His eyes darted frantically, cataloging every potential betrayal. The drawer filled with the records of exiles loomed in his peripheral vision.

Seek and find, his young voice said in the back of his mind. *We were playing a game of seek and find.*

"Blythe, *out. Now,*" Denali forced out.

She continued to thumb through the book. She licked a finger, turning a page.

The room tilted, and Denali's grip on the doorframe tightened.

"I'm fine," she said. "Your father can't hurt me." Another page turn. "Not more than he already has."

Footsteps echoed in the corridor. Denali's heart leapt to his throat, choking off his breath. "Guards," he rasped.

Blythe held up a finger, leaning closer to inspect the book. She set it down and reached for a small drawer beneath the bookshelf, tugging the jammed compartment.

"Blythe," his voice cracked.

"Hold on, I just need to get this open!"

The footsteps grew louder. They would be at the entrance to the library any second. Terror overrode Denali's paralysis. He dove into the room, wrapped an arm around Blythe's waist, slammed the drawer shut, and lifted her off her feet.

They burst out of the room and Denali sprinted toward their original spot, tripping on his way and sending them both tumbling to the ground. Two guards turned the corner right as they fell. Blythe was on her back and Denali was holding himself up over her. They both stared up at the guards, wide-eyed and pale.

One guard quickly averted his eyes. "Oh . . . uh. Sorry, sir. We didn't mean to intrude." He bowed his head, nudging his companion. They both retreated hastily.

Denali's muscles went slack, a trembling sigh escaping as his forehead lowered to Blythe's shoulder. Slowly, he lifted his head, meeting her gaze.

Blythe raised a slim, black leather book between their faces. "I found it."

Denali sat up, moving off of her but remaining on the floor. His fingers shook as he ran them through his hair. He focused on each breath.

In, out. In, out.

Gradually, the room stopped spinning. His voice came out low and strained. "You can't do that, Blythe. I'm not messing around."

She sat up and Denali looked her square in the eyes. "What did you mean earlier, about my father?"

Blythe's expression faded, her features going distant.

A sickening feeling settled in the pit of Denali's stomach. "If he's ever hurt you—"

She waved her hand dismissively and let out a small chuckle. "I wasn't talking about physical pain, D. That's *nothing*."

She had to be talking about her uncle. Denali opened his mouth to ask more, but she cut him off by pressing the book into his line of sight.

He hesitantly took it. There, etched on the cover, was a handwritten note: *Journal of Lucien Darkov*. His heart skipped.

He flipped through the first few pages, consisting of sloppy black sketches of the syphon and . . . mushrooms?

Blythe dramatically stroked her blue hair behind her ear. "Am I the best pal ever or am I the best pal ever?"

Denali continued to flip through pages hungrily. There were more sketches of the syphon and little notes pointing at it. One of them read, *Turns different color when absorbs a memory.*

Another note was scrawled hastily in the margin: *Substance moves toward offered memory. It's drawn to it like a magnet.*

Denali cupped a hand over his mouth. "It's the journal he kept when he created it."

"Yep. And you don't have time to read it right now."

Denali shot his head up at the clock hanging on the far wall. He cursed. He was supposed to be at the cave in twenty minutes, and he still needed to change into his black suit.

"Luckily for you, I've got loads of time." Blythe reached for the journal.

Denali lifted it above her reach. "Don't even think about it. This does not go out of my sight."

He tucked the book in his bag, knowing his research would have to wait. He grabbed the key and did a final peek in the forbidden library, ensuring that every book was in its place.

Every paper in its rightful position.

Every drawer closed.

✦

Denali sat quietly in the cave, fixed on the ritual unfolding before him. Since arriving, he had witnessed two syphonings. The latest session had lasted three long hours, involving an elderly woman who wished to forget her deceased pet bird, Coco. Rather than merely removing the memory of her pet's death, she proceeded to eliminate all memories of Coco, erasing his entire existence from her mind.

It was rather extraordinary, the will power it took to erase such deep and ingrained memories. Even Cronian appeared impressed— a sight that Denali had seen only twice in his life. Ghandrians had tried to erase memories of those who were exiled, but none had ever fully succeeded, at least not without going crazy. One man had nearly done it, but during one of his final sessions, he went full on looney. It was too much to obliterate. The emotional fabric of those memories were too dense, too interwoven into their beings.

Denali straightened his back when Finnian, his schoolmate, was the next to walk in. Denali had asked his father to get him in sooner, but he had declined. Finnian bowed before Denali and Cronian. They were the only two there today. Morianna was busy manicuring her garden and Archaelus had likely dozed off somewhere.

Turning to face the syphon, Finnian knelt and raised his palms. He began:

"In release, we find freedom. In forgetting, we find . . ." he paused and his forehead creased. "Uh . . . we find peace. Praise the syphon. For through it, we are healed."

He opened his eyes, seeking Cronian's approval. Cronian shook his head and Finnian lowered his hands and started again:

"In release, we find freedom. In forgetting, we find peace. Praise the syphon. For through it, we are healed."

This time, Cronian gave a curt nod. Finnian turned his head back to the syphon. The cave darkened and murmurs of his memory began to echo.

A woman was yelling. "You dare defy my rules?"

"It was an accident, Ma."

"Don't call me that."

"Forgive me, ma'am."

"Listen to me, scum," she spat. "You were your father's mistake, not mine. Children are a rot, spreading through Ghandria, weakening us all. I should have stayed firm, should have never given in to his sniveling pleas."

Denali shuddered at the tone. It was too similar to Cronian's.

The woman's words repeated while Finnian lowered them to the syphon. It began to slowly absorb into the inky substance, but then paused before the transition was complete.

Strange.

Denali had never seen the syphon hesitate like that. It had part of the memory in its grasp, but it waited there, and the cave's atmosphere shifted. The shadows deepened and a particular aura enveloped Finnian, casting him in an obsidian glow as the syphon decided whether or not to accept the memory. Denali's eyes moved to Cronian, but his father merely raised a hand to silence his questions. A knot of unease began to tighten in Denali's stomach.

Something wasn't right.

Finnian's head began to twitch as the memory hung in front of him. Denali inched forward in the silence of the cave. Suddenly, a shriek eroded from the syphon. Its tendrils jutted around violently before striking Finnian's hand. Finnian cried out as black substance began to absorb into his skin.

FIFTEEN

"Get down!" Cronian yelled.

Denali dropped to his knees, shielding his ears from the high-pitched screech, but remained transfixed by the scene before him. Finnian screamed as the black substance seeped into his flesh, spreading from his fingertips up to his elbow. The pitch rose higher and higher until it finally shattered into silence.

The cave stilled.

Denali and Cronian withdrew their hands from their ears. Denali's eyes widened on his classmate. Finnian's pupils had glazed over white, his face stripped of all expression. Though the syphon had returned to the cave's center, Finnian's hand remained devoured by shadow. He wavered on his knees for a few seconds and then dropped face down with a thud.

Denali jumped to his feet and ran over to him.

"Get away from him!" Cronian yelled.

Denali grabbed Finnian's arm. Now that he was close, he could see the darkness coursing through his veins. Denali fumbled for a pulse. Seconds stretched.

Nothing.

"He's not breathing!"

The guards rushed in and lifted Finnian's limp body from the ground.

"Where are they taking him?" Denali demanded.

Cronian grabbed Denali by the back of his neck. "Listen carefully," he growled. "You are not to repeat this. Do you understand? The syphon is stable. That is all you are to say."

Denali's mind was still reeling with panicked thoughts. Finnian had stopped breathing. He looked at the guards as they disappeared around a curve in the walls.

With a violent grip on Denali, Cronian shook him, snapping him back to the present. "Do you understand, boy?"

Numb with shock, Denali could only nod.

Cronian released his hold and followed after the guards, barking orders at them. Denali looked back at the syphon. It floated normally in the room, like nothing had happened. He approached it slowly, peering into it. Shadows swirled in its core. Something about the scene made his skin crawl. He stumbled back and fled the cavern.

Three Ghandrians were rushing toward him as he emerged from the cave. "What's happened to the syphon?" one of them asked.

Denali stared at them, still reeling. When he didn't answer right away, they moved closer to the opening.

"Stop!" he said. "There are no highborns in there. You can't go in." He lowered his tone. "You've nothing to worry about."

Then, he began to utter his father's lie. "I assure you, the syphon is . . ."

He froze. The syphon was *not* stable. And that was exactly what he wanted people to know. But he needed to play this game right. If people started to doubt the syphon now, Cronian would only do more to hide its secrets. Denali needed more time to truly undermine him.

"The syphon is well."

✦

Nova sat slumped at the kitchen table. Her body ached from taking the full force of a waterfall for eight days. Not to mention her training in the pit Taos so graciously forced her to continue. Xander hadn't shown up ever since Nova was revealed to the town. That was no surprise.

What did surprise Nova was that Kiera and Gus acted no differently toward her. Drills in the pit were much easier when defending against three attackers rather than four.

"Liam quits!" a child yelled in the courtyard.

"That's enough, Liam," Taos said.

Nova stood and tiptoed to the archway to peek out.

Taos bent down next to the boy. "I don't train quitters. Stand up and come back to the circle."

Liam sat on the floor, arms crossed.

A shadow fell across the archway. Nova whirled around and found Berkshire standing there. His eyes moved from her to the children and back.

"Sorry—I, uh, I didn't mean to get so close."

"You may join them."

Nova searched his face. "But . . . you promised to keep me away from the kids?"

"So long as you were a threat, yes."

Without waiting for a response, he turned and began walking down the hallway.

Warmth bloomed in Nova's core. She smiled, wondering why his permission to meet the children meant so much to her.

As he disappeared around the corner, she whispered, "Thank you."

She took a moment to collect herself, then turned on her heels and crossed into the courtyard. Liam still sat with his arms crossed while Taos led others through their practice. Nova plopped down beside the young student. Taos paused and glanced at them, then got back to his lesson.

"Wow," Nova said, using Denali's old trick for cheering her up when she was down. "Wowwwww."

Liam's attention shifted to her, but he said nothing.

"I have never seen such valiant soldiers before. Are you a soldier too, Liam?"

He hesitated.

"You want to know Nova's favorite thing about soldiers, Liam?"

His head tilted slightly as he awaited her response.

"Soldiers have duties and honor. They never give up. They are the world's most heroic and important people."

He scowled. "Kid soldier not important."

Nova crossed an X over her heart, just as Denali always had. "Honest, Liam. I swear. They are *so* important."

He slumped. "It hard for Liam."

"That's what makes soldiers so special. They fight through those hard things."

He scrunched his face, pondered for a few moments. "Is Nova soldier?"

Nova was taken aback by his question. She bit her lip and looked at Taos, who continued to glance at them while he sparred with students.

"I suppose I am, yes."

"Nova fight what?"

Nova mulled over the boy's question. She tugged Rita's arm coverings up. Liam's jaw hung open when he saw the faded, jagged scars across both of her forearms. Where Father's whip tore through her skin, the scars were widest, puckered and twisted like angry seams sewn into her flesh.

Liam reached his fingertips to touch. "Whoa."

Nova couldn't feel his fingers tracing her arms. She'd lost all feeling there a long time ago. She looked up and caught eyes with Taos. Suddenly, the tip of a wooden sword jabbed into his ribcage. He grunted, and then chuckled at the little girl who had taken advantage of his distraction.

"Boom. Ninny got Tao," she said.

Nova bit back a smile.

"All right, soldiers," Taos said. "It's time to test our vision. Liam, will you be joining us?"

Liam glanced up at Nova, uncertain. She gave him an

encouraging smile. He brightened and then stood and walked over to the other kids. Nova observed as Taos demonstrated his stretching of hearing and then vision. She was surprised to see it. For some reason, she had assumed sense enhancement was his indiscretion. He seemed too confident in sparring for someone who couldn't heal themselves. For the next thirty minutes, the kids took turns practicing honing their senses. Berkshire had mentioned that teaching the children was how he earned his keep in Nadir. For some reason, Taos had taken over his job since he'd arrived. It appeared they worked out a trade between themselves, one that remained a mystery to Nova.

Berkshire stepped under the far archway of the courtyard and Nova whined, "I need a longer break before we go back to the falls."

"Not today." He motioned for her to follow.

Nova perked up and walked to the meditation room, plopping down on the mat. Berkshire lit the candles and enveloped the room in a warm glow. "Breathwork," he said.

Nova followed his instruction, drawing air in through her nose, holding, and then releasing out her mouth and holding. The tension in her shoulders eased with each exhale.

Berkshire spoke again. "Tell me about the holes in your memory."

Nova's mind reeled back to the occasions Denali had taken her to practice at the syphon.

"Everytime I tried to make an offering," she began, "it was like . . . fog in my brain. I couldn't fully grasp what I was trying to project."

Berkshire contemplated for a moment. "Choose a memory you remember fully. Walk me through it out loud"

Nova nodded. Speaking memories aloud had been one of the first techniques Denali had taught her—a beginner's way to practice until the process became natural. Nova cast her mind back. "There's one," she said. "I'm twelve years old. I'm in my father's chamber."

"What are you feeling?"

Nova twitched when she thought about it. She forced out the word: "Fear."

"What else?"

"I'm just terrified. I'm about to be punished. That's all I can think about."

Berkshire paused, studying her face, and then asked, "When recalling this memory, are you looking down at yourself, or are you seeing it through your younger self's eyes?"

"I . . . I'm looking down. I can see myself in the chair."

It was silent for a minute. Then Berkshire prodded further, "What do you hear?"

"Father's footsteps. He's pacing in front of the fireplace. He's upset with me for staining my new dress at dinner. He's holding . . ."

A swell of anxiety filled her chest, throwing off her breathing. Her concentration broke and she snapped back to reality. The projection of her memory flickered in front of her, threatening to dissipate.

"Stay with it," Berkshire cautioned. "Center yourself."

Nova closed her eyes again and calmed herself. When the world stopped spinning, she was back in her mansion.

"I get four lashes today."

Cronian lifted the whip into the air and little Nova winced, ready to take the pain.

But then the doors to the room burst open.

"Denali is here," Nova narrated. "He's come to take my place. I'm begging Father not to let him."

Little Nova was crying, pleading with both Denali and Cronian.

"It's okay, Nova," young Denali said, grabbing her by the shoulders and looking down into her eyes. "I will always take your place. No matter what you did. Do you understand? *Always.*"

Nova shook her head. Denali tenderly brushed his thumb against her cheek, wiping a tear away. "Lu mea evoradara, kid sister." He pulled her close, tucking her head under his chin. "I will *always* give you my light."

"Enough," Cronian spat.

Denali's frame tensed. "Go wait in the study room. There's a surprise for you there."

The projection wavered, and it skipped to a new scene. Nova was curled into a tight ball outside the chamber doors. The sound of the whip cut through the air. Each crack was followed by Denali's grunt of pain. Nova flinched with every lash.

Present Nova felt Berkshire's eyes on her. She let the projection dissipate and wrapped her arms around herself. She hadn't been lashed by her father in years because Denali came to take her place every time. Watching those scenes was more painful to her than taking the whippings herself. Once she learned to syphon, his cries of pain would be the first thing she would erase.

"I have found the issue," Berkshire said.

Nova's head snapped up. "You have? What is it?"

His expression remained neutral as he stood up. "We're done for today."

"But—" Nova started. "Wait. You can't just—"

Berkshire was already out of the room, leaving Nova alone with her unanswered questions.

The next couple of weeks Nova's routine became a cycle of waterfall meditation, projection practice with Berkshire, and sparring in the courtyard. Despite her repeated attempts to get Berkshire to explain what he had discovered, he remained frustratingly tight-lipped. Instead, he introduced new techniques during their sessions.

"Don't describe what you see," he'd say. "Tell me what you feel against your skin. The temperature of the room, the weight of your clothes."

Other times, he'd have her focus on her other senses: "What do you smell? Is there a taste in your mouth? Can you hear your own heartbeat?"

He even had her practice recreating physical sensations: "Tense your muscles as if you're about to move. Feel your breath catch in your throat."

Though Nova couldn't understand the purpose behind these exercises, their impact was undeniable. They demanded intense concentration, draining her energy far more than simple recollection ever had.

As she stood in the courtyard, Nova stared down at the pit. The sight still sent a shiver down her spine, making the hair on her arms rise. There were only six days left until her trial. She drew in a deep breath, steeling herself, then stepped down.

Taos, Kiera, and Gus took their places around her.

Here goes.

"Starting without me?" a voice called out. They all turned. Xander stood in the courtyard, arms folded. He tapped his foot on the ground.

His eyes locked on Nova and she braced for the worst. Was he going to yell at her? Fight her? Try to *strangle* her?

To her surprise, though, he only winked. "We're not taking it easy anymore, rookie."

Nova stared in bewilderment. *That's it?*

She had expected a confrontation about his hatred for her family. His absence from their training sessions had made it clear that her presence affected him. Perhaps he had moved past it by now. Still, Nova wondered about his story and who the highborns had separated him from.

Xander took his place in the ring as if he had never left.

"Let's get on with it, then," Taos said.

Nova took a moment in the middle to subtract her hearing and enhance her vision. Kiera had given her that bit of advice after the last training session. She had scowled at Taos for withholding that tip. "Real fights don't come with advice," he had said. She rolled her eyes, replaying his favorite phrase.

The courtyard snapped into focus. The patches of grass beneath her feet became a forest of individual blades. She could see every vein, every cell structure. Some green blades stood tall.

Microscopic droplets of dew clung to their tips. Interspersed among them, she spotted yellowish stalks, edges turning brown and crisp.

Her comrades, circling around her, moved in slow motion. Nova could detect the slightest twitch of their muscles, the barely perceptible shift of weight from one foot to another as they prepared to strike. Their skin became a landscape of pores and fine hairs.

As they swooped with their blades, Nova effortlessly sidestepped their attacks. She could see their movements unfold before they even fully committed to them, giving her ample time to react and counter.

With each successful defense, Nova's confidence soared higher, her movements becoming fluid and instinctual. She flowed seamlessly from one defense to the next.

Two blurs of motion broke her rhythm. Taos's blade lashed out at the same time as she reached to block a blow from Kiera. She reacted, but not fast enough to avoid the grazing cut that sliced across her upper arm. She hadn't expected two people to attack at once.

"Hey!" she said. "That's against the rules."

Taos slid his sword into its sheath. "Real fights don't come with rules," he said. "You have to be prepared for anything."

Kiera reached a hand out to her. Nova took it and stepped out of the pit. Xander gave her a pat on the back. "Not bad, rookie."

Kiera handed Nova a strip of cloth and Nova quickly wrapped it around her wounded arm, pulling it tight to cut off any seepage. Berkshire, already heading to the meditation room, beckoned for her to follow him.

Once in the room, she positioned herself on the mat in front of him.

"It's time."

A cold knot formed in her stomach. "I don't think I can."

"You can."

Nova's lips tightened as she braced herself. Delving into this particular memory demanded immense effort and often felt futile. It was as if her mind, guarding its secrets, pushed her out whenever she neared the truth. Each attempt left her drained, weary in both body and spirit.

Berkshire tapped a finger on his knee, waiting for her to begin. She closed her eyes.

Immediately, she hurled into the familiar memory where she lay on the crimson-streaked marble floor of her mansion. She could hear the projection take form in front of her, but it was flickering, unstable from the start.

"Hold on, Nova," Denali's voice warped as if traveling through water.

There were drowned out yells from Cronian in the background. The projection pulsed, sections of the image disappearing and reappearing at random. Young Denali began to lift Nova up, but as he did, the entire scene started to fracture. Nova hadn't even realized she had stopped breathing until the projection collapsed entirely. Her body shuddered as oxygen flooded back in.

"You lost your breathwork," Berkshire said.

"I can't see past this."

"You can," he said. "Your conscience is shielding you from something. You're pushing this away just like you were doing in your first lesson. Surrender or you will fail."

Nova closed her eyes again. She brought her mansion back to her mind, but this time she wasn't lying on the floor. This was an earlier memory.

Little Nova was standing outside the door frame of Cronian's library . . . his *forbidden* library. The smooth floor felt cold beneath her bare feet and her toes were on the invisible line the doorframe drew, not daring to cross. The slight draft from the open door chilled her skin. She could smell the musty scent of old books and papers wafting from the room.

"Nali," she whispered, her voice quivering, "You're scaring me."

Denali paid her no heed as he ransacked the room, his fingers sifting through piles of papers. Nova focused on the sounds—the rustle of papers, the frantic movements of her brother. She tensed her muscles, mirroring her younger self's anxiety, feeling her heartbeat drum in her bones.

"Quiet, Nova!" Denali snapped. "Go away so I can get this done before Father gets home. I have to find something for my classmate."

A look of triumph crossed his face as he brandished a sheet of paper. "Found it!"

He traced his finger over the document, scrutinizing its contents.

Nova pleaded, "Please come out. If Father sees—"

Denali was still transfixed by the paper. "That . . . doesn't make sense."

"Please, Nali."

Their world crumbled into eerie silence, interrupted only by the ominous creaking of a door on the floor below. Nova's bones stiffened, terror paralyzing her. Denali's reaction was swift. He shoved the paper back into the drawer and tiptoed to the door, closing it softly and securing it with a key.

Footsteps echoed up the staircase, each thud making Nova's heart lurch. Denali dug the keys into the plant pot beside the door.

Nova's voice cracked. "He's coming."

Cronian's shadow darkened the doorway. Denali turned away from the pot.

"We were playing a game of seek and find," Denali said nonchalantly.

Cronian studied Nova intently, panic thrumming beneath her skin.

"I just caught her," Denali added hastily.

Cronian's eyes narrowed at Denali, lingering for a moment before he spoke. "Come," he said. "Dinner is prepared."

Denali rushed to follow Father, but Nova hesitated for another second, casting a glance back at the library on her way out. Her world tilted when through the window, she spotted a solitary sheet of paper protruding from the very drawer Denali had been plundering.

SIXTEEN

The library scene distorted, stretching and warping like reflection in rippling water. Nova opened her eyes, returning to the present, her body tense as if she had truly just lived through the event. The projection before her was clearer and more stable than any she had ever seen.

This was a memory she had never accessed before.

What could that mean?

Berkshire shifted forward. "Are you still seeing yourself from above?"

Nova paused, considering. "I . . . I'm still looking down on myself. Is that wrong?"

His expression remained neutral. "In order to erase a memory, you cannot be an observer. You must be the memory itself."

"Be the memory itself?" Nova repeated. "What does that mean?"

Berkshire started to stand.

No, Nova thought. She wasn't ready to be done. Not yet. She had just made a major discovery. Whatever the reason was that she couldn't syphon, it was connected to this memory somehow. It had to be.

"Let's go again," she said.

"No."

Nova straightened. "What? Why? I can do this."

"We're done for today," he said, his tone final as he left the room.

Nova let out an exasperated sigh, and she pushed herself to her feet. She was so close to the truth. Waiting was unbearable.

Sounds from the courtyard pulled her from her thoughts. Taos and his friends were still there, gearing up to leave. Kiera was busy packing a bag.

Where could they possibly be going this late?

Gus's voice rang through the yard. "Nova come?"

Taos didn't even glance up from his packing as he dismissed the idea with a firm, "No."

Nova crossed her arms. Gus persisted. "Nova is friend. Nova come."

Taos finished tying a knot on his bag. "It's dangerous, Gus. She's not coming."

Xander and Kiera exchanged glances as they followed Taos to the front door.

Taos stopped to check on Gus, who remained stationary in the courtyard.

Gus took a few steps backwards until he was standing beside Nova. "No Nova, no Gus Gus."

Nova was stunned. How could Gus be so kind to her? Maybe he didn't fully understand who she was.

"Ease up," Xander said to Taos. "The rookie can come."

Kiera pointed up at the cloudy night sky. "We need to go or we'll miss the rain."

Taos ran his hand down his face and let out a sigh. "Keep her in the middle."

Xander perked up. "Peachy. Let's go, then."

Gus tugged Nova's hand with a beaming smile, following the others out the door.

They moved into the cool night and Nova found her gaze wandering across the dark silhouettes of the cottages, their outlines barely visible under the moon's soft glow. The world paused, the silent night wrapping around them like a cloak. A soft patter of rain began to fall, its droplets clanking on the cottage roofs.

"Where are we going?" Nova kept her voice low as she spoke to Kiera, who was right in front of her.

Kiera turned around and walked backwards as she talked. "The ridge. It's the area that divides the spora forest from the waterfall forest." She faced forward again and fell into stride beside Nova and Gus. "Krall don't typically go near the falls. They stay in the spora forest by the beach where the boatman comes. We need to cross over tonight but we won't get too close to that area."

"I thought we weren't supposed to go near the spora at night?" Nova asked.

"Since when do we follow the rules, rookie?" Xander said. "Consider this your initiation."

Nova cocked her head, glancing down at his feet. "You're not going to wear shoes?"

Kiera chuckled. "Xander doesn't believe in shoes."

"They're just a crutch." He swung his right foot into the air. "I'm toughening up my soles."

Nova crooked her eyebrow. It sounded so silly.

A cottage shutter swung open, making Nova jump. A woman leaned out and cast a stern glance their way. "Shush!" she hissed.

Kiera lowered her voice as they continued to walk. "Helga encourages people not to come out because the spores release toxins that can mess with your brain and affect the way you think and act. That's why the Krall start to look the way they do. It's also why people who grew up here speak a little differently. It takes a lot of exposure for that to happen, though. One night won't hurt you."

"Helga Gus mom," Gus pitched in.

"Your leader?" Nova asked.

"Helga was the first child born and raised in Nadir," Kiera said. "So yeah, she has a lot of influence."

"And Helga have big family."

"Whole lotta redheads," Xander said, winking at Gus.

A smile flickered across Nova's face, her thoughts wandering to the families in Ghandria. The notion of a large family invited scorn and disdain, even the birth of a second child stirred discomfort. But, within Nova's heart, the idea of having another sibling—of having another *Denali*—seemed quite all right to her. Most people, though, thought of children as an inconvenience. Families often chose to have a single child solely to preserve their lineage.

Taos halted and turned, making them come to a stop. "Are we here to do our job or are we here to play catch-up?" He looked directly at Nova. "There's a reason I didn't want you to come."

Nova bit down hard.

Taos pointed to the spora forest. "In a few minutes, we'll be coming up on the ridge, right beside the spores. Krall could be listening, so keep your mouths shut. The spores make a puckering noise before they release the toxins, so if you hear it, run and don't breathe it in. Don't bother the lumicats. They'll ignore us if we ignore them."

Nova chewed on her lower lip, her hand halfway raised before Taos cut her off with a scowl. "No questions."

Nova spoke anyway. "What if the cats *do* bother us?"

She shuddered. Her hand moved to her side, where a cat had pounced on her first day here.

"Oof," Xander said. "Were you wearing purple? Rookie move, rookie. Never wear purple around the lumicats."

Nova's forehead creased as she tried to recollect what color she had been wearing. "Why do they care about purple?"

Xander's eyes twinkled. "I tried asking them once, but they weren't very talkative. Turns out cats make terrible conversationalists. Who knew, right?"

Taos pinched the bridge of his nose and inhaled sharply. "Everyone, shut up and follow Kiera."

Kiera pushed ahead, then turned on her heel, motioning for them to follow.

Nova gave a slow nod, unsure of what she was getting herself into. They made their way up the slope of the ridge that rose barely five feet above the forest floor. The natural barrier stretched across the landscape like a long, narrow spine, offering views of both sides of the forest.

To their left, a dense canopy of trees cascaded down the slope, punctuated by the silvery ribbons of distant waterfalls. The air from this side carried the crisp scent of pine and the faint roar of rushing water.

To their right, massive mushrooms sprawled out in mesmerizing complexity. Their shapes emerged through a veil of mist. Some of their caps pulsed with an amber glow.

Nova walked in silence behind Gus. The rain grew into a steady downpour, drumming on the soil and masking the sound of their footsteps. Now, she understood why they did this during rainstorms.

As they progressed, Kiera slowed her pace. With a hand gesture, she motioned for the group to veer right, down off the ridge. Nova's heart quickened as she realized they were about to enter the spora forest.

Carefully, they picked their way down the incline, leaving the relative safety of the ridge behind. The ground beneath their feet changed from hard-packed earth to a softer, spongier texture.

The massive mushrooms loomed around them. Something moved in the corner of Nova's eye and she jumped. A lumicat bounded away from them.

The rain tapered off as they walked another five minutes. Nova stretched her vision along their path to make sure they were clear of any Krall. Suddenly, her gaze fixed on a figure in the distance behind them. It wasn't a creature . . . It appeared to be a man, and he was wearing a deep violet hazmat suit. Nova lifted a finger to tap Kiera, but before she could, a gentle popping sound broke the quiet. Nova's blood ran cold.

A soft hissing filled the air and yellow mist began to seep from a nearby mushroom. The group took off into a sprint, but Nova stayed locked in place. She looked back to where the strange figure in the hazmat suit had stood, but he was gone.

Taos's hand shot out and circled Nova's wrist. He yanked her and they broke into a run. Her senses returned to their normal states and the forest came alive as more puckering sounds punctuated the night. The toxic fog filled the air with a sickly yellow hue.

Faint noises seeped into Nova's ears as they ran—a woman's panicked voice, a baby crying, then a *tick-tick-tick*.

Nova caught only fragments . . .

"It didn't have to be this way . . ."

She filled her lungs with one last breath before she and Taos hurtled into the yellow fog. The seconds stretched like hours until they barreled on the sandy shoreline of the beach. Taos released her hand and they plunged into the ocean. Nova dunked all the way in, letting the water wash away any traces of the toxic mist.

One by one, the others surfaced, wiping water from their faces.

Above them, the clouds were parting, revealing the most stunning display of the night sky that Nova had ever seen.

"Nova pass," Gus said

"Nova did *not* pass." Taos turned to her. "You froze. What were you thinking?"

"I . . . I thought I saw someone back there," she said. "And the voices . . ."

Kiera traded a silent look with Taos, then looked back at Nova. "There were no voices, Nova."

Nova drifted backwards a step, a small wave lapping at her back. "But . . ."

"That's the toxins playing tricks on ya," Xander said.

"Come on." Kiera took Nova's arm. "Time for the best part." She led her back to the shore.

"Not yet," Taos said. "We have to search first."

Kiera hoisted the backpack from off her shoulders and started to untie it. "I'm making an executive decision to stargaze first tonight."

She pulled a blanket from her bag and laid it on the sand. She sat down and patted a spot for Nova to join her.

"That's not the plan, Kiera," Taos said.

Xander stretched lazily. "It's the rookie's first time. Cut her a break."

Nova inspected the blanket, beckoning her to lie down. Oh, how she missed stargazing with Denali. "What about the Krall? What if they come out here?"

179

Gus shuffled forward and plopped down on the blanket.

"The Krall haven't ever harmed us. They are after Ghandrians," Kiera said.

Nova bit her lip. *Not in my experience.* She worried Kiera was underestimating just how shaken up the Krall had become since her arrival here. Still, she moved forward and slid between Kiera and Gus.

"What are you looking for, anyways?"

Kiera let out a weary sigh. "A way out . . . a way home. If you can even call it that."

At the mention of "home," a sharp pang of longing twisted inside Nova. The concept of home felt like a far-off dream. Almost eight weeks had passed since she had been separated from Denali. It felt like fragments of another life. She tipped her head back, willing the moisture in her eyes to recede.

Taos pulled a blanket from his bag, stretching it out beside Kiera. They all lay back, surrendering to the vastness above. Nova focused inward, dimming her auditory senses. She then opened her eyes and stretched her sight into the sky.

The stars transformed from distant pinpricks to vibrant beacons. Nova felt as if she were floating among the constellations. Planets shimmered faintly, and the misty arm of the Milky Way reached out and swirled around her like a cosmic embrace.

Nova's heightened vision caught a subtle movement. A streak of light blazed across the night sky. A soft gasp escaped Nova's lips as she witnessed a shooting star leaving a luminous trail in its wake. She held her breath, making a wish in that fleeting moment.

A wish to go home.

Her gaze followed the trail of stardust. Maybe Denali was looking upon these very same stars. The thought brought an unexpected comfort, a feeling of closeness despite the circumstances and distance that separated them.

Beside her, she could feel Gus staring. She brought her vision and then hearing back to normal and looked at him. Something soft and understanding lived in his eyes.

"Nova miss home," he said.

Those three words pierced something raw inside her. Nova sat up and wiped at her running nose.

"Yes, Gus. Nova misses home."

She noticed Xander sitting far off. He was in a criss-cross position, breathing deeply. It was the healing position Ghandrians were taught at a young age.

"Him no see."

"What?"

"Xander can't enhance his senses." Kiera sat up, joining their conversation. "That's his indiscretion."

The casual way Kiera mentioned it jarred Nova. Indiscretions were private things, secrets everyone fought to keep buried. Nova knew better than most.

"Tell me about yours," Kiera said.

Tension coiled in Nova's gut. The idea of discussing it openly felt wrong, *dangerous* even. She'd spent her entire life guarding it. Her eyes darted around, looking for an escape, a way to change the subject.

"Hey, it's okay." Kiera placed a gentle hand on her arm. Then she pulled up the corner of her shirt, revealing a blood-stained bandage underneath. "You don't have to hide it here."

Nova lifted a hand over her mouth. "You can't heal."

Kiera dropped her shirt back over the bandage. "No, but I don't know the difference, so it doesn't bother me much."

Nova looked down and traced the damp sand with her fingertips, wishing she felt the same about her indiscretion.

"We aren't defined by the labels they give us."

Nova gave a bitter laugh. "That's exactly what we are defined by. That's why we're here." She dug her finger deeper into the sand. "A miscreant as a daughter is one hell of a disappointment."

Kiera frowned. "A father that would banish his own daughter sounds like one hell of a disappointment."

Her words sliced through the air with an intensity that caught Nova off guard. The sucking sound of a whirlpool in the distance filled the silence between them. Nova pulled her knees to her chest and focused on a point in the darkness, fighting the sting in her eyes. She searched for words that wouldn't crack her voice.

"My brother can heal unlike anything you've ever seen," she said. "He can close up a cut just as fast as it takes to make it."

Kiera raised her eyebrow. "How is that possible?"

"Like any other ability, I suppose." Nova's attention drifted to where the waves met the shore. "It takes practice."

Still evading Kiera's gaze, Nova took a moment to steady her voice before continuing. "I practiced, too. Syphoning, I mean. My brother would take me to the cavern when nobody was there. He was trying to teach me before anyone became suspicious."

Kiera was quiet for a minute. Finally, she asked, "How did you go so long without being caught?"

"I didn't have to be tested," Nova said. "Youngborn privileges."

"So, what happened?"

Nova opened her mouth to respond, but the words lodged in her throat. Her fingers twisted into the sand. "I don't know," she managed. "It was just me and Denali that knew. We never told anyone." She closed her eyes briefly. Her voice cracked. "Somehow . . . someone found out."

Desperate to change the subject, Nova turned to Gus.

"What about you, Gus?" she asked, her voice steadier now. "What's your indiscretion?"

He shrugged. "Gus Gus perfect."

"Gus wasn't exiled. He was born here."

"Yeah, but you still have an indiscretion, right?"

He shook his head.

"Children of miscreants are labeled as the same," Kiera said. "Morianna believes that allowing miscreant offspring to reside in Ghandria would pollute the gene pool." She leaned back on her hands. "She can't have us passing on our 'flawed' genes and undermining the evolution of their society."

Nova's expression fell, the light dimming in her eyes as she processed Kiera's words. Girls were tested at the age of thirteen—young enough to be removed before they could bear children if they failed to manifest all three abilities. Boys had until adulthood to prove themselves. Nineteen was the age they were tested at, but girls . . . Her stomach churned as she thought of the calculated cruelty of it. She had never considered the implications for the children born here in Nadir. If Gus was able to evolve like everyone else in Ghandria, he should be able to live there. Nova struggled to find the right words. "That's . . . not right," she finally said.

"It's not," Kiera said. "But what's new? We've all been erased because of things that are out of our control."

The quiet lingered between them. Nova tucked a section of her wet hair behind her ear. "What were your parents like?"

Kiera patted the sand off her hands. "Let's just say they weren't exactly devastated by my exile."

The corners of Nova's mouth tugged downwards. Gus scooted closer to Kiera and placed a hand on her knee.

"Kiera is family."

She smiled at him. "Life here's not too bad, anyhow." She flung an arm around Gus's neck. "I get to crash with the Goodfellows, after all."

Nova returned the smile, but doubt festered in her mind. It was impossible that anyone could truly prefer living here. She glanced at Taos. He was still stargazing. He and Kiera probably bonded all the time over sharing the same indiscretion. A prick of jealousy took Nova completely off guard. Mentally, she laughed at herself.

One moment I'm jealous of those who have control over their abilities, and the next, I envy two miscreants who can't heal.

Taos sat upright. Something shifted in his expression as he caught Nova's eyes. She quickly looked away.

"We should get moving," he said.

"Ugh," Kiera whined. "Can we just relax for a bit and give Xander more time to heal his poor feet?"

Taos's attention moved to the shoreline where Xander sat.

"I still don't get it," Nova said. "Why no shoes? What's the point?"

"He calls it 'callus cultivation,'" Kiera said.

"Callus cultivation?"

"Yeah," Kiera said. "It's TOE-tally ridiculous if you ask me."

Gus burst into laughter that sounded more donkey than human. It was so obnoxious that it caught Nova completely off guard. She traded a startled glance with Kiera and then they both erupted into laughter. Gus's body was shaking so hard he let out an accidental toot. Kiera doubled over, gasping for air between fits. Nova was wheezing, clutching her sides.

Taos scowled. "Seriously?"

His disdain only heightened their giggle frenzy. Laughing felt so new. Nova couldn't remember the last time it had come so easily, so genuinely. It felt . . . liberating.

But the moment ended when Xander cried out. The four of them looked over right as his figure was dragged into the water.

"Xander!" Kiera screamed.

While the others rushed to the water, Nova made it to her feet before her body betrayed her. Her muscles locked into place, every nerve ending screaming *danger*.

A slender, shadowy figure emerged from the water—a Krall. Moonlight glinted off its elongated nails, which were embedded into Xander's side. He struggled to stand while clutching at the Krall's grip. Taos reached for his sword. The Krall lashed out with its free hand, knocking Taos off his feet and back into the water with a splash.

Gus stepped forward with his dualfate, but the creature caught his hand before he could strike. The Krall sent Xander flying onto the shore and sank its claws into Gus's arm instead. Gus let out a hoarse cry. He was flailing his arms, trying to break free as the Krall dragged him out of the water, past Nova, and into the forest.

Nova looked back to where Taos and Kiera were running to Xander, who lay on the sand. Taos's right arm bled where the Krall had struck him.

Nova's eyes darted back to the shadowy threshold of the forest. The urgency in Taos's voice, the fear in Kiera's motions—everything slowed down for a heartbeat. Then, Nova snapped out of her paralysis. She turned on her heel and took off after Gus at full sprint.

SEVENTEEN

"Nova!" Taos yelled, but she was already deep in the forest by the time she heard it. She brushed past mushrooms, following the howls of pain from Gus.

The dim moonlight barely filtered through the canopy of mushroom caps above. The toxins no longer filled the air, but a soft glow emanated from some of the fungi. The spongy ground beneath her shifted with every hurried step. Gus's anguished cries grew louder, guiding her through the maze.

Bursting through a clearing, Nova skidded to a stop. The Krall was crouched over Gus, who lay sprawled on the ground. One of the creature's clawed hands pinned Gus's shoulder, while the other was raised high, poised for a strike. Nova yelled out.

"I'm a Darkov!"

The Krall jerked its head up, fixing its gaze on Nova. Its throat convulsed, unleashing a chilling sound—part growl, part clicking. It pulled back from Gus, releasing its grip on him. Gus sucked in a sharp breath. Then, a chilling sound began to unfold in the depths of the forest. Screeches began to vibrate from every direction. It was the sound of an alarm, a signal that roused the others. Soon, the drumming of bodies, relentless and increasing in number, filled the air.

What have I done?

"Go!" Gus yelled.

The creature lunged at Nova and she took off, barely dodging its razor-sharp fingernails. Before she could make it far, another Krall leaped at her, wrapping its claws around her ankle. Nova stumbled to the ground.

She kicked her other foot into its face, then sprang to her feet and ran. With a quick glance over her shoulder, dread slithered beneath her skin—a pack of three Krall bounded on all fours behind her.

The arm Nova had yet to finish healing from the pit throbbed, but she pushed her pace faster. At the very least, she needed to lead the Krall away from Gus.

She made a quick turn around a mushroom and lengthened her strides, hoping to gain ground. Yet, in the blink of an eye, a Krall materialized from the shadows in front of her, lunging at her with predatory precision.

The impact was brutal, the Krall colliding with Nova's body like a boulder from a cliff. The world spun as she crashed to the forest floor, the wind violently expelled from her lungs. In that disorienting moment, Nova fought to regain her footing. Before she could, the Krall pinned her to the ground and its ghastly sneer revealed a mouth dripping with inky black saliva. The creature raised its bony arm high above her.

Time slowed to a painful drag as the Krall swung its claw downward, slicing into Nova's abdomen. Searing pain ripped through her. Her screams split the air.

Agony radiated from the wound. The creature lifted its hand for a second strike, but was thrown off Nova when another slammed into it.

Then another.

And another.

Nova couldn't tell how many bodies were on her, but her chest was being crushed by the weight. A sharp, tearing sensation exploded across her thigh as another claw gouged her flesh. She tried to scream, but the sound was smothered beneath the crushing weight of bodies. Her vision was lost in a tangle of limbs and torsos.

Through the haze, Kiera's voice was barely audible.

"I'm a Darkov!"

More screeches tore through the night and Nova began to feel the relief of the bodies jumping off of her. Dark spots crept into the edges of her sight. The last thing her mind registered was a steady beat.

Tick-tick-tick.

Then, she slipped out of consciousness.

"Twenty-nine percent, merciful Magnus! I dare say the rest of you could learn a thing or two from Mr. Rogan." Professor Cleghorn's brown mustache twitched as he spoke. He held up the neurotuner to show the class Bram Rogan's numbers. The crystal-faced gauge showed the needle resting just above the quarter mark.

Cleghorn had devoted his entire life to researching Magnus Bloodthorne's discovery of the ability to enhance the senses. He practically worshiped the soil that Morianna's grandfather had walked on.

With a flourish, Cleghorn raised his mug to his lips, but paused and scowled. He shook the empty mug upside down and gave a dramatic sigh.

"Dude." Blythe leaned over to Denali. "Did you hear about Finnian?"

Denali's heart skipped a beat. Could she know about what happened?

"He dropped dead a few days ago. Some crazy sickness, I guess."

Denali's fingers gripped the table. "A sickness?" he repeated, his voice carefully neutral despite the disbelief coursing through him.

"Crazy, right? We talked to him a few weeks ago and he was totally fine."

Denali's mind reeled as he grappled with the half-truth. The image of Finnian's sudden collapse flashed before his eyes. Anger simmered within him at his father's audacity to spin such a lie to Finnian's grieving family. They deserved to know the truth. Denali's expression faltered as he relived the event. He had never seen the syphon make contact with someone before. It had gone *into* Finnian.

Lucien's journal entries surfaced in his mind. Before class, Denali read a section where Lucien had documented mysterious behavior of the syphon. The entries had grown increasingly urgent —describing high-pitched screams from the syphon and violent spurts of energy. Then finally, a breakthrough scrawled in hasty writing: the syphon had a capacity. When it reached its limit, it became unstable.

That must have been what happened with Finnian.

Denali's attention was drawn away as his professor approached Blythe's table. "Miss Pierce, I believe you forgot to turn in your last assignment," he said.

"Oh, no, I didn't forget, Cleghorn," she said. "I just didn't do it."

Cleghorn's smile faltered slightly, and he lifted a pointer finger. "*Professor* Cleghorn, if you please. And Miss Pierce, we mustn't miss out on opportunities to further our education. Every assignment is a stepping stone to greater understanding and achievement."

Blythe sat back, arms crossed. "School's a scam, dude. It's just busywork that'll be irrelevant the moment we get out of here."

Cleghorn sighed, his voice carrying a note of disappointment. "Shame."

He then placed a hand on Denali's shoulder. "Ah, Mr. Darkov! How would you like to play professor for a spell? I need to step out and wrestle with the coffee machine. That infernal contraption seems to think it's smarter than a room full of alchemists!"

He raised his mug, adorned with the title "Magnus's little helper," and shook it in the air.

"But alas," he said, "'tis not so!"

Denali took his spot at Cleghorn's desk and Cleghorn shuffled out of the room, swinging his elbows dramatically at his sides. The rest of the class relaxed in their seats and began talking to their neighbors.

"Oh, merciful Mr. Rogan," Slater taunted Bram after their professor was gone. "Lookie, twenty-nine percent. That's nothing to boast about. Once, I got my vision down to twenty-one percent."

"That's enough," Denali said. "We aren't supposed to go past thirty percent, it's dangerous."

"Yeah, that's exactly what we'd expect from Sir Goody Two-Shoes. The rest of us like to push our abilities," Slater said.

Bram shrunk in his chair.

"Oh, lighten up, you dainty little yellow-belly." He held up the neurotuner in front of Bram. "See if you can best me."

Denali stood from the desk. "Slater, I'm warning you."

"Hey, I'm not forcing him to do anything. I'm just saying, if he wants to be called the best, he has to *be* the best." He rested his elbow on Bram's desk. "That's what you're trying to do, right? You're trying to make Mommy and Daddy proud? Since your brother was a miscreant you have to prove—"

"I said that's enough!" Denali shouted.

Bram slowly raised his head and met Slater dead in the eyes. A fiery resolve burned within them and it brought Denali to silence. Bram reached forward, snatching the device from Slater. He tilted his head back to thread the first nerve fiber through his nasal cavity. Then he guided the second one into his ear canal.

Slater grabbed another neurotuner and mirrored the action. "And, we're game."

"Come on, guys," Blythe said. "Don't be idiots."

"Shut it, blueberry," Slater said.

The class held their breath, watching the silver gauges on both devices. The needles trembled at their center marks before beginning their leftward sweep. Slater's was already plummeting to seventy. Their gauges moved in a race downward, neither of them hesitating until they both crossed thirty percent. Denali exchanged a concerned glance with Blythe. Two classmates took turns reading off their numbers.

"Twenty-four . . ."

"Nineteen . . ."

"Sixteen . . ."

"Twelve . . ."

The needles stilled. Bram hesitated. He adjusted the fiber at his nose.

"You want to be the best, right?" Slater said. "Prove it."

His needle dropped again.

"Slater's at nine."

"Bram's still at twelve."

Bram squeezed his eyes shut. His number dropped lower.

"Bram's at seven."

Whispers snaked through the class.

"Impressive." Slater's grin grew wider as his own needle dipped farther left.

"Slater's at five."

Denali hesitated, a sense of unease creeping over him. He looked around to see if anyone else would intervene, but the room fell into an anxious hush as everyone watched. Even Blythe, who had earlier warned against it, stared on with disbelief.

Denali crossed to Bram's desk and lowered beside him. "Bram, you have nothing to prove."

"Yeah, it's not like he has a miscreant for a sibling, bringing the entire family name down. You wouldn't know anything about that, would you, Darkov?"

Denali ignored Slater's comments. His worry deepened as he observed the determination etched on Bram's face. As he reached an unprecedented four percent mark, Denali's lungs seized. He scanned the room, noting how still his classmates had become.

"Bram's at four."

Slater hesitated to go any further.

"That's enough, Bram. You've won," Denali said.

When Slater didn't interject, a smile tugged at Bram's lips.

Slater's gauge needle moved smoothly back to the center, settling at the one hundred percent mark.

Denali let out a relieved breath, suddenly aware of the stiffness in his muscles. The class erupted into applause.

"Bram, the legend!" someone yelled.

Denali scoffed and lifted himself from Bram's desk. He stood and placed a hand on Bram's shoulder. That's when he realized how tense Bram was. Tremors were coursing through Bram's hands. Denali looked at the gauge. The needle still quivered at four percent.

Bram was muttering something, but Denali couldn't hear it over the clapping. He leaned closer.

"It's stuck . . . I can't see." His words were acid, burning through Denali's every nerve.

"Bram, focus."

Suddenly, the classroom door swung open and Professor Cleghorn shuffled through, brandishing a steaming mug like a trophy.

"It's stuck!" Bram yelled. He struggled to stand from his chair, but fumbled aimlessly with outstretched hands.

Cleghorn nearly dropped his cup as he took in the scene. "What in the name of Magnus's menacing monocle is going on in here?"

"Look!" One classmate pointed to the neurotuner's face.

The needle jerked erratically—jumping to nine . . . three . . . six . . . two. The fiber in Bram's nostril twitched with each wild swing.

Then, the needle hit zero.

The room fell deathly quiet.

The silence crystallized around Denali as he waited. The seconds stretched into an agonizing moment of suspense, and then, Bram opened his eyes.

A collective gasp echoed through the room and a chill ran down Denali's spine. He had warned against this, but now, as he witnessed the consequences unfold, a profound sense of regret settled in. He should have done more to stop it.

Denali's gaze remained fixed on Bram, who was grappling with the realization of what he had just lost. His irises had been replaced by a haunting vacancy. His pupils were shrouded in a ghostly white film.

He was blind.

"Miscreant!" a classmate yelled.

Students shrieked and took steps back to distance themselves from Bram. Blythe and Denali stayed put. Blythe was tense, unable to pull her eyes from the scene.

Bram's hands trembled as they reached out, searching for something to anchor him. He fumbled to the floor beside Cleghorn's feet.

"Merciful Magnus!" Professor Cleghorn squealed as he jumped up on his table for safety.

He reached under his desk, fumbling for a second before his hand found the hidden button. With a firm press, he triggered the alarm. Immediately, sirens blared through the school, accompanied by flashing lights. Denali flinched at the sound—Nova would spiral into a panic attack from the noise, he had to get home to her—

He froze.

No.

Nova wasn't home.

She hadn't been for a long time.

The familiar hollow feeling returned.

Denali dropped to one knee beside his classmate. "You're going to be okay," he said. "Just breathe."

Three guards burst through the door and Cleghorn pointed to Bram. Denali squeezed Bram's arm once before retreating. The guards removed the neurotuner and lifted Bram from the floor. He hung limply from their arms, his fingertips still trying to touch his eye sockets, as if feeling them could bring his vision back. They dragged him into the hallway.

More screams came from students in the hallways. Cleghorn shuffled after the guards. "Straightaway to Morianna's grounds then? I shall accompany you. Might I quickly change my unmentionables?"

The door shut behind them. Denali looked out the classroom window. Sirens were ringing through the streets. Ghandrians were rushing into their houses and locking their doors. The last time the alarm had sounded was for Nova. Denali's blood became hot. He turned to face Slater.

"This was your doing."

Slater scoffed. "I didn't make the freak do anything." He picked up Bram's bag and started sifting through it.

Denali clenched his fists. "Do you have any idea what you've done? To him? To his family?"

"He should thank me. I've reunited him with his brother." He pulled coins out of the bag and stuffed them into his pocket. "But I understand your sensitivity toward the situation, what with your miscreant little sis and all."

Denali lunged, his fist crashing against Slater's mouth, sending him sprawling to the floor. Some students jumped back while others leaned in.

"Man, D," Blythe said.

Slater dabbed at the blood on his mouth, then chuckled. "Have I touched a sore spot, Darkov? Or maybe you're angry because it's not my fault, but yours."

Denali's next words died on his lips. Something cold settled in his stomach.

"You were in charge of the class, right? Just like you were in charge of your pathetic little miscreant sister?"

Denali's jaw tightened and a muscle twitched along his cheek.

"Slater," Blythe warned. "Shut up."

"Am I wrong?" He wiped at his mouth again. "Isn't that the reason you stopped going out with friends? You were staying in to *hide* what she was. Or maybe you were trying to teach her? You thought if you gave her enough lessons you could *cure* her."

Denali ground his teeth together. He reached down and grabbed a fistful of Slater's shirt. His eyes flashed with a dangerous intensity as he stood over him.

"Ah, so that's it then." Slater chuckled. "What a waste of effort. People like her can't be cured. The only thing more pathetic than what she is, is how you keep pretending she's still your sister."

The world went red.

Denali's fists found flesh, bone, blood.

Again.

Again.

Again.

A guttural scream tore from his throat as he struck. Slater managed to block a few blows, but Denali left little room for recovery. The classroom watched in stunned silence, the only sounds the brutal rhythm of fist meeting flesh.

A hand tugged Denali's arm from behind. He shoved the person trying to get him off. Blythe stumbled backwards and fell to the floor. Denali went still, horror dawning on his face as he realized what he had done.

She frowned. "He's had enough, D."

Denali glanced around the classroom, taking in the horrified expressions of his classmates. His chest heaved and he looked down at Slater's bloody face, now distorted and swollen beyond recognition.

Denali's fists loosened and Slater dropped back against the floor.

He turned to Blythe, but she broke eye contact, shrinking away from him.

"Blythe, I . . ." He hesitated and averted his gaze. Then, he fled the classroom.

The path home passed in a blur. Not even the wailing sirens could penetrate Denali's thoughts as he navigated the narrow cobblestone streets of Ghandria.

That night, he paced back and forth in his bedroom. Bram's trial had taken place that afternoon, but Denali hadn't attended. He ran his fingers through his dark hair and pulled at its roots.

Was Slater right?

Was it his fault?

Seeing Bram's transition hurt somewhere deep inside Denali. In an instant, the entire class had turned on Bram the way they had turned on Nova. It had been Denali's duty to protect her. He'd dedicated his life to it. All the years spent training, practicing, and hiding had been in vain. And it was all his fault. Nova was gone because of him. His family was ruined because of *him*.

Why couldn't he have been better for Nova?

She deserved so much more.

Now, she only had five days left to learn an ability that deep down, Denali wondered if she even had the capability to learn. Unable to contain his frustration, Denali grabbed a nearby vase and hurled it against the base of the wall near his feet. The shattering crash filled the room. Shards of glass scattered across the floor, three of them digging into the flesh of his legs. He ripped them out and healed the gashes as he walked across the room and sank into a nearby chair, dropping his head into his blood-stained hands.

EIGHTEEN

Distant whispers pulsed with Nova's heartbeat. Warmth surrounded her, along with the scent of healing herbs and earth. Light pressed against her closed eyelids. She shifted, and pain flared through her body. Her eyes fluttered open. She was in a small, tented room. Plants and herbs dangled against the fabric walls. Nova traced her fingers along the bandages that wrapped her abdomen. Each touch sent ripples of discomfort through her.

"You didn't tell me she was Darkov," came an urgent voice from outside the tent.

"Doesn't change anything."

"I used good herbs on her. Those treasures are sparse, Berkshire!"

"We don't decide if one's life is more deserving than others."

"Oh, but, we do, Berkshire! If it's a Darkov, we do!"

"Enough. She's awake."

Nova pulled herself up as Berkshire parted the entrance to the tent and walked in, followed by a short, bald man wearing thick goggles who seemed intent on staying hidden behind Berkshire's frame.

Berkshire came closer and inspected the bandages around Nova's abdomen and leg. He had a grim look on his face and Nova was unsure whether he was angry at the doctor or angry with her.

"What happened?" Nova asked.

"You were foolish."

Her head felt foggy. There were flashes—shouting, running, pain—but nothing concrete would form. She touched the edge of her bandage with her fingertips to peek under it.

Berkshire smacked her hand. "Don't touch."

Nova flinched and massaged her fingers. "It's fine. Now that I'm awake I can heal it."

"Doc?" Berkshire said.

The man shuffled forward until he was safely behind Berkshire again. He plucked a germbayne root from his white coat pocket and stuck his arm out dead straight. As he held it out, he peeked one eye around Berkshire.

"I'm fine," Nova said. "I can get this healed by the end of the day."

"Quiet," Berkshire snapped. "Eat it."

Nova complied and took the root from the doctor's shaking hand. As soon as she had it, he yanked his arm back. Nova gnawed her teeth into the squishy base. Liquid spilled from the corners of her mouth. It had an awfully bitter taste, but it would stop any infections from spreading.

The doc tugged on the bottom of Berkshire's shirt. "Sparse, Berkshire," he whined.

Berkshire shushed him and led him out of the tent.

Nova was still chewing on the root when Kiera and Xander ducked in.

"The rookie lives to see another day," Xander said.

Nova inspected them as they walked up to her bed. Her attention caught on Kiera's face—dark bruises bloomed along her jaw, a deep gash stretched from cheekbone to chin, and a white bandage wrapped her bicep. Last night's events flooded her mind—stargazing, the forest, the Krall.

"Gus," Nova said. "Is he okay?"

"He's fine," Kiera assured her. "All healed and back to his usual cheery self."

"And Taos?" Nova asked, noticing his absence.

"He'll . . . be alright."

"Haven't seen him around much." Xander dropped into the chair beside her bed. "The guy has been spending all his time in the 'sentimental' garden."

Kiera rolled her eyes. "Would you stop calling it that?"

"That's what it is, blondie," he said. "I get he's upset, but you can't bring 'em back. Best to move on."

"Bring who back?" Nova asked.

"The creepy crawlers."

"Taos had never harmed a Krall before, let alone . . ." Kiera trailed off, leaving the rest unspoken. "I know he's been by, though. Caught him sneaking out of here yesterday."

Nova's mind pieced together that night—when three Krall had her pinned down before Kiera baited them off. Her gaze traced Kiera's injuries. She and Taos must have faced them after Nova blacked out. How bad were Taos's injuries? She hated the idea of two people who couldn't heal battling the Krall.

The tent flap rustled and stole her from her thoughts. Gus waddled in and relief flooded Nova at the sight of him whole and unharmed.

"Gus Gus bring surprise."

"You best get yourself healed up, rookie," Xander said. "We have a celebration tonight."

"A celebration?"

Kiera sat on the edge of Nova's bed. "To welcome a new arrival."

Nova scrunched up her face. Thankfully, she had stayed under the radar when she arrived. Drawing that kind of attention right off the bat would have gotten her killed.

The three of them stared at her, waiting for an answer. Nova sighed. "Listen, guys. I'm not really up for it right now."

"Good luck with that," Xander said. "I've tried to get out of the past four celebrations. They are *relentless*."

"Gus already made your outfit," Kiera said.

Made?

Gus revealed a tank top denim dress from behind his back. The tiered, flowing fabric cascaded to ankle length, its hem embroidered with small black flowers. The stitching was slightly sloppy.

"Gus Gus know Nova like black."

Nova's face lit up. "Oh, Gus! You made this?"

He smiled sheepishly.

"We had a lot of downtime," Kiera said. "Especially with training canceled."

"Downtime?" Nova asked. "What do you mean? How long have I been out for?"

Xander and Kiera exchanged glances.

"Guys?"

Xander rubbed the back of his neck. "Two days, rookie."

Nova shot upward and winced from the sharp pain.

"Whoa, whoa." He moved toward her, extending his hands in a calming gesture. "Easy."

"That only gives me three days—" Panic stole her breath. "I don't have enough time—"

She gripped the bed rails until her knuckles blanched.

Kiera scooted closer. "It's okay, Nova. There's still time."

Her grip tightened. Pressure began to build behind her eyes.

Building.

Building.

She squeezed her eyes shut. She needed them out. She needed them out *now*.

"Out," she said. "Please get out."

Building.

Building.

Kiera tried again. "Nova, we can help—"

"I said get out!" Nova screamed, fingers digging into metal.

Finally, silence filled the room. Nova, shaking with the force of each breath, dared to look. The scene before her twisted the knife of guilt deeper into her heart. Kiera nodded and slowly began to retreat. Gus and Xander hadn't moved, their expressions stunned.

Gus dropped his head and placed the dress on the corner of a chair. Kiera and Xander stood, and they all slipped out without another word.

Nova released her grip on the rails and sank back against her pillow, pressing her palms into her eyes. Kiera's hurt expression and their shocked faces gnawed at her memory, twisting her insides.

"Wait." The whisper died in the empty room. "I didn't mean it."

Why couldn't she have acted differently? They were only trying to help.

Someone walked back into the tent and Nova slid her hands down her face and peeked through her fingers.

"Speak, kid," Berkshire said as he lowered to the chair beside her.

Nova dropped her hands into her lap, fiddling with her fingertips. "I'm going to fail at the final trial," she said. "I've lost Denali, haven't I?"

There was a pause—three breaths of silence.

"Yes."

Nova furrowed her brow. "Berkshire?"

"You said you will fail, so you will." He sat back in the chair. "Words have power, kid. If you fail, it is because you chose to."

Nova sat still, contemplating for a few seconds. "But, I'm doing all I can."

"I don't care," he said. "Don't tell me. Tell yourself."

She felt small beneath his words. He stood from his chair.

"Berkshire, wait." Nova dropped her head as she replayed her lashing out at Kiera. "I've ruined everything."

"Yes, you have," he said, earning another amazed look from Nova. He tapped his forehead twice. "Change your mind."

He picked up the dress Gus had left and threw it at Nova. She flinched, catching it before it hit her face. Her fingers twitched against the fabric as she wrestled with her decision. When she looked over the makeshift stitching, a small smile formed. A spark of confidence ignited within her. With a resolute nod, she made her choice.

"Berkshire!" she exclaimed.

But he was gone. He'd disappeared without a word, like he always did. She shifted to jump out of bed, momentarily forgetting her injuries, and let out a cry of agony.

She glanced through a slit in the tent. The sun hung low in the sky, signaling the late afternoon. She still had enough time to heal herself and make it to the celebration.

An hour and a half later, one of her wounds was completely closed. She had made good progress on the gash on her thigh, but it would take more time, and the sun was starting to set. She wrapped a cloth around it and slipped into the dress Gus had made her, then grabbed a brush from a nearby stand. She cursed as she tried to tame the knots, realizing it might take just as long as the healing did.

A trumpet sounded in the distance, signaling the start of the gathering. Nova hastily fixed her hair into a single, thick braid, then set out to find her friends. The streets led her to the town center, where the celebration was in full swing.

Humble cottages framed the square, their window boxes spilling over with flowers. Overhead, paper lanterns hung on crisscrossed strings, painting everything in a warm glow.

Nova stepped into the throng. A fiddler's tune wove through the crowd, accompanied by the sharp slap of a hand drum. On a rickety wooden stage, two musicians swayed to the rhythm.

The air was thick with the scent of fried dough and blooms. Couples spun past, their feet scuffing the worn cobblestones. Children darted between the dancers, their faces sticky with fruit preserves. Laughter bubbled up between the notes. Although Nova could appreciate the music, the volume scraped against her nerves. She adjusted her hearing to a more manageable level.

"Nova in Gus dress."

Nova's heart leapt when she heard Gus. She turned to find him, Kiera, and Xander approaching her. Taos emerged behind them. To her surprise, he appeared unscathed—no cuts or bruises from the battle with the Krall. She could have sworn she'd seen the Krall in the water claw his arm, but it must have been Xander's blood.

"I uh . . ." She bit her lip. "About earlier—" She fidgeted with the hem of her dress and cleared her throat. "Well, what I'm trying to say is—"

Kiera's arms wrapped around Nova. Nova kept her arms down at her sides, completely unaware of what to do next.

Was Kiera really hugging her? After she had yelled at her?

Gus joined in on the hug.

"Remind me never to sit through an apology with you, rookie," Xander said.

Gus and Kiera released her.

"As far as we're concerned, it never happened," Kiera said.

"Now, don't go speaking for all of us," Xander said. "I, for one, was traumatized by the whole thing. In fact, I may need to sit this whole celebration thing out and take some time to recover."

Taos scoffed. "Get over yourself."

"If you try to get out of this one more time, Xander, we'll stay an extra hour just to spite you," Kiera said.

Xander threw up his arms in surrender.

Kiera linked her elbow with Nova's. "Come now," she said, leading her into the crowd. "I heard the new guy is cute. I want to see him."

Gus snorted. "Him no see you."

Kiera punched his arm. "Cruel joke, Gus Gus. Just cause he's blind doesn't mean he's not cute."

"He's not here," Taos said.

Kiera groaned. "The new people never come to their own parties."

"Yeah, well," Nova turned as she inspected the gathering. "It's not something they want to celebrate."

The balls at home were much more extravagant. There were colorful suits and gowns crested with real crystals. Here, everything was muted and handmade. Nova looked down at her dress. The embroidery was far from perfect, but the fact that Gus had made it for her made it special. A smile tugged at her lips. Nobody had ever made anything for her before.

As she followed Kiera and Gus into the throng, a subtle shift swept through the dance floor. Curious glances were exchanged between couples, conversations ended, and heads turned as the collective realization of Nova's presence permeated the celebration.

The lively swirls of skirts and the rhythmic footfalls slowed to a hesitant shuffle.

Every eye felt like a piercing spotlight, scrutinizing her every move. Nova's chest tightened, and an uneasy knot formed in the pit of her stomach.

The musicians on the makeshift stage gradually faltered. The tambourine fell silent, and the lively melody drifted away with the last rays of sunset. A small circle of space formed around Nova as people backed away. Gus, Kiera, Xander, and Taos all stayed beside her.

One man stepped forward. His whole body was quivering. His eyes were red, a deep-seated trauma evident in his stare. He began to sign with his hands, his fingers jabbing in the air, his gestures exaggerated and forceful.

As he signed, he spoke. "You not welcome here." The words were slightly muffled, with softer consonants and drawn-out vowels.

"Who let her in?" Quentin pushed his way to the front of the line.

Blood rushed to Nova's ears. Their scrutiny pressed in from all sides. *Please, no. Not now.* She pleaded with her body to avoid another episode.

The crowd began to part, and a plump woman stepped into the circle. It was the same woman Nova had seen in the Garden of Remembrance. She wore a loose, burnt orange dress with a crown of colorful blooms. The gatherers bowed their heads in respect as she passed. Nova eyed them and realization dawned on her—this was Helga.

She walked to Gus and wrapped her arms around him, then backed up and looked at Nova.

"Helga says anyone who saves her son is welcome."

"But Helga, she—"

"Helga don't repeat herself," she snapped. "Quentin have a problem, Quentin leave."

She cupped her hands around her mouth and yelled, "Music!"

The band picked up the music and people began to fall in line with the dance again.

Helga lifted one hand to pinch Nova's cheek softly. Her eyes conveyed deep gratitude, expressing her thanks without any words at all.

Nova stared at her in disbelief. She was too shocked to form a sentence so she studied Helga's face, taking in the gentle determination in her round, freckled features. This was a woman who had been forced to grow up here because of the highborns. She had every right to hate Nova. Instead, she was sticking up for her. She'd even threatened to kick one of her people out.

Helga patted Nova's cheek, offering a tender smile before turning and walking away.

"I'm surprised she didn't offer you a meal," Xander said as he draped his arms around both Nova and Kiera. "Welp. Time to partay!"

He grabbed both of their hands and spun them out, then back into him. Nova exchanged a glance with Kiera, and their laughter bubbled up.

In that fleeting moment, Nova sensed a weight lifting from her shoulders. For once, she felt okay to stay. True, most people didn't want her here—their stares and the deliberate space they left around her group made that clear. But right now, with her small circle of friends, she didn't care about the others.

She smiled at the thought of having friends. *Real friends.* She watched the four of them laughing and spinning. Well, Taos wasn't technically doing it on his own. Despite his best efforts to get away, Xander had grabbed him and twirled him around. Taos's scowl deepened.

"Gus turn!" Gus grabbed Nova's hand and pulled her into a waltz. He laughed as he led them through their dance.

"What's so funny?" she asked.

"Nova bad dancer."

Nova shot him a hurtful expression and turned to Taos for support. He smirked. "Gus only speaks the truth."

Gus raised his hand to give her a twirl. As Nova turned, her eyes caught on something. Immediately she stopped and stumbled in her dance, breaking free from Gus. Taos mumbled something else about her dancing, but it didn't register.

The world stopped. Nova rubbed her eyes to double-check it was real. Across the way, looking straight at her, stood her older brother.

Denali.

NINETEEN

I n the midst of the jubilation, Nova's surroundings blurred, and the music faded into the background as she met eyes with the spectral image of Denali. The weight of the banishment pressed heavily on her shoulders, and she took a step back, a mix of emotions swirling within her.

Her hand flew to her heart as if to restrain its wild beats from leaping right out of her ribcage. Her feet carried her forward in a burst of speed. As she neared him, her pace decelerated to a cautious approach, noting his stillness—an unsettling calm that was out of place.

Something didn't feel right.

She drew closer. There was no shock or surprise etched on his face.

How was he here?

Why wasn't he excited to see her?

His eyes showed a hollow emptiness that chilled the air between them. Nova's steps faltered to a halt inches from him. His gaze didn't meet hers. It pierced through her, fixed on something beyond her presence. His complexion was ashen, the color drained as though he'd witnessed something horrific. Then, he fixed his eyes upon her with such profound sorrow that it penetrated Nova to her core.

"Hold on, Nova," he said. "I can fix this."

Nova tilted at his words. That was exactly what he had said in the memory her and Berkshire had been working through. Pain shot through the back of Nova's skull. She grabbed her head. She had felt pain like this before, from loud noises and bright lights, but this one was different—deeper, *hotter*. She must have hit her head when she got pummeled by the Krall.

"Nova!" Kiera's voice shook her from her trance. Nova turned to look at her.

But when she turned back, Denali wasn't there.

Nova scanned the crowd for his face. "I . . ." She whirled around. "I thought I saw . . ."

Kiera took Nova's hand. "Come on," she said as she gently pulled her back to the dance. The music surged, stabbing through her head like needles, but she barely registered it. Her hand, shaking slightly, moved to cover her twitching mouth. Xander pried her fingers away, leading her back into dance. She twirled in his arms and accidentally stepped on his bare foot. "Easy, rookie."

Her mind was elsewhere, lost in what she'd seen. Beside them, Taos was watching her with concern, but her attention stayed fixed on the crowd, searching for Denali.

Her heart thudded when she caught a glimpse of him again.

There, in the middle of the celebration, stood Denali once more. This time, though, he was younger. The air stilled in Nova's lungs, longing and dread tangling in her chest.

Young Denali's gaze held wisdom far too deep for his years, carrying the same weight of sorrow that had haunted her during his previous apparition. Nova backed out of Xander's grasp and strolled toward Denali. Once she reached him, she dropped to her knees so they were face to face.

He stared back at her, a perfect picture of his younger form. Nova reached out a finger to touch his face, to make sure he was real. Before she could, he said, "We were playing a game of seek and find." Once again, heat shot through the back of Nova's skull. She winced, but didn't take her eyes off Denali.

Tears spilled down his cheeks. Snot ran from his nostrils as he cried, "Hold on, Nova. I can fix this."

"Fix what, Denali?"

He looked straight at her when she asked the question. The heat in the back of Nova's head turned scalding. She squeezed her head with both hands and closed her eyes. Then, the pain vanished.

She opened her eyes and now Denali's back was to her. She reached out and grabbed his shoulder, but when he turned around, it wasn't him. It was a little boy Nova recognized as one of Taos's students. The boy's mother shrieked and pulled him away.

"Keep your filthy hands away from my son!" she yelled.

Nova shivered. "I'm sorry, I didn't mean—"

"She grabbed my son!" the woman announced.

Her accusation rippled through the gathered miscreants, eliciting a wave of murmurs. They shifted away from Nova in collective retreat.

Strong hands wrapped around Nova's waist and pulled her up. "Time to go," Taos said.

"I saw . . ." She sniffled. "I thought I saw . . ."

Her voice trailed off as she looked around, swallowed by the crowd. Helga pushed her way back through and covered Nova with her arms. "Come."

Helga shepherded her and her friends away from the scene, leaving behind the whispers and stares that clung to the air. Nova moved as if in a trance, her mind replaying the impossible vision she had witnessed.

How could she have seen him? Was she hallucinating? It seemed so real.

The cottages of the town square began to dissipate, replaced by the expansive breadth of the forest. The air grew fresher, filled with the scent of pine. Night was settling in as Helga guided them to a clearing that existed in a world apart from the town.

Kiera tugged on Nova's hand. "Hey," she said. "Forget about the celebration."

Nova's gaze remained unfocused. She gave a small, almost imperceptible nod. It wasn't the people at the celebration that bothered her. It was seeing Denali that left her so unhinged. She cast one final glance back at the tiny cottages that were now disappearing behind the trees. A part of her felt tethered there, stuck in the middle of the celebration.

Kiera squeezed Nova's hand and brought her mind back to the forest. "Look," she said.

Nova turned back around and took in the sight of the structure before her. A home rose organically from the very ground it stood on. Constructed entirely of wood, it harmonized with the natural world in a way that took her breath away. At the heart of the property stood an ancient, thick whispering oak tree, its sprawling branches and deep roots intertwined with the cottage. Candlelight winked through the windows nestled among leaves. Above the doorway hung a hand-carved wooden sign that read, "Goodfellows is most happiest when we has guests." Someone had endearingly carved every E backwards.

Xander whistled. "Welcome to the nest."

"It's made out of a tree?" Nova asked.

"It was the first house built here. It was before they figured out how to make bricks," he said. "Personally, I prefer this."

Helga led them through the doorway. The kitchen was the grandest part of the house, featuring a massive oak table at its center, with enough chairs to seat sixteen people. From exposed wooden beams crisscrossing the ceiling, bundles of herbs had been hung to dry, filling the air with a blend of aromas. A staircase spiraled up and around the tree's trunk, leading to treehouses that served as bedrooms. One of the bedroom doors swung open and out spilled two, short, plump girls, shoving and elbowing each other as they squabbled down the hallway.

"Sister Agatha hogs all the blankets!"

"Gwendolyn sleeps like a starfish, she does! Agatha needs warmth!"

"Does not!" Gwendolyn retorted, her nose scrunched in defiance. "Agatha snores like a grumpy troll . . ."

Nova watched as they bickered. *Three children?* She had only seen that once before. She envied that Gus had one more sibling than she did. One more *Denali* than she did. She noted how much Gus and his family looked alike—all short with the same roundness and bright red curls. The girls continued to bicker while they walked down the stairs.

Helga made her way to the stove and poured water into a pot. "Helga think you all hungry."

Xander rubbed a dramatic hand over his belly. "Helga, have I ever told you you're my favorite?"

"Gus Gus work on rolls," Gus said.

Nova took a seat at the table and let the smell of the food invade her senses.

"Uh oh." Xander's expression turned warning.

Nova looked up at him curiously. Helga was already on her way over. She grabbed Nova's arms and lifted her up from the chair. Then, she plopped a strange little tool into Nova's hands.

"Nova don't sit until Nova help," she said.

Nova was taken aback. At home, the servants had always made her food. She didn't know the first thing about cooking. "But I—"

Nova's protests were cut short. Helga gave her a shove into the kitchen. Nova approached a sack of potatoes on the counter, the tool poised awkwardly in her hand. She rotated it carefully, trying to make sense of its peculiar shape. Meanwhile, Helga placed rags in Xander's and Taos's hands and had them wipe down the table. She nudged Kiera toward Gus to join in on the task of arranging the rolls.

At the foot of the stairs, Agatha and Gwendolyn stood, fighting over what task they would take. "Agatha should help with the salad. Gwendolyn cuts vegetables too chunky."

Gwendolyn gasped. "Gwendolyn cuts perfectly well!"

Helga swiped the tool from Nova's hands. She shuffled over to the girls and smacked it on the back of each girl's bum.

"Agatha and Gwendolyn both do dishes," Helga scolded.

Agatha rubbed her bottom with her right hand. "Dishes? Agatha is a creator, not a cleaner!"

The sisters eyed each other warily, but accepted their fate with a dramatic sigh.

"Gwendolyn call drying!" With that, the two of them raced over to the sink.

Helga plopped the tool back in Nova's hands and then wrapped her hand over hers, roughly positioning Nova's fingers around the handle. She guided Nova's hands to drag the blade across a potato's skin, leaving a clean strip of white flesh beneath. "Nova finish," she said, and then went back to her own work.

As Nova peeled, Agatha and Gwendolyn continued to shove each other beside her. She couldn't help but stare at the scene. She scrunched her face as they continued to fight.

Maybe all siblings aren't like Denali.

Thirty minutes later, the front door swung open and a man ducked under the door frame. Nova's gaze traveled upward, and upward still, as she took in the newcomer's height. Although his stature was completely out of the ordinary, his red hair and facial features left no doubt that he was related to Gus.

"Babs set table," Helga said to the giant.

Nova looked at Taos. "*Four* kids?"

"Not four—six."

She nearly choked. "Six?!"

"Ethel no live here no more," Gus said. "Hognose still at party."

Nova cocked her head at the recognition of that final name. At that moment, her familiar friend waddled through the door. He inspected the kitchen with a grin on his face, sniffing in the scents and rubbing his protruding belly. He seemed even shorter now that Nova was really seeing him. He paused as he looked everyone over, freezing on Nova. He jumped behind Babs and shrieked. "Her attacked Hognose!"

Nova glanced nervously at Helga, waiting for a reaction. She didn't give one. Hognose yanked on Babs's arm.

"Attacked!" he repeated.

Babs raised an eyebrow. Taos started to chuckle.

Helga finally turned to Hognose. "Hush, you ninny. Food is ready. Sit."

Hognose pointed a trembling finger at Nova, nostrils flaring. "Hognose no sit with her!"

"You'll be fine, Horace," Taos said as he whipped a rag over his shoulder. "Just make sure there are no sticks nearby."

Nova scowled at him.

Helga rushed everyone to take a seat, ordering Agatha and Gwendolyn to opposite ends of the table. Although, Nova wasn't sure if that made their bickering better or worse, because now they were yelling across the table.

The door swung open and another man walked in. He was much older and covered in soot. As he approached, Helga lifted her chin up. He bent down and landed a tender kiss on her lips. Taking a seat beside her, the sooty smell that accompanied him wove into the aromas of roasted vegetables, simmering stew, and fresh bread.

He smiled warmly. "Lovely to have so many guests."

Helga smiled in response. Her expression dropped when she saw Hognose picking at his food. She smacked his hand and he shrieked.

"Mom attack Hognose!"

"Nova give grace?" Helga asked.

Nova shifted uncomfortably. She had never given one, nor had she ever learned how. Her face drained of color. Gus's father studied her, waiting expectantly. She swallowed hard.

Luckily, Xander spoke up. "You know how I always like to do the honors, Mr. and Mrs. Goodfellow. May I?"

Nova exhaled softly, relief washing over her as the attention shifted away from her.

Helga gave a pleasant nod and everyone bowed their heads. Nova glanced to her side, noticing Gus's outstretched hand. Looking around the table, she realized everyone was joining hands.

Uneasily, she slipped her hands into Gus's and Kiera's. Once she did, Xander began reciting a ritual that was foreign to Nova's ears. Her eyes swept across the table as each of them kept their heads bowed. She shifted uncomfortably as she watched.

Once Xander's words faded, the group burst into a frenzy. Plates clattered and utensils clicked against bowls. Nova flinched as hands darted to snatch up rolls and spoon heaping servings of mashed potatoes. Gus piled his plate high with food. Nova hesitated, then quietly reached for the ladle and served herself a modest portion of potatoes. As Xander shoveled food into his mouth, bits tumbled back onto his plate only to be scooped up again. Nova grimaced. He grinned at her, showing the mashed food in-between his teeth as he shrugged. "What?"

"Small bites at a time," she murmured to herself, her tutor's words echoing in her mind as she brought a small forkful of potatoes to her mouth.

Across the table, Hognose stared Nova down as he demolished his meal, each bite more aggressive than the last. He gripped his fork like a weapon.

"Pass potato!" Agatha yelled as she got up from her seat and marched over to the other end of the table where Gwendolyn sat.

Without waiting for a response, she reached across Gwendolyn.

Gwendolyn snapped back, yanking the bowl from Agatha's reach.

Nova flinched at the sudden argument, her fork pausing midair.

Is this . . . normal? she glanced around at the others who seemed unfazed by the sisters' bickering.

She had barely made her way halfway through her small serving when the second wave began. Hands darted across the table, snatching up the remaining food. In seconds, not a crumb was left. Nova blinked in surprise, her fork still poised over her partially finished bowl.

Her stomach grumbled softly, and she couldn't help but feel a twinge of regret for her careful eating. She took a bite of her food, reconsidering her earlier wish for more siblings.

Maybe one is enough.

"Sister Agatha take the last roll! That three rolls for Agatha. She eats like a pig, she does!" Gwendolyn pointed an accusing finger at her sister, who was back in her seat nonchalantly buttering her ill-gotten gains.

"Agatha needs her strength. Gwendolyn must go faster next time. Not Agatha's fault she is slow."

Gwendolyn squinted her eyes and flung her spoon in the air, sending a blob of butter right into Agatha's hair. Agatha slammed her hands on the table and sent her roll flying at Gwendolyn. Gwendolyn caught the roll and gave a smug grin, biting into it and holding her nose high.

Agatha's face turned a deep shade of red.

Helga yelled, "Husband Phillip, handle this!"

A mild headache pulsed behind Nova's eyes. The volume of voices, the sounds of their chewing, and the clattering of dishes drummed in her skull. She massaged her temples. Amidst the chaos in the room, Nova caught Gus watching her. His expression softened and he carefully split his roll in two, dropping a half into her bowl. Nova offered him a grateful smile.

Suddenly, the front door swung open and a family of three walked in. The young mother's appearance fit right in with Gus's family. Her baby's wail joined the other sounds in the house.

Helga rose from the table and splayed her arms out. "Ethel here!"

TWENTY

"Hold on, Nova." Denali's young face flashed in Nova's mind. "I can fix this."

She woke to a mouse nibbling on the corner of her blanket. She rubbed her palm over her face. She had been having nightmares of Denali all night. What she really needed was sleep, especially after such an exhausting night at Gus's house.

Shadows in the hallway stretched and twisted, playing tricks on her eyes. She swore she saw Denali's shadow standing in the kitchen, but it disappeared as soon as she turned her head. The wind whistled as it flowed through the cracks in the brick cottage. Nova stood, pacing the small space of the hallway in an attempt to shake off the clinging remnants of her dreams.

With a sigh, she stopped her pacing and looked out the kitchen window where silver light spilled in. A screech fractured the silence, and Nova dropped to the floor.

A shadow stretched across the kitchen wall, elongated in the moonlight. The Krall made a clicking noise before running off. Nova stood and secured the window. They were getting closer now and she couldn't help but wonder how much longer it would take for them to find her.

Or for someone to give her away.

Nova rubbed her temples. Staying on her meager bedding would only bring more dreams of Denali. Instead, she sought solace in the quiet of the house, wandering through the courtyard and hallways. Eventually, she found herself back in the kitchen. She sifted through the cabinets and made herself a cup of tea. Sitting at the table, she let the silence envelop her. The warmth from the cup cradled in her hands fought against the chill that had settled in her bones.

"Want to play a game of seek and find?" someone whispered.

Nova spun around, scanning the darkened kitchen, searching for the source. But there was nobody there—only shadows. She wrapped her hands tighter around her steaming cup. The tension in her shoulders eased as she took a sip. She rested her head against the back of the chair and set the cup on the table. Her eyes, heavy with the day's fatigue, drifted closed.

✦

"Wakey, wakey."

At the sound of Taos's voice, Nova shot upwards, her head lifting from her arms on the kitchen table. The abrupt transition from the depths of sleep to the brightness of the morning stabbed through her brain. She dug the heels of her palms into her eyes.

Berkshire stood beside Taos, arms folded. Taos grabbed her cup and took it to the sink.

Nova squinted at both of them. "What is it?"

Berkshire pulled the other chair beside her and took a seat. "You neglected to tell me what happened to you yesterday."

"I don't know what you mean."

Taos's voice went flat. "You were talking to the air."

"It wasn't the air." Nova hesitated, not wanting to sound crazy. "It was my brother. I saw Denali."

Berkshire tapped his finger on the table.

"How is that possible?" Nova asked. She twisted at a piece of loose thread on her dress where Gus's stitching was coming undone. "Am I going insane?"

Taos observed the interaction, shifting his gaze from her to Berkshire.

"No," Berkshire said. He stroked his beard. "I supposed this might happen."

Nova waited for him to go on, but he didn't. Trying to get this man to explain anything was like pulling teeth. "You supposed what might happen?" She pulled at the thread, breaking it from the dress so it would stop unraveling.

"Was the celebration the only time?" he asked.

Not exactly.

It happened again last night.

Berkshire reached out and snatched the piece of string she had been fiddling with. "You've begun unraveling a memory that's been hidden all your life. Your conscience is telling you there is more to see."

Nova looked at Taos, who was deep in thought.

"Until you resolve it," Berkshire said, "you will keep seeing this ghost."

"What does that mean?" Taos asked.

Berkshire pinned Nova with his stare. She felt exposed now that she had nothing to fidget with.

"It means you're ready."

Nova settled herself opposite Berkshire, crossing her legs and resting her hands on her knees, palms open to the skies. She only had two days left before her trial. The reason for her inability to syphon was in this memory. Today she would confront it. Today she would finally get her answer.

A faint shimmer appeared in the air between her and Berkshire. As Nova focused, it intensified into a hazy image. The projection flickered, but Nova gritted her teeth, pushing through the resistance.

Gradually, the image stabilized. The blurry outlines sharpened and Nova's bedroom materialized in the air. She saw her younger self perched on the edge of her bed. Nova could feel the tension in her body. She smelt the faint scent of sweat that clung to her skin.

"I remember this night," Nova whispered. "Father is walking toward his library. I'm worried he'll know Denali was in there."

She strained to listen. When her father's scream ripped through the silence, she felt it reverberate in her bones.

"Who's been here!" Cronian's voice thundered through the corridors. Heavy footsteps shook the foundation of the house.

The creak and bang of Denali's door made her flinch. Denali's scream pierced her ears, and little Nova leapt from her bed and raced into the hallway.

"He grabbed Denali first . . ." Nova narrated. "Then he came for me."

Cronian's hand shot out, fingers tangling in young Nova's hair. Pain exploded across her scalp. He dragged them both to his chambers. Nova's feet barely touched the ground as she struggled to keep up.

The scene shifted again to their father's chamber. He threw them both on the floor. Then he yanked Denali up from the ground and pressed him against the wall. The room seemed to shrink.

Nova's concentration faltered. The memory was slipping away.

"I can't . . . I can't breathe," she choked out as Berkshire and the meditation room came back into focus. The projection was flickering. Nova's hands shook as she clawed at her top, desperate for air. Then her fingers moved to circle her neck.

"I can't breathe," she gasped. Tears spilled down her cheeks.

"Easy," Berkshire said. "Remember your first lesson."

Nova glanced at the rice box in the corner of the room. She thought about all the voices she had tried to fight for so long when all she needed to do was to surrender.

To accept the past instead of trying to silence it.

Closing her eyes, Nova loosened her grip around her throat. She took one slow, shaky breath, then another.

Stop fighting, she reminded herself. *Surrender.*

One finger at a time, she unballed her fists, allowing her hands to rest palm-up on her knees. She focused on the sensation of air entering and leaving her body, not trying to control it, but simply observing.

The tightness in her chest began to ease and the projection reformed. This time, instead of trying to grasp it, to force her way through it, Nova let it take shape naturally.

And something shifted.

The ceiling of her father's chamber loomed above her, impossibly high. The elaborate chandelier, usually so far away, now filled her entire field of vision.

Nova blinked, disoriented. Her perspective had changed. The cold marble floor pressed against her back. She tried to lift her hand, and a tiny, trembling fist came into view, so much smaller than she'd expected.

The acrid taste of fear coated her tongue, her pulse pounded so hard she could feel it in her fingertips. For the first time in her life, Nova wasn't just seeing the memory—she was *reliving* it.

This was it. She had *become* the memory, just as Berkshire had said. This was her key to return home, to finally being able to syphon. Triumph overcame her. "Berkshire, I'm doing it!" she tried to shout, but the words came out as a choked sob instead. A heavy, settling feeling took root deep in her gut.

Cronian's massive form filled her vision as he held Denali up against the wall. "I'll ask one more time," he hissed. "Who was in my library?"

Tears started to well up in Denali's eyes. The sound of Cronian's fist pounding against the wall shook the room, the vibrations traveling through the floor and into Nova's small body.

Cronian's grip shifted, now tightening around Denali's neck. He lifted his other hand into the air. The first punch landed with a sickening thud.

"No, please!" The words burst from Nova. She scrambled to her feet and tugged frantically at the fabric of Cronian's pant leg, but it was like trying to move a mountain.

Nova craned her neck to see his face and begged, "Let him go!"

But Cronian's attention never wavered from Denali.

Denali's struggle for air became more frantic. His heels kicked against the wall beneath him.

"Who!" their father yelled.

Denali clawed at Cronian's grip. His face started to turn purple and his eyes filled with fear as he rasped, "Nova."

In an instant, Cronian released his hold on Denali, letting him crumple to the floor. Before Nova could process what was happening, she was yanked into the air and strapped into the chair. Cronian's grip clamped around her wrists, squeezing them until she cried out.

He secured them tightly in the strap holders on the arms of the chair, the constriction already cutting off her circulation. He snatched a case from the fireplace mantle and slammed it onto the table with a deafening thud.

The blood drained from Nova's face, her gaze locking onto Denali. He was the one who had sneaked into the library. Her tiny fingers curled helplessly around the arms of the chair. She was trapped, exposed, forced to watch as the brother who had been her whole world crumbled into a stranger.

He was shaking, choking on his sobs. "Wait," he stammered. "Wait!"

The whip whistled through the air. Fire erupted across Nova's arms, stealing her breath before her scream could form. This wasn't like Father's other lashes—this was different, deeper, meant to break something inside her. Before she could recover, another lash bit into her flesh. This time, her screams cleaved the air.

Denali's voice rose above her cries. "It wasn't her!"

Cronian's anger remained unyielding. He lifted the whip again, poised to strike, but Denali leaped forward, shoving Cronian to the side just as the whip was descending. It struck the side of Nova's head with a sickening snap, and darkness claimed her world.

As Nova regained consciousness, a throbbing ache pulsed through her skull. Her mind struggled to focus, vision blurring as she tried to make sense of her surroundings. The fireplace, usually upright, now appeared horizontal in her field of vision. She was on the floor, still strapped to the arms of the chair. Someone unbuckled her wrists, then gentle hands gathered up her fragile body.

A low, mournful sob reached her ears. The sound was distant at first, but it grew louder. Denali's tear-streaked face hovered above her. He choked on his words as he sobbed.

"Hold on, Nova." He cupped her tiny face in his hands. His fingers were painted in her blood. "I can fix this."

TWENTY-ONE

Nova's sight returned to the meditation room. She felt Berkshire's steady gaze on her. He was still, watching her like she was a thin piece of thread that was about to break. An intense heat shot through the back of Nova's head, the same as it had when she saw Denali's ghost at the celebration. She reached her hand back to feel the side of her head, tracing what she had always assumed was a birthmark. The ridged indentations there felt suddenly alien under her fingers, proving that what she had seen was true.

"Is that why?" she whispered.

Berkshire stared at her, his silence heavier than any response could be.

Nova's heart pounded. His focus on her made her feel like she was suffocating. She sprang to her feet and ran out of the room and through the courtyard. As she reached the front door, she hurtled into a figure—Taos was standing in the doorway.

Nova stepped around him and ran out of the house. She sprinted through the village, ignoring Xander as he called out to her, "Where you off to, rookie?"

Her feet carried her into the forest, toward the falls. At first, her pace was frantic. As the path stretched on, her sprint slowed to a jog. Tears flowed freely, blurring her vision as she pressed on.

Her legs ached, but she couldn't bring herself to stop. Finally, she broke through the treeline and the misty spray of cascading water cooled her flushed skin. A protruding root snagged her foot, and she stumbled. She hit the ground hard, skidding to a stop on the riverbank. Pebbles dug into her palms and knees as she caught herself.

The reason she couldn't syphon, the reason she had always felt like an outsider, was not some quirk of birth or a mistake of nature like she had always believed. Instead, it was the result of a brain injury from Father and a betrayal from the person she loved most in this world.

It was the reason she was banished.

They were the reason she was banished.

Tears filled her eyes as she clutched her head, trying to make sense of it all. How could Denali, the person who had sworn to always be there for her, hide this from her?

The pain was not just physical, it was a deep, searing ache in her soul. Her dreams of standing alongside her family had been shattered. The very essence of who she was had been stolen from her.

The worst part, though, was the overwhelming sense of isolation. She was an outcast in her own family. Denali was the only person she'd truly trusted. But he'd lied. He'd lied to her since she was five years old.

The entire time she was struggling in her classes and facing persecution, Denali had come to her side to reassure her. She finally realized why he always took her whippings, why he tried so hard to teach her in the cavern, why he stayed home from being with friends to help her . . . he felt guilty.

Was that the reason for all his love?

Because of his *guilt*?

Nova pressed the palms of her hands into her eye sockets, wishing she could take back everything she had seen. Then, a new thought struck her.

What if Denali didn't tell her because he didn't remember?

He must have syphoned the traumatic memory. The thought of it made her blood hot. She never had that luxury growing up.

She folded into herself, face pressed between her knees, fingers laced tight behind her head. Her temples throbbed with each heartbeat.

How could he keep such a terrible secret?

In Ghandria, she was cast out. In a family tainted by secrets, she was a stain. In Nadir, she was reviled. The only certainty left was that she didn't belong anywhere.

Something moved through the forest, crushing leaves underfoot. Nova dragged her head up, fighting against her own weight.

Branches parted and Xander stepped into the clearing. Nova slumped down again. She didn't bother to look up when he planted himself on the ground next to her. He said nothing for a few minutes, and Nova appreciated the lack of conversation. She wasn't ready to talk.

"My brother was sent here," he said finally. "He was labeled a miscreant a few years before me."

Nova remained still, but continued to listen.

"It made my exile a little bit easier, knowing he would be here . . . that I would see him again."

Nova raised her eyes to meet his, wondering what had happened to his brother. "What was his indiscretion?"

"Same as mine."

"What happened?"

Xander stared forward. "He was hiding it for a while, I think. One day, I did something stupid that got him caught. When I was banished here, I couldn't find him anywhere. I thought he had died." Xander picked up a rock and hurled it into the water. It skipped four times before sinking. "I was out with Kiera one day and I saw him in the forest, digging his claws into the corpse of a cat."

Nova covered her mouth. "Oh, Xander."

"I didn't recognize him at first." He grimaced. "He wasn't my brother anymore. When that *thing* looked at me, it had no idea who I was."

Nova tried to imagine seeing Denali that way. The image made her squeeze her eyes shut.

"How could someone erase their memories of their brother?" His voice barely carried over the rush of the waterfall.

"Xander, I . . . " Nova began, then faltered. Words seemed inadequate in the face of this kind of loss. After a moment, she simply said, "I'm so sorry."

The roar of the falls filled the space between them. Nova's mind replayed what he had said about his brother. A realization struck her.

"Your brother," she said hesitantly. "He erased his memories here?"

Xander nodded as he hurled another skipping rock.

"But, how? There's no syphon."

Xander stopped mid-throw. "What are you talking about?"

"You can't erase memories without the syphon."

His eyebrow lifted. "The syphon is an energy source, rookie. Nothing more."

"Energy source? What do you mean?"

He waved his hand around. "Everything around you is an energy source. The water, the ground, the trees. When you erase a memory, it can't just disappear. That would go against the laws of the universe."

Nova gave him a questioning glance.

"Did you not learn this in school?"

"I didn't exactly go to school."

"Gee, you really are a rookie," he went on. "Every action has a reaction, right?"

Nova scrunched her face, still not understanding.

Xander chuckled and pressed his pointer finger to her forehead. "When you remove a memory from your mind, it doesn't vanish into thin air. It has to go into something else. Basically, it gets a new host. In Ghandria, they use the syphon. For everyone here, they can use the trees or the water I guess. I don't actually know about water so don't quote me on that one. I wasn't exactly a straight-A student.

People here use the spora, though. It's much easier that way. You can tell the ones that have stored memories because they glow."

He extended his hand and pointed toward the spora forest. "My mushroom is right over the ridge. It's kind of an unspoken rule here to not use the ones that are already glowing. Sort of like a territory thing."

"So . . . people here are still syphoning? Without the syphon?"

"Yep, not as much as you're used to in Ghandria, of course. The actual syphon makes it a lot easier. Doing it any other way takes more practice and a lot of effort. And then, of course, there's Berkshire, always rambling on about how it corrupts your soul and loses your identity and whatnot. Personally, I think it's just a way to . . ."

His voice drowned into the background as Nova pieced together information. She really was the only person who hadn't syphoned. All this time, she'd thought the miscreants here couldn't erase their memories, but they could all along. *That* was why Berkshire said she was their only hope. *That* was why he was so adamant about teaching her.

"Xander!" Nova inhaled sharply. "Xander, we have to go!"

She leapt up, taking his hand and yanking him with her as she broke into a run. "Come on!"

He stumbled, trying to match her pace. "Uh, where are you taking me, rookie?"

Nova ignored him as she ran. She let go of his hand and he followed her over the ridge and into the spora forest. Through the stillness came the sound she'd been waiting for—a baby's fading cry and a *tick-tick-tick*.

Her eyes darted from one mushroom to another as she sprinted, following the sound.

Where is it?

Come on. Where is it?

She skidded to a stop in front of the pair of mushrooms fused together at the stem, and scanned around the forest floor. Beyond the conjoined giants, she spotted the glowing mushroom marked by the shreds of purple cloth at its base. A clearer whisper reached her ears. *"It didn't have to be this way."*

"What are we doing here?" Xander asked. "Did you not learn your lesson last time?"

Nova felt a twinge in her abdomen remembering what had happened last time she was in the spora forest, but she ignored it as she stared at the mushroom in amazement. "My first day here," she said, "I saw a vision. I thought it was a warning . . . but it wasn't a vision, Xander. It was a *memory*."

He shook his head. "Nobody can see memories after they are erased, rookie. You can see them once, as they are being offered. After that, they belong to their new hosts."

Nova's lips pressed into a thin line as she absorbed his words. She knew what she had seen. It had happened both times she had touched the spora. It was the same experience she had every time she reached out to the syphon, too.

"All I know is that I see memories every time I touch this spora."

"Every time?" Xander asked. He reached out and touched the base of the mushroom, his hand resting on its surface for a split second. He looked back at her. "See?"

Nova frowned. The veins of the mushroom pulsed. She felt it pulling at her. It was luring her in the same way the syphon had. Subtle whispers pulled her closer . . . *"It didn't have to be this way."* Followed by a *tick-tick-tick*. Xander's protests drowned out behind her as she reached her fingers to touch it.

TWENTY-TWO

Nova was cradling a child to her chest. It was too dark to make sense of her surroundings. The sound of pounding filtered through the walls. Gradually, her eyes adjusted and she saw one vertical slant of light. She was in a cupboard.

A paralyzing fear gripped at her. A door swung open and footsteps sounded in the room. She hugged her baby close.

"I know you're in here." A familiar voice shook the room.

Cronian.

Something flew across the room and hit the wall. Nova winced. He was overturning furniture. "It didn't have to be this way," he said. "You could have lived here with your family."

Another heavy object hit a wall and the cabinet doors shook. The baby started to fuss and Nova covered his mouth to keep him quiet. She heard the cabinet doors beside them swing open.

She froze. Cronian's shadow moved over to their cabinet, blocking the little light that came in from the crack. It felt like a heavy blanket had draped over her, suffocating her.

"Cronian," another voice called out. "Over here."

When Cronian's shadow retreated and disappeared into another room, Nova released her hand from the child's mouth. A few minutes passed and the voices of the men faded completely, leaving only the sound of a clock ticking.

Tick-tick-tick

Her body drew in a shaky breath. Then, a rancid scent began to tickle her nose. At first, it was a faint hint of something burning, barely perceptible. Then her nostrils flared, and goosebumps prickled along her arms. She shifted to peer through the crack in the cabinet door at what she could see of the room. Smoke was seeping in from beneath the door, crawling along the floor like a sinister snake.

Fire.

Nova's maternal instinct screamed at her to protect her child. Holding her baby tight, she burst from her hiding spot. She cast a desperate glance at the door, but the heat rising from beneath made it clear that escape in that direction was impossible.

Her body moved toward the window. She pulled at the seal with all her might but it wouldn't budge. Heat radiated from the floor, singeing the skin on her ankles. She was coughing, choking on smoke. The child was wailing now. She lifted her dress, revealing a silver dagger holstered on her thigh. A sapphire gem gleamed at its hilt, catching the firelight. With trembling hands, she took aim and hurled the blade at the window's weakest point. It struck with precision, sending cracks spiderwebbing through the glass.

She scanned the room for a safe place. Her eyes fell on a heavy wooden chest in the corner. With utmost care, she placed the crying boy inside. Then, she seized a nearby chair and thrust it forcefully into the damaged window. Glass shattered and the room was swiftly overtaken by the encroaching smoke.

She rushed back to the chest, scooping up her baby. She dragged the chair to the base of the window and climbed up. Flames licked her heels as she balanced precariously, clutching her child tightly. She thrust her arms through the jagged opening, lowering the baby as far as she could before she let go. Then, she clawed her way through the shattered remnants of the window.

Shards of glass sliced her legs as she squeezed through, but adrenaline numbed the pain. She bit down on her teeth as she tumbled to the ground outside. A series of raspy coughs wracked her body, leaving her throat raw and her eyes teary. Her lungs felt as though they were filled with hot embers, and every breath seared through her like a branding iron.

She spotted her baby lying below the window, right beside her dagger. With quivering arms, she reached for her child, her fingers outstretched, their tips brushing the soft fabric of the baby's clothing. Before she could grasp him, a grip closed around her wrist. Cronian's laughter rang through the air.

He lifted her arm into the air, hoisting her upper body off the ground. Nova's heart pounded as she struggled against the fiendish grasp, her eyes darting desperately between Cronian, his accomplice, and her helpless baby. Nova wrenched her arm out of his grasp and dropped back to the ground.

Cronian's command was cold, detached. "Take him."

Her voice cracked as she screamed, "You can't take him from me!"

A savage, feral energy surged through her body. Every muscle coiled, every nerve blazed. Heat flooded in her veins, rage and terror fusing into a molten force that could burn worlds. Her hand flew to her dagger, fingers curling around the hilt.

Cronian's accomplice bent to snatch her child, but before he could, Nova launched herself forward. She brandished her weapon with wild grace and the man blocked every strike. Their struggle played out amidst the raging inferno, the baby's cry barely audible over the roar of flames.

As the man pounced, Nova sidestepped and used her foot to shove her baby, sending him rolling away from the flames. She turned back to her assailant and aimed a lethal blow for his neck, but he captured her wrist and twisted it. Pain exploded through her arm and her weapon clattered to the ground.

Then, he yanked her toward him and head-butted her in the bridge of her nose. The world fractured, pain radiating through Nova's skull. She staggered back, the heat of the engulfed house scorching her skin. Her assailant charged at her, but she dropped and swept his legs from beneath him. He crashed to the ground, inches from the raging flames. As he tried to stand, Nova tackled him, pinning him down against the fiery debris.

The man's clothes caught fire, the blaze devouring him inch by inch. As the fire spread, it consumed Nova's left hand. Gritting her teeth against the pain, she maintained her grip. His howls filled the air as he writhed in agony beneath her.

With a strong heave, he shoved her off. He pushed himself to his feet and stumbled a few feet away from the fire, then dropped to the ground and rolled frantically.

Nova staggered to her feet, nursing her burned hand close. She spun around, looking for her baby. There, on the ground, the child wailed. Cronian stood between them, her own dagger glinting in his hand.

She lunged at him, but Cronian sidestepped and plunged the blade deep into her side. Nova gasped. He grabbed her shoulder with his other hand and held her while he twisted the dagger deeper, the blue jewel now slick with her blood. She choked on the pain. Cronian grabbed onto the back of her hair and pulled her face close until they were inches apart.

"It's time for our people to witness the consequences to those who challenge the syphon." He released her hair and she crumpled to her knees.

The baby wailed on the ground, reaching his tiny hands out for his mother. A lone tear traced a path down Nova's cheek. Her trembling fingers inched toward the knife, to pull it from her stomach, but Cronian kicked her to the ground. Through blurring vision, she saw her son lifted into the air, his cries fading as darkness crept in from the edges.

Everything faded to black.

Nova hurled forward in ragged breaths. Darkness now engulfed the forest, and Xander was gone. Fog was oozing between the mushrooms. She grabbed her spinning head, processing what she had seen.

Had Father killed this woman?

Was he truly *that* evil?

The revelation started a maelstrom of pain and betrayal swirling through her mind. The weight of the thought made her head spin.

He was a *murderer.*

Did Denali know?

Was this another secret he had kept from her?

She turned at the pounding of footsteps to her left where Xander ran toward her. Berkshire and Taos followed closely behind.

When they saw that she was all right, they slowed their pace.

Nova held out her hands for them to pull her up. Her entire body ached. All she wanted to do was collapse into sleep, and she nearly did as Taos carried her back cradled in his arms. It felt like minutes later she was in a bed at the cottage, succumbing to her exhaustion.

✦

Denali carefully pinned a note to the wall of his room, adding to the growing collage of information he had gathered from Lucien's journal. The wall was a tapestry of questions, theories, and snippets of text. He drew back, his eyes roaming over the chaotic display, trying to make sense of the rubble of thoughts that buzzed in his mind. The recent revelation about the syphon's capacity limitations kept circling to the forefront.

The incident with Finnian, where the syphon had spiraled out of control, must have been a result of it reaching its capacity. The erratic behavior, the violent tremors—it was the only explanation.

But then, as quickly as it had started, the syphon had calmed, returning to its usual state. The change left him with a nagging question: how had Cronian managed to stabilize it? According to Lucien's journal, the syphon's power was tenuous at first, unable to accept memories from more than a few people. He searched for a remedy and discovered a solution in the toxic compounds of certain mushrooms. This toxin, which he called 'fed' to the syphon regularly, fortifying it. Increasing the amount could expand the syphon's capacity. So it stood to reason that Cronian must have access to a supply of the toxin, and had been using it to keep the syphon in check.

Denali began to pace, his mind whirring with possibilities. If he

232

could find a way to cut off Cronian's supply of sitheus, the syphon would inevitably start to act out again. And if he could orchestrate a situation where people witnessed the syphon's instability firsthand, it could cast doubt on the validity of Nova's banishment. Her trial was only two days away, so he needed to be ready.

Exposing the syphon's flaws would be a dangerous game, one that could easily backfire if he wasn't careful. If it meant saving Nova, though, and righting the wrongs that had been done to her, he would take that risk.

Denali's gaze drifted to his own sketch of the spora mushroom. The key to his plan hinged on understanding the fungi—where it grew, how the toxin was extracted, and how much of it Cronian had access to. If he could unravel those secrets, he might have a chance at this.

As he walked past his vanity, he caught a glimpse of his reflection and paused. The person staring back at him was unrecognizable. His bloodshot eyes were surrounded by sagging dark circles. The constant stress and lack of sleep had started to take their toll, leaving him haggard and gaunt. His hair hung in limp, unkempt strands around his face.

Studying was easier when he'd had Blythe's company. His stomach twisted, remembering their last interaction—the way he had lashed out in class, the look on her face after he had pushed her. She had only been trying to help, to keep him from making a mistake, but in the moment, blinding rage had consumed everything else.

His reflection mocked him, a twisted, distorted version of himself. He had hurt Blythe. Just like he had hurt Nova. The pain on her face was imprinted in his memory. His fingers curled into a tight fist at the memory. It was the same look Nova had given him when—

With a growl of frustration, he threw his fist into the mirror, shattering it against his knuckles. The sharp sting of pain barely registered.

He heard a vibrant voice yelling in the hallway. "Hey, rock-for-brains! I said move!"

233

Denali opened his door and peeked out.

"Get this imbecile out!" a guard yelled, grabbing Blythe by the wrist.

She yanked her hand from his and held a finger up at him. She had to be two feet shorter than him. "Touch me again, *bonehead*— see what happens. My uncle taught me well." She did a thumb gesture in the air. "Straight for the eyes."

The guards exchanged uncertain glances.

Denali spoke up. "She's with me."

Blythe huffed as she stomped past them, her blue hair bouncing with each step. She spun around to shoot them an exaggerated mock salute before ducking into Denali's room. Denali shut and locked the door behind her. "How did you sneak in?"

Blythe whirled around, her hand on her popped-out hip, and fixed Denali with a glare that could melt steel. "Oh, no. You don't get to ask any questions, dude."

Denali flinched as Blythe's finger appeared inches from his nose, causing him to stumble back a step.

"You've officially pissed me off. First, you go all berserker mode with Slater, and then you ghost three classes? It's a freaking miracle Pippington hasn't failed you yet. Then again, I suppose it's normal, given her favoritism toward you. It's barf-worthy, man. Even when you're gone, she still talks about you . . ."

Blythe's voice trailed off and her expression shifted, melting into something more somber. Confused by the change, Denali followed her line of sight, his stomach dropping when he realized what had caught her attention.

The shattered mirror.

Blythe dropped her finger and looked at Denali's hand. He had already healed it, but the dried blood was still crusted over his knuckles. He quickly hid it in his pocket, his face burning with shame.

"What's going on, D?"

He shifted, his gaze ricocheting off the walls, the floor, the ceiling—anywhere to avoid Blythe's eyes. Anywhere to escape the sight of the person he'd hurt. The silence between them stretched out. A sandpaper sensation scraped the back of his throat, tempting him to cough.

Blythe lifted an eyebrow. "Really? You're gonna shut me out? A lot of good that's doing you." She took a whiff of the air. "You stink."

Denali did his own scent check of his armpits and grimaced.

Blythe walked over to the wall and started inspecting the notes. "Hmmm," she said. "Interesting." She plucked one note off the wall. "Where is the sitheus supply coming from? Certainly not from an underground tunnel. That would be insane."

Denali cocked his head to the side. "How did you know about sitheus?"

Blythe shrugged. "Certainly not from reading the journal. That would also be insane."

Denali shook his head, remembering who he was talking to. "I should've known you'd steal it."

"I didn't *steal* it, I *took* it." Blythe put her hands on her hips. "It was back in your backpack before you even realized it was missing. And you're lucky I did read it because while you were alienating me, I was out doing my own research and guess what I found?"

"What?"

Blythe smirked. "You first."

Denali exhaled. "I . . ." He hesitated and sat on his bed. "Finnian didn't die because of a sickness."

"What do you mean?"

Denali dug his palms into his eyes, wishing he could unsee all of it. "I was there."

"If it wasn't a sickness, then what was it?"

"The syphon."

Blythe's eyes widened. "Whoa, D. That's seriously twisted."

Denali's fingers started to tremble. "That's not all."

Blythe shifted more toward him, waiting for him to go on.

He took a deep breath, forcing out the words. "I'm the reason Nova's a miscreant."

Shame heated his face. The words hung in the air. Part of him wanted to take them back. Another part felt a sliver of liberation after saying them aloud.

He had never told anyone before.

Blythe's silence stretched. She sat down beside him.

"I was just a kid. I didn't think . . . I wasn't . . ." Denali fumbled over his words. "I never meant to hurt her." He pressed his hand against his face. "It's my fault."

Blythe spoke softly. "D, whatever this was . . . whatever you did, you were a kid."

"I hurt her. If she ever remembered what I did . . ."

Blythe took his hand in hers. "If she remembered what you did she would *forgive* you, D. She loves you."

"What if what I did was unforgivable?"

She shook her head. "Don't do that. You're taking her choice away. Forgiveness is a decision Nova has the right to make."

Blythe leaned forward, catching his gaze. "Holding this guilt inside is only hurting you. Nova wouldn't want that."

"I hurt her, Blythe. In class, I hurt you too. Both times, I couldn't face either of you, so I hid." His eyes found his broken reflection. "What if I'm no better than my father?"

Blythe scowled. "D, if you ever say that again, I'll uppercut you. For real. I might do it right now just because you thought it. You are not like Cronian. And you never will be."

"How do you know?"

"Hasn't anybody told you?" She flicked her hair back. "Girls with blue hair know everything."

Denali chuckled. "And what does this girl with blue hair know about this valuable piece of information she found?"

"Not 'what.'" Blythe smirked. "Who."

Nova woke in an unfamiliar space. Her eyes adjusted to the daylight and the room came into focus.

236

She was lying on a wooden platform, cushioned by a thin layer of cloth padding.

Taos's bed?

The gentle flicker of a fire danced in the hearth, which was nestled against the wall opposite from where she lay. Near the door, Berkshire spoke in low tones to Taos.

"It appears her lack of syphoning has allowed her to do more than I had anticipated."

"Hold on," Taos said. "You're saying she can see memories after they've been erased?"

"One more reason I'm a freak," Nova muttered.

They turned sharply at her voice. Nova craned her neck to see them better.

"That doesn't make you a freak, Darkov," Taos said.

She dropped her head back on the pillow. "Then why do I feel like one?"

Just when she had succeeded in projecting a steady memory, she had found another thing that singled her out as different. At least Xander wasn't alone in his indiscretion. The inability to manipulate the senses was the most common indiscretion. Kiera and Taos shared their inability to heal. Nova had seen Kiera with multiple cuts and bruises, but Taos . . . never seemed to have any. The thought snagged in Nova's mind. Her eyes traced over him.

"What's your indiscretion?"

Taos's posture stiffened, but he said nothing.

Nova pushed herself upright. "I've seen you enhance your senses." She stared at his arm, remembering her surprise when his skin wasn't marked with any scratches, cuts, or blemishes. "And I don't believe that you made it out of the Krall attack unmarked. So . . . what's your indiscretion?"

Taos shook his head. "You don't know what you're talking about." He opened the door and Berkshire stepped aside to let him pass.

Nova stood from the bed and followed him down the hallway.

He passed the kitchen where Xander was sitting and went

straight for the front door. Nova pressed her palm against it before he could leave.

"Please, Taos. I need to know," she said. "Is your indiscretion the same as mine?"

Taos exhaled. "You think I can't syphon?"

Nova considered. "But . . . if you can syphon, enhance your senses, *and* heal, then you don't have any indiscretion."

His eyes met hers for one heavy moment. Then he pulled the door open just enough to slip through, letting it close with a soft thud.

Xander let out a low whistle. He was sitting back in a chair with his feet propped up on the table. "He's a little worked up, huh?"

Nova made her way over to him. "I don't understand. If he doesn't have any indiscretion, why is he here?"

"Not my story to tell, rookie. Sorry."

"Xander, please. Is this the reason he hates me so much?"

Xander stared at her for a few seconds while he contemplated. Finally, he sighed. "All right, rookie. But it didn't come from me."

Nova took the seat beside him.

"Brace yourself," he said.

Nova leaned in.

"Our boy is not a miscreant," he whispered.

"That's impossible. Only miscreants are sent here. Taos was labeled one."

"Yes, he was *labeled* one—for his indiscretion of healing to be exact. But you and I have both seen that he can do it."

Nova scrunched her face. "So, what? He *faked* it?"

"Atta girl."

Her lips parted slightly, her head tipping to one side. "Why would he do that?"

"Why would he fake it? Why did he take Berkshire's place? What is Berkshire looking for every day? We'd all like to know. Unfortunately, they keep to themselves."

Berkshire cleared his throat behind them.

Xander stood from his chair. "Welp, time for me to sprint. Glad you're okay, rookie. Don't do that again. Seriously. Me coming back here and asking for help isn't a good look. Sort of ruins my reputation."

He winked as he closed the front door behind him.

Nova passed Berkshire and walked through the courtyard to Taos's room. She sat on his bed, contemplating her conversation with Xander. Nothing made sense. After a few minutes of thinking, she surrendered and collapsed against the pillow. A glint caught her eye from Taos's shelf and she winced. She rose and approached the source of the reflection. It was a silver dagger. She picked it up, running her thumb along the dull edge. Her fingers went numb when she saw it. Embedded in the hilt was a jewel.

A sapphire.

"What are you doing, Darkov?"

Nova startled, nearly dropping the dagger. She hadn't heard Taos come in. "Did . . . did you really just leave the front door and come in through the back window?"

"I'm trying to *avoid* you, Darkov." He shook his head and mumbled under his breath, "Not that I've ever been successful."

"Taos," Nova said, her voice softening. "Where did you get this?"

He held out his hand, and when she gave him the dagger, he tucked it away. "Leave it alone."

She looked back up at him. "Why did you come here?" she asked. "I spent my whole life trying to hide that I was a miscreant. You spent yours trying to convince people you were one." She paused, realization dawning on her. "You think she's here. That's what Berkshire's been doing everyday. He's trying to help you find her."

A flicker of surprise crossed Taos's face.

Nova bit her lip, choosing her words carefully. "But, Taos. Your mom isn't here."

"I know what the records show, Nova. You shouldn't believe everything the highborns say."

Nova shook her head gently. He couldn't possibly know what the records had shown. Those files were kept in Cronian's forbidden library. "Taos, I saw your mom . . . I mean, I saw what happened to her."

Taos's head snapped up, his eyes boring into hers.

Nova's mind recoiled from the truth, the horrific images of the woman's death burned into her memory. Taos looked so hopeful—how was she supposed to tell him that her father had set their house on fire, stabbed his mother, and left her there to die?

Wait.

She had seen that memory through his mother's eyes, which meant that she had to have been alive to syphon it. Here, in the spora forest.

"She *is* alive." A disbelieving laugh escaped Nova's lips. "Taos, she's alive. And she's here!"

"Whoa, Darkov. Slow down."

Nova brought her hands to her forehead. The memories she had seen flashed through her mind. The baby she had seen was *Taos.*

He grasped her shoulders, bending slightly to meet her gaze. "Darkov, please. Talk to me."

Nova's attention shifted to a fleck of ash drifting from the fireplace. As it floated toward her, an image stirred in her memory: her hand aflame, pressing an ignited man into the ground.

Nova inspected her hand. The phantom sensation of burning persisted, though her skin remained unmarked. As she flexed her fingers, she recalled a woman she had met on one of her first days here.

A woman with burn scars covering her left hand.

Nova's hand shot to her mouth. She grabbed Taos's arm.

"We have to go!"

TWENTY-THREE

Nova pulled Taos by hand to a distinct spot in the marketplace.

"What are we looking for?" he asked.

"Shush!"

She surveyed the area and found a woman she had seen her second day here. "Do you remember me?" she asked her. "You're Clara's friend, right?"

The lady looked up at them.

"Can you bring us to her?"

The lady gave them a puzzled expression, but after a moment's hesitation, led them through dozens of cottages until she stopped at one that stood out from the rest. The front door and windows were decorated with freshly picked flowers.

"Darkov, what is this?" Taos said.

"The memories I have been seeing of a baby boy . . . I think they might have been about you."

He shook his head. "Berkshire's already gone through these doors. Let's go."

Nova scrunched her face. "What? I don't understand. I want to help—"

"I said let's go." He started backing away from the door.

The maiden watched.

"Taos, don't give up now," Nova said.

"Think about it, Nova," he said. "If you saw her memories . . . what does that mean?"

Nova couldn't understand why he wasn't happy about this. "It means we might have found your parents."

"You shouldn't have brought me." He turned on his heel, then stopped short.

A tall, slender man was approaching the doorway, holding a bundle of logs. He halted when he saw the two of them at his door. His face was framed with a scruffy brown beard. His clothes, a raggy tan shirt and trousers, were covered in a fine layer of reddish-brown soil, the knees and elbows particularly caked with dirt from a day's work in the fields. The earthy aroma of freshly tilled soil and sun-dried wheat clung to him.

Taos stopped breathing altogether as he stared at the man.

"Them is looking for Clara," the maiden said.

The man inspected Taos.

Nova nudged Taos in an attempt to snap him out of it. When he still didn't move, the man nodded. "Please, come in."

He opened his home to them, and Nova and Taos both took a seat on his couch. The man held out a cup of water and smiled. "I'm Nathaniel."

Taos didn't reach for the cup. "Did you have a son?"

Well, that's one way to do it, Nova thought.

Nathaniel's hand, still outstretched with the unclaimed cup, trembled slightly before dropping to his side. He lowered himself onto the couch opposite them and the silence stretched as he studied Taos's face.

When Nathanial finally spoke, his voice came out as a ragged whisper. "It seems like another life."

"So you do remember?" Taos asked.

Why was he being so blunt with this man?

Nathaniel dropped his head and whispered, "Of course I do."

"It's just her that doesn't?"

Nova creased her brow in confusion. Then, it struck her. Taos's words rang through her mind.

If you saw her memories, what does that mean?

A chill ran down her spine as the answer crystallized.

It means she erased her memories of you.

Taos had said that Berkshire had already been through this area, but if he had talked to Clara, it was possible that she didn't remember her son. Erasing an entire person from one's memory wasn't impossible, but the willpower it took was far more than most could handle. The process had lasting effects, causing long-term damage to the brain.

Nathaniel sniffled and brought Nova back to the scene in front of her. His eyes roamed over Taos's face, taking in every detail. His lips quivered, caught between a smile and a tremble.

"You . . ." Nathaniel started, then tried again. "You've grown so . . ." He trailed off.

Taos clenched his jaw.

Nathaniel swallowed hard, his hands fidgeting at his sides. "How—" He paused and started over. "How are you?"

"Why did she do it?" Taos asked, ignoring his question.

Nathaniel's face closed off. "We don't have to go over that now."

"Answer me," Taos said, "or we leave."

Nova frowned. She parted her lips to say something to him, but his glare stopped her from doing so.

"We tried to get back," Nathaniel said. "We tried to get on the Marmoris. We made our own boat to try and cross. We fought to near death to get back to you for *nine years*."

He looked up, meeting Taos's gaze. "Clara . . . she couldn't handle it. The spora toxins were affecting her. Some nights, she would scream for hours. She was *changing* . . . turning into one of those *creatures*. We never agreed with syphoning. That's what got us exiled. But I had to make a choice to watch my wife turn into one of them or . . ."

"Or to erase your kid?"

"If I had ever thought there was a chance of seeing you again . . ." He choked back his emotions. "We were going to *lose* her. She was driving herself mad. She wouldn't be here today if she hadn't done it."

Taos stared past the man, his jaw locked.

Nathaniel started to reach out to him, but Taos shook his head. Nathaniel sank back into his seat.

Nova bowed her head, feeling the pull of gravity as if it had suddenly intensified.

Nathaniel broke the silence and spoke again. "After she did it, she wasn't the same. At first, she was angry all the time. She developed a temper unlike anything I had ever seen. She wasn't my Clara anymore. Over time, glimpses of the woman I married began to resurface. She came back to me, bit by bit, but she was never the same as before. She lost a part of herself when she lost you."

Taos said nothing.

"I'm not trying to make excuses, son. I just want you to understand—"

"It's 'Taos.'"

Nathaniel closed his eyes and exhaled. Then, he looked at Taos and continued. "Taos, Clara fought fiercely for her beliefs. She was one of the only people brave enough to stand against the syphon, and Cronian nearly killed her for it. He called it mercy that he kept you there to give you a better life. The most sickening part of it was that he had a kid too."

Nova's face fell. *Denali.*

"How could a father take a child away from another father?" Nathaniel said. "We had to start our lives over. It was the only way for us to move forward."

Taos stared forward. "Start over how?"

Before Nathaniel could answer, the door opened and Clara slipped in, carrying her basket of flowers. One hand clasped the hand of a boy, no older than three. He looked almost identical to the boy from the memories. Nova watched as Taos's eyes unraveled the information, shifting from the boy to Clara. Taos remained stiff, staring at her. Clara pulled the child closer, her arms encircling him protectively.

Taos stood up and approached her. She swung the child behind her, shielding him. Nathaniel rose from his seat, gesturing with open palms to assure Clara that everything was okay. Taos studied her as if he were trying to inspect every freckle on her face. A small, hopeful smile tugged at his lips.

"Do you know me?" Taos asked, his voice filled with desperation, a vulnerability Nova had never witnessed in him before.

Clara blinked up at him, curiosity washing over her features. Taos delicately lifted his hands to her face, cupping her cheeks. "Do you know me?" he whispered this time.

Clara looked down at her basket of flowers. She picked a single yellow one and held it out to Taos, drawing attention to her hand with scars webbed across her skin.

The scars that came from her fight in the house fire.

The scars that were caused by Father.

She parted her lips to speak and Nova held her breath. The words came out impossibly soft. "The stars like to steal my flowers at night. Twinkle thieves, they are." She looked at Nathaniel. "But I don't mind. I grow them to share."

Taos's fingers, still hovering where they cupped Clara's face, curled inward slowly. The soft curve of his hopeful smile wavered, then crumpled at the edges. He inspected her face for a few moments longer. His hands fell to his sides and he stepped back, nodding his head.

When he finally spoke, his "Okay" was a broken thing.

"Taos," Nathaniel begged.

Taos ignored him. Nova watched as he straightened his shoulders. Then, he turned and walked toward the door, leaving the flower in Clara's hand. The door opened and closed with a soft thud, and Taos was gone. An awful silence hung in the room.

Nova watched, heart aching, as anguish consumed Nathaniel's features. The corners of his mouth twitched in an attempt to compose himself.

Clara was still looking out the window after Taos's retreating figure. "A silly color for gardening, don't you think? Smells a lot like chocolate."

Nathaniel sniffled and smiled at his wife. "Yes, my darling."

She turned to Nova with an innocent smile. However, as she continued to look, her expression gradually dropped. A subtle change overtook her and she squinted slightly. "Those eyes," she said. "I know those eyes."

Nova's frame tensed. Chills blanketed her skin. Surely, she couldn't know Nova when she didn't know her own son. Nova peeked at Nathaniel. Luckily, he wasn't fazed by it. He was slumped in his chair, his face buried in his hands. Nova shifted beneath Clara's unwavering stare. The child started tugging at her arm, but she wouldn't budge.

"I should go," Nova said.

"We did everything we could to get back to him." Nathaniel sniffled. "Please make sure he knows that."

Clara tilted her head as she continued to study Nova. Nova shivered and forced herself to move. She pushed the front door open to follow after Taos. She cast a glance back and found Clara framed in the window, still inspecting her. The intensity of her stare made a feeling of unease settle over her.

✦

The rhythmic pounding of a sword striking its target echoed through the courtyard, drawing Nova's attention as she stepped back into the cottage. Her eyes found Taos, who was in the midst of a fierce battle with the training dummies. One by one, the wooden targets fell victim to his assault.

Taos finally plunged his blade into a rice bag, leaving it impaled, and turned his focus to delivering a series of punches to the bag's surface. His shirt hung loose, buttons undone, skin damp with exertion. He ceased his onslaught when he noticed Nova approaching, but he kept his eyes fixed on the bag.

"You can't be here right now," he said.

Despite his words, Nova advanced. "Taos—"

He spun around, seizing her shoulders firmly. "I said leave! You can't be here, Nova! I'm not messing around!"

Nova asserted her stance. "I'm not leaving."

Taos spun her around, pressing her back against the rice bag. "You're a highborn. You don't care."

"I do," she said. "Taos, I care."

He pounded a fist into the rice bag, the force of the blow sending tremors through it.

Nova winced at the power of the impact, but she held his gaze. Taos's expression softened as his eyes traced her face, lingering on each feature.

He placed his hands against the rice bag, one on each side of her face, effectively caging her in. Nova's heart hammered against her ribs. Gently, Taos leaned in, resting his forehead against hers. Nova's eyes fluttered closed, aware of nothing but his breath on her skin.

"Don't blame her." She struggled with the words. "It's not her fault."

They stayed there for a moment before Taos lifted his head and looked back at her. He was so close now, Nova could see the golden flecks around his irises.

Nova broke eye contact as Quentin's words came back to her: *Can you really look at her without seeing* him?

Suddenly, the closeness felt suffocating. She placed her hands on Taos's chest and gently pushed, creating space between them. She slid out from under him.

"I should go," she said. She crossed to the archway, then stopped and turned back. "She fought against my father with everything she had. I felt it. She would have died for you."

Taos remained silent. He kept his back to her and she could see his muscles tensing visibly under his shirt. He ran both hands through his hair, leaving strands sticking up wildly. When he turned to Nova, his jaw worked silently, as if he was chewing on words too painful to voice. Then, he spun on his heel and strode toward the opposite archway, disappearing into his room.

TWENTY-FOUR

Nova stood in the center of the meditation room. "I go back tomorrow."

Xander leaned against the wall, arms crossed, observing. Gus fiddled with the rice box. Kiera stood to Nova's side, her expression a mix of concern and skepticism. Taos hadn't come. Nova hadn't seen him since their tense moment in the courtyard earlier that day.

"This is my final night to learn levitation. I'll go back and convince my father of everything Berkshire has said."

Kiera paused, considering. "What if he doesn't listen, Nova?"

Of course he won't.

The only time Nova had seen a highborn's decision swayed was during her trial, when Denali had lifted an appeal. To get the highborns to listen, she needed to make their people question them.

"I have to turn Ghandrians against him."

"*If* you can do that, then what?" Kiera asked.

"Then the people start to question the system . . . and whether or not the exiles are effective."

"You haven't even mastered your levitation. You can't prove anything to them." Kiera threw her hands into the air. "We don't even know if Berkshire's theory is right!"

"I have to try. I'm running out of time."

"No."

The firm voice came from behind her. Nova spun around. Taos was standing under the archway.

"You saw what he did to Clara when she challenged him," he said.

The room fell silent. Xander let out a whistle. Gus stopped fiddling with the rice box. Nova's gaze fell to the floor.

Surely her own father wouldn't try to kill her.

"Taos is right," Kiera said. "Challenging the highborns is too dangerous."

Xander shrugged. "I say let the rookie make her own decisions."

"I'm close to levitating, I can get it," Nova said. "I have one more lesson with Berkshire and we'll figure it out."

Taos shook his head.

"I don't understand," Nova said. "I'm trying to do what you and Berkshire have been training me for."

"But it didn't work, Darkov." He stepped into the room. "It's too dangerous."

Nova's expression dropped. "Let me worry about that."

"But, Nova?" Kiera said. "You have the choice to stay there if you show them you can syphon. Our plan didn't work, but yours still can. You can be home with your brother."

Nova fidgeted with the black fabric of her top. Kiera was right, and of course Nova had thought about it. The ability to erase memories was all she ever wanted. Now that she could control her projections, she could offer them to the syphon. She wished she could tell her friends that she wouldn't syphon, that she would throw it all away and live out her days here with them. She wished she could tell Berkshire that she would take his advice and never erase a memory, no matter how much pain it caused her.

But that would be a lie.

Instead, she said, "I will do everything I can to bring you guys back."

"Gus no leave."

Nova looked at him. "What?"

"He's right," Kiera said. "Some of us built our lives here. Not everyone wants to go back. Especially not after our own families threw us out."

"Speak for yourself," Xander said. "I'm outta here the first chance I get."

"Right now, we need to focus on getting Nova back," Taos said.

"How *do* you get back?" Kiera asked.

"Morianna said the boatman would come for me," Nova said.

Taos crossed his arms. "How do you plan to make it through the forest teeming with Krall, and then make it to the Marmoris while they're swimming out to it, too."

"By tying my dress to a lumicat and sending the Krall after it."

"That's not a plan," Taos said.

"It's what got me here."

"Which is why it won't work," he said. "They won't be fooled again."

Xander chuckled. "We'll get it taken care of, rookie."

"How exactly are we supposed to do that?" Kiera asked.

"That's what our commander friend is for." He patted Taos on the back. "He'll come up with something."

"I can come up with something, sure, but that doesn't mean you'll like it."

"Just hold on," Nova said. "Don't do anything until we all agree on it."

Taos nodded toward the door where Berkshire waited. Nova watched her friends file out, still debating their next moves in hushed tones.

She settled onto the mat, crossing her legs beneath her. This was her final lesson, her last chance to prove herself in an ability she had yet to master.

Levitation.

Berkshire stood before her, his tall figure casting a long shadow in the soft glow of candlelight. The scent of burning incense filled her nostrils, soothing her nerves. She turned her palms upwards, resting them on her knees.

"Focus, kid."

Nova drew in a breath. "On what?"

"What you've learned," came the reply.

Nova began to think about her time in Nadir. She thought of her rice counting. *What have I learned?* she asked herself. Her answer came to mind moments later. She'd learned to stop fighting what she was . . . a miscreant. But she wouldn't be for much longer.

She breathed again, in and out. She thought about her training and how far she had come since she first endured the pit. She thought about her new friends, Xander, Kiera, Gus . . . Taos. She surrendered to the smile that spread across her face. She thought about meditating under the crushing weight of the waterfall and how it had become weightless when she learned to master her technique.

She'd learned to find strength within herself.

She thought about how she'd helped Taos find his parents and about how Gus had made her a dress using her favorite color. Then, she thought about Denali's betrayal. Her fingers curled against her knees. The pain of it still felt raw. She had trusted him.

What had she learned?

The answer was simple: her family was not who she thought they were. She peeked an eye open. Berkshire stood across from her, stroking his beard.

Nova halted her breathwork. She was still firmly planted on the floor. "I don't understand," she said. "I've done everything you said, but I'm still not levitating, and I'm out of time."

"What is holding you back?"

Denali's betrayal flickered in her mind, gnawing at her from within. She chewed on her inner cheek.

"You must work through it," Berkshire instructed. He took a seat in front of her. "You must *forgive* him."

Nova's expression contorted. *Forgive Denali?* Without even an apology, harboring secrets all her life?

"You're saying that's what is stopping me from levitating?"

"I cannot say what it is. I can only tell you that there is something left for you to learn. You are the one who must figure out what it is," Berkshire paused. "It would do you good to hear him out."

She scowled. "I don't want to."

"Then you are a fool." He frowned. "Not everyone receives such an opportunity."

"I'm just not ready."

With a heavy sigh, Berkshire rose. "Then, it is your pride that will be your undoing."

✦

The first light of dawn painted the sky with strokes of pink and orange. Nova stepped outside, expecting a quiet departure with her friends. Kiera and Gus stood outside the door, waiting to see her off.

Kiera offered a smile that was tinged with sadness. Gus's shoulders were hunched, making him even shorter. He perked up when he saw Nova's outfit.

His eyes grew large. "Nova wear Gus Gus dress."

Nova smiled down at him. "Of course, Gus. It's my favorite dress."

She grabbed the denim fabric in her palm, running her thumb over the sloppy but endearing black stitching of the flowers. She had made sure to wash it the day before and lay it out to dry overnight. If she could bring one thing home with her, it would be this dress that was made specially for her.

Noting the absence of two familiar faces, Nova asked, "Where are they?"

"Taking care of the Krall. They've been at it all night," Kiera said calmly, though she did a poor job of hiding her concern. "I wouldn't expect them back anytime soon."

A nagging feeling tugged at Nova. The realization that she was leaving without a proper goodbye hurt more than she cared to admit. Turning away from the door, Nova stood tall, ready to depart. To her surprise, a small group of miscreants began to trickle in and gather around the cottage, stopping right in front of Nova. She recognized a few individuals while noting the majority were strangers.

Nova leaned into Kiera. "What's going on?"

Kiera took Nova's arm. "They are here to support you."

"Support? For *me*?"

"You gave them hope, Nova," Kiera answered. "Hope to somehow get back home."

Nova chewed on her lip as she surveyed the faces in the crowd of twelve people. They were all so full of longing. Nova's heart ached for them.

The group parted and Helga walked to the forefront. With her ever-present smile, she held out a bag. Nova took it and peeked inside. It was filled with apples, vegetables, and a steaming muffin.

"Helga won't have Nova go hungry on her trip."

Nova's fingers tightened around the bag. The generosity of this woman was overwhelming.

Kiera embraced her tightly. "Be careful, Nova."

A tear slipped from Gus's eye. "Gus Gus miss Nova."

Nova swallowed, fighting against the lump forming in her throat. Her voice came out hoarse. "Nova will miss Gus too."

She took a final look around, trying to etch every detail of the cottages and her friends into her memory. Berkshire shifted, signaling that it was time to depart. Nova turned toward him, ready to go.

A small figure suddenly broke free from the farewell gathering. "Wait!" Liam sprinted forward and wrapped his arms around Nova's waist, nearly knocking her off balance. She held her hands in the air, unsure where to place them. The young student tilted his face up at hers. "Nova is soldier," he said.

Heat pricked behind Nova's eyes. She knelt down and hugged him properly. Words failed her as his small arms wrapped around her neck.

When she stood, Liam ran back to where his mother waited. Her face tight with worry, she quickly drew him behind her skirts, though she managed a stiff nod to Nova.

Nova squared her shoulders and turned to go. She and Berkshire made their way through the village, the cottages growing sparse as they approached the spora forest.

Despite her friends' assurances, the question of how they planned to clear the path to the boatman gnawed at her. They had been purposely vague, leading her to believe it was a dangerous plan that she wouldn't have agreed to. When they reached the edge of the forest, Nova couldn't help but look back. Kiera's and Gus's figures were smaller in the distance, but no less significant. Kiera's hand was lifted in a farewell gesture, her other arm wrapped around Gus. Nova willed herself to face forward.

To her astonishment, there was no sign of any Krall, only lumicats. The air was clear, the path ahead visible. She half-expected a Krall to leap out at any second. As she and Berkshire walked silently, side by side, it dawned on her that the forest was indeed clear. Somehow, Taos and Xander had fulfilled their promise.

Instead of gratitude, though, a smidge of bitterness took root in the pit of her stomach. Taos hadn't even bothered to say goodbye or see her off. He likely still hated her, and he had every reason to. But to leave knowing they might never see each other again? It felt like a low blow.

A faint *tick-tick-tick* wove through the forest, followed by a quiet wail. Nova glanced in the direction, but forced herself to keep walking, falling into step beside Berkshire. The unsettling melody continued for the next ten minutes, accompanying her until the forest finally thinned, revealing the shoreline.

Waves whispered against the sand. The Marmoris bobbed on the water, the hooded boatman waiting at its tip.

Nova's shoes sank into the sand as she reached the water's edge. She turned, meeting Berkshire's gaze one last time. Without thinking, she threw her arms around him. Berkshire stiffened, his arms hanging awkwardly at his sides, but Nova held on.

Pulling away, she avoided Berkshire's eyes and she climbed into the vessel. The boatman's hook swiveled, and the vessel lurched forward. Nova gripped the sides to steady herself. She looked back, hoping to see Berkshire, but the beach stood empty and still.

He was gone.

Water lapped against the boat's side and the Isle of Nadir grew smaller against the darkening sky. Strange, how she'd once wanted nothing more than to syphon her memories of Nadir. Now the thought of erasing it all left a bitter taste in her mouth.

Still, nothing compared to the dread of facing Denali.

Would he even remember the incident between them and Cronian?

The disappointment in Cronian's face flashed in her mind's eye. But for once, his judgment didn't make her shrink—it made her cheeks burn with anger. She bit down hard. Cronian would do anything to protect his syphon. Memories of his cruelty surfaced— lies, families torn apart, *Taos* stolen from his mother, Gus and his family shunned and forced to live in exile—all in the name of the highborns' game.

Nova stared in the direction of Ghandria as nature itself began to mirror her fury. Storm clouds gathered overhead and whirlpools churned in the channel waters. The Marmoris fought through the waves, and Nova welcomed the vessel's defiance.

She would make the highborns face every exile, every broken family, every lie they'd buried. The syphon's secrets wouldn't stay hidden forever. Not anymore. They had played their games in the shadows for too long—now she would drag them into the light.

Now, Father would play *her* game.

TWENTY-FIVE

"You still haven't told me what we're doing here," Denali said. Blythe knocked firmly on the stranger's front door, for the third time.

"If anyone knows where the sitheus supply is coming from, it's them. It has to be." She knocked again.

"It's *who*, Blythe? Who are these people?"

"The Eldens."

Blythe reached for the door handle and found it unlocked. She pushed it open and started to step inside.

Denali grabbed her by the wrist. "Whoa. What are you doing? You can't just break in."

"I'm not. The door's unlocked."

"That's still—" Denali shook his head. "We can come back later, when they're home."

"Nova's trial is tomorrow. We don't have time."

Denali hesitated. He looked around to make sure nobody was watching. Then, he followed her inside.

A pair of heavy, mud-caked boots stood next to the door. The air in the house was thick with the scent of earth and dampness. Blythe moved into the front room and began searching through shelves and drawers.

A sharp crack echoed through the house as a floorboard

splintered. Denali whirled around as a figure crept around the corner and pressed the tip of her crossbow to the back of Blythe's neck. "I didn't answer for a reason."

Blythe froze, her hands still buried in a drawer. Denali inched forward and raised his arms in surrender.

The woman's dark skin gleamed with a sheen of sweat. Toned muscles rippled beneath her olive-green utility vest, her powerful biceps exposed. Her gray afro stood out against the dim light.

"We don't mean any harm," Denali stammered. "We're looking for information about the tunnels. I'm a Darkov."

"I know who you are," she mumbled, keeping her weapon aimed on Blythe. "Do not mistake yourselves into thinking I won't shoot a highborn."

Denali raised his hands higher. "We're only trying to help a friend. We thought you might have information that could be valuable."

The woman glared. "The tunnels are *my* business."

"Well," Blythe said as she turned to face the woman, "whatever we find may just be the key to ending the syphon—"

"Blythe!" Denali yelled.

She couldn't be saying these things. If any of the highborns found out about this, the consequences would be severe.

Blythe stood her ground, facing off against the stranger. "What if it doesn't just save our friend from Nadir, but some of yours as well . . ." She lifted a picture frame showing an aged photo of two kids. "Berkshire, maybe?"

Something shifted in the woman's eyes.

Blythe flipped the picture around and read the note on the back. "Berkshire and Imani. First day of meditation class. That's you, right?"

"Burn it for all I care." She placed her finger on the crossbow's trigger. "He left us."

Denali tensed. "Blythe, maybe take a step back." He reached for her arm, but she yanked it away.

"No."

Denali stood helpless, unsure of what to do next.

"I'm sick of this," Blythe said. "Aren't you, D? Of all the exiles? Of letting the highborns pick and choose who gets to stay and who has to leave? My uncle, your sister . . ." She looked at Imani. "Your brother."

Imani narrowed her eyes.

"If you don't have the balls to do something to help them then you're just as bad as those self-serving highborn cowards." Blythe was practically spitting the words at the woman.

Denali's gaze locked onto the weapon that was still pointed straight at Blythe. His fingers twitched at his sides, torn between the instinct to reach out and the fear of making any sudden moves.

Imani's voice was cold. "Get out."

Denali reached for Blythe's hand.

"Yeah, yeah," she said. "I'm going."

Once they were out, the lock clicked behind them.

"What were you thinking!" Denali said.

"Did you see her boots?" Blythe asked, ignoring his question. "The mud on them was fresh."

"Okay . . . so?"

"So . . . do you see any mud around here?"

Denali took in their surroundings. Besides the fact that most of the roads were paved, it hadn't rained in days.

"She's been digging," Blythe said.

"How would we find out where?"

Blythe grinned. "I can think of one place we could check."

Denali's restless steps traced a path across the wide expanse of the grand hall, situated on the third level of his home. His footsteps resounded off the high, ornate ceiling. Seven steps, turn, nine steps, turn—his body finding the old pattern it knew for when thoughts of the library became too heavy to hold. And now Blythe breached those same walls he'd learned never to cross.

He drew in a steadying breath and looked out through the large, arched windows, waiting for any sign of Nova's arrival. On the grounds below, guards were ordering people into their homes. The weight of a miscreant's return seemed to loom heavily in the air.

Today would be the day he would tell Nova the truth.

Cronian watched Denali's movements with a cold detachment. "Control yourself," he said. "The very idea of allowing a filthy miscreant back into my home—"

Denali stopped in his tracks, his gaze snapping to his father. "Do not speak of her that way."

Cronian's lips twisted into a sneer. "Your 'sister' ceased to be a part of this family the moment she was exiled. Her return is a blemish on my name."

Denali gritted his teeth together. "She is no 'blemish' on our name, you pompous—"

"Hold your tongue, boy." Cronian tugged at the cuffs of his suit to straighten a single wrinkle. "I can send her back as easily as I did the first time. You would do well to remember that."

Denali's fists clenched at his sides. "You can at least allow me to escort her from the dock."

"No one is to be at that dock when she arrives. We've no idea what diseases she might have caught there. You should thank me for allowing her back inside my home at all."

The guards began to line the path leading from the dock. The town was eerily silent, the residents hidden away as if Nova's return was a harbinger of doom. Then, Denali saw her. The moment he spotted her among the guards, tension drained from his body.

Seeing her, alive and walking toward their home, ignited a spark of joy. For a moment, Denali allowed himself to bask in the simple happiness of seeing her again. Then fear began to consume him.

After I tell her, will she ever be able to look at me the same?

Will she ever trust me again?

At the sight of her passing, Ghandrians snapped their windows shut. A guard, one of many along the path, broke rank and spat at Nova's feet. Color rushed to Denali's face, his hands balled into fists so tight his knuckles whitened.

He rushed for the stairs, prepared to confront the guard's behavior head-on. Before he could get far, Cronian's hand clamped around his forearm, halting him with an iron grip.

"Enough," he hissed.

For a second, father and son faced each other, a battle of wills raging between them.

Cronian snapped his head toward Merek. "See that the maids get her filth cleaned up."

Denali tightened his jaw. Blue hair caught his eyes. Blythe was coming down the hallway. She gave Denali a single nod and he could breathe again. He hoped he had distracted Cronian long enough for her to find where the tunnel led out.

"Oh," Cronian turned to Merek. "And be sure to keep the miscreant off my floor."

Merek bowed his head as Cronian strode from the hall.

Denali descended the staircase, his anticipation mounting as he neared Nova. He reached the entrance and paused for a fraction of a second, collecting himself.

He flung the door open. The sight of her—alive, standing before him—unwound the tight knot that had been suffocating him since the day she'd left.

Denali moved to inspect her. As he grasped her by the shoulders, he quickly took in the state of her appearance. She was skinnier now, her cheekbones more pronounced than he remembered. Her skin bore freshly healed wounds, visible on her bare arms. The denim dress she wore was crusted with salt from the ocean. He lifted her chin, but rather than looking him in the eyes, she drew back. His hands fell away as she stood there, motionless, her eyes not quite meeting his.

"Nova?" His voice softened. "What happened there?"

She didn't respond immediately, her posture rigid, her silence a barrier as tangible as the walls around them. It was like her to be silent, to be still, but not with him . . . never with him.

What had she been through? What had she seen?

As the silence stretched on, Denali took a hesitant step forward, his hand outstretched, yearning to bridge the gap between them, to dissolve the iciness with a touch. But Nova's slight shift backwards was a clear rebuff, sending a message that stung more sharply than words could.

Had he done something to upset her?

His mind raced through their last interactions, searching for a clue, but finding none. The shadow of her stillness seemed to seep under his skin. It was then, watching her carefully guarded expressions, that a sliver of dread pierced him.

Could she know?

The thought was a whisper at first, but it grew louder, more insistent. He studied her, really looked at her, and saw the storm brewing in her eyes. It was a storm of hurt, of betrayal, a storm that knew the truth. Denali's heart sank. The realization hit him like a physical blow. Nova knew. Somehow, she had uncovered the truth about that day.

"Nova, please," Denali found himself saying, his voice tight. "Let me explain."

The words felt hollow even to him. How could he explain the inexplicable? How could he justify his actions that day, when he had allowed his fear and selfishness to hurt the person he loved most in this world?

Nova finally looked at him, and her pain was a mirror to the guilt that had been eating away at him for *thirteen* years. He realized then that there was no excuse, no explanation that could erase the damage he had caused.

Nova's voice thickened. "How could you hide this?" she whispered.

Denali's eyes sealed shut against her words. All those years fighting against becoming Cronian, and here he stood, hiding his darkest secret.

Proving blood would tell.

He lowered his face to hers. "That was the worst moment of my life, Nova."

She stood still, but there was a slight tremor in her hands.

"I've lived every day with that guilt. And I'll carry it for the rest of my life."

Nova's eyes were fixed on the floor, avoiding Denali's gaze. "Why didn't you erase it?"

Denali drew in a heavy breath, his tension slightly easing as Nova spoke to him, a sign that he hadn't entirely lost her.

"I thought about erasing it every day for weeks. Months. But . . ." He paused, looking away as he grappled with his memories. "I worried that if I did, it might happen again."

Denali's voice faltered, choked by the vividness of his haunting memories. His hands curled into fists at his sides as he fought against the surge of emotions. Then slowly, he forced his fingers to unfurl, trying to physically let go of the pain as he continued.

"The only way to ensure that it never happened again was for me to remember." His eyes met Nova's again. "I vowed that I would never offer a memory of you to the syphon. Those memories are too valuable to me."

Tears flowed down Nova's cheeks now. "I just need a moment."

She moved around him and began walking to the grand staircase, the guards following a few paces behind. With each step she took toward the third floor, Denali's heart grew heavier, sinking to his stomach. He started forward, then stopped, caught between the urge to follow after her and the need to respect her request. So he stood there, rooted to that spot in the front room as he listened to the sound of her footsteps fade.

The moment Nova's hands were unbound, she closed her bedroom door behind her. The facade of strength she had tried to hold onto crumbled. She slid down against her door. As she collapsed onto the floor, tears streamed down her face, not from anger or resentment toward Denali, but from a deep, aching love for him.

The revelation of his long-held guilt, his confession and his vow to protect her, had dissolved her resolve to be angry with him. It was overwhelming to realize the extent of his remorse, to understand that he had been punishing himself all these years for a mistake he'd made when he was just a child. She thought about all the times he had taken her place in the whipping chair and started shaking with sobs.

He had been living with this guilt, allowing it to eat away at him in silence. He had taken upon himself the role of her guardian, her protector, ever since he was six years old. Him believing that he deserved to bear the consequences alone cut deep, especially when the real person who should have taken the blame was their father. She wished she could have lifted some of Denali's pain the way he had lifted hers for so many years.

Deep in the back of her mind, she heard Berkshire's voice: *forgive him.*

Nova wiped her tears from her cheeks as a dawning comprehension washed over her—forgiveness wouldn't require the drawn-out process she had anticipated because she had already been working through it for years. Though her mind had blocked out the memory, her subconscious had been processing it all along.

Every time Denali had come to take her whippings in her place, she had forgiven him a little bit.

Every time he had rushed to her room to hold her during her panic attacks, she had forgiven him a little bit.

Each night as he had sat beside her bed, telling her stories of the stars when she couldn't sleep, she had forgiven him a little bit.

Nova realized that through her whole life she had, without knowing it, forgiven him completely.

A soft knock sounded on the door, stealing her from her thoughts.

"Miss?" a voice called from the other side.

Nova pushed herself up from the floor. She quickly wiped the rest of her tears with the back of her hand and managed a quiet, "Come in."

The door opened and Nova's maid entered. She gave a small gasp when she took in Nova's appearance. Nova glanced down, inspecting herself. Despite rinsing at Berkshire's before her journey home, the day's travel had taken its toll.

Her hair hung in salt-crusted tangles around her face, still damp and matted from the ocean spray and thick fog. The dress Gus had given her was wrinkled and stiff with dried seawater. Dirt clung stubbornly beneath her fingernails.

Nova's body ached from the constant tension of the journey from Nadir. The return home had thrust both her and the boatman into the heart of a storm. First came the grip of violent whirlpools, then the winds rose, bringing waves that crashed over their heads. It was nothing short of a miracle that the vessel had brought them safely to shore.

"May I?" the maid asked.

With a silent nod, Nova granted permission.

In the bathroom, her maid filled the bath with warm water. Steam rose in gentle swirls, warming the air and fogging the mirror. The maid tested the water's temperature before motioning for Nova to step in. The first touch of hot water against her toes gave her a jolt of pleasure.

As she submerged herself deeper into the bath, the warmth seeped into her bones, loosening muscles that Nova hadn't even noticed were tight. The maid retrieved a soft sponge and began the task of scrubbing Nova gently, starting with her arms. She poured warm water over Nova's head and massaged a rich lather of soap into her scalp, her fingers working through knots and tangles. Nova closed her eyes and soaked in the feeling.

Thirty minutes later, Nova stood before the mirror, draped in a flowy dress of midnight black. Her hair fell in soft, natural waves reaching down to her hips, blending seamlessly into her dress. The maid lifted her hair to begin a set of elaborate braids, but Nova waved her hand to stop her.

"No braids today, thank you."

The maid bowed her head and silently began to exit the room, grabbing the dress Gus had made for Nova on the way out.

"Wait!" Nova called out to her.

The maid halted, alarmed by Nova's actions. "Uh," Nova fumbled for words. "Don't throw it away, please. Just wash it."

The maid inspected the gown another time and scrunched her face. "Are you sure, miss?"

Nova smiled at the black flower stitching that was beginning to unravel. "Yes, I am sure."

With that, the maid left. Nova ran her hands over the soft, silk fabric. This dress was a masterpiece. Only the very best for the syphon.

The syphon.

Reality settled back in. Nova still had a job to do. She lifted her skirts off the floor and made her way down the hall toward Denali's room. She raised her hand to knock and paused. Her fist hovered in the air before his door. Doubt crept in, weaving its cold tendrils around her thoughts. She had come to tell him she'd forgiven him, but what if the words wouldn't come?

Nova let Denali's words replay in her mind. *Stop thinking the worst.*

Finally, she tapped on the door and pushed it open. Denali sat on the corner of his bed, pulling his head up from his hands when Nova entered. She took in the scene around him. Open books were sprawled across the floor, their pages filled with dense writings and markings. She sank to her knees, tracing lines of text that spoke of the syphon, its properties, its mysteries. Denali's handwriting was scrawled across the pages in blue ink.

Nova continued to study the scattered research, then she looked up to meet her brother's gaze. He held it like something breakable. She frowned at his forearms, wrapped in cloth bandages to conceal his scars that far outnumbered her own. He'd taken every single one of her lashes since the accident.

Nova peeled one of his notes from a book page and turned it over. She grabbed a pen and wrote a few words. Then, she stood and placed it in his palm.

He opened and read, *Lu mea evoradara.*

Denali seemed to deflate, a visible sigh of relief escaping him. The tension in the room dissipated and he stood. Nova closed the distance between them, wrapping her arms around him, tucking her head under his chin. Denali's frame trembled in Nova's as she held him.

He backed up, searching her face. "There are so many things to say."

"No." Nova shook her head. "There is *one* thing to say."

She took Denali's hand in hers. "You have spent your whole life caring for me and raising me. You took on responsibilities that never should have been expected of you. I'm the one that's sorry, Denali. I'm sorry you have had to do all of this on your own."

Something almost like a smile touched his mouth, gone before it fully formed. "Taking care of you was never a burden."

"But it wasn't meant to be your job."

Denali went quiet. The way he looked at her reminded her of when they were children, before the weight of everything else.

"There's something I've been working on." Nova lowered to the floor and scooted the books aside, making a clearing for herself. With their relationship beginning to heal, she was certain that the shackles which had grounded her to the earth were finally gone. Today, she would levitate. She settled into her meditative position, palms turned upwards. Closing her eyes, she inhaled deeply, drawing in the peace and serenity of her surroundings, and released slowly, letting go of any lingering doubts.

Focus, Nova, she told herself.

Her mind wandered through her journey in Nadir, not to dwell on the pain or the betrayals but to acknowledge her growth, and the strength she had found within herself. And in finding herself, she had forgiven Denali.

Surely, this act of letting go, of overcoming such a deep-seated emotional hurdle, would be the key to unlocking her ability. With another breath, Nova concentrated on the feeling of lightness, imagining herself rising from the floor. She waited, expecting any moment to feel the distance between her and the ground increase, to experience the exhilarating sensation of defying gravity.

But nothing happened.

Nova remained firmly seated, as connected to the ground as ever. Confusion clouded her mind. She had done everything right, had worked through her emotions, had practiced diligently. She had even forgiven Denali, something she'd thought would take years. Yet, gravity held her as tightly as it always had.

Nova opened her eyes. Denali watched quietly. The certainty she had felt was replaced by a plague of questions.

Have I truly forgiven Denali?

Is there something else, some other lesson I need to learn?

She searched for anything Berkshire had said to explain why it might not have worked, but she had done everything he'd instructed. She dropped her head in defeat. Maybe Berkshire's theory was wrong. Denali crouched down beside her.

"It didn't work." Her voice was barely a whisper. "I don't know why it didn't work."

Denali took Nova's hands in his. She blinked back tears. Without levitation, she would never be able to get the highborns to listen. Her friends were counting on her. Now, she had no way to help them.

She had failed them.

Words have power, kid. Berkshire's voice drifted through her memory. *If you fail, it is because you chose to.*

Nova sat in silence with Denali, turning those words over and over. She glanced at the window and noticed a small, potted plant that sat in the frame. It was scrawny, but something about it resonated with her. She reached out and grabbed it, noticing the bud that was beginning to bloom—a tiny, lavender flower. Her fingers traced it delicately. When Denali saw it, he snatched the pot from her and brought the flower up to his right eye. "It's not decaying," he said. "It's *blooming*."

Nova gave him a wild look. "Yeah . . . I can see that."

Denali jolted into action. He grabbed his bag from across the room and put the plant in it.

"What are you doing?" Nova asked.

The bathroom door swung open and Nova spun around.

"Welcome back, little Darkov," Blythe said. "For the record, I told him you'd forgive him."

Nova's surprise softened into relief. Denali rarely brought

Blythe into their home, but Nova had always loved when she came around. There was something freeing about her absolute refusal to tiptoe around anything.

"Eavesdropping, are we?" Denali asked.

"I wasn't eavesdropping. I was *listening*. I have ears, D—that's kind of what they do." She turned her attention to Nova again. "Hate to ruin the moment, Little D, but I gotta know. Did you learn to syphon?"

Instead of answering, Nova met her gaze with a quiet confidence. She brought a memory to the forefront of her mind. The projection materialized before her effortlessly—the scene of young Denali in the library.

Awe spread across Denali's features. "Nova, you're doing it."

"I've learned a lot," she said.

Blythe dropped a small book onto the floor. "So have we."

Nova's projection dissipated as she stared at the book, transfixed by the words "Journal of Lucien Darkov."

Denali mumbled, "'Don't take anything' was my one rule. Do you ever follow the rules?"

"Rules are for boneheads," Blythe said. "I found some real creepy stuff on the Bloodthornes too."

Denali sighed, rubbing his forehead. "Did you at least find any information on—"

Blythe shushed him and pressed her finger to his lips. She pointed up to where Cronian's floor was. Then, she switched on a music player in the room. "Just in case."

Denali repeated his question, lowering his voice this time. "Any information on the sitheus?"

Blythe shook her head. "No. There were no tunnel plans or any hint of where the spora would be."

"Spora?" Nova pipped her head up. "You mean like the ones in Nadir?"

Denali and Blythe both sat up. "What?" Denali said. "There's mushrooms in Nadir?"

"Only a whole forest of them."

Blythe and Denali turned to face each other.

"Do you think . . . ?" Blythe asked.

"No way," Denali said.

Blythe tilted her head with a questioning glance.

"Even if there was," Denali said, "we have no idea where the opening is."

Nova raised her hand in the air. "What am I missing?"

"Yes, the highborns know. Cronian ordered me to tell everyone it was stable."

"It actually absorbed *into* someone?" Nova clarified.

Denali nodded.

She pressed her fingertips to both temples as she processed the new information.

Denali stood. "If we can find the tunnel and figure out a way to cut off their supply—"

"D, there's no time. Even if we found it, who's to say there's not another one somewhere else?" Blythe said.

Sighing, Nova slumped onto Denali's bed. If everything in the journal was true, that meant Ghandrians were sneaking into Nadir and taking extractions from the spora. How had nobody noticed? She tried to think of a place the tunnel might lead out to—any hint. It would have to be in the forest so they could slip in and out without being noticed.

Something clicked.

"Wait."

She recalled the night she and her friends had an encounter with the toxins. "Never wear purple around the lumicats," she repeated Xander's words to her that night.

Now she understood why the lumicat had attacked her on her first day in Nadir. Her dress had been the same purple shade as the hazmat suit. The cat must have mistaken her for one of them. It wasn't a mindless attack. The cats had learned who their enemies were. They were protecting their land.

Denali and Blythe exchanged glances, their raised eyebrows silently urging her to explain.

"I saw someone one night," Nova said. "I thought it was a trick of my mind at the time, but someone was there in a biohazard suit. They must have been there for extractions."

There were a few seconds of silence. Blythe took a seat. She shook her head and started to chuckle. "There's been a tunnel to Nadir *all this time*? A connection from here to there? From me to my uncle?" Her laugh died down. "Let's get these bastards."

"We need a plan," Denali said.

Nova stood and surveyed the jumbled board on Denali's wall. They needed to find a way to stop the extractions. If they could show the syphon having one of its outbursts, then it would help the people see how dangerous it was.

Wait.

"Cutting off the supply isn't the only way to show the syphon is unstable." Nova looked at them. "Round everyone up. We're moving my trial."

TWENTY-SIX

Nova winced at the onslaught of sunlight as she was led out of her home. The rough fibers of the rope bit into the tender skin of her wrists. The guards escorted her toward the syphon for one final test. She kept her gaze fixed straight ahead. It was a weird hazy deja vu feeling, kind of like she never left. Like the last sixty days hadn't happened at all. Everything looked the same, yet everything felt different.

Cronian and Morianna led the way to the cavern. A guard wheeled Archaelus beside them. His head rested against his wheelchair and his eyes were open only a crack. Nova couldn't tell if he was asleep, or . . . something else. The town was unnaturally silent. There were no people staring from their windows, no kids playing out front.

Morianna scanned the vacant doors. "Where are my Ghandrians?"

The guards came to a halt. Cronian paused, taking in the still town. His gaze landed on Nova, boring into her with unsettling intensity. She kept her expression carefully neutral as she shrugged in response to his unspoken question.

He commanded the guards behind Nova to search the area. Then, faintly at first, a low murmur began to build in the distance. Cronian whistled and the guards resumed their positions in formation around the highborns. Their hands reached for their dualfates and they moved toward the sound.

The murmurs grew clearer as they left the abandoned streets behind, following the sound along the forest path. In the distance, a seething mass of humanity surrounded the cavern's entrance. The entire town had come.

Good.

Cronian's focus settled on Denali, who was positioned in the gaping mouth of the cave. Blythe stood beside him.

"What is this?" Cronian snarled.

"Ah, Father. Running a little late, are we?" Denali said. "Now that our beloved highborns are here, we may proceed."

Morianna cocked her head to the side. "Proceed with what exactly, child?"

Denali moved to address the crowd. "The highborns have graciously asked me to preside over this trial. I will now ask my sister to come forward."

Cronian took one step, his expression hardening.

Denali held his father's stare. "The people have come to witness her syphoning. They are anxious to clear the Darkov name. And I have seen her newfound ability with my own eyes."

The assembly stirred. Cronian measured the gathered witnesses, his rigid stance easing.

"By all means, enlighten us," Morianna hissed. "We would love nothing more than to clear the Darkov name."

Archaelus's head fell back in his chair and everyone turned their attention to him. A guard placed two fingers against his pulse point. After a few seconds, the guard nodded and the group's focus returned to Morianna.

Nova watched Blythe at the front of the gathering. At her signal, Nova took her place at the yawning entrance of the cave. She stood at the threshold and the cool shadows from within reached out to her. The syphon itself remained hidden in the depths of the cave.

But not for long.

Denali's readings of Grandfather's journal had taught them that the syphon was drawn to offered memories like a magnet. She needed to coax it out and make it visible to everyone for this to work.

Nova faced the people and, for a few seconds, the weight of their judgment pressed down on her. It felt as heavy as when she'd sat under the full force of the waterfall in Nadir. She closed her eyes and let the world fall away as she honed in on her breaths. The noise and the pressure faded into the background and when she opened her eyes again, she was ready.

She lifted her palms in the air, not bothering to kneel before she began. "In release, we find freedom. In forgetting, we find peace. Praise the syphon. For through it, we are healed." The ritual words carried their usual weight, but this time she proceeded without looking to the highborns for permission.

She poured her energy into the memory of Denali's young face and it took shape before her.

"Hold on, Nova," he sobbed. "I can fix this."

Crackles from the fireplace emanated from the projection.

Then, a new sound began to fill Nova ears—the soft, insistent hum of the syphon. It was a siren song, whispers that tugged at something deep within her. Nova focused harder.

Slowly, almost imperceptibly at first, the syphon began to move. Nova felt it like a physical thing, a magnetic pull that drew her forward. The soft voices from the syphon grew clearer. The Ghandrians fell into a hush, as if they could feel it in the air. The clouds darkened the atmosphere around them. And then, the syphon emerged from the cavern, its dark, swirling form filling the entrance like a living shadow. Awe swept through the crowd as they watched.

Nova felt the eyes of the highborns boring into the back of her head. She stared straight into the syphon. The blackness writhed in front of her, inches from her projected memory. Her fingertips tingled from the sensation. Her memory played through again. There were no flickers, no breaks. It was a flawless projection. No fighting or rejecting—Nova had accepted this memory. She was taken aback by an urge to give in, to drain it into the syphon. If she held it there a little bit longer, it would belong to the syphon, instead of plaguing her thoughts. She would never have to think about the accident or about how her father could do something so cruel. She could forget all of it and then she could belong here. *Really* belong. As a highborn with Denali. That was all she'd ever wanted.

The syphon began to unfurl, its black tendrils stretching toward her memory. Nova felt herself sway forward, drawn in by the promise of oblivion, of a fresh start. No burden of her past following her anymore.

Don't try to silence the past. Taos's words cut through the temptation. *That's what he's trying to teach you.*

The faces of her miscreant friends rose to her mind. Taos, with his devotion to finding his family. Berkshire's loyalty to meditation. Gus and Kiera's kindness toward her when she had done nothing to earn it. They were outcasts, like her. *They* were the ones who had shown her a different meaning of belonging.

And she had made them a promise.

With a sudden, wrenching effort, she withdrew her memory from the syphon's grasp, and the projected image dissolved into the air.

The town erupted into a frenzy of murmurs. Cronian's lips curled in disgust. "What are you doing?" he snarled. "Finish it."

She looked squarely at her father. His jaw muscles twitched beneath the skin. His nostrils flared as he drew in a breath. A veil lifted, and Nova saw the monster from Clara's memories.

"And if I don't?" she asked.

A shadow passed over Cronian's face. His voice was a low, menacing hiss. "When a threat comes to the syphon, I will not hesitate to eradicate it." He ground his teeth together. "Finish it, *girl.*"

"No."

Cronian's hatred bore into her soul. "I will ensure you spend the rest of your pathetic days on that accursed isle," he spat. "You will be forgotten by all, pruned and left to wither and die as an outcast . . . a *miscreant.*"

Nova braced herself for the familiar sting of his words, the shame he'd always made her feel. To her surprise, though, the blow never came. Instead, a sense of peace settled over her. She *was* different, a miscreant in the eyes of all. She'd rather be a miscreant to these strangers, though, than a highborn in the eyes of her friends. And she'd rather keep every single memory with Denali in it. Those memories, no matter how painful, had shaped the person she had become. They had shaped her and Denali's childhoods. Erasing them wouldn't be true to who she was. She looked up at her brother and felt a lightness seep into her being.

And then Nova's feet began to lift off the earth. She rose inch by inch as gravity released its pull on her. Her hair floated freely above her shoulders, reaching toward the clouds as if drawn up by some invisible force. Nova stared around her in awe at her ascent. She surrendered to the sensation of weightlessness.

The sensation of freedom.

Below, Ghandrians stood speechless. Blythe's jaw hung open.

Nova's voice rang out clear and strong, cutting through the stunned silence. "The syphon is not what you think."

Cronian was seething. Morianna placed a steadying hand on his arm.

Nova fixed her father with a piercing stare. "But you already knew that, didn't you? You knew syphoning was the reason people lost their ability to levitate. You knew, and you banished them anyway."

The crowd fell deathly silent, all eyes fixed on Cronian, waiting for an answer.

"Cronian," Morianna growled in warning.

A voice rose from the mass. "That's why he banished the professors?"

The accusation sparked an explosion of whispers.

"Silence!" Cronian roared.

Morianna leaned closer to him. "I told you we should have erased the memories of levitation all together. Deal with this."

Nova remained suspended in the air. She lifted her chin, her gaze steady on Cronian's face. "Have your lies finally caught up to you, Father?"

A dangerous glint crossed Cronian's features. "You don't know the things of which you speak, miscreant."

"Don't I?" Nova's voice carried a sharp challenge. "What about Clara?"

Cronian's reaction was immediate. His head jerked upward.

"It was the strangest thing, meeting her and Nathaniel in Nadir, both very much *alive*."

A dark-haired woman stepped forward. "Clara? But her family was taken by the disease . . ."

"Yes, explain that, Father?" Nova said. "Explain how I met her, her husband, *and* her son."

The color drained from Cronian's face. He looked from her to Denali, and then to the people.

"And Finnian?" Denali announced. "Another 'illness,' Cronian? Or will you confess it was the syphon that truly killed him?"

"What did he say?" A man with a long, bushy beard pushed through to the front. "What about my boy?"

"When it comes to protecting the syphon"—Cronian darkened —"I will not hesitate."

Unease settled over the crowd. "That's my son!" the man yelled.

Denali lifted his chin. "It's time for the highborns' reign to end."

Malice glinted in Morianna's eyes. "*You* are a highborn, child."

"I resign," he said.

Morianna cackled into the cold air. "This reign cannot end. Our society, our *existence* relies on our ability to prune and evolve."

"You're wrong, Morianna." Denali reached into his bag. "You view the miscreants as the problem, as the thing leaching our roots of their energy . . ."

"And who else would be to blame, young Darkov?"

He pulled the plant from his bag. The small twig's flower was beginning to bloom. Recognition flickered across Morianna's features.

"A flower cannot sprout from poisoned roots," Denali said.

Morianna stiffened. Ghandrians blinked back at her. There was a look of venom in her eyes—for the first time, her subjects were questioning her.

She turned back to Denali, her face like ice.

"Grab him," she said to the guards. Immediately, two guards seized Denali, pulling him down to his knees.

Nova dropped back down to the earth. "Wait!"

Behind her, Merek grasped her hands and lowered her onto her knees beside Denali.

A woman pushed through the onlookers and grabbed Blythe by the wrist. Blythe yanked her hand back. Shortly after, a man joined. Nova watched their bickering. The woman turned to Morianna and bowed her head. "Excuse our daughter. She is not a part of this."

Blythe scoffed. "Screw off."

"It was her miscreant uncle," her mom said. "He's responsible for filling her head with this nonsense."

Blythe's body tensed. She spun to face the people. "Look around you!" she yelled. "How many of your loved ones have you lost because of these *tyrants*! We can't keep living like this!"

A hush fell over the crowd. Heads turned, eyes looking to neighbors and friends.

Blythe's mother begged, "Blythe, stop this madness."

Morianna surveyed the scene with cold calculation. She turned to the guards. "No one escapes."

The guards moved as one at her command, their weapons drawn as they encircled the Ghandrians. The gathered people looked frantically between each other and the advancing guards.

Cronian strode forward and grabbed the woman who had spoken out about Clara. The woman cried out as he dragged her by her arm. He threw her at the feet of the syphon.

"Erase it," he said.

The woman shook her head, her lips moving in a silent plea for mercy.

Cronian snatched a dagger from his waistband and leveled it at the woman's jugular. She whimpered when its tip bit into her flesh.

"Erase it," Cronian repeated. "Or I will paint the walls of this cavern with the crimson of your blood."

Tears streamed down her face. Shakily, she lifted her palms upwards and brought a projection into view in front of her. It displayed the entire scene of Nova levitating and the discussion of

Clara. Nova watched in horror as the syphon claimed her memory. Afterward, the woman sat still, her eyes blank.

Panic exploded through the crowd like a wildfire. They pressed against each other, strapped in a suffocating mass of humanity. The guards stood like an impenetrable wall. A woman screamed. Others took up the cry. Their hands beat uselessly against the hard metal of the guards' armor, but the guards did not flinch.

Morianna stood beside Cronian. Her eyes glinted with cruel amusement. She motioned a guard forward. "Bring us more."

TWENTY-SEVEN

Ghandrians pushed and shoved, seeking any gap or weakness in the guard line. In the crush, some lost their footing. Women stumbled. Children wailed, their small hands clutching at their parents' clothes as the surging mass of bodies threatened to separate them. The air grew thick with the stench of sweat.

One by one, people were plucked from the throng and brought before the syphon, placed in front of those who lined up willingly. It baffled Nova that some of them stayed loyal to the syphon and the highborns after everything they had just witnessed.

Among the willing stood Hubert, a man Nova had seen syphon more than anyone else. His decision was no surprise to her. Blythe's father stood in line behind him while Blythe's mother continued trying to pull Blythe in. She was yelling at Blythe now. The rest of the line was filled with unfamiliar faces, except for a couple tutors and one of Denali's professors who stood calmly, stroking her fingertips over the fur of a fluffy white cat in her arms.

When their erasure was finished, they were led away by the guards. Through it all, Morianna and Cronian watched with cold, pitiless eyes. They stood like kings surveying their subjects. The guards continued to add to the line behind the syphon. One by one, each of them was forced to erase their memory of the recent events.

The syphon absorbed each memory effortlessly.

Come on, Nova begged. *We have to be close. Just a few more memories.*

She looked at Denali, seeing her own tension mirrored in his face. A bead of sweat trickled down his temple as he watched the syphon . . . waiting. She followed his gaze there, acutely aware of the tightness spreading through her. The truth was, they had no idea how many memories it would take for the syphon to reach its capacity, but if a whole town of people couldn't overwhelm it, they would have to find another way. With each memory absorbed, the syphon's glow intensified slightly. Was it her imagination, or was the surface beginning to roil more violently? Nova held her breath, waiting for the moment when the syphon would finally reach its breaking point.

Beside Cronian, Morianna gleamed as she scanned the crowd for the next participants. A subtle smirk played at the corners of her mouth. She was reveling in the control, completely unaware that each command played directly into Nova's plan.

Morianna's attention settled on a small figure huddled amongst the chaos, and with a flick of her wrist, she signaled to the guards. They reached out like talons to seize their prey. A high-pitched scream pierced the air as they dragged a young boy forward. He thrashed and wailed. Dread punched through Nova. The boy couldn't have been more than six years old, his cheeks still round with baby fat. His lower lip quivered as he clutched a wooden toy soldier.

Nova's eyes burned with unshed tears. She had felt the boy's terror herself. She could taste the metallic tang of his panic on her tongue.

With a grunt, Nova wrenched herself free from the guards' grasp and jumped forward. Her fingers had barely brushed Morianna's sleeve when the guards caught her again. "End this, Morianna!" she screamed, still fighting their grip.

"Well, well." A grin spread across Morianna's face as she purred. "It appears our little Darkov traitor has a soft spot for children. Now that you can erase your memory, let's put it to the test."

280

"I will *never*."

Morianna threw her head back and unleashed a burst of laughter. "These miscreants . . . these *creatures* that seem to have swayed your allegiance?" Her laughter dwindled to a menacing quiet, her gaze hardening into a mask of cold contempt. "They are nothing but carrion to be picked clean, mere scraps to be scavenged by the elite. They are *abominations* against our divine order."

She pulled out a dagger and pressed it against Denali's throat. Nova's whole body went rigid.

"Do not underestimate me, youngborn," she said. "Choose now with whom your loyalties lie."

Nova opened her mouth to speak, but Blythe's voice cut through the tension. "You know, Morianna, I was doing a bit of light reading and I stumbled upon something interesting."

"Quiet, child. I have no time for your antics," Morianna said.

"It appears that your grandfather had some misgivings about you becoming a highborn, but he passed away right before you took the throne," Blythe said. "Funny timing there, don't you think?"

Morianna's face paled slightly, her composure slipping for a split second before she regained control.

Mrs. Pierce's hand tightened around Blythe's wrist. "Blythe, stop it," she warned.

Morianna's eyes darkened. "Bring her to the front of the line," she said to a guard.

He took Blythe's arms, separating her from her mother, and dragged her to the front of the line.

Denali broke free of his captor. His fist connected with the guard's jaw, sending him reeling. Two more guards tackled him from behind. He roared as he twisted and bucked against their restraint, but they held firm. They forced Denali to his knees again, pinning his arms behind his back.

In front of Blythe, the young boy held his palms up to the syphon. Nova couldn't bear to watch. She turned her head from the scene, but Morianna's fingers were suddenly digging into Nova's jaw, gripping it with an intense strength as her long nails tore into Nova's skin. Morianna forced Nova's head back toward the boy.

Her breath was hot and foul against Nova's cheek. "Do not turn away from our utopia."

She pointed one long, bony finger at the boy, at the projection that hovered before his face. He was sobbing openly now. Snot and tears mingled on his chin. The sight of it, the raw, primal desperation, was like a knife to Nova's gut.

"Those emotions don't ever have to be felt here. In a few seconds, that boy's memory will be free of this burden. He won't be afraid anymore. The syphon is not the villain, Bellanova. It is our *savior*."

Nova watched helplessly as the boy's projection faded into the syphon and the light drained from his eyes, replaced by a milky white until he blinked it away. A guard hastily led him out while another one pushed Blythe into position.

When she refused, the guard pulled out his dualfate. Blythe spat at his feet, the glob landing with a splat on his polished boot.

He tightened his hand around his weapon, and Morianna's cool voice wound between them. "Now, now," she said. "Let's not be hasty, Miss Pierce. We wouldn't want any *accidents* to happen to your parents, would we?"

Nova's eyes snapped to Blythe's parents, who were now being restrained by guards.

"Blythe, please," her father entreated in a low tone. "End this nonsense."

Blythe slumped, and then fixed Morianna with a hostile stare. "You'll pay for this, you psychotic wretch."

Morianna clicked her tongue.

Blythe turned to face the syphon.

✦

Denali strained against his captors. He watched as Blythe knelt down.

282

From somewhere in the crowd, a familiar sneering voice called out, "Not so tough now, are you, Darkov?"

Slater.

Denali ignored the comment, keeping his focus on Blythe. She projected her memory, the shimmering image hovering in the air before her. The syphon reached its tendrils out to consume the memory, but when it touched her projection, it paused. Denali went still. The image hung in the air, tantalizingly close to the syphon's writhing surface. A sudden, high-pitched whine pierced the air. The shoving among the Ghandrians halted.

Come on. Let this be it.

He glanced at Nova. She gave him a hopeful look and then turned her attention back to the syphon. The sound grew louder, building to an unbearable shriek. Everyone clutched their ears.

The syphon's surface began to ripple and distort. Black mist churned.

Morianna's triumphant expression faded.

Then, with a shattering wail, the syphon erupted.

Jets of inky black mist shot out in all directions, enveloping guards and citizens alike. The mist seemed alive, coiling and twisting as it sought out victims. Ghandrians screamed and ran in all directions, colliding with each other in their desperation to escape. Slater plowed through the mob, knocking women and children aside.

At the edge of the crowd, Professor Cleghorn was knocked onto hands and knees. "Merciful Magnus!" he squealed.

"Hold them!" Cronian shouted.

Archaelus jerked upright in his chair, gasping at this interruption to his slumber. He squinted, surveying the area. He started to yell but then passed out again.

Denali's eyes widened as a bolus of black mist headed straight for him.

"Duck!" Nova screamed.

He dropped, feeling the rush of the air as the mist passed overhead, striking one of his captors instead. The guard's hold loosened, and Denali saw his opportunity. He drove his elbow back into the guard's unprotected midsection. Then he spun around and head butted the other guard. The man staggered back.

Denali's eyes found Nova, still held firmly by Merek. Denali paused, muscles tense, his mind racing as he assessed the situation. Merek was stronger, more experienced. But he held the one thing that Denali had fought for his entire life.

Nova.

Denali charged forward, feinting left before diving right. Merek, anticipating the move, released Nova and shifted his stance. His experience showed—he countered Denali's moves with practiced ease.

Merek reached behind him, drawing his dualfate from its harness. The blade whistled through the air, slicing across Denali's arm. The fabric of his shirt split open, revealing a deep gash underneath. Blood welled up, staining the torn edges of Denali's sleeve. Before the crimson could spread farther, the wound sealed itself shut.

Merek pressed on, screaming as his weapon found Denali's side, then his shoulder, then his waist. Stars exploded in Denali's vision. He fell to his knees, clutching his stomach. The taste of blood filled his mouth.

"Such weak blood from such strong stock." Merek leveled one tip of his dualfate at Denali's throat. "The great Cronian's legacy, reduced to this—two mewling failures."

Denali's hand shot up, fingers wrapping around the naked blade inches from his neck. He clenched his fist, letting steel bite deep into his palm, and wrenched the weapon from Merek's grasp. Then, Denali drew in a deep breath, summoning his remaining strength. The gashes on his side, shoulder, waist, and hand began to knit themselves shut in unison. He lifted his palm to the air, inspecting it as the fresh cut sealed itself into a faint line and then disappeared entirely.

Merek stumbled backwards. His eyes darted from Denali's healed side to his palm, pupils dilating in shock. "Impossible," he breathed.

Denali raised the dualfate at Merek. His own blood trickled

down the length of the blade. The tattered remains of Denali's shirt revealed his newly healed skin underneath. Merek's face drained of color and he staggered back, his legs giving way beneath him. He crumpled onto the ground and lifted both hands to shield himself. Denali scoffed and threw the weapon to the side.

Merek's face flushed bright red, veins protruding from his neck. He sprang to his feet again, yelling out in the process.

A blur of blue flashed in Denali's peripheral vision. Blythe launched onto Merek's back. She dug her fingers deep into his eye sockets.

"Straight for the eyes!" she yelled.

Merek howled as he threw her off. His hands flew to his face, clawing at his eyes. He cursed and felt around blindly for his dualfate.

Blythe scrambled to her feet.

"Get Nova!" Denali yelled.

Merek began to stand and Denali shifted his stance.

This ends here.

✦˙

Nova was wiggling, trying to free her wrists from the tight bindings Merek had tied around them. Blythe's fingers worked quickly at the knots, but just as Nova's bonds fell away, a hand shot out from behind her and grabbed a fistful of her black hair. Cronian yanked her back, eliciting a cry of pain.

Blythe sprang forward, but Cronian caught her by the throat and tossed her to the side.

He pulled Nova closer to his face. "You ungrateful little *nothing*. This is how you repay me for all I've endowed you with? By trying to destroy my good name! You are a Darkov. Your blood is *mine*." His grip tightened around her hair and she winced. "Your hair is *mine*." He dragged her toward the syphon.

Nova caught sight of the dagger attached to his belt. She shot her hand out, grabbing it from his scabbard. She swung the blade upward, slicing through the hair that Cronian clutched tightly. A chunk of her dark locks fell away, freeing her from his grasp.

Cronian stumbled back, stunned, still holding the severed fistful of Nova's hair. Taking advantage of his surprise, Nova spun around, the dagger now pointed directly at her father.

Cronian's face contorted with rage. "You dare turn on your own blood?"

Nova flinched at his words. "You've established a society that tears families apart. You banish innocents you deem lesser than yourself. How dare *you*, Father? How dare *you* turn against *them*."

She lifted the dagger higher. "Back away or I will show you how much I can turn on my own blood."

Cronian's eyes flashed with hatred. "Everything I do is for our blood . . . for Lucien. The syphon enables this utopia."

"Look around," Nova said.

The syphon shrieked, spewing black mist in violent bursts. Ghandrians continued to run in panic. Guards wrestled with citizens, forcing them to submit. Four bodies lay motionless on the ground.

"You've created a world where people can silence their past, erase their pain . . . and lose themselves in the process," Nova said. "Every memory offered to the syphon takes a piece of who they are. This isn't the utopia Lucien dreamed of, Father. We're not healing people—we're *erasing* them."

Something flickered in Cronian's eyes—doubt, perhaps, or a glimmer of realization. But it was quickly consumed by something else. "I've created a world where we are on top!" he screamed, spittle flying from his lips. "You cannot take that from me!"

He lunged and seized Nova's wrist, twisting it violently, and forcing her to drop the dagger. Pain shot through her arm as she struggled against his grasp. Then, a new voice penetrated the chaos.

"Enough."

Nova whipped her head around to see a stranger—a muscular dark-skinned woman with a striking gray afro—standing a few feet away, her crossbow aimed steadily at her.

No . . . not at her.

At Father.

His grip on Nova's wrist loosened and Nova jumped away from him, stumbling back to where Denali and Blythe were now approaching. Both of them halted at the scene. Denali reached out and grasped Nova's hand.

Cronian's voice dropped to a sinister whisper as he advanced on the woman. "*Imani Elden.* For this treachery, I'll find the remains of your pathetic family—"

An arrow sailed through the air and sank into Cronian's thigh. Seething through clenched teeth, he took another step. The woman cocked her weapon back and sent a second arrow in his other thigh. He grunted and dropped to his knees. Blood seeped through his clothing. Nova's eyes doubled in size.

Cronian glared at Imani, each word dripping with venom, "First you expose her secret, now you play the savior. Which betrayal will be your last, I wonder?"

The color drained from Nova's face as she stared at the stranger. This was who had exposed her?

Beside Nova, Denali stiffened, his hold on her hand tightening. Blythe slowly shook her head. "That's messed up, dude."

Nova searched Imani's face for any kind of emotion, but found only an unreadable mask. The woman's gaze remained fixed on Cronian, her crossbow still trained on his kneeling form.

"Come." She then lowered her crossbow and turned.

Nova, Denali, and Blythe stood motionless. Cronian was clutching his wounded legs and yelling for the guards. Nova looked back to see Imani disappearing into the cave behind the erupting syphon. Snapping into action, she rushed after the woman. Denali and Blythe followed close behind. As they entered the cave, the air grew cooler. Imani moved fast, and they struggled to keep up.

Nova's mind raced. How had Imani seen her and Denali that night? Why was she helping them now, after exposing their secret?

Imani stopped and knelt down. In the dim light, Nova barely made out her hands moving across the rocky terrain. There was a soft scraping sound, and then a section of the ground lifted, revealing a trapdoor.

Realization dawned on Nova. This was how Imani had witnessed their practice that night without being noticed.

"In," she said.

Denali went first, lowering himself into the dark opening of a tunnel. Blythe followed, her vibrant hair disappearing into the shadows.

Nova hesitated for a split second, casting one last look toward the cave entrance. Screams still sounded outside. Nova turned back, coming face to face with Imani and pausing. "Why are you helping us?"

Without a word, she reached out, offering Nova a folded piece of paper. Nova took the note and opened it. It was identical to the one she had been given sixty days earlier. Only, this one read, "Goodbye, brother."

Nova's fingers went numb around the paper. "You're the one who gave me that note on the day of my exile . . . You're Berkshire's sister?"

Imani stared at her blankly. "In."

Nova obeyed and descended into the tunnel. As soon as her feet touched the ground, footsteps thundered from above. The guards were coming.

Nova craned her neck. "Hurry!" she said.

Imani remained above ground, her crossbow at the ready.

"Come on, we have to go!" Nova yelled.

The woman stared down at her, expressionless. Then, she closed the steel hatch, plunging Nova into darkness. Moments later, the muffled sounds of shouts and crossbow bolts penetrated the earth above.

Denali lit a small lantern and an amber glow illuminated the path ahead. He zipped up his backpack and slung it over his shoulders. It was the same backpack he had brought when they first tried to escape Ghandria. The lantern's glow revealed a corridor that stretched into the darkness, the ground sloping steeply downward. The dirt walls were lined with ribbed metal arches and intermittent concrete pillars. The air was musty and stuffy, filled with the scent of damp earth and the faint, metallic tang of rust.

"Where's Imani?" Blythe asked.

Nova frowned and squoze the note in her palm. It would feel cruel giving this to Berkshire. If Imani knew there was a tunnel leading to him, why had she never gone to see him? Her heart twinged with pain.

"She's not coming," Nova said.

"We need to go," Denali said. "Now."

Nova hesitated, her eyes traveling back up to the trapdoor. "But Imani—"

"Nova," he interrupted. "We have to move."

With a last, pained look at the ceiling, Nova nodded.

"Okay," she said. "Let's move."

Denali's frantic sprint had long since slowed to a steady walk behind Nova and Blythe. The lantern had gone out, and he paused to relight it, carefully cupping his hand to protect the fragile flame as it took hold once more. They had been running for hours and the aching in his joints told him that it was long past bedtime. Blythe was running her fingertips along the side of the tunnel. As they walked in silence, Denali took in the reality of their situation.

They had left home.

Challenged the highborns.

Revoked their titles.

Now, they were headed to the last place he had ever thought to find himself.

The Isle of Nadir.

Denali straightened. Fear was only meant to be felt behind closed doors. For now, he would push his emotions aside and make sure Nova felt safe.

"Don't be afraid," he said.

"I am not afraid."

Her response jarred him. The old Nova would have curled into herself by now, needing hours of gentle coaxing before she'd speak a word.

A tear slipped down her cheek. "I'm sorry."

"For what?"

"You lost everything because of me. Our father, our home." She wiped at her nose. "It's all my fault."

Denali smiled. "And I would give it up over and over again."

"What about your friends?"

He gestured toward her and Blythe. "They're all here."

"Touched, D," Blythe muttered from behind them, still tracing a finger along the wall.

Nova sniffled and wiped at her nose.

"Wow," Denali said. "Wowwwww."

Nova rolled her eyes. "Not this again."

"You know my favorite thing about tunnels?"

"What?"

"They always lead somewhere better than where you came from."

"Once again," she said, "you made that up."

Denali crossed an X over his heart. "Honest, I swear."

The look she gave him was one he remembered well—pretending to be annoyed while failing completely.

As they pressed on, he sifted through his bag and pulled out a book.

"What's that?" Nova asked.

"I found it in the library and held onto it. It has some information on the lost power."

"Not a power," Blythe mumbled from behind them.

Nova ignored her and reached out to take the book from Denali. "I would have thought Father'd had all of those burned."

Denali shrugged. "He missed one."

Nova opened the book, her fingers delicately turning the pages. She leaned in closer to the text.

"Look at this," she said.

Denali moved closer, peering over her shoulder as they walked. She pointed to an illustration of a figure floating on the page, strikingly similar to Nova's form outside the cave. Beside the central figure, the artist had sketched additional sets of arms, showing multiple positions of limbs in a single image. The extra arms floated alongside the body, as if capturing different moments of movement in one static picture.

"What does that mean?" Nova asked.

Denali offered a reassuring smile. "I guess we'll find out."

Then, his smile faded. Internally, he was still grappling with the reality of what he'd witnessed. The ability of levitation had been lost for nearly fifty years because of the syphon.

There were so many things to say, so many questions to ask about levitation and the miscreants Nova had met.

He opened his mouth to ask, but before he could, Blythe spoke out. "D and Little D, as much as I love our little underground escapade, my legs are waving the white flag."

Nova nodded and snapped the book shut. "We should rest."

Once they said it, it was like the fatigue hit Denali in full force. He set the lantern down.

Nova curled up on a relatively smooth patch of ground, turning to face the wall.

Blythe sat a few feet away, her knees drawn up to her chest, staring into the flickering light. Denali rummaged through his backpack and pulled out some energy bars.

"What's up?" he asked, holding a bar out to her.

Blythe took it. "Whole lotta nothing."

"You haven't been this quiet since . . ." His voice trailed off before he finished the sentence.

She tugged at the collar of her jean jacket, as if it had become too tight against her neck. "I never thought I'd see the guy again, ya know?"

"This is good, right?"

Her fingers worked at the wrapper of the energy bar, but she made no move to eat it. "What if he doesn't want to see me?"

Denali waited, giving her space to continue.

"At his trial . . . I . . . froze." Her voice cracked. "He looked right at me, told me he was sorry, and I just stared back. Didn't even say goodbye." She squeezed her eyes shut. "My parents *mocked* him, and I still did nothing."

"You were in shock, Blythe," Denali said. "It's normal to act that way—"

"No," she cut him off. "It's not. He was my family, D. And I let him go without a word."

She looked at Denali squarely. "When it was Nova, you didn't freeze. You didn't sit back. You stood up and risked everything for her. Nova will never forget that. Why couldn't I have been *that* person?"

Denali's mouth twitched as he fought back a smile.

Blythe stared at him. "What?"

"I've always wished I could be more like you." He shrugged. "You're not scared of the highborns, you call the guards 'boneheads,' and you're not even afraid of mouthing off when there's a crossbow aimed at your head."

A soft laugh escaped Blythe's lips.

"You're not afraid to say what others won't," he said, "no matter how much trouble it gets you in."

Blythe bobbed her head up and down slightly. "I made a promise after that day . . . that I would never hold back what I really wanted to say. Not to my parents. Not to the highborns. Not to anyone. No more filters." She pursed her lips together and continued. "I knew it wouldn't make up for what I did, but it felt like a way to tell my uncle I was sorry." She breathed out a laugh. "It doesn't exactly make me the teacher's pet."

Denali bit back a smile. In their classes, he tended to be the favorite while Blythe was the student that professors would interrogate. Once, when they were called out for talking in class, their professor had made Blythe sit in the corner while Denali was given the professor's desk.

"Blythe, if you wanted one of my silver stars, you could have just asked."

Blythe laughed, took a bite of her bar, and spoke with her mouth still full. "Keep Pippington's 'sparkling pupil' stars to yourself. That's all you, man."

Suddenly, a loud snore reverberated through the tunnel, startling them both. They turned to see Nova, fast asleep, her mouth slightly open as another snore escaped.

For years, since the accident, she'd had trouble sleeping. Relief flooded Denali at seeing her rest, but it was mingled with a deeper pain—he should have been there in Nadir, watching her heal, watching her grow. Instead, she'd transformed without him. Their old roles—him the protector, her the protected—had dissolved while he wasn't looking. And he could never get that time back.

He pulled a thin blanket from his backpack and carefully draped it over her sleeping form. Then he turned to Blythe. "Don't be scared to face him. Seeing you again is all he thinks about."

"I hope you're right, D."

He looked back down at Nova, safe beside him. Warmth spread in his chest, the same warmth he'd felt when he saw her safe again when she returned to Ghandria.

"I am."

A chilling growl echoed through the tunnel, startling Denali awake. He bolted upright, disoriented in the darkness. The lantern had long since burned out.

His hands fumbled to find it.

A screeching noise bounced off the walls.

Denali finally managed to relight the lantern, its flickering flame casting their shadows along the tunnel walls. As the light spread, he saw Nova already on her feet, her body tense. Blythe was awake too, frozen beside her. Their eyes were fixed on something behind him.

He shifted, stretching his vision in the same direction. His eyesight zoomed through the tunnel. Finally, in the distance, he saw the outline of a figure.

Someone had come in behind them. A guard?

As he watched the man walk, Denali tilted his head. There was something eerie about the way he moved. The top half of his body hung to the side at an unnatural angle.

He parted his lips to say something, but Nova's hand clamped over his mouth. She pressed her pointer finger to her lips. Denali's heart started to race. He nodded and Nova lowered her hand.

With exaggerated care, she motioned for them to move. Denali's palms grew clammy with sweat. He stayed behind Nova and Blythe, placing each foot with deliberate precision and occasionally glancing back to stretch his vision. The man continued his strange, loping walk, oblivious to their presence.

Time stretched endlessly as they crept through the tunnel. Denali's calves burned from the constant tension. Sweat trickled down his neck and back.

The floor beneath them began to slope upward. The unexpected incline caught Denali off guard. His foot slipped on the steepening surface and he stumbled. He shot his hand out to catch himself. There was a sharp slap as his palm hit the tunnel wall. His stomach dropped.

The three of them went still. Blythe covered her mouth.

A bone-chilling noise split the silence. Denali stretched his sight in the direction. The man's head shot up. A clicking sound escaped his throat. Then, he picked up his pace, barreling toward them.

Denali's eyes grew wide. "What the hell?"

"Run!" Nova yelled.

She grabbed Blythe's hand and they sprinted through the tunnel. As they struggled against the incline, the growl morphed into a series of rapid, thudding footsteps—closer, louder. The man . . . the *thing* was gaining on them.

The tunnel narrowed, forcing them into single file. Ahead, it opened to a spacious room.

The exit?

Denali's hope turned to despair in an instant. The tunnel ended abruptly and a wall stood before them, mocking their efforts with its silent, impassable presence. Blythe screamed as she beat her fists into the wall.

The creature's cry grew louder, more excited, as if it could sense that they were trapped. Denali's eyes darted around the chamber, searching for any sign of hope, any sliver of an escape they might have missed.

Nova snatched the lantern from him and raised it high. There, bathed in the flickering light, was an escape hatch, barely visible against the ceiling. Hope blazed through him. He interlocked his fingers, creating a step for her. Nova dropped the lantern, placed her foot in Denali's hand, and propelled herself upwards, her fingers grazing the edges of the hatch. She started to push at it, but had no luck.

The growls of the creature filled the tunnel, its presence ominously close now. Denali, glancing at it, could see its claw-like hands.

"Any day, Little D!" Blythe yelled.

Nova secured a new hold on the metal hatch and pushed. It finally swung open.

Below, Denali braced himself, digging his feet deeper into the damp dirt to support her as she lifted herself through the opening. Blythe was next, and he boosted her up—all ninety pounds of her. Nova helped from above until Blythe was up and out. Then, Denali jumped up, securing his hands around the metal frame. Blythe and Nova grabbed onto his arms.

He pushed a foot against the wall, the weight of his bag making it harder to elevate himself. With a desperate push, he managed to get his waist through. Then, pain seared through his leg.

He bit down hard.

The creature's claws dug deep into the flesh of his calf. For a heart-stopping moment, Denali feared it might succeed in dragging him back down. The pain was blinding, his leg aflame with agony.

Nova and Blythe both dug their nails into the skin of his arms. With a strangled grunt, he kicked at the creature's face with his free leg. It loosened its grip and Denali summoned the last reserves of his strength to haul himself up. The creature's claws tore through his flesh as he pulled free of its reach.

As soon as he was out, the sound of rushing water overtook his senses. Nova let the trapdoor shut and Blythe dragged a large rock over the top of it.

✦

Nova watched as Denali healed himself. Usually he could heal in seconds. This, she imagined, would take more time. The tunnel had led them to a pocket behind a waterfall. A curtain of water created a barrier between them and the outside world. Nova held in an absurd laugh. This was *her* waterfall.

There was the rock at the base of the breaking water where she had spent weeks meditating with Taos. All that time, a hidden tunnel to Ghandria was right beneath her nose.

Denali's clamp on Nova's hand relaxed, and he let out a long, exhausted breath. Nova inspected his leg. It was completely new. She blinked in disbelief. He had become even more skilled in the time she was away.

Blythe put her arms around them. "We made it."

Denali ran his palm down the length of his face, a sound between a laugh and a sigh escaping him.

As Nova rose to her feet, another screech rent the air in the cavern of the waterfall, stopping her mid-motion.

That one didn't come from beneath them.

She moved toward the translucent sheet of water. Blurs of figures made her heart thud. Cautiously, she peeked through a break in the side of the water. Dozens of Krall roamed around the waterfall.

Nova chewed on her lip and looked at Denali.

"What is it?" he asked.

"What was that you said about a tunnel always leading to somewhere better?"

TWENTY-EIGHT

K rall cries filled the world outside. Nova's expression hardened, the gravity of their predicament sinking in. They were trapped.

She turned, assessing their surroundings for any possible escape, but the cavern was completely enclosed. The metal trapdoor to the cave thudded beneath them, budging, but secure thanks to the heavy rock on top. The Krall must have used its claws to scale the walls. Nova shuddered, becoming more and more aware of what the creatures were capable of.

Denali pushed another rock onto the trapdoor as an extra precaution. As he did, Nova looked out of the falling water one more time. Her eye caught on something gleaming in the trees. She stretched her vision and her face brightened at what she saw.

A single-blade sword.

There was only one person who still used those.

Taos crouched in the tree, inspecting the Krall. Nova noticed more movement beside him. Xander huddled on a nearby branch.

They must have rallied the Krall here to help Nova get on the Marmoris safely. She realized now that they were keeping them here in case she came back today. Only . . . she was back, just not in the place they thought she would be.

So much for that plan.

The metal hatch began to thud harder. Nova searched for anything that she could use to send a signal to her friends, but there was nothing besides rocks and dirt.

Think, Nova.

Blythe and Denali reached for the grate to hold it down. That's when Nova noticed the glint from Blythe's earrings—several small diamond studs. She bit her lip, an idea forming.

"Blythe," she whispered. "I need to borrow your earrings."

Blythe looked confused, but quickly complied, removing two studs up one ear and handing them to Nova.

Nova carefully positioned the earrings, angling them to catch the light. Filtering it through a pocket to the side of the waterfall, she aimed the reflected beam toward Taos and Xander. At first, nothing happened. Nova adjusted the angle slightly. Xander raised his hand, shielding his face from the flash. He squinted in her direction.

As she moved to signal again, something else caught the light. A pair of reflective eyes snapped toward her. Then, three more Krall's heads jerked in her direction.

Oh no.

There was a blur of motion from the tree Xander was in. He leapt from his perch and hit the ground running. "Over here, you uglies!"

The Krall's heads swiveled toward the new disturbance.

Then, a soft, persistent scratching rose from beneath Nova. Denali and Blythe exchanged a glance.

The soil beside the base of the metal hatch began to shift and tremble, small clods of dirt and stone tumbling away as it was being pushed from below. Before them, a new hole began to form. For a moment, there was silence, a tense, suffocating quiet that hung in the air. Then, with a guttural growl that scraped against the walls of the cavern, the Krall began to emerge.

Its limbs, grotesquely elongated and covered in soil and debris, grasped the edges of the hole, pulling its body into the light of the cave. Its eyes were fixed on Nova and Denali.

There was no time to hesitate. The three of them took off, their feet pounding against the wet rock as they navigated the cave's exit. The Krall followed closely behind them, but slipped on the rocks.

Nova, Denali, and Blythe burst through the cave's opening. The creatures outside turned as one toward the mouth of the cave, their eyes pinning Nova and Denali. For one terrible moment, everything stilled. A Krall cocked its head back to the sky and let out a long-breathed screech.

Then, they all surged forward. Nova spun and began scaling the cliff of the waterfall. It was a steep incline, but it was their only chance. Denali and Blythe immediately began their ascent beneath her. Climbing was a battle against both the pull of gravity and the spray of water that sought to dislodge them. Each handhold was a major victory. The Krall began to follow, their claws scratching the stone. Some fell to the waters below, taking out more beneath them in their descent.

Nova neared the top, and she glanced down. Time slowed as Blythe's hand slipped from the wet rock. She hung from one arm, swinging to the side. Then, with a cry that was swallowed by the roar of the waterfall, she fell.

Denali reached a hand out for hers, but missed. "Blythe!" he screamed out.

Nova's heart stopped as their friend plummeted. She hit the water with a splash. Five Krall were in the waters right beside her.

Nova and Denali clung to the rocks, frozen in horror. Blythe surfaced and coughed water from her lungs as she was swept downstream. She was carried straight toward two of the monsters, their arms slashing at the water. Instead of attacking Blythe, though, they moved past her, their focus unwavering as they continued after Nova and Denali.

A Krall reached out for Denali's foot. He kicked its face and sent it hurtling to the ground. "Go!" he yelled.

Nova reached for the ledge above. With one final effort, she pulled herself over the edge, collapsing onto solid ground. Denali was seconds behind.

Krall were climbing like ants behind them, inching closer to the ledge. Nova caught sight of a new figure running up below—

Berkshire. He was beside Xander. In his stare, there was a silent urging, a reminder of their lessons. Her pulse raced with equal parts fear and determination as her new ability surged to the forefront of her mind.

Berkshire was right. About levitation, about who she really was, about forgiving Denali . . . about *everything*.

Nova took Denali's hand, her fingers intertwining with his. She focused on the energy that had coursed through her yesterday. And then, her feet lifted from the ground and they began to rise. As they ascended, she heard Denali's sharp intake of breath. "Whoa."

Below them, the Krall's piercing cries rose to a fever pitch, but those sounds faded away, becoming nothing more than background noise as student levitated in front of teacher.

Nova felt the energy of Denali's hand in hers. She surrendered to the sensation, letting it seep into her skin. With each inhale, the feeling spread, resonating through her bones and raising goosebumps along her arms. The air around her crackled with an invisible force, making the hairs on the back of her neck stand on end.

The Krall twitched and shuddered. One by one, they started to back away from the waterfall. Some of them lost their footing and tumbled to the ground. Others let out low, guttural sounds of distress. The retreat turned to a frenzied escape, with the creatures scrambling over each other in their haste to flee. Taos and Xander sprang into a fighting stance, but the Krall rushed past them too, disappearing into the direction of the spora forest.

Nova lowered herself and Denali away from the waterfall's edge until they touched down beside Taos, Xander, Blythe, and Berkshire.

Denali rushed to Blythe, examining her for wounds.

She rolled her eyes. "D, I'm good."

Nova looked up at Berkshire. He bowed his head ever so slightly.

"Classic move, rookie," Xander said, "making an entrance in the only place you were supposed to stay away from."

Nova shifted uncomfortably on her feet as she caught Taos's

gaze. There was a certain look in his eyes, a depth she had only seen when he had her pushed up against the rice bag. For a fleeting moment, the air around them hummed. Then she watched as Denali gave Taos a subtle nod, which he returned.

Nova did a double take. "Wait? You guys know each other?" She turned to Taos. "You didn't tell me you knew my brother."

He shrugged. "You never asked."

Nova stood there, mentally retracing every interaction they'd had. Surely that detail should have come up in one of their conversations.

"Son," Berkshire called out for Taos.

He turned and walked toward Berkshire. Xander followed, leaving Nova alone with Blythe and Denali.

"Is that who's been teaching you?" Denali asked.

"Berkshire? Yeah," Nova said distantly as she eyed Taos and Berkshire's conversation.

"Imani's brother, Berkshire?" Denali asked.

"He was one of the levitation professors," Blythe said. "You know, back before it was banned and stuff."

"Uh, yeah. Cool." Nova was still watching Taos as he talked. "So, Denali, were you and Taos, like, friends?"

Denali scoffed. "Taos isn't friends with youngborns. He thought Father lied about his parents' deaths. I snuck into Father's library to find the records—"

"Wait." Nova shook her head, drawn back into their conversation. "*That's* the reason you snuck into Father's library?"

Denali scratched the back of his head. "Uh . . . yeah."

Blythe whistled nonchalantly as she removed herself from the conversation, pretending to find the waterfall very interesting.

"Wow," Nova said.

"I'm sorry, Nova. I never meant for any of this to happen—"

She held up her hand to silence him. "No, it's not that. It's just crazy how everything led us here."

She took in her surroundings, soaking in every sound of wind that whistled through the leaves, the crashing of the waterfall, and her friends' conversations. "It feels like I'm exactly where I'm supposed to be."

Denali stared at her in bewilderment.

"What is it?" she asked.

"Nothing. It's just . . ." His voice softened. "The sun doesn't hurt you anymore."

Nova tilted her head as her mind wrapped around the significance of his statement. The sun wasn't affecting her. At least not like it had before.

Not like it had her whole life.

She was standing in broad daylight and the sun's embrace felt surprisingly gentle against her skin. The corner's of her mouth stretched into a smile, and she couldn't pull it back in.

"The sun feels good, Denali." She let out a breath and laughed when she did. "It feels so good."

He smiled at her. It was her favorite smile—the kind where his eyes were smiling too, saying everything that needed to be said without uttering a single word.

✦

"Show Gwendolyn again!"

Nova laughed as she landed back on the wooden floor of the nest. That was the third time the sisters had asked to see her levitate.

Helga grabbed hold of them both. "Helga says stop pestering. Dinner time. Sit."

After they said grace, the table erupted into its usual chaos. Nova watched in amusement as Denali recoiled slightly. His gaze darted from person to person, trying to track the flurry of movement as dozens of hands reached across the table at once. Someone knocked over a glass of red juice, staining the wood surface of the table and splashing Hognose's brown shirt.

"Attacked!" he yelled.

Blythe was unfazed, tracing her pointer finger in an endless circle around the rim of her bare plate. She had a far-off look.

Two hours had passed since Berkshire left to fetch her uncle.

A knock at the door cut through the chatter. Nova looked at Blythe, who had suddenly gone stiff. Gus's father opened it.

When Nathaniel walked in, Blythe's shoulders sagged.

Nathaniel removed his hat. "May I?"

Everyone looked to Taos for approval. He gulped and then gave a subtle nod. Blythe's gaze fell back to her plate, resuming her mindless tracing.

Then, two more figures appeared in the doorway. Berkshire entered first, followed by a man Nova didn't recognize.

Blythe went completely still, her eyes locked onto the guest who was not much taller than herself.

He was barely breathing when he whispered, "Bean?"

Blythe launched from her chair. She threw herself into the man's arms, the force of her embrace causing him to stagger back. His arms tightened around her and his face buried in her blue hair, tears streaming down his cheeks.

Nova looked at Denali. He smiled. They turned back to the table, ready to eat, but their jaws dropped at what they saw. Empty plates littered the surface, not a morsel left on any of them. Hognose licked grease and crumbs from his fingers and let out a belch.

Nova glanced at Denali, who was equally bewildered. Kiera, Gus, and Xander leaned back in their chairs, patting their full bellies with satisfied grins.

Helga stood and wiped the crumbs off her apron. "Helga make more for new guests!"

Gwendolyn and Agatha cheered.

"Not for you," Helga scolded. "Bedtime."

A tangible wave of disappointment washed over Gwendolyn and Agatha. "Aww," they both sighed in unison. They cast longing glances back at the kitchen, their shoulders slumped as they trudged to the base of the stairs. When they reached the bottom of the stairwell, Agatha's eyes lit up with a mischievous gleam. "Agatha calls first shower!"

Gwendolyn's head shot to face her. "Agatha shower first last time!"

There was a moment of hesitation. Then, both of them burst into action, their feet pounding against the wooden steps as they raced each other up the stairs.

Nova bit back her laughter.

As the commotion settled, Nova looked across the table to Taos. His posture was stiff as Nathaniel tried to make conversation beside him. He met Nathaniel's friendly overtures with wooden smiles and one-word answers, clearly uncomfortable despite his attempts at being polite.

Suddenly, as if sensing her stare, Taos's eyes met Nova's. Her heart gave an unexpected thud. Flustered by her own reaction, Nova quickly broke eye contact. A warmth crept up her neck and she focused intently on her empty plate. When she dared to look up again, Taos had returned his attention to Nathaniel, but there was a slight smile playing at the corner of his mouth.

An hour later, Nova and Denali helped the others clean the dinner mess. Blythe was still at the table with her uncle, arms sprawled out, acting out her conversations since he had lost his hearing. While Nova was washing dishes, Gus approached with a grin that spread from ear to ear. "Ma says Nova and brother live here with Gus Gus!"

Nova, taken aback, tried to protest. "Oh, you don't have to do that."

"Hush," Helga said. "Helga won't have it any other way. Nobody bother you here."

Hognose folded his arms and turned his nose up in disdain. "Us have no extra room."

She patted his back. "Them take Hognose room."

Hognose's jaw dropped. "Hognose is appalled! Where will Hognose live!"

"Oscar has extra bed ready for Hognose."

He gasped. "Hognose is outraged!"

Their bickering faded as Taos drew closer to Nova. "I, uh . . ."

He rubbed the back of his neck. "I'm sorry you didn't get your wish."

Nova gave him a blank stare.

"When we were stargazing," he clarified.

Nova's mind flashed back to that moment, when Gus had called her out for her wish to go home. *So he had been listening.*

Her eyes wandered across the room, taking in the scene before her: Helga wrapping Gus and Hognose in a warm embrace. Blythe animatedly catching up with her uncle. Kiera and Xander laughing with Denali. Warmth spread through her chest, filling her with a sense of belonging she'd never known in Ghandria.

Then, Nova's eyes lost focus and her smile faded.

"What is it?" Taos asked.

She turned to him, her forehead creased. "I can't stop wondering . . . how was there a Krall in the tunnel? It came from behind us . . . from Ghandria."

"Well," he said, "if everything you mentioned about the sitheus supply is true, they've been coming here for years, right under our noses. Who's to say they haven't taken more than just sitheus?"

"You think they've been taking Krall?" She searched his face, her voice dropping to a whisper. "What would they want with them?"

Taos shook his head. "I don't know."

Nova chewed on the inside of her cheek as she raced through possibilities. Cronian sending a Krall down the tunnel after them didn't surprise her. It was exactly the kind of ruthless tactic he'd employ. Having access to a Krall in the first place, though? That was unexpected.

The highborns didn't take such drastic measures without a plan. And whatever they were planning, it couldn't be good.

"So they banish us and tell us we'll never see our families again, while all along there's been a secret passage they use to come and go, *stealing* from the miscreants?"

"It's not unlike them to have a hidden passage."

"Well, now so do we."

Taos cocked his head. "What are you saying?"

"They're not the only ones with access to that passage. Not anymore." Nova stood taller. "We can find out what they're doing. We can end the exiles."

"Whoa, Nova," he cut in sharply. "You can't just march everyone through the tunnel into Ghandria. The highborns' soldiers are probably waiting." He leaned in. "You can't start a war that way. Uprisings have rules, systems."

Nova's eyes drifted across the room, lingering on each face. Her attention landed on Berkshire, who stood apart from everyone. He was by the fireplace, staring at the note from Imani. Nova frowned. She had found her home. She had found her *people*. But this wasn't just about her and Denali anymore. It was about all of them—the exiled, the forgotten, the miscreants who had been cast aside, those who had been *pruned* from society, ripped from their families. It was about the Krall who lived in oblivion, wasting away from the futility of hope of making it back home.

This was worth fighting for . . . for all of them.

"Real fights don't come with rules." She turned back to Taos and held his gaze. "It's time to bring everyone home."

ACKNOWLEDGMENTS

There are many people to thank throughout this four year process. I have been blessed with an incredible support system and I try not to take that for granted, but somehow always do.

First and foremost, I give thanks to God. Without His constant presence and inspiration, this book would remain unwritten.

Thank you to my parents, who have been just as excited for this book as I have. Thanks, Mom, for reading through my entire manuscript in its early stages and gushing over it. There isn't a woman in this world who embodies the mother star, Cassiopeia, more than you do.

Thanks, Dad, for teaching me the true meaning of perseverance. Your work ethic inspires me. Your and Mom's phone calls to me where we discuss the future success of this book have made me feel so loved. Thank you for always being there to talk about my dreams.

Thank you to my little sisters, especially Kendra and Kianna, this journey would not have been the same without you. Sitting together, each working on our own books while bouncing ideas off one another—those moments were precious to me. I can't wait to cheer you on with your own novels and accomplishments. Thank you to Karissa and Kinlee for being my cutest little supporters.

Thank you to my brother, Cody. You inspire me daily as you fight your battles, and our experiences together are woven into every page of this book. You mean everything to me.

Thank you to my good friend Lindsey for helping to create the perfect cover, helping to inspire my characters, and saving my butt when it was crunch time. Thanks, Dakota, for always being so willing to help with my books while working hard on your own. Thank you to my editors, Marcelle and Lia, to Lauren Kay, to Bekah, and to Robert Gurr and his legal team. Some others who have helped me tremendously throughout my education that I want to mention: Jason, Dr. Provost, my incredible coworkers, my mentors, the Cox family, and the entire Hatch family.

Finally, to the loving indie author community I found on Instagram, to my ARC readers, and to you. I've poured years into crafting this world, but as a reader, you're the one who makes it real. Thank you.

ABOUT THE AUTHOR

Kynsie Cole was raised in both Gilbert, Arizona and
Saint George, Utah. She holds a bachelor's degree in
Communications. When she's not weaving stories of sibling
bonds into fantasy, Kynsie enjoys playing ping pong and
going to the gym. Miscreant is her debut novel and she is hard
at work on the rest of The Darkov Series. Follow her writing
journey and behind-the-scenes peeks on Instagram
@kynsiecole

*Did you enjoy Miscreant? As an indie author, your review on
Amazon would mean the world to me (trust me, I read them all).
Thank you for your support!*

JOIN MY NEWSLETTER!

I like to send free gifts this way...

www.ingramcontent.com/pod-product-compliance
Lightning Source LLC
Chambersburg PA
CBHW050018120726
47903CB00006B/1819